WESTAVAHN

EMBERS

B. ADAM WARK

ISBN: 979-8-9955091-0-3

Published by Balderdash Studios™

CHAPTER ONE

The wind didn't howl. It whispered.

Snow sifted between the pine boughs, drifting onto branches heavy with frost. The air was sharp, scented faintly of resin and iron-cold earth.

A raven called from its perch high above. There were no other sounds.

Rodrik crouched beside a snow-draped boulder, one knee buried in powder, the other braced behind a shadowed fir.

He flexed fingers stiffened by the cold, stretching old scars that crisscrossed his knuckles—trophies from past hunts and battles.

His breath was low and shallow, rising in pale ribbons that vanished almost at once.

Three days he had tracked the beast. Twice Rodrik had come close enough to draw. And twice he'd let the string settle back without loosing. It was not yet ready. The kill had to be clean. Had to be right.

This was no yearling, no half-lame trail-bleeder with its hide already half-promised to wolves. This one was older than most ever lived to be. A twelve-point monarch, a scar notched deep across its left flank, one antler slightly bowed from a break long healed.

The buck stood in a shallow dell below, half-draped in low mist, its flanks rising and falling in rhythm with the wind. Each of its motion was careful—hooves testing ice before weight followed, ears turning, wary, cautious.

Rodrik drew the string back. The bow creaked softly—an old sound he trusted. His breathing steadied, eyes calm yet fiercely focused, his senses sharpened to every subtle shift and sound.

The buck turned its head up, and in that still second, the sunrise broke clean across the ridge. Light caught the antlers, blazing gold and amber through the thinning morning mist.

The weight of something older than instinct settled—discipline learned long ago.

With a final steadying breath, Rodrik freed the string, the arrow whispering forward. Tension left him as it flew.

The arrow struck just behind the shoulder. The buck staggered once, gave no cry, and folded into the snow.

Rodrik waited, motionless.

Three breaths.

Four.

He rose and crossed the distance quietly, with neither glee nor pride—only the habit of ritual.

Rodrick knelt beside the fallen beast and placed one hand on its neck, feeling the warmth there begin to fade. A faint scar along his cheekbone tensed slightly as he whispered the words.

"Thú gav vind, mìn brór. Nú gav eld. Gakk mjúkt til rót," he murmured softly in Hraven, the old words rolling off his tongue with practiced reverence. -*You fed the wind my brother, now feed the fire, go gently to the roots.*

Above, the sky gradually brightened. Muted gold and orange streaks painted the horizon, ushering in morning.

He moved with the calm of long habit, selecting two young pines nearby and limbing them with quick, efficient strokes. Strapped together with rawhide cord drawn from his pack, they became a narrow travois, light enough to drag, strong enough to bear the weight.

Kneeling again, Rodrik drew his knife and dressed the deer where it lay. The work was swift and respectful, practiced enough to need no thought beyond the blade. He kept the heart and liver, setting them aside in clean snow, and wasted nothing that would serve later.

He stepped out from the line of frost-coated trees, the deer trailing behind him on the travois. He paused briefly, stepping from shadow into the open.

Standing tall and broad-shouldered, his figure softened by a thick cloak shedding snow and frost. Beneath the fur lined hood, strands of prematurely silvered dark hair framed a face etched deeply by harsh winds and sharp cold. Hardened leather bracers encased his forearms, scarred and darkened by years of use and hardship. His furs were rugged—wolf, bear, elk—patchworked, not pretty, but practical.

On his back, secured with straps of oiled leather, rode a double-headed axe. Its crescent blades bore age without dullness. The leather-wrapped haft rose above his shoulder, occasionally brushing the hood of his cloak as he walked.

In his hand, a longbow carved from aged ashwood, etched with markings worn smooth by time and weather. A Nuvareki seal-hide quiver hung at his hip, partially filled with arrows fletched with black raven-feathers.

The path beneath him was barely that—a thread of compacted snow between jagged rock and tree roots, leading toward a cliff that broke the forest like a scar.

The day pressed on, and Rodrick measured it in steady miles.

The sky had climbed to a pale, hard blue, the sun riding high and thin above the trees, and the scent of cold rose from the earth—the metallic bite of frost and the faint promise of distant snow.

His cabin crouched low beneath the pines, snow and shadow half-swallowing its form. Its roof bore a thatch of frost-silvered branches. Smoke curled thinly from the stone chimney, carrying the scent of peat and pine. Moss grew in the seams of the stacked-stone foundation, and antlers crowned the lintel above a sturdy, iron-banded door.

He set the travois aside and went to work again, stripping the hide and quartering the carcass beneath a simple tripod lashed from poles. The meat was hung by the hind legs to chill, the cold doing its work quickly. When the cuts were clean, he carried the quarters to a shallow stone-lined hollow in the frozen ground, covering them with slabs of shale and packed moss to keep them cold and scentless.

Only then did he take a thick hunk from the haunch. It was dark and dense, streaked with pale fat. Then he turned to the cabin.

He pushed the door open without ceremony, hinges complaining softly as it swung inward. Pausing on the threshold, allowing his eyes to adjust to the dim interior before stepping fully inside.

Warmth gathered slowly—not from roaring flames, but from the steady heat of a long-burning hearth tucked into the far wall.

A single table stood in the center, rough-hewn and scarred from years of use. A raised bed of thick pelts and straw lined the corner. Bundles of dried herbs hung from the rafters—heather, thistle, juniper—alongside smoked fish and strips of salted venison.

Everything was arranged to hand. Tools and stores sat where they were needed; nothing more, no space wasted.

Kicking snow from his boots and stepping to the hearth, he speared the meat onto an iron skewer. Then he rested the skewer across two flat stones set at the edge of the fire.

Outside, the wind shifted against the cabin walls, setting the rafters to a low creak.

While the meat cooked, he placed the longbow, then the axe—each on its own designated hooks with a steady hand. The axe especially—he handled with care, its leather wrapping worn smooth where fingers had long gripped it. Each time he hung it up, he touched the haft briefly, a reflex learned long ago. Eirik had once said a man should greet his weapon like an old friend.

He took off his cloak, then his gloves—callused fingers flexing in the warmer air. Then the fur-lined coat and leather jerkin. Beneath, a torso marked by a life far from peace.

His arms, corded with muscle; not the bulk of a brawler, but the dense, precise strength of a man who worked with tools and weapons alike.

Pale skin, kissed by the cold, stretched over scars both new and faded. One curved beneath his ribs like a hook—old, angry, half-forgotten. Another slashed across the collarbone, clean as northern law.

His face, carved from stone, caught the firelight in harsh angles and shadow. Eyes like glacial runoff, unyielding, not easily thawed. Even in rest, those eyes remained watchful, set beneath a heavy brow. His beard, neatly kept but thick, ran the length of his jaw, dark with flecks of grey.

He rubbed his hands briefly above the fire, chasing away the last of the stubborn cold. Then, from a shelf near the bed, he grabbed a clay flagon sealed with beeswax, cracked it open, and poured himself a measure into a horn cup. The mead was thick, golden, and strong. He drank like a man thawing from the inside.

Then he turned to the bones—laying them out one by one on a flat slab near the fire.

The long bones he split with a smaller axe kept near the hearth for such work. He scooped the marrow—rich, steaming—with callused fingers and sucked it clean. His first meal of the day. The hollowed shafts were set near the flames to dry; later they might be carved into needles, fishhooks, or whistles—each a tool to be traded or used. Even the sinew was stripped and set aside.

By the time the meat was ready, the marrow bones had cooled, and every tool hung back in its place.

He pulled the skewer from the fire and tore into the meat without ceremony, biting through char and heat without flinching. No plate. No fork. Just fire, flesh, mead, and comforting quiet.

He sat chewing, staring into the flame. Silence held—until it didn't.

Three knocks—sharp and hard. Rodrik froze mid-bite, the last scrap of venison still hot in his mouth. He chewed once, slowly, then stood. Eyes narrowing, he crossed to the door in three steps, right hand drifting toward the axe hung by the frame.

Another knock—quieter, but no less sure.

He unlatched the door and pulled it open in one swift motion.

Cold surged inward, wind tearing through the cabin and scattering snow across the warmth and shadows. The sharp scent of frost and pine momentarily overpowered venison and smoke, a blunt reminder of the world beyond these walls.

A man stood at the threshold, bundled in heavy wool and cured leathers, ice stiffening the hem of his cloak. A scarf masked the lower half of his face, but his eyes were sharp.

His gear was simple but well-maintained. Strapped across his right shoulder was a hardened leather pauldron, intricately etched with clan patterns, dyed with pigments drawn from mountain lakes. Upon it—darkened by time and fire—gleamed a familiar mark: the personal seal of High Chieftain Eirik, pressed into the leather and ringed in runes of authority.

It had been years since Rodrik had answered a knock bearing that mark.

His hand tightened briefly on the axe handle, then relaxed.

The messenger's eyes flicked once to the weapon, then back, shifting his stance with practiced ease, fingers brushing the edge of his cloak. His voice cut through the wind, steady and respectful.

"Síra Stormviðr," he said firmly, shifting effortlessly into the old Hravn tongue with proper respect. "The High Chieftain begs audience. As soon as you are able."

Rodrik remained silent.

The messenger thought briefly, as though weighing his next words carefully. "There have been whispers, Síra. Something stirs beyond the mountains. The High Chieftain believes only you can see clearly through this storm."

Rodrik considered him in silence.

The messenger reached into his cloak and produced a scroll, sealed in dark wax, and held it out with both hands—one gloved, the other bare and red with cold.

"A summons," The messenger said, holding the scroll steady. "Written by the High Chieftain himself."

Rodrik accepted the scroll. The wax seal was flecked with crushed ironroot. His thumb brushed the mark—and stilled.

Blood in the snow.

Friends lost.

He did not need to study the seal.

The messenger's gaze drifted past him into the warmth of the cabin. His eyes caught on the fire, then the half-eaten skewer of venison resting near the hearth. He blinked once.

Rodrik noticed. "Come in," he said, voice rough from disuse. "Eat. Then take my answer back to Eirik."

The messenger stiffened—not at the invitation, but at the name. He paused, just long enough to mark it.

Rodrik stepped aside. Smoke and the scent or roasted meat rolled into the cold behind the messenger, followed by the dry, bitter scent of hanging herbs.

He stamped snow from his boots and knelt by the hearth. The warmth loosened his shoulders as he pulled off the widowed glove with his teeth and reached for the skewer. Rodrik handed it over without comment.

The younger man ate in steady, efficient bites. Grateful, but measured.

Rodrik returned to the table. He set the scroll down unread. Sitting, he poured himself another cup of mead. He drank slow and considered the High Chieftain's summons.

Outside the wind howled and tested the shutters. Inside, the fire snapped softly. When the messenger finished eating he asked, "Should I tell him to prepare for you?"

Rodrik looked at the scroll. His hand rested flat on the table beside it. He didn't need to open it. He knew what was inside.

"I'll go," he said at last. "But I don't like being summoned."

The messenger hesitated, unsure what to do with that.

"Eirik knows that." Rodrik's gaze dropped briefly to the fire. "Which means this isn't politics."

The messenger leaned back slightly; warmth had returned to his face and hands, his eyes remaining sharp.

Rodrik poured a second cup and set it within reach. The younger man accepted it with both hands, paused, then drank.

"Didn't expect mead," he said. "Most offer cold stew—if that."

Rodrik grunted. It wasn't agreement. Or disagreement. Just a sound.

They sat in quiet for a while, the wind muttering at the eaves.

"I should leave soon," the messenger said, setting the empty horn down on the stone shelf. "The snow's easing, but not for long." He hesitated, eyes fixed on the fire.

Rodrik studied him in silence. The fire popped once, and he didn't look away.

"Then you'd best leave prepared," he said, rising. He took a spare cloak from its peg and crossed the room, setting it into the younger man's hands. After a beat, he added a pair of fur-lined gloves. "Take these. Two gloves are better than one."

Then he added in the old tongue, low and even: "Snær skeldr ei húgr—aðeins klæðá." – *The snow doesn't care how brave you are—only how well you are dressed.*

The messenger nodded, pulling the gloves on, fingers stiff at first, then steadier as warmth crept back.

"Stay off the lower trail," Rodrik said. "Snow's drifted deep. Ridge path is safer."

The messenger pulled the cloak tight over his shoulders and moved to the door.

Before stepping out, he paused. "Síra—when should I tell High Chieftain Eirik to expect you?"

"Full frost. After the sun sleeps."

The messenger blinked, the old phrase unfamiliar to him.

The corner of Rodrik's mouth twitched. Then he clarified. "The evening after you should arrive in Thorenfell."

The messenger pulled the cloak tight and stepped outside, unhitching his horse. He mounted and tipped his head toward Rodrik before turning the animal toward the forest trail.

Cold rushed in, sharp and brief, before Rodrik could closed the door. He latched it, then stood where he was, hand still on the latch, until the fire cracked.

The cabin settled around him—wood, smoke, and the low sound of wind pressing at the walls. Rodrick returned to the hearth and sat, hands resting on his knees.

His gaze stayed on the coals.

The scroll remained on the table, unread.

✶

The sun hung low over the western rim of the world, bleeding gold across the snow-crusted ridges of the Boulderfist Mountains. Their jagged edges caught the light like the teeth of some ancient beast, long asleep but never forgotten.

Below them, the forests of Hravnskot stood black and silent, their snow crusted pine-needled spires trembling in the evening wind.

Rodrik moved steadily, breath fogging the air as pale light sifted through the branches around him. Firelight played in fractured patterns across the frostbitten ground, broken and scattered across the snow.

He'd traveled fast—faster than he liked—but the messenger's words pressed at him all the same. *Beg* was not a word the old wolf used lightly. The summons carried an echo of old debts and unanswered questions, and that was enough.

As the trees thinned and the slope dropped toward the valley, a low, rolling sound greeted him—half music, half laughter. It grew louder with each step. Then came the scent—roasted meat, woodsmoke, pine sap, and mead-thick breath.

Thorenfell Hall rose from the frost like a ship breaching the sea—broad and tall, made from whole trees felled by men who feared no foe. Its roof was steep and thatched with pine-bark and snow, supported by beams the size of oaks, and none spared the axe.

The outer wall was adorned with skulls—massive elk, black bear, a dire wolf or two, and one polished dragonhead carved from mountain stone—truth or legend, depending on the ale and the mouth telling it. Between the bones, iron sconces burned low with orange fire, their smoke trailing into the darkening sky.

Rodrik slowed from familiarity, not awe. He had walked this path before, many winters ago, when younger bones carried lighter burdens. Then, he had come as a shield-brother, a hunter, a clansman.

Now he came alone—summoned. That was the colder road.

He pushed open the thick doors and stepped into warmth. The noise rolled over him—laughter, boots, the clash of horn-mugs—a cacophony after so long with only wind for company. Heat sank into muscle and bone as his eyes adjusted to the blaze and motion.

Inside, chaos reigned with practiced grace. Thorenfell's great hall was alive—dancing, drinking, wrestling. A bonfire roared in the central pit, flames licking at the smoke-hole far above. Songs were half-sung and half-shouted.

A grizzled skald beat a drum carved with clan runes, his fingers ringed with iron, face tattooed with stories only he knew. Beside him, warriors laughed, their hair braided with colored thread signifying clan, victories, and blood debts yet unpaid.

"Wind's biting tonight!" one warrior shouted over his cup, eyes gleaming mischievously. "Best drink enough to drown it out!"

"Better to drown yourself," came the dry retort, "lest the wind claims you first!"

Meat turned on iron spits near the fire, fat dripping into the coals with a satisfying sizzle. The aroma of roasted boar, garlic, and smoke wrapped around him like an old friend's embrace. The hall radiated warmth, alive with the blended warmth of bodies, fire, and spices—a sharp contrast to the chill still clinging to him.

He paused at the threshold, letting his vision adjust as the sounds of revelry washed over him. Beneath the clamor ran a steady rhythm—the heartbeat of Thorenfell Hall, resonating through stone and beam, carrying echoes of ancient courage and simmering grudges.

Behind him, the doors groaned shut, muffling the distant wind.

The rhythm of laughter and song stumbled as heads turned—some curious, others quietly recognizing. Conversations faded to murmurs; the lyre strings hesitated briefly, and mugs hovered uncertainly.

His silhouette stood unmistakable in the blaze—broad-shouldered, wolf-cloaked, shaped from the same granite as the encircling mountains.

A few men whispered his name, while others quickly averted their eyes. Reputation moved faster than wind here, always preceding him.

Without haste, he moved forward, acknowledging each nod and glance with a brief tilt of his chin—recognition without warmth. Men and women shifted aside without being asked, opening space as he passed.

His boots echoed softly, worn leather meeting stone polished smooth by countless footsteps and spilled mead. At the aisle's end, wide timber steps ascended toward the raised dais and the seat of power embedded in the hall's bones.

The hall slowly resumed its murmur of conversation, cautious voices blending with a softer minstrel tune meant for listening rather than shouting. Attention shifted away from the dais, settling back into cups and plates—though a few eyes lingered longer than they meant to.

Not far from the central hearth, at a long table cluttered with half-gnawed bones and overflowing mugs, four figures leaned close—three men and a woman, each somewhere between tipsy and warmly flushed from the mead.

One man, thick-necked and red-cheeked, thumped his cup down and jerked his chin toward Rodrik's retreating form.

"You know who that is, right?" the thick-necked one whispered loudly enough to carry beyond their table.

The woman—freckled, sharp-eyed, sober enough for genuine curiosity—tilted her head. "Storm-something?"

"Stormviðr," the third man interjected, grinning broadly through boar grease and bravado. "They call him the Stormwalker. Makes thunder seem courteous."

The first man leaned in, eyes wide with theatrical seriousness. "He talks to mountain spirits. Lives where even clouds fear to tread. Sleeps with one eye open, and the other fixed on the horizon—just in case trouble finds him."

The older man, grizzled and contemplative, squinted through the smoky haze, mug paused halfway to his lips.

"My cousin reckons Rodrik hasn't aged since Thorenfell was just stones and ambition. Says he drove a spear straight through a Jötnar king's neck at the founding—and kept the spear as a walking stick."

Lysa blinked rapidly, eyes wide, voice hushed. "Truly?"

Her earnest question briefly froze the table in a tight, expectant silence.

Then laughter erupted—loud, rough, but good-natured, the kind reserved for legends, potent ale, and sweet fools who believed both.

"He's not that old, Lysa," the red-cheeked man chuckled, wiping foam from his mouth. "But by the gods, if he ever looked straight at me, I'd feel colder than a White Howler's backside on Highcrown Peak."

Lysa giggled despite herself, flushing warmly as she tucked a stray curl behind her ear. "Well—even the fiercest beasts probably think twice before crossing him."

"Nah," the older man corrected gently, smirking into his ale. "Trouble follows him around like ravens after battle, waiting to see who's fool enough to stand in the way. Wherever he walks, danger trails like wolves behind wounded prey."

Lysa glanced toward where Rodrik had disappeared, her voice quieter now, layered with thoughtful seriousness. "Maybe trouble isn't following him. Maybe he brings it."

"You're not wrong in that, girl," the older man half laughed, half shouted, spilling ale across the table. "And gods know we Hravn chase trouble like drunkards chase mead!"

The conversation flowed naturally—part jest, part reverence—circling truths no one cared to settle.

Rodrik moved through the hall without hurry, his presence drawing space as he passed.

Glances followed him; whispers shifted and died. Tales clung to his name, tightening and twisting into legend. Some claimed he'd slain a mountain bear alone. Others insisted he'd died three winters past.

Rodrik advanced toward the dais, the hearth's glow playing along his shoulders. Despite the attention upon him, his face remained impassive, back unyielding, gaze steady.

Above, banners of the great clans fluttered gently from the high rafters—wolf, raven, skull, hammer—their colors softened by years of smoke and time, yet their significance undiminished. They hung silently, sentinels to a hall well-acquainted with both revelry and bloodshed.

At the hall's head sat Eirik Storrvaldr, High Chieftain of Hravnskot, upon a throne of pine raised on a dais of dark stone beneath an arch carved from rock. He filled the throne as naturally as if it had grown around him, draped in dark wool edged with silver-threaded dara and shield knots.

A massive bearskin adorned the throne, its claws arched above his broad shoulders. His limbs were thick, his beard thicker, silvered by age.

Though relaxed in posture, beneath Eirik's calm demeanor lay quiet alertness. His storm-lit eyes missed nothing. They fixed steadily on Rodrik, acknowledgment flickering there.

A faint smile softened the old chieftain's mouth as he raised a horn of mead in greeting.

"Well met, Rodrik Stormviðr," he spoke, voice resonating with quiet authority.

"Your arrival is a boon," Eirik said, his voice carrying across the room, quieting nearby chatter. "We have much to speak of."

Rodrik approached, rushes whispering beneath his boots. At the dais, he accepted the horn, their gazes locked, neither blinking.

Rodrik drank deeply. The thick mead warmed muscles numbed by snow.

Eirik studied him carefully, fingers tapping lightly against the horn. After a moment, he spoke again, voice softened by memory.

"Remember the Rime Vale? First snow camp we raised? Gods, we believed it unbreakable. Then those bastards tore through the frost like wolves desperate for blood."

Rodrik gave no reply, though a faint tightening around his eyes spoke volumes.

"Hrolf took an arrow through the throat—still kept fighting." Eirik chuckled softly, without humor. "Didn't realize death had found him 'til he ceased yelling."

Rodrik nodded slightly.

Eirik swirled the mead thoughtfully, eyes distant. "Few remain who remember those days."

"Few," Rodrik murmured quietly, eyes briefly shadowed by memories.

Rodrik straightened slightly, voice calm yet edged with quiet intensity. "I am honored by the summons, High Chieftain. But I traveled hard, slept little. What storm draws me from the mountains?"

Eirik exhaled sharply, almost a laugh. "You'd slice right through the table if I let you." He gestured casually with the horn, a subtle smirk forming. "Fine. Let's cut to marrow."

"Conquest," Eirik stated plainly, leaning forward, thick forearms resting comfortably on the throne's armrests.

"The southern kingdom rots like driftwood abandoned to the sea. I've heard the cracks—nobles devouring each other like starving wolves. They forget that swords rust when unused, that iron grows brittle without being tested."

He paused, gaze shifting briefly to the hearth. His calloused thumb traced the rim of his mug—weighing his words carefully.

"A few nights ago, a little bird made of wind and ice visited me. It whispered of fractures in Eldaraine."

He took another slow drink. The scent of burning logs mingled with rich mead, filling the hall with warmth edged by the chill outside. When he spoke again, his voice deepened.

"Go south. See what they've become. Gauge their strength, sense their fear. Bring me answers—not blood. Not yet."

Rodrik's jaw tightened. The words settling heavily between them.

He held still, eyes fixed on Eirik.

The Chieftain leaned back, fingers drumming gently against the throne's armrest in a slow, deliberate rhythm.

"I'm not asking you to raise banners, Rodrik. Just read theirs."

Eirik continued evenly. "No howling winds, no pounding war drums. You're the shadow before the strike, not the hammer's blow. Walk soft, see clear, and if you speak—let your words bite deeper than your blade."

"What exactly would you have me do?" Rodrik asked quietly, arrows carefully aimed in fading twilight.

"Fínn sprúng, prófa vǫll," Eirik said firmly, invoking a Hravn saying as old as their mountains.

"Test their foundations. Learn if their roots run deep or shallow, and how quickly their leaves scatter in adversity. Remember, even the mightiest tree falls when the roots are weak."

Rodrik turned and moved towards the fire sipping his mead. He watched the firepit crackle, logs snapping and sparks leaping high.

He had not stepped into those lands for years. The thought of returning pressed heavily all the same.

Eldaraine lingered between them, unspoken.

Finally, he nodded decisively. And looked back to Eirik.

"I'll see it done."

Eirik thumped his mug down on the thick armrest, mead splashing on to the worn furs that covered it.

"Good. Leave as soon as the snow relents. Take whatever you need—provisions, weapons, horses. I've seen too many caught unaware by sudden gales."

Rodrik raised an eyebrow slowly, like a cautious hunter scenting the air. "And yet you're sending me directly into one."

Eirik's familiar grin appeared again, edged with authority and dry humor. "Aye," he said simply. "But the storm doesn't fear the wind."

Rodrik moved through the Chieftain's stores with quiet precision, knowing exactly what he needed.

The chamber had a low ceiling, the air cold with frost, filled from floor to ceiling with practical provisions.

Lanterns hissed and smoke drifted as Rodrik navigated shelves worn smooth by generations of hands. Distant sounds from the hall seeped faintly through thick stone walls—a pulse of warmth stark against the storeroom's chill.

Shelves displayed dried meat, flint, waxed cord, smoked fish, hard bread, and bundled herbs—provisions meant to last, not to comfort. Fur-lined cloaks hung quietly from iron hooks, like soldiers waiting patiently for orders long overdue.

He moved by them silently, breath forming brief clouds in the air, passing by extravagance in favor of dependability. Selecting only what was familiar and trusted.

He reached for boiled leather bracers, a horn-and-gut waterskin, salt, and bitterroot. A small iron kettle was secured to his pack with a pouch of charcoal and a flint stored inside.

Then a bone-handled knife, he tested its edge—dull yet reliable. He placed the blade into its sheath and attached it to his belt. A ring or iron nails and a wrap of ermine pelts, small items for trading.

At a shelf stacked with herbs wrapped in waxed linen and labeled in faded script, he chose Roseroot, spruce sprouts, and one more—Tukrahlin Thyme, bound in rust-colored thread. In the corner were travel packs sewn from seal-hide, some marked with faded clan runes. Rodrik selected one unmarked, cinched the straps tight, and placed it all carefully into his pack and closed the flap.

A steward entered, shivering despite heavy furs. Young and uneasy, his gaze flickered between Rodrik and the exit, hands shifting at his sides.

"A horse is ready," the steward announced, voice tight with tension. "Northern stallion. Sure-footed."

Rodrik didn't look up. "Too loud. Too hungry."

The boy hesitated, anxiously tugging his cloak. "There's a mule—stubborn but reliable in snow."

Rodrik turned slightly; lamplight highlighted the frost lingering in his beard.

"I'll walk."

The steward shifted uneasily, fingers tapping nervously. "Mule's half-blind, mean-tempered. Kicked me right in the—"

"No mule." Rodrik silenced him with a look.

The boy snapped his mouth shut, bowed, and withdrew.

Rodrik adjusted the kettle's strap and inspected the gut-skin stitching on his pack. Everything was in its place. Satisfied he shouldered the pack and stepped out beneath Thorenfell's carved threshold into the cold; the air braced him, biting through his layers.

Outside, snowfall whispered—steady, relentless. At the forest edge, Rodrik brushed his thumb across familiar scars, a brief, practiced gesture before stepping forward. The wind had shifted, cutting against his cheek.

Behind him the hall's light faded to a dim glow in the frost.

Ahead lay Eldaraine.

With a last glance skyward toward the silent ravens, he moved steadily into the gathering dusk.

✶

CHAPTER TWO

The fire in Lady Elara Icewind's study had burned low, coals sleeping in the grate. The room bore the quiet wealth of a house that had not yet begun to starve: ashwood panels polished and unwarped, velvet chairs set with deliberate care, shelves of leather-bound volumes kept in quiet order. Small silver-framed portraits watched from their places along the walls, her family preserved in stillness, where feelings were kept contained.

Beyond the window, Icewind Manor sat along the Murkher Coast, west of Oakenrest, its stone silhouette clean against a bright full moon.

Alerick stood near the window, half-shrouded by curtain and shadow, watching the grounds where frost silvered the courtyard stones and the last patrol lantern swayed in the wind. He hadn't spoken since entering.

Elara sat at her desk—once her father's—the polished oak worn smooth by years of use, faintly scented still with the ghost of his pipe tobacco.

The pipe itself rested exactly where he had left it, untouched—a silent monument not only to memory, but to a promise she struggled daily to uphold. Her sleeves rolled to the elbow, ink smudged the corner of her mouth—a lingering habit from childhood, born from chewing on quills when deep in concentration. A wax seal shimmered pale blue beside her hand, a six-point snowflake—House Icewind's sigil, pressed clean into its face.

Behind her, Alerick finally shifted slightly, the floorboards creaking softly beneath his weight, breaking the silence.

"You sent it?" Alerick said at last, voice low but not surprised.

Elara didn't look up, her fingers spinning the pewter die slowly, half lost in concentration.

"Hawk first, then rider at Frostmere Tower. It should have reached Thorenfell by now."

Alerick turned from the window, the folds of his dark cloak catching briefly in the fire glow. His face, angular and travel-worn, gave little away.

"So, you called for aid," he said bluntly.

"I insinuated rot," she corrected gently, with careful formality. "I advised High Chieftain Eirik that the kingdom stirs with division—that certain houses hunger for something more than what Castellon offers. I suggested that a storm gather south of the Ironback. I implied—"

She paused, choosing her words with care.

Alerick finished her thought.

"You implied—war," his voice was cold. At his side, his fingers flexed briefly.

Elara met his gaze. Her composure held, eyes steady as they met his.

"Not war," she corrected, softly insistent. "Just tension. Enough to divert eyes from my ledgers. Enough to unsettle the crown so deeply they fail to notice the cracks in my walls."

"You think High Chieftain Eirik will oblige you with theater?" Alerick asked, voice low, resonating with the certainty of past gambles lost. "He doesn't bluff. If he marches south, it won't be for appearances. It will be to spill Eldarin blood."

She stood slowly. The fire behind her cast a long shadow toward him. She looked smaller than usual, despite the stiff set jaw and stubborn chin.

"What choice do I have? Lord Valen circles like a dog in heat. The crown's coins don't reach as far as their threats. Lord Caerlyn pulls away from every agreement like it carries plague. If I wait, I lose the estate. If I deal with Valen, I lose my soul."

Alerick nodded slowly. "So instead, you light a signal fire and hope the wind doesn't carry it to the whole forest. You have a great deal of faith in the King's Guard."

Elara did not argue the point. "If the Guard falters," she said, "Valen will learn that neutrality is a luxury he can no longer afford."

She folded her hands together deliberately, steadying herself before she spoke. "One he will no longer be able to afford."

Alerick chuckled without humor, shaking his head slightly. "You always were a little too clever for your own good."

Her lips curled into a tired smirk. "You keep saying that as if it's a warning."

"It always was."

She looked at him then. "I learned from the best, did I not?"

He allowed a faint smile to crease his lips—not fond, not amused. Just sad.

"You were twelve when I pulled you from the smoke. You clung to my wrist with a strength that didn't belong in a child. I'd never seen anyone hold on that tightly."

Elara looked into the fire. Pushing back memories she had no time for now. "And I never thanked you."

"You didn't need to," Alerick replied. "You built a life. You survived. That was thanks enough."

She looked at him again, meeting his eyes. "You were the only one who stayed. Even when they whispered. When the other children found new names for me and tested them aloud. You taught me how to walk past them without flinching."

"I taught you how to disappear."

"No," she said firmly. "You taught me how to wait until they forgot to look." She let the silence settle, briefly allowing the old pain to fade. Then she straightened slightly, forcing her thoughts back to the room, the ledgers, and the cold arithmetic of survival.

Alerick sensed the shift. When he spoke again his voice was edged with dry skepticism. "You really think they'll buy it? The Hravnskot don't send ravens just to chat about snowfall. If Chieftain Eirik believes your words, he'll send men and steel—not a polite letter."

Elara set the seal die down, unaware she still held it, and turned fully toward him. "That is exactly what I'm counting on."

"So, a war." Alerick confirmed, his gaze returning to the window.

Silence stretched, the embers sighed softly, smoke curling upward in thin, unsettled threads.

Elara turned slowly back to her desk, picking up another sealed letter. "I have a contingency, in the event Eirik doesn't act. This one is for the Storm—assuming he's still breathing."

"He is," Alerick replied, his tone flat but certain.

She shot him a look, eyes sharp. "And you know that because?"

Alerick took one more look at the moonlit waters of the Cold Sea, then turned to meet her gaze. "He got a summons from Eirik himself. The messenger should deliver it in a few days."

Elara lowered herself into her chair, exhaling quietly. "Then it's begun." She turned the sealed letter over in her hands thoughtfully, then tossed it into the fire without another glance. The paper curled and blackened, the wax bubbling and melting into the flames.

"Not yet," Alerick corrected, his eyes fixed on the smoldering parchment. "But it's definitely in motion."

She rubbed at her temples, sighing. "I just need time. A year, half that even. Time to fill the granaries, fix the damned ledgers. If the north keeps the crown's attention long enough to delay the audit—and if Wynmere plays along with the grain supply—I might scrape by. Maybe."

Alerick leaned forward, resting a hand on the desk to catch her attention. "And if it all goes sideways anyway?"

Elara's eyes held steady, exhaustion edging into stubbornness. "Then at least I won't have sat around watching everything collapse from behind a locked door."

Alerick stared, his voice dropping, losing its sarcastic edge, turning serious. "What's your limit here? How much are you willing to lose? The estate, your title? Your soul?"

Elara looked away, jaw tightening. Her hand unconsciously clenched at her side.

Alerick turned to her now.

He reached inside his coat and withdrew a cold brass coin etched with a raven clutching a dagger, its edges uneven, dented. Elara stared at it, her expression tightening.

"A precaution," he said simply. "If the storm does come, you'll want someone in the rain who knows how to keep you dry. Storms have a habit of growing once they start."

He turned toward the door. Leaving the coin on the desk.

Elara's voice caught him as he reached the door.

"Three nights from now, usual spot," she added, looking up.

"I'll be there," he replied, over his shoulder, voice steady.

Alerick slipped out without saying another word, the door closing softly behind him.

Long after he had gone. Elara remained at her father's desk.

The brass coin lay on top of her untouched papers, catching the last light as the fire sank to embers.

Picking it up, she flipped it over with her fingers, feeling the weight. Physical and symbolic.

Then she placed it in the desk drawer.

Next to another that had rested there as long as the pipe on her father's desk.

Castellon, capital of Eldaraine, rose in disciplined tiers around the Flamebound Order's Grand Citadel, streets coiling outward as veins from a still-beating heart. Frost held the highest towers hostage in winter's shadow, while the merchant stalls and forges below woke to warmer life: iron-scented steam from smithies, flickering tavern lanterns, and wooden wheels rattling over frost-slicked stone.

Faileas moved through it all with the idle grace of a man on no particular errand. His boots struck the cobbles soft as a rumor, his cloak cut from dark-dyed wool that blurred rather than billowed, clean but unadorned. No sigil, no sash, no mark of trade save the brass-rimmed folio under one arm—the sort a scholar or scribe might carry, stuffed with half-written ideas or whole stolen truths.

Vendors were already setting up their stalls, voices hoarse from the morning chill. Faileas passed among them with a nod here, a coin there—pausing not because he craved food, but because they expected it. To them he was a historian: harmless, charming, obsessed with dead monks and forgotten orders.

"Morning, Master Faileas!" called a heavy-jowled spice-merchant near the Westgate rise. "I've got fire-pepper and frost-leaf from the south—care to warm your tongue or chill it?"

Faileas smiled with only one corner of his mouth. "Not today, Eldrin. Your fire-pepper still makes my stomach plot revenge—and I've no time for mutiny below decks."

Laughter rippled from surrounding stalls—the kind that masked suspicion behind familiarity. Faileas offered no explanations for his daily wanderings, so Castellon filled in its own. Some said he was writing a book on the Flamebound Order; others whispered he had once belonged to them. Still others insisted he was nobility in disguise, playing author to avoid a betrothal.

All were wrong. All were useful.

He ascended the cobblestone path slowly toward his destination, letting the city reveal itself street by street. Steam from the Metallurgical Academy to the north rose like banners of pale smoke. Children chased a dog through slush near the Royal Library, their laughter scattering crows from the roof. Ahead of him loomed the central power of Eldaraine—Castellon Shield—all precise angles and watchful eyes, waiting like a closed palm ready to clench.

Faileas passed the guards at the portcullis with a polite nod, needing no words. The King's Guard had grown used to him—he bore no title or crest, but familiarity could be sharper than any blade, in courts as much as alleys.

Through the inner doors, the stone gave way to polished marble. Cold light spilled through stained glass set high in the vaulted walls, and the air took on the measured hush of a place that expected secrets to walk it.

He crossed the antechamber unhurried. Pages scurried past in green-and-black livery, scrolls in hand, voices clipped and urgent. Courtiers clustered in loose knots, draped in silks of winter bloom and dusk-purple, conversations masked by civility but edged with implication. Faileas offered a half-bow to Lord Berwyck, a white-bearded minor noble, and moved on without slowing.

The throne room doors stood open—he stepped through the arch like a man entering a familiar chapter in a book he'd already rewritten.

Inside, warmth bled from braziers of perfumed coal, and the scent of lavender and parchment curled through the air. Gold-threaded banners hung heavy from the walls, each bearing the crest of a noble house, the Thornsword sigil blazing highest—a dark green and black shield bearing a pale stag poised before a thorned tree. At the foot of the dais, a chorus of conversation rippled like wind through leaves.

Faileas did not approach the throne. It sat conspicuously empty, as it too often had of late—a silence more telling than any herald's cry. Drifting along the chamber's edge, he studied its tone and tempo, letting the undercurrent of power seep through him.

No one stopped him. A few nodded. One merchant-prince greeted him by name and began a familiar joke. Faileas smiled at the right moments without listening.

Instead, his attention snagged on a conversation to the chamber's east—close enough to overhear, too distant to invite address. A tall man in dark leathers and a woman in pearl-threaded green and silver stood with the distance civility demands, but the familiarity disagreement breeds.

"Lord Valen's grain stores are not your jurisdiction," Lord Lanyard Darkoak said with the crispness of a blade still in its sheath.

"They are if they threaten the supply chain from Highfield to Tarnhollow," replied Queen Avanna, calm but unyielding. "I will not have another winter rationed on rumors and promises."

Faileas listened while nodding absently to the merchant, cataloging the tension rather than tasting it. Lanyard's voice was hard, and Avanna's was harder.

The merchant finished his joke and chuckled. Faileas smiled. "Clever as always, Master Linden."

And then the room resolved itself. At the far corner of the hall, beneath a mosaic depicting the founding kings, stood the reason he had come.

"Excuse me, I have important business to attend to." Faileas nodded politely and turned away, the merchant's laughter trailing off behind him, already forgotten.

She wore steel-blue silk that caught the brazier-light like water in moonlight, layered with a white velvet mantle clasped by a snow-lily brooch. The cut was exact, the effect deliberate—softness tempered by restraint.

Lady Elara Icewind.

Faileas approached her with the calmness of a man greeting a storm he had studied but never seen break.

"My lady," he said with a bow. "You requested a quill with legs. I presume you still require delivery?"

Elara's eyes, a cool blue-grey that never quite warmed even when her lips curled, flicked over him.

"Master Faileas," she said evenly. "Prompt as ever."

"Promptness is a courtesy many rarely offer—but always expect." Faileas said, pressing his hand to his chest and giving another dip of his head.

She handed him a scroll—aged just enough to seem authentic. The wax seal gleamed gold, pressed with the unmistakable crest of House Caerlyn: a fox with nine tails encircling a full moon.

"Signed as Lord Quentyn would," Elara said, voice precise and cold. "The seal must convince him."

Faileas tilted his head slightly, a half-smile tugging at the edge of his mouth. "Careful, my lady. Doubting my credibility might hurt my feelings—if I had any left."

She didn't smile. "Convince Lord Valen this is genuine. Once signed, it goes directly to the Storm—no detours."

With a nod, Faileas slipped the scroll into the folio, fingers brushing briefly over the wax seal.

He let his tone soften just enough to invite—but not demand—more. "And, if Lord Valen asks questions?"

Elara's voice sharpening by a hair, "You are carrying a scroll. Nothing more. It is signed as House Caerlyn would sign, sealed as Valen expects to see. Your task ends and payment will be made the moment it reaches the Storm with Valen's seal and mark. If it strays—or is unmasked early—there will be no distance left between flame and ash."

She paused, ensuring he understood. Then she looked away, just briefly, toward the west-facing window. "I hear a storm moves south."

He bowed—slow and deliberate. "Then I suppose I'd best be swift."

Faileas turned and left with the same relaxed ease as he'd entered. He inclined his head to passing courtiers without breaking stride, adjusted the position of his folio, and vanished back into the ordered flow of the court—another harmless fixture moving through Castellon Shield, practiced calm intact.

Moments after Faileas slipped from the hall without a ripple, Lady Elara Icewind made her own measured exit—less retreat than calculated drift, as though seeking to pass unnoticed through a room that watched everything.

She moved through court like a figure carved from frosted glass—elegant, precise, slightly apart. Her steps were measured, unhurried, hands clasped gently before her, white velvet mantle trailing a half-step behind. She had made it halfway across the chamber—nearly free—when her name caught the air like a hook.

"Lady Elara."

She turned.

Queen Avanna Thornsword stood near the dais, Lord Lanyard Darkoak at her shoulder—silent, attentive, already aware.

The queen's voice was warm, her smile warmer still. "That mantle—Icewind blue, isn't it? Only your house ever makes velvet look like steel."

Elara bowed her head, her smile practiced. "Your Majesty honors me. The seamstress deserves the credit."

"Nonsense. It takes a certain *bearing* to wear steel with grace."

Avanna extended a gloved hand. Elara approached slowly, carefully, curtsied, hands steady. When she rose, the queen's gaze lingered just a heartbeat longer than comfort permitted.

"And how fares your estate?" Avanna asked, as if inquiring after a garden. "I hear the late frost was unkind this year."

Elara's mind flickered to the books—grain tallies revised downward, losses marked to spoilage rather than field, the quiet cost of keeping stores dry and vermin-free. Her heart tightened once. Her face did not.

Elara smoothed a sleeve. "Our reserves remain sufficient. We reinforced the lower granaries early and rotated stores before the damp set in."

"Mm. And the stables? I remember your mares were expecting several foals this season."

"Five." A beat too fast. "One lost in the cold. The others are strong, though fodder has been—carefully managed. The stablemaster remains confident."

Avanna's smile stayed carefully fixed. "Even a handful can tip the scales, Lady Elara. Good horses have a habit of outrunning misfortune."

Elara inclined her head slightly. "We all do what we can, Your Majesty."

"And the elk herds?" Avanna's tone was honeyed. "The mountain passes were cruel this winter—I hope your herds fared better than Tarnhollow's cattle."

Elara paused just briefly, as though selecting her words with care. "Fewer sightings than I'd prefer, Your Majesty, though not unusual for this time of year."

Darkoak said nothing. He didn't need to—his presence beside the queen was comment enough. Arms folded behind his back, expression unreadable, he watched Elara in silence.

Avanna tilted her head thoughtfully, tone delicately weighted.

"These are lean years indeed." Avanna let the words settle, just long enough to be felt. "Sometimes it's the quietest houses whose ledgers speak loudest. Your ledgers, I trust, are in order?"

For a split second, Elara paused. Then she drew a steady breath, her expression settling back into practiced composure.

"Of course, Your Majesty," Elara said, her voice smooth.

Darkoak's gaze didn't waver. When Elara briefly met it, she found no threat—only cold, measured assessment.

"Well," Elara said with the soft grace of retreat, "I fear I've kept your attention longer than I should. No doubt there are matters more urgent than the ramblings of a minor house."

"Nonsense," Avanna said. "Every house matters—particularly those wise enough to speak softly."

Elara bowed again. "Your Majesty. Lord Darkoak."

Darkoak offered a nod—precise, cool, final.

Elara turned, her pace just as graceful as her entrance. She inclined her head to a passing courtier, adjusted the fall of her mantle, and rejoined the slow current of the hall—another noble retreating, nothing amiss.

The lower east side of Castellon was quieter by midmorning—less ringing steel, more cooling soot. Faileas climbed narrow stone steps two at a time, boots barely scuffing, until he reached the second floor of a weather-stained building tucked between a candle-maker's shop and a weaver's guild hall. He turned the key smoothly, entered, and shut the door with the practiced care born of years needing silence more than safety.

He bolted it behind him.

The apartment was small but not squalid—too tidy to be poor, too cluttered to be noble. Shelves sagged under the weight of unorganized scrolls, ink bottles, and stray feathers from quills left half-carved. Canvases leaned against the far wall, some blank, some bearing half-finished landscapes or portraits scratched over in black.

A basin below a cracked mirror caught the morning light, full of water gone cold. Three small glass jars sat beside it: one for oil, one for ash powder, one for a concoction that smelled faintly of lemon and vinegar. Identity, in liquid form.

The table was scarred, wax-stained, holding a folio identical to the one he carried—one real, one empty. A single chair, a small fire grate, and a narrow balcony overlooking the cobbled street completed the scene. A writer's room, perhaps. Or an exile's. Or simply a place to disappear.

He pulled off his cloak and hung it on a peg near the door. Then the vest, the tunic, the boots—the careful outer mask of Faileas. One by one, he shed posture and expression along with the fabric.

In the cracked mirror above the basin, Alerick looked back at him. The face was plainer, harder, the eyes less forgiving.

Elara, he thought, dipping fingers into the skin tonic and rubbing it along his jawline. She hid things well—but he was trained to notice seams. The game wasn't about power. Power could be seen, stolen, stabbed. Leverage whispered while the knife was still in its sheath.

He examined a small leather roll of false moustaches and trimmed hairpieces. Paused. Considered. Then exhaled through his nose—a slow, precise breath—as though committing to a recipe.

He chose a fine dust of ground kael-root to deaden the natural sheen of his skin, applying it in delicate, swirling passes across cheekbones and jaw with a worn silk puff—clockwise, always clockwise.

He dabbed faint red beneath his eyes and between the knuckles, just enough to suggest a day's ride, not a fever. The palms were stained with a smear of saddle dye—his own blend, baked into the calluses.

From a lacquered box, he lifted a worn patch of a courier's guild outpost, crest intact but threadbare.

He stitched it onto the satchel flap with a bone needle and vinegar-aged thread to mimic sun-fading. It had to pass inspection—but not draw attention. That was the balance.

Then the tunic—brown, two years out of fashion, loose at the shoulders. He rubbed the collar against a beeswaxed windowsill, picking up just enough grit to fray the edge. The boots were scuffed precisely, mud reapplied from an old jar labeled *"Stonewatch–spring flood."*

He adjusted his gait once, twice, in front of the mirror. A hesitant shuffle. A slightly bowed head. A nod rehearsed until it vanished into instinct.

Finneas the messenger, he thought, fastening the buttons with the kind of care a surgeon might envy. Earnest. Timid. A little pinched in the gut. Certainly, beneath notice.

Any spy could vanish into a crowd, he reminded himself. But to vanish into memory—that took skill. They'd recall the satchel or the patch, perhaps, but the face? The name? Never.

He moved to the balcony and looked out across the street—narrow, crooked, a clothesline stretched across it like a loose smile between tired buildings. No one watched. Not now. Below, the street murmured—distant voices, the slow creak of carts over cobblestones, a breath of woodsmoke in the chill air.

He liked this moment—the in-between. The breath before the lie. It was a cleaner feeling than truth.

He smiled.

Finneas never smiled.

So he stopped.

Lord Circus Valen's estate made no effort to blend into the kingdom that tolerated it.

North-east of Castellon, just beyond the capital's respectable shadow, Goldacre manor rose from a bend in the stoneway, positioned where the land grew rich and scrutiny thinned. Unlike noble estates tucked behind cliffs, rivers, or old forests, Goldacre sprawled brazenly across fertile plains, its walls built more for spectacle than war. Pale limestone facades, gilded window frames, imported glass, and towers—too narrow to be practical, too tall for safety. It looked less like a home, more like a boast written in stone.

Surrounding the manor were the Goldacre fields: vineyards, barley farms, and almond orchards worked not by the house's retainers, but by laborers from villages Valen had quietly indebted. His grain was the main supplier of the realm, his wine cellars were older than most noble bloodlines, and his shipping contracts along the Murkhar coast served as the invisible veins of the western trade route. He was not beloved. But he was needed. And in Eldaraine, that was a better kind of power.

Beyond the arched gates—polished bronze engraved with House Valen's sigil, a weasel entwined in grain, cunning elevated to heraldry—lay the estate grounds: manicured hedges clipped into symbols of rule and submission—crowns, scales, kneeling figures—fountains that ran with scented water even in the cold, and sculptures of himself scattered across the gardens with no regard for subtlety.

One featured Valen standing among Flamebound monks, his attire richer, his posture elevated—scales resting in his grasp while the others bowed their heads in study. Visitors did not linger outside long.

Inside, the discomfort worsened.

Goldacre's interior was a clash of color and ego—purple velvet drapes trimmed in gold fringe, mosaics depicting battles Valen had never fought, walls crowded with paintings that placed Valen at the center of moments he had financed rather than lived—treaties signed, verdicts rendered. One showed Valen grappling a stag whose antlers echoed the king's sigil—close enough to be recognized, distant enough to deny. Another, hung prominently above a marble hearth, depicted a family scene that had been carefully altered—two figures scraped away to leave Valen standing alone where others once belonged.

The corridors smelled of myrrh, oil, and something sweeter, almost cloying. Every room echoed with the hush of servants trained to move like ghosts. Those who spoke without being spoken to rarely remained employed—or visible.

The drawing room—a cavernous chamber crowded with mismatched chandeliers, and a ceiling fresco depicting Valen ascending into clouds while winged scholars wept. Below, sat a long iron-banded walnut table that sprawled beneath this absurd grandeur.

Lord Valen reclined against a high-backed chair with peacock feathers wired into the headrest. He wore a coat of deep plum, edged with silver fox fur, open just enough to show the gold chains looping across his robust torso. A crystal goblet twirled between his fingers, half full of pale wine and wholly ignored.

Across the table stood Rennic "Smudge" Stride, perfectly poised, hands clasped behind his back. His suit was three days newer than the current fashion, which meant it would be the trend tomorrow.

His gloves were off, revealing the telltale smudges on his fingers—ink and old blood that even olive oil and lime couldn't hide.

Rennic adjusted his cuffs with precise, measured movements—left sleeve first, then the right—each tug exactly the same length, each crease aligned with painstaking accuracy.

"I've taken the liberty," Rennic said, "of correcting House Morwell's ledger. Again. Their second son seems to believe brothels operate on trust."

Valen grunted. "If they did, I'd be bankrupt. Now—what about House Varrin?"

"Collapsed under their own debts. Their daughter is being married off to a cousin to consolidate titles. The son is rumored to have taken work as a traveling harpist."

Valen laughed—low, indulgent. "A harpist? Flame take me, the nobility never tires of disappointing me."

"You do set the bar rather high," Rennic said mildly.

Valen's smile thinned. "Board up the house. Absorb any staff worth keeping. Sell the furnishings that won't embarrass me, burn the rest—or throw it into the river, I don't care."

Rennic inclined his head. "I'll see to it personally."

They fell into a silence broken only by the hearth's crackle.

A knock interrupted the fire's rhythm—a soft, hesitant tap from one of the inner doors.

Rennic glanced at Valen, who raised a single finger. "Enter."

A breath later, the door creaked open, just enough for a servant to peer in—barefoot, dressed elegantly in soft gray linen.

"M' lord," she said softly, eyes respectfully downcast, voice clear and composed, "a messenger has arrived. From House Caerlyn. Should I show him in?"

Valen arched a brow. "From Caerlyn? Uninvited? How refreshing."

He drained the last of his wine and set the goblet aside.

"Yes. Show him in. But clear the parlor first. I want him alone with the echoes."

"Yes m'lord." She gave a quick bow and vanished with the speed of one trained to avoid lingering.

Valen tapped his finger against his chin, then flicked his gaze toward Rennic.

"Bring a fresh bottle—the amber I think."

Rennic inclined his head and turned, boots whispering across tile.

The air changed the moment Finneas crossed the threshold into Goldacre Manor.

It wasn't the warmth—though there was plenty of it, pumped from perfumed hearths, heavy with pressed figs, amber oils, and something faintly metallic. It was the sensation beneath the warmth, a pressure that had nothing to do with heat.

He maintained an even pace, shoulders slightly hunched, messenger's satchel tugged forward just enough to suggest awkwardness. The boots were scuffed, the tunic lowland-plain and half a size too loose. His hair, darkened by herbal cream, was combed with blunt professionalism. No cleverness here—just delivery, parchment, and respectful bows.

His eyes—those remained sharp.

The entryway was an assault of bad taste: marble floors inlaid with twisting, gold-veined vines, ostentatious enough to feel punitive. Along the corridor stood a single statue of Valen, rendered in pale stone—one hand raising a ledger upright like scripture, the other relaxed at his side. Tucked into an arched alcove, framed by two golden palms.

The servants, however—they gave him pause.

All of them were women. Young and old alike, moving with efficiency through the halls, eyes downcast, voices measured.

They moved silently on bare feet across marble floors. Fine fabrics caught the lamplight as they carried polished silver trays, eyes lowered, steps measured—presence shaped into trained invisibility.

One of the servants approached him with silent, careful steps across the marble.

"Sir, master Valen will see you. Please, follow me." Then she turned and started walking in the direction she came from without waiting for him.

He followed her—a quiet figure who moved ahead without looking back. She led him down a hall lined with portraits of Valen in grandiose military poses.

When they reached the door, Finneas adjusted the satchel and made sure the scroll was precisely visible.

The servant pushed and the door creaked open on a gust of lemon oil and road musk. He stepped inside.

Valen reclined deeper into his chair, watching the figure enter.

The messenger was exactly what Valen expected—lowborn posture, plain tunic smelling faintly of saddle and soap. Clean, but not overly so. He walked with the careful stiffness of a man who had memorized when to bow.

Which he did.

"My lord," the courier said, voice subdued. "Scroll from House Caerlyn."

Valen extended a hand, not rising.

"Caerlyn," Valen scoffed. "Maybe Quentyn's finally offering that sister of his—flame knows she's better bred than his grain."

He took the scroll and turned it slowly in his fingers. Gold seal. Crisp. The kind of crisp that came from cold vaults, not warm hands. His eyes flicked up, briefly, noting the courier's composure.

Nothing special. No scent of fear. No stammer. No real presence at all.

"Thank you. You may wait outside. If I find the offer interesting, I may even sign it in front of you. What a moment that would be, eh?"

The messenger gave a dutiful nod. "As you wish, my lord."

Valen waved a dismissive hand, already unrolling the scroll.

Outside the parlor, Alerick, in his guise as Finneas, lingered, feeling the weight of the silence close around him like a cloak.

The door shut behind him softly, a whisper of oak and iron that sealed him in Valen's strange domain. Through the corridors, serving women drifted in wool and shadow, their footsteps hushed as snowfall. They bore silver trays and rolled parchments with smooth, practiced movements, faces composed into quiet dignity.

One passed by carrying a gleaming comb and a goblet of something pungent, her eyes respectfully downcast, her expression inscrutable. Another padded by in the opposite direction, carrying an iron pot full of charcoal and cinders from a hearth in the next room; a subtle smudge of ash upon her sleeve the only hint of imperfection.

And then something stirred.

A memory, unbidden. He'd been ten, maybe. Time blurred the image—but not the smell: cedar and ash.

His father sat in a carved chair, reading aloud—his face lost to memory, just firelight and silhouette.

His voice was deep and sharp-edged, carving words into air like commandments—lessons about the Flame, about how ash must come after fire.

Ash is the memory of fire. It teaches us that nothing forgets.

The words struck harder than the voice. He hadn't understood them then. He wasn't sure he wanted to now.

His father had spoken of fire as inevitability. Every lesson circled back to ash. Alerick had dismissed it then as obsession.

But the words lingered.

His father had always spoken as if fire were inevitable—as if every path ended in ashes. Perhaps he'd been right, and it was only ever about choosing which fires to walk through.

Valen watched the door click shut, then broke the seal with his thumbnail.

The scroll resisted before giving way, wax snapping like a twig bent too far.

He read in silence.

For a fleeting second, suspicion crept behind Valen's practiced smirk. Quentyn had never been bold—clever, certainly, but this felt different.

He dismissed the thought with a sip of wine. Then a slow, incredulous chuckle rose—dry and sharp.

Rennic leaned slightly closer, silent, patient.

"Well?"

Valen handed it over. "Read it. I want to know if madness now prints its own stationery."

Rennic scanned the page. His lips thinned.

"They want you to store your grain in Caerlyn's silos," he said slowly. "All of it. This year's harvest, next year's reserves… even the unreaped oats from Hillmere."

Valen stood, his robe whispering across the stone like a dragged banner.

"They'll stockpile it and starve everyone else," he muttered. "Classic Caerlyn—turn scarcity into gold, and blood into margin."

Rennic's eyebrow lifted a fraction. "Twenty-three percent markup on all current ledgers. Waiver on southern tariffs. Generous—if you're stupid."

Valen laughed—sharp, delighted and savage.

Rennic returned the scroll to Valen's hands adding, "He speaks of new blood and loyalties. Interesting."

Valen sat back at his desk, the seat creaking under his weight, "Oh, Quentyn. You greedy little fox. You're trying to build a famine and sell me the crown for hosting it."

He picked up a plumed quill and moved towards the ink well. "Let's not ruin the scene. Let them believe I dance when they whistle." Then stopped, considering.

Valen briefly touched the corner of his mouth, checking for imagined imperfections before allowing a satisfied smile to settle.

He set the quill aside, still smirking, and glanced toward the door.

"Smudge," Valen said lightly. "Have her return."

Rennic inclined his head and signaled toward the hall.

The doors opened again moments later. The servant returned and stopped just inside the threshold.

"Yes, m'lord?"

"Fetch the courier. I want him to observe the finale."

She nodded and turned, vanishing through the tall double doors without a sound—silent as smoke.

Rennic tilted his head. "You want him as a witness?"

Valen chuckled. "Oh please, he's not a witness—he's a satchel with legs. Let him carry back the illusion that I signed with reverence."

She returned to the messenger and stood framed by the doorway, hands folded. Her voice was softer this time, barely audible.

"Sir, Lord Valen is waiting."

Alerick blinked once, feigning boredom then nodding with practiced awkwardness.

He adjusted his satchel and followed her.

She glanced back briefly before pushing open the tall doors. The hinges whispered gently, echoing the quiet atmosphere of Goldacre Manor.

Alerick—wearing Finneas's borrowed face—stepped inside.

He caught the tail of a chuckle—conversation between men who had never feared being overheard.

Valen waved a dismissive hand, unrolling the scroll.

He dipped the quill with theatrical flourish, then swept his name across the parchment—bold, looping strokes carved like a brand, the ink bleeding through the parchment, thick and black.

He paused, then lifted a stick of deep red sealing wax over a quiet flame until it dripped hot onto the page. The ring followed, pressed with deliberate slowness into the red wax, it took his mark cleanly, like skin accepts a scar.

He rolled the scroll, the wax seal still soft at the edges. A black silk cord followed—not for courtesy, but because deals, like blades, looked sharper when sheathed.

He held it out with a faint smirk.

"Return this to Lord Caerlyn. And give him my regards."

He paused. "Also… remind Quentyn that I've already priced his loyalty into the margin. He'll find it there—between desperation and silence."

Alerick took the scroll with both hands, tucked it into the satchel, bowed again and retreated without a word.

The door closed with a hush. Valen didn't bother to watch him leave.

The light in Goldacre's drawing room was low and amber-rich, cast not from candles, but from twisted glass globes that glowed like embers trapped in honey.

Lord Valen leaned against the edge of his writing desk, a glass of Westmere amber cradled like a secret.

Across the room, Rennic stood at the window, eyes flicking over the fog-drenched vineyard outside. The journal he held was half-open, but his mind was already ahead of it.

"Six invitations," Valen said. "Five that matter, and one just for the hell of it."

Rennic's brow lifted slightly. "You're inviting House Lesserin?"

Valen's smile widened. "Why not? Let Quentyn see his little nephew paraded beside the lions. It'll make him nervous. Or stupid. I'm satisfied either way."

Rennic turned a page. "The others?"

"Quentyn. And Narcona, of course," Valen said, swirling his wine. "Dravik will come because he believes in duty—and because he's too proud to let anyone else represent the Shelf."

Rennic nodded.

"Lady Wynmere," Valen went on. "She'll come for the wine, stay for the spite. I'm told she loathes me, but respects my taste in musicians. Branik as well. His loyalty has been questionable of late. I want to measure his backbone."

Rennic looked up. "And Icewind?"

Valen's grin thinned. "Ah, Lady Elara. She will send a reply penned in frost and forged in manners. But she'll come. She's too careful not to."

He gestured toward the stack of sealed parchments. "I've drafted the invitations myself. Subtle enough not to be treason, pointed enough to make them wonder. Each scroll sealed with my crest, scented with myrrh and just enough truth to be dangerous."

Rennic picked one up reading it.

'To the Lords and Ladies of Esteemed Lineage—

An Evening of Reflection and Reckoning. Goldacre awaits your presence beneath an unclouded moon. Discussion. Delicacy. Direction.

—Lord Circus Valen of Goldacre"

He set it down. "Poetic. Cryptic. Almost sincere." Rennic carefully aligned the parchment, adjusting it fractionally to ensure the edges were precisely parallel with the edge of the desk. His fingertips lingered just a moment longer, confirming perfect symmetry before withdrawing.

Valen raised his glass. "Exactly the flavor of bait they can't resist."

Rennic clasped his hands behind his back. "And if the queen hears of this?"

Valen smirked. "She's not invited. Let her learn secondhand. Let her wonder why five great houses are drinking my wine while she recites grain tallies."

Rennic paused. "It's dangerous. Even for you."

Valen drained the glass and set it down with a soft *clink*.

"Everything worth doing is."

Outside, the air tasted cleaner yet still carried Goldacre's subtle perfume—figs and secrets clinging stubbornly to fabric and memory alike. Castellon's distant towers shimmered gold in the haze, dusk bleeding into rooftops like spilled ink over old parchment. The shadows lengthened, and with them, the rhythm of the city shifted—lanterns lighting, shutters closing, voices lowering.

Alerick crossed the lower city on foot; a carriage would have been faster—and raised questions.

So he walked.

The distance gave him space, time to consider all the players on the board.

He turned corners without thinking, cutting through courtyards, slipping past gates and shuttered stalls like he'd lived here all his life. He hadn't. But the lie felt good under his heels.

By the time he reached his apartment, the sun had fallen behind the city wall, a soft, hazy orange rim lit his window.

Inside, the room greeted him with its usual chaos: the half-painted canvases, the cold basin still flecked with yesterday's dust. He closed the door, bolted it, and let the stillness settle.

He hung up the satchel carefully, almost reverently. The scroll went atop the writing desk, still warm from his hand. Still sealed with Valen's ring, the red wax catching the fading sunlight.

One piece at a time, he peeled the courier away.

He removed the tunic and boots, shed the posture. Rubbed off the stubble. Combed out the dye.

Splashing water over his face, he watched it drip Finneas from the man looking back in the cracked mirror above the basin.

The mask was gone.

He dried his face with an old cloth and saw his own reflection, Alerick now. Not Faileas. Not Finneas.

The accent, he shed with a muttered curse.

And then—those words again.

Ash is the memory of fire. It teaches us that nothing forgets.

Why now?

He braced both hands on the rim of the basin and stared into the blur. Not his father's face. That was lost.

But the scent of him lingered in memory—cedar and ash. Always ash. A fire never seen, but always implied.

Another phrase surfaced—older, colder, pulled from a corner of the mind he barely dared disturb.

A Flamebound king… a flame never lit.

He didn't know why the words echoed now, or what they meant. He frowned—not at the phrase, but at the silence it left behind.

He didn't remember when he'd first heard it, or whether it came from his father or some ruined text.

But it stayed. Not loud. Not urgent. Simply there.

He stood still a long time.

Then, with no great flourish, he poured a glass of Wynmere dry—earthy, a little bitter. He stepped onto the narrow balcony, leaned one arm on the railing, and watched the sun paint Castellon's rooftops in rust and flame.

He sipped the wine and stared into the dying light.

CHAPTER THREE

The Royal Library of Eldaraine breathed out the weight of centuries with every creaking shelf. Dust hung in sunbeams like old secrets, spinning above shelves that climbed toward the vaulted ceiling. Thick tomes lined every wall, bound in cracked leather and stitched parchment, their spines inked with titles in three dead languages. Candles wept wax in iron sconces.

Prince Baldrik Thornsword lounged in a high-backed chair with all the grace of a man punishing furniture for existing.

His doublet—green, gold-threaded, and twice as regal as he felt—hung on him like a borrowed title. A history of maritime treaties lay open, unread. His boots sprawled across a low table, flanked by ledgers lined up like loyal fools—still waiting on a commander who'd rather be anywhere else.

Across from him, Queen Avanna stood—rigid grace coiled around steel restraint, the kind that cracked stone given time.

"You are the heir to Eldaraine," she said, voice clipped but calm. "Your kingdom will be won or lost not on the battlefield, but here—between parchment and policy."

Baldrik let the weight of her words settle briefly, feigning contemplation before flipping another page with all the interest of a monk proofreading fish tallies.

"Should I duel the tax code first, or would the port tariffs prefer jousting at dawn?"

Avanna's brow twitched—just enough to signal the storm gathering behind her eyes.

"This isn't a jest, Baldrik."

"You sure? Because it reads like one."

She cut across the room, slammed the book shut, and leveled a stare sharp enough to draw blood from vellum.

"The Stonewrights demand tariff rollbacks. Westmere's wine district has militias settling land claims with swords instead of seals. Poachers—Flame burn them—are emptying our forests of elk and deer.

If Scorchland raiders choke the southern roads, the eastern free-villages starve before thaw. Hillmere's roads can't carry grain, Highfield's stores are already rotting, and Icewind's tidy little ledgers hide empty harvests."

Baldrik hesitated. "And that's… genuinely bad, I take it?"

Avanna's voice dropped, sharp with measured patience. "Starving villages lead to riots, Baldrik. And when hunger comes, they won't curse poachers or Scorchland raiders. They'll curse the king. Your father."

"Ah. Then yes, probably bad."

Baldrik's jaw tightened slightly, her words pressing into him like thumbs into a fresh bruise.

Avanna's voice dropped further, carrying the full consequence of the words. "If the populace struggles to feed themselves—their children. It will lead to unrest. Not rebellion. But something close enough to bleed for."

Avanna turned, pacing between towering shelves. Her fingers brushed spines, briefly trembling, as if daring the histories to judge queen and mother alike.

"Your father forges the steel," she said quietly, pausing as if measuring each word. "I bend the quills and bribe the wolves. Someday, both weights will fall onto your shoulders—ready or not."

Baldrik watched her pace. The smile was gone. Just the unreadable stillness of someone weighing the cost of speaking.

"I'm eighteen. That buys me at least a few more mistakes, doesn't it?"

She turned on her heel—sharp, sudden, as if the past had struck her first.

"Mistakes crown kings, Baldrik. Your grandfather didn't get a choice either. Your great-grandfather—King Maldran—slipped during the River Avahn's thaw—foot caught on wet stone. A misstep ended him there. No glory. No hero's death. Just gravity doing its work."

She didn't need to say more. The shame wasn't in the mourning—it was in the absurdity. Baldrik could hear it in her voice: the insult of randomness. That a king, descended from conquerors, could be ended by a riverbank and gravity itself.

"They pulled your grandfather straight from the training yard. Still had a wooden sword in his hand when they named him king."

Baldrik held still. His stillness was sharp now—no longer bored, no longer mocking. He stared at the edge of his boot, as if it might speak.

"And he ruled for forty years," Avanna continued. "Not because he was ready. But because someone had to remind the realm: even when fate mocks kings, the crown does not slip."

Silence settled between them, thick with more history than Baldrik had ever bothered to read. Then came the smirk—slow, deliberate, far too pleased with itself.

"Was that a pun? Great-grandfather slips, crown slips… I mean, it's pretty poetic for a tragedy. Almost like the Flame was making commentary."

Avanna narrowed her eyes, brief confusion shadowing her composure. "Is this a game to you, Baldrik?"

"What? I'm putting a lot of thought into it. That's how seriousness works, isn't it?"

She didn't sigh. But something flickered behind her eyes—a fracture carefully concealed, a moment of weariness quickly shuttered against a brewing storm.

Baldrik opened his mouth, one more quip loading, but he saw it. The change. The weight she didn't show unless it cracked through.

He let it die there.

His brow furrowed. His voice was quieter now.

"That's not in the histories."

"No," she said, voice soft but cutting. "It shames the court. Not the boy—the death. A king lost to wet rock and a foolish step. No last words. Just blood on stone, and a kingdom left grasping for dignity."

She stepped closer. Her voice didn't rise, but each word cut cleaner than the last.

"He ruled for forty years, my son—not because he was ready, but because someone had to show the world: Eldaraine does not flinch."

Baldrik stared at the floor for a long moment, then leaned back. His fingers tapped the ledger, testing its rhythm, as if one misplaced note might let him laugh it away.

"Still sounds easier than negotiating with the Stonewrights."

Avanna exhaled through her nose—not sharp, not tired—*contained.* Like someone keeping the fire from catching the curtain.

Baldrik glanced away, suddenly aware of the invisible tension coiled between them.

"You think this is beneath you," she said. "You think your path leads somewhere else. But a crown isn't worn when you want it—it's *thrown* at you when the kingdom needs it. And you will wear it, Baldrik. Or it will grind your name into the dust beneath it."

He met her gaze then. Really met it. And for one small, traitorous moment, something flickered behind his usual smirk. Not surrender—never that. Then it vanished again, tucked behind the practiced shrug of boyish charm.

"Maybe I'll just become a librarian," he said. "I am already dressed like one."

Her hand twitched—barely. Toward a book thick enough to teach lessons the old way.

Baldrik's smirk vanished—briefly revealing the uncertainty lurking beneath. A shadow of fear he quickly buried.

He glanced away, toward the stained glass, the tension slipping from confrontation into something profound. The etched glass of the Flamebound window hung unmoving—patterns of flame, sword and balance. Crimson and gold bled across his boots and the shelves beside him.

"You know," he said—his voice lighter than it had any right to be, like someone skipping stones over ice they suspected was thin, "the Flamebound say true purpose isn't inherited. It's chosen. Or revealed, if you're listening hard enough."

Avanna froze—not visibly, not dramatically, but with the tension of someone hearing a blade drawn behind her, uncertain if it meant protection or betrayal.

"I've been listening," He went on. "And what I hear doesn't sound like scrollwork and grain taxes."

"The monks," she said slowly, "do not choose their priests from thrones, Baldrik. They choose from ash and flame. You were born to bear the fire, not walk in it."

"You don't know that," he said. Not louder. Just sharper. Like a blade testing its own edge.

"I—do."

It wasn't shouted. It was final. The library had held its breath long before now, but her voice—steel rasped along stone—made even the fire falter.

She crossed the room and planted both hands on the long table between them, knuckles bone-white.

"You want purpose?" she said. "Then read the names inked into these books. Every one of them breathes because this house—*our house*—holds."

She leaned in. "This isn't a calling you walk away from because riddles and incense feel safer than names carved in blood and barley."

Baldrik remained silent.

His fingers curled around the armrest, not in rebellion, but to steady himself. The boy who wanted to speak vanished. The prince remained. What came out wasn't venom—it was truth.

"You've already chosen my life for me."

Avanna flinched—not visibly, but a tremor passed through her, quickly masked. Just a catch behind the eyes. Words she couldn't swallow and couldn't say.

Then came the sound of a door opening—quiet, precise, slicing through the silence. No announcement. No fanfare. Just undeniable *presence.*

Lord Lanyard Darkoak stepped into the library like a shadow across stone—slow and inevitable. The high-collared black of Castellon's inner court accented the sword at his hip, looking more ornament than threat. But everyone knew better.

His eyes—grey, sharp, and void of mercy—landed on Baldrik first. Then shifted to Avanna.

He offered no greeting.

His arrival sank the room into quiet. The tension between mother and son, already pulled taut, froze into something brittle.

Avanna straightened subtly, hands folding in front of her like ribbon over parchment. Her gaze flickered briefly to Lanyard, a brief acknowledgment of the balance he represented—stability bought with steel and silence.

Baldrik stood with a sigh, brushing off the dust.

"The Sword of the King," he muttered. "Right on time."

"Poor timing is youth's privilege," he said. "And the burden of those who clean up after them."

He stepped closer, voice like dry slate.

"Your training master has been waiting on the grounds since midday. He's not known for his patience."

Baldrik grimaced. "Flame forbid I keep a man waiting just because his sword's sharper than his wit."

He moved toward the exit with deliberate reluctance, pausing only to pluck the Maritime Treaty of Vara Archipelago from the table and toss it toward the shelf. It landed sideways in a pile of ink-stained scrolls.

He didn't move to fix it, just shrugged and slipped through the far doors.

The moment the latch clicked behind him, a hush reclaimed the room.

Lanyard turned to Avanna—quietly, but not gently.

"He still thinks the world will wait for him to grow up. As if it ever would."

Avanna's gaze lingered on the door.

"No," she said. "He thinks it won't notice when he doesn't."

Lanyard gave no reply.

She turned to the table, fingers brushing the spine of the abandoned archive, then stopping, as if the weight of it resisted her touch.

Outside, sunlight bent low through the stained glass, gold deepening into brass. The symbols on the window—stone, flame, balance, sword—hung in silence, as they always had.

Lanyard waited a breath longer before speaking, his voice low, steady, and unyielding.

"He goes to the yard often enough. Though I sometimes wonder if he's training to fight his enemies, or just to escape them."

Avanna gave a faint smile—tired, sharp, unfunny—then let it fade into something quieter, something closer to acceptance.

"At least the sword doesn't ask him questions he can't answer."

The training yard of Castellon was a scar of churned earth, slush, and sweat—ringed by sparring posts, weapon racks, and the echoes of bruises not yet earned. Noon light lay pale and unforgiving between the towers, catching on blades, helms, and the bald head of the yard's most terrifying resident.

Commander Elessan Cinquedea was mid-rant, which meant the old gods themselves were ducking for cover.

"You lazy-eyed, slack-jawed bucket of goat piss!" he roared, hurling a practice sword into the mud with such force it stuck upright like a grave marker. "That wasn't a thrust!"

A boy of maybe fifteen stood wobbling in mismatched greaves, one arm raised too high and the other clinging to his blade like it might fly away if unobserved.

Cinquedea stormed toward him, limping not from pain, but from muscle memory—like a man whose body had long since forgotten how to break down.

The boy swallowed visibly, his face pale beneath dirt and shame, desperately trying not to let the sword slip further in his trembling grip.

"You're not fighting for your life. You're not fighting for your name. You're fighting for my patience, and son, that's a battle you already lost!"

The boy tried to reset his stance.

"Oh! What's this now?" Cinquedea gestured theatrically, spinning on one heel and miming court applause. "Look at him! A miracle! A stance so crooked it's pissing sideways!"

From behind a stack of weighted shields came a sound Baldrik hadn't expected: a muffled *bawk.*

Cinquedea's eyes narrowed.

He reached down, hauling something dramatically from a nearby crate, pausing just long enough to ensure every eye was riveted before raising it—like a heretic triumphantly unveiling a forbidden relic.

Baldrik leaned slightly forward, curiosity edging past his practiced boredom. Whatever came next promised to be anything but ordinary.

It was a chicken. Feathers fluffed, eyes wild.

The yard froze. Even the wind seemed to pause.

"This," Cinquedea declared, brandishing the bird like it was an unpaid debt, "is your opponent now."

The boy's eyes went wide. "What?"

The commander didn't blink.

"You heard me. If you can't outmatch a cockerel with more spine than you, then maybe you should marry it and breed warriors with better instincts!"

The chicken flailed.

Cinquedea flung it.

The bird exploded into flight with a shriek of wings and indignation—beak-first toward the boy, who screamed, dropped his sword, and fell backward into the half-frozen mud with a wet, humiliating sprawl.

The bird landed on his chest flapping it wings and strutted off like it had won something sacred.

Baldrik felt laughter rise—unbidden and impossible to contain—releasing a tension he hadn't realized he was holding.

Not a chuckle. A sharp bark of amusement—unwelcome and too loud.

Every face turned—mud-streaked, bruised, exhausted—united in disbelief, relief, and wary anticipation.

Cinquedea turned last, slowly, deliberately, his single good eye narrowing with the dangerous curiosity of a predator spotting unexpected prey.

"Ah," he said. "The princely turd finally floats to the surface."

Baldrik's smirk faltered briefly, masking a pang of genuine irritation beneath practiced humor. "Good to see your charming disposition survived the morning."

"You're late."

"I'm royal."

"You're useless."

"You're limping."

"I'm winning."

Baldrik descended the steps, removing his cloak. The cold courtyard pressed against him, damp and raw.

Cinquedea leaned on a wooden post, thick arms folded across his chest—every inch the battle-worn terror he meant to be. "You think you're clever. You think your blood gives you license to be soft."

Baldrik paused at the edge of the training circle, sizing up the master-at-arms with wary respect. The easy banter faded as reality pressed closer.

"Soft?" Baldrik rolled his sleeves, the coarse fabric chafing his skin. His eyes darted briefly to the scattered feathers on the training ground, a wry smirk tugging at his lips. "I just watched you declare war on poultry."

"Bird has better reflexes than half my squad," Cinquedea growled. "And more guts than your cousin before he pissed himself during jousting drills."

Baldrik stepped into the ring, a corner of his mouth twitching before he smoothed it away. "Which cousin?"

Cinquedea didn't answer. He tossed a blunted practice sword at Baldrik's chest.

The prince caught it—barely.

"You come late, you bleed early," Cinquedea said. "Lesson one. No warmups. No welcomes. Just pain."

Baldrik's jaw tightened slightly; a quiet defiance flickered in his eyes. He turned the blade in his hand, getting a feel for the weight.

"You always this poetic?"

The commander's grin cracked wide, all yellow teeth and scar-twisted cheek.

"Only when I smell failure."

He turned to the rest of the trainees, most of whom were still staring at the chicken, now roosting proudly on the weapons rack like a usurper god, drawing suppressed laughter and sidelong glances from the trainees under Cinquedea's glare.

"Form pairs!" Cinquedea bellowed. "Except for our royal blossom here. He gets—me."

One of the younger recruits whispered something and got backhanded with a gauntlet.

Baldrik's grip tightened. "I didn't come here for special treatment."

Cinquedea stepped into the ring and drew his own blade. Not a blunted one—real steel, chipped and ugly.

"No," he said. "You came to prove your mother wrong." Baldrik stiffened, his breath briefly catching in his chest. His shoulders tightened as his gaze hardened.

The yard fell silent again; the pale winter sun hung high and unkind, casting sharp shadows across frost-slick ground.

Baldrik's smirk vanished, like warmth on cold iron.

Cinquedea's tone dropped. "You think this court will wait while you figure out who you are? It won't. It'll kill you, grind up your corpse, and feed it to the next pretty heir with softer hands."

Baldrik's jaw tightened; unease flickered through his eyes. "There isn't another heir."

Cinquedea's grin twisted, sharp and humorless. "Then you'd better learn to fight, or you'll be taking more than a sword to your backside."

Cinquedea lifted his weapon.

"So let's find out if you bleed blue, or just leak privilege."

Baldrik raised his training-sword, gripping it tightly; uncertainty trembled through his stance.

The circle of trainees tightened around them.

Baldrik moved first—impulse driving instinct. His boots scraped sharply against slick stones as adrenaline surged through him, breath fogging faintly in the cold air.

A sharp thrust aimed at Cinquedea's midsection, blade straight and true.

But Cinquedea had seen better lies told by dying men. He angled sideways, caught the thrust on his guard, and twisted.

Steel clanged and sparks kissed the dirt as Baldrik stumbled—but recovered, barely, eyes flashing.

He came again, low this time, sweeping for the knees. A clever strike. Smart.

Too smart.

Cinquedea stepped in, batted the blade aside with his forearm, and buried his hilt into Baldrik's stomach—just below the ribs, where breath turns to fire.

The prince doubled. The blow that followed was worse. A punch. Straight to the jaw. No finesse. No warning. Just the commander's knuckles, calloused and uncaring, colliding with princely pride.

Baldrik hit the ground hard; pain radiated, ears rang as humiliation burned through him.

Stone kissed spine. Icy grit and mud splashed up.

Just like that, the ring stopped watching a prince.

They started watching a boy.

Tunic damp with sweat, he rolled and came up swinging—only to have the weapon slapped from his hands. It skittered across the stone.

"Get up, princeling," Cinquedea snarled, contempt sharp enough to cut stone. "Or is the dirt your throne now?" His voice was gravel soaked in vinegar.

"Pitiful," he barked, looming over the prince, his jaw clenched tight. "I've seen better form from a dead squirrel being fucked by a goose."

Baldrik groaned, spitting blood onto the dirt, tasting iron. His head spun slightly, pain throbbing through every muscle.

Cinquedea turned to the squires watching from the sidelines. "You lot see that? That's a Thornsword. Royal blood."

"Bleeds like the rest of us, shits like the rest of us, flailing like a boy trying to outswim piss in a bathhouse."

He looked back at Baldrik, eyes hard as steel. "Pick it up."

Baldrik staggered to his feet. "What—"

"I said pick it up, not piss about." Cinquedea bent, grabbed the fallen blade, and chucked it at him.

Baldrik caught it by instinct, the hilt slamming painfully into his palm, sending a jolt of shock up his arm as he fought to keep his grip firm.

"Good," the commander snapped. "At least your hands know what they're for."

He circled Baldrik slowly now, tapping the edge of his own blade against the back of the boy's legs, shoulders, ribs. Each spot he touched drew a flinch.

"You want to wear a crown? Learn to wear a bruise first. You want to give orders? Learn how to take a hit and stay standing. You want glory?" He snorted. "Find a bard."

He stopped in front of Baldrik and lowered his voice so only he could hear.

"Out there, it's not your name that'll keep you alive. It's your footwork and how fast you remember what pain tastes like. Forget that, and I'll dig your royal corpse out of a ditch myself and use it to train the next idiot who thinks the Flame owes him something."

Then louder, to the yard: "Again!"

From the overlook above the training yard—a narrow gallery beneath the eastern rampart—two men watched the prince bleed. Lord Darkoak stood arms crossed against his chest, eyes fixed on the ring below, his face betraying nothing despite the chill breeze.

King Harald leaned against the balustrade beside him, arms folded, one boot resting on the lower ledge. The wind teased at the edges of his cloak, whispering coldly around him, but the king did not shiver.

Below, Baldrik rose—slower this time. Commander Cinquedea barked something unintelligible, and flung the fallen weapon at the boy's chest.

The prince caught it, stumbling slightly as he fought to regain his balance. His stance was improving, but not fast enough; each misstep tightening Harald's jaw imperceptibly.

Harald exhaled through his nose, the sound closer to a grunt than a sigh.

"He's trying," the king said.

"He's flailing," Lord Darkoak replied. "There's a difference."

"Sometimes they look the same," Harald muttered.

Below, Baldrik lunged. Too wide. Too eager. Cinquedea pivoted, smacked his wrist with the flat of his blade, and sent the prince spinning.

"Good!" Cinquedea shouted. "Better! Now you might even fend off the squirrels nibbling at your ash-damned nuts!"

A ripple of nervous laughter drifted through the slush-churned yard, mingling with distant sword clashes. A scowl from Baldrik. Another fall.

Lord Darkoak didn't blink. "His reach is poor. His balance worse. He reacts, but does not read. Still too proud to anticipate the blow."

"Still eighteen," Harald said, his voice calm.

"That's not young for a battlefield. Or a throne," Darkoak replied.

"I know."

They stood in silence a moment longer, watching Baldrik stagger upright. Sweat matted his hair, his face flushed with frustration as he struggled to regain his footing.

Harald's gaze remained fixed.

"He doesn't want it," he said at last, a subtle note of disappointment threading through his voice.

"The throne?"

Harald nodded.

"I've seen men fake loyalty. I've seen men fake faith. You can't fake hunger. And he's never once looked at that chair like it was his to take."

Lord Darkoak's eyes never left the ring. "Then where does his hunger live?"

"I don't know," Harald said.

"That should concern you."

"It does."

Cinquedea advanced again, boots kicking up icy grit and filling the air with the sharp scent of sweat and stone.

The rhythmic clang of swords echoed as his blade cut quick, precise arcs through the air.

Baldrik parried once—twice—then dropped low in a clever pivot, managing to tap the commander's leg with the tip of his sword.

Cinquedea stopped. Looked down.

Grunted.

Then whacked the prince across the shoulder so hard he crumpled like a tent in wind, pain jolting through his shoulder, a bitter taste rising in his throat.

"Better," the commander said. "Still shit. But better."

Lord Darkoak's mouth twitched. "He learns. Slowly. Under pain."

"Most of us did." Harald said.

Another pause followed. Below, Cinquedea hauled Baldrik to his feet by the front of his tunic and shoved him back into stance.

Then Lanyard spoke quietly: "The other boy…"

Harald's jaw tightened, an uneasy shadow flickering behind his eyes. For a brief moment, the rhythmic clash of swords and distant murmurs filled the pause. "What of him?"

"He learns faster. No sense of entitlement to shed. Nothing to prove but the steel in his hand."

A long silence followed. The wind moved past them like a disapproving ghost.

Harald didn't look away from the yard, the wind tugging at his cloak. His voice dropped—lower, colder. "Do you think he'd take it?"

Lord Darkoak didn't answer right away. The pause itself was answer enough.

Harald's lips pressed into a thin line.

"I want him trained harder," he said.

Lord Darkoak's brow lifted, just slightly. "Harder than this?"

"I'm not talking about Baldrik."

A pause.

"Push him. Not past breaking. Just far enough that he must decide whether to."

"And if he does?"

"Then we'll know what kind of steel he's made of."

Below, Cinquedea barked another insult and hurled another chicken. It clucked indignantly.

"There's talk in the court," Lord Darkoak said. "Quiet, but growing."

"Let them talk."

"They question the heir's fire."

"It's not their fire to question."

"But they'll ask anyway."

Harald's hands settled on the balustrade.

"They asked the same of me."

"You had a command by nineteen."

"I had a war."

"You had clarity."

Harald gave the faintest nod. "That, I did."

He turned only halfway. "He's not weak. Just wandering."

"He can't afford to wander much longer," Darkoak said.

"No." Harald conceded.

Silence followed again.

Then Harald added, almost carelessly, "If word gets out about the other boy—shut it down."

Lord Darkoak didn't nod. Didn't speak.

But the message landed.

Below, Baldrik slipped again and hit the ground with a groan. He did not rise immediately.

Cinquedea stood over him, panting, sweat darkening his tunic, blade lowered.

Waiting.

Baldrik still didn't move.

"You rest when you're dead, your highness. Or when I am. And I'm not dead yet."

The yard swirled with dirty slush, and the stink of hard-earned failure.

"Keep pushing him," Harald said quietly. "We may need more than one name ready when the crown weighs in."

Then, without another word, he turned and walked away. The wind rushed down from the north, chilling the air.

Lord Darkoak remained a moment longer, watching the prince below fail again—less dramatically this time.

Below, Cinquedea straightened and raised both arms like a prophet in a pit of mud.

"That's it!" he bellowed, his jaw tightening. "Training's done! Go soak your bruises, wipe your tears, and if you see that ash-damned chicken—salute it! It fought better than half of you!"

The trainees scattered, boots sloshing through mud and slush as the yard began to empty.

Lord Darkoak turned and followed his king.

Still silent. Still watching.

High above the training yard, in a crescent alcove of stained glass and ashwood lattice, Queen Avanna Thornsword watched her son fall—again.

The pane-glass nearest her cast gold across her cheekbone—warm. Deceitful. Below, Baldrik rose slowly, blade dangling from slack fingers, shoulders tight, jaw clenched. His tunic clung darkly at the ribs where the blows had landed.

The boy did not cry out. He did not curse. But he did not rise like a prince either.

Avanna's hands remained folded at her waist. Only her fingers tightened.

The yard rang with Cinquedea's voice—mockery wrapped in gravel. Laughter followed.

She turned from the window.

Not with anger. Not with despair.

With calculation.

Her chambers lay quiet behind her: silk sliding softly against stone, the faint creak of the casement, the familiar scent of ink and parchment. A ledger lay open on the table—grain tallies from Hillmere, unsatisfactory. Ashbriar reports waited beneath a paperweight, unopened.

A smaller note lay beside them, hastily penned by a mayoral steward from Tarnhollow:

Storm sightings. Northwind merchants growing quiet. Roads soft. Roads dangerous.

She touched none of it.

Instead, Avanna moved to the low shelf beneath the casement. Behind a carved ashwood screen rested a narrow teak case, unmarked and unsealed.

She opened it.

Inside lay a bundle of corded strands—dark ash-fiber and drift-pearl thread, looped and knotted with deliberate care. A Flamebound measure-string, gifted long ago.

She drew it out, letting its weight settle across her palm. Her thumb found the first knot by habit, then the next, the cord sliding through her fingers in measured rhythm.

Avanna let the cord move, knot by knot, the discipline of measure and order settling into her hands.

Below, steel rang again. Someone groaned. Cinquedea barked.

She returned the measure string and closed the case.

Only then did she speak—quietly, without turning back to the window. "If you fall, my son, I will still build a crown. Even from the ashes."

Avanna stood at the long reading table, scrolls unfurled before her—grain counts, border disputes, tariff negotiations dressed in calligraphy and quiet contempt. Her fingers moved with the meticulous grace of one tutored in patience and diplomacy—elegance honed not for beauty, but for survival.

She scanned the latest report from Highfield—supply shortfalls creeping like slow poison, minor raids stirring discontent. Troublesome, but nothing she couldn't bend quietly with coin and a carefully placed word.

The next scroll bore the plum wax of House Tyrenth—petitioning for a larger share of Castellon's sea trade.

She set it aside dismissing it. They always asked for more. They rarely earned it.

Her hand hesitated.

A letter lay among the scrolls—smaller, folded thrice, sealed in plain wax. No crest. No flourish. Its anonymity was louder than any sigil.

Her brow knit, subtly. The script on the outer fold was elegant, unhurried—masculine, perhaps. Unfamiliar. But not careless. Her fingers paused on the parchment—just long enough to feel the texture beneath it—before moving again.

To His Majesty, King Harald Thornsword—

She did not open it. That was not her place.

But her thumb slid along the edge, and she noted something strange: the parchment was doubled. A second layer folded inside, tighter, thinner.

She lifted the letter toward the candlelight, careful not to break trust, but keen enough to trace subtle secrets hidden in shadow.

The inner sheet was narrower. Different grain. Slightly older.

She placed the letter aside, top corner facing down, marking it for later.

The next scroll bore the dark green wax of House Thornsword.

She broke the seal and read.

Her lips thinned.

Arrowhall Tower reports Hravnskot activity increasing on the Eastern Ironback Pass.

That region was meant to remain dormant—a trade corridor wrapped in frost and monotony, not suspicion. But the Thornsword scouts had spotted movement: *warbands shifting*, not posturing. Clans that had no reason to coordinate were suddenly seen traveling the same routes, setting the same campfires.

No raids. No attacks. Just—presence.

Pressure.

A line at the bottom, scribbled in haste:

"Not sure what they're after. But they're looking south, not east. And they're not hiding it."

Avanna reread the sentence twice.

Then she folded the scroll.

And here she stood, the weight of the court pressing in without a single voice raised.

She turned back to the sealed note to Harald. Tapped it twice with an obsidian-painted nail.

Then she walked to the side table, retrieved a slim silver case, and placed the letter inside.

For now, other things demanded watching.

She moved to the hearth, staring into the coals, their faint crackle whispering empty promises, the scent of charred wood steadying her thoughts.

Clans didn't move without cause—not in winter's dead grasp, not in careful coordination, and certainly not toward her throne.

She thought of the Storm—rumors, myths, exile-born names rising in taverns and travel songs. Thought of Baldrik—still nursing bruises. And thought of the strange letter, sealed but humming with weight.

Then another absence pressed at the edge of her thoughts:

Still no missive from Vara.

Not unusual, not entirely. The island kingdom had always kept its own rhythm—trade partners, naval allies, but never vassals. Miroray would say as much with a smile and a tilt of her crown.

Weeks had passed without word from her sister—no comforting line, no reassuring sails on the horizon, not even a whispered rumor to ease her growing unease.

"Strange."

Avanna reached for her ink-set, hesitated, then let her hand fall back to her side. It was late.

"Tomorrow," she told herself. "I'll write her tomorrow."

Baldrik said nothing as he left the training yard.

He didn't nod to the squires. He didn't thank Cinquedea. He didn't even roll his shoulders like usual—his quiet defiance, his *I'm still standing* flourish.

He just walked.

Past the stone barracks, their roofs rimmed with frost. Past the kennels, where the warhounds didn't bark for him anymore, breath steaming faintly. Past a servant girl who curtsied and looked away too quickly, her cloak drawn tight against the chill.

He found the garden court just before dusk—a half-forgotten quadrant beneath the eastern towers, where rosewood trees leaned bare over cracked, frost-slick tile and the air smelled faintly of cinderpetal and old frost. Distant castle sounds drifted through the leaves, muted.

Here, at least, the walls didn't expect him to win.

He slumped onto a bench rimmed with chill, wincing as pain rippled through his ribs and shoulders. He pressed a hand to his side, then let it fall. His jaw throbbed where Cinquedea's knuckles had kissed it.

"You want glory? Find a bard."

He huffed a breath that might have been a laugh. It hurt.

A crow landed nearby, talons scraping against frost-dusted stone. It tilted its head, watching him, and hopped along the stone.

Then came footsteps.

The soft scrape of woven, sandaled soles on tile.

Baldrik kept his gaze lowered. "If you're here to tell me I'm disappointing the realm, take a number."

The voice that answered was quiet. Male. Neither young nor old.

"I've no numbers. Only questions."

Baldrik glanced up.

A figure stood a few paces away—plain ash-grey robes, hood low. A satchel at his hip, a twist of incense braided into his flame-spun belt. No weapon. No crest.

"You're Flamebound," Baldrik said.

A nod. "For a time."

Baldrik wiped sweat from his brow, breath fogging as he exhaled. "What, come to check on the faithful? Or recruit?"

"Neither." The monk's gaze didn't waver. "I saw a prince walk like a beggar. I thought perhaps he needed something."

Baldrik snorted. "What I need isn't something incense can fix."

"No," said the monk. "But fire isn't for fixing. It's for revealing."

Baldrik watched him a moment. "And what exactly do you think's being revealed?"

The monk breathed in slowly, as if testing the air.

"That you are angry. Not at the blade. Not at the bruises. But at the weight no one asked you if you wanted to carry. What weight are you willing to carry? What weight do you want to shed?"

Baldrik offered no reply.

After a moment the monk went on.

"Ash remembers. It remembers what has burned. And why."

Then he stepped back and bowed once—not deeply, but with precise stillness.

"When the fire finds you," he said, "don't run from the pain. Follow the smoke."

Then he turned and walked away, passing between hedge and hall until he was simply gone.

Baldrik remained on the bench.

He didn't call after him.

The crow took flight.

The garden dimmed as the light shifted from pale amber to grey. Baldrik's breathing slowed. The ache in his ribs dulled, settling into something heavy and constant, made sharper by the cold.

He reached down and picked up a fallen blossom near his boot. Cinderpetal—black-edged, red at the core. It crumbled between his fingers, leaving a faint scent of ash.

Baldrik brushed his hands together and stood.

He had no answer.

But for the first time, he didn't turn away from the question either.

CHAPTER FOUR

The sun didn't simply shine over the Vara Archipelago—it performed.

It spilled molten gold across the jungle canopy in long, theatrical sweeps, igniting dew-beaded leaves like fire across emerald glass. The air shimmered with heat and promise, thick with the scents of ripe firefruit, crushed lemongrass, and distant brine.

Below, the sea spoke in a dozen tongues—lapping at reefstone, slapping against hulls. The waters here were rarely just blue—celadon near the shallows, rich lapis farther out, and near-black beneath the drop-offs where the reef gave way to the open sea.

Princess Kirahnae—sixteen and already carrying the weight of a crown not yet hers—paused on the terrace overlooking Vael'Shura, her breath catching at the rippling waters below. She straightened her spine. Today required strength.

On the cliffs of Vael'Shura—the Crown Isle—woven banners danced on poles carved from storm-felled teak. They snapped in rhythm with the wind; each stitched with the serpent-vine sigils of royal blood. From the canopy terraces of Shan'Telune to the misted lower groves, the island stirred as Kirahnae watched.

It was wedding day.

Far beneath, the harbor sang, and Kirahnae's gaze lingered at the horizon.

White-hulled longships trimmed in reefbone and jungle bark bobbed in their moorings. Sails painted in dusk reds and seabird silver caught the warm wind as if aching to leave port even before the feast. Some bore the crests of high bloodlines—Reefkin, Tidecaller, Flamegrove. Others, older still, were marked only by shark teeth and storm glyphs, painted by hands that remembered bloodier ages.

Princess Kirahnae stood at the coral-edged balustrade, her green-gold eyes tracing the fleet's rhythmic movements below. Rowers moved in rhythm, oars cutting arcs into the surf. Drummers signaled from prow towers, calling to islanders on shore with beats meant for celebration and coordination. Bells rang from towers carved directly into coral cliffs, their notes tuned not to chime but to *hum*—a sound that resonated in the ribs and teeth.

From the lower terraces of the capital, plumes of scented fire drifted upward—thin braids of spiced palm oil, ground clove, and roasting sweetroot.

Women sang as they cooked—melodies woven from sea chants and birth hymns, passed down not in notes, but in breath and word.

In the palace above the jungle court, the air changed.

The open terraces gave way to stone corridors and carved thresholds where wind softened into breath and sunlight fractured into ashlight. Outside, the island dressed itself for ceremony—drums rising, banners snapping, the sea answering in rhythm. Inside, the work became quieter. Heavier.

Queen Miroray watched silently from her place within the chamber, eyes observing the dignitaries gathering below. She felt the island's subtle shift, that shared inhalation before action—a reminder that even beauty carried sharpened edges.

The chamber was warm with ashlight and perfume, sweetened by incense coils smoldering in shells along the walls. Scents of firefruit, char-root, and woodsmoke clung to the air, stirred only by the quiet hands moving around her.

Miroray stood at the center of it all, clad in a flowing island gown of layered silk and gauze, the fabric draped loosely over her form and catching the light as if it breathed. Her skin was polished in sun-oil and dusted with ceremonial shimmer.

Light from the terrace licked across her shoulders, catching the blue-black sheen of her Jagua tattoos—glyphs of reef, flame, and storm worked onto skin and fabric alike, not as decoration, but declaration.

Miroray's gaze flicked briefly toward the horizon, where ships gathered with sails full of promises and threats.

A fire-dyed silk sash was knotted low and long over her left thigh, the gown parted to allow the markings beneath to remain visible. It was ceremonial rather than modest, and it was enough.

The gown's color bled between coral and dusk-orange, fluttering with her every breath like something alive. She dressed to command, not to flatter.

Two attendants flanked her with bowls of fruit-pressed pigment, dabbing the final ink across her shoulders. They told the story of the day. Each meaning something only the gods and the Queen were meant to fully understand.

Every mark traced upon her skin carried the weight of her people's expectations—and the sharper edge of her own concerns.

"Slower," Miroray said. "If you rush, the pattern will break."

"Yes, my Queen," one whispered, instantly adjusting.

The open archway filled with the sounds of the capital drifting upward—drums from the harbor, wind-chimes of the tower groves, the low call of a sea-horn marking the turn of the tide.

From the terrace, Miroray could see the Island-Goers' Fleet arriving in waves. One by one, their longships kissed the reef docks, each carrying a name, a vow, or a challenge.

She exhaled slowly, letting the drumbeats below steady her pulse. The time for ceremony would soon pass; the time for careful words and watchful eyes would swiftly follow.

Outside, the scent of sea salt and crushed orchid drifted through the open terrace. Somewhere below, the drums changed rhythm—ceremony was closing in.

The veil parted behind her, and Miroray did not turn.

"You're late," she said, smoothing the edge of her sash. "That, or the sun has learned to lie."

Bare feet padded over the lacquered floor. A chime of ankle bells. A laugh sharp as salt.

"And you're still half-naked. Not exactly keeping up the image of a divine bride."

"Queens are not brides," Miroray replied. "They are storms. The vows don't crown *me* today. They just catch him in the rain."

She turned, slowly.

Princess Kirahnae stood in the threshold. Her hair was half-unbraided; her dress wrinkled from the wind.

"You're not ready, the priestesses will not be pleased," Miroray noted.

"I have time, they are still setting out the food and decorating the arch," Kirahnae replied, combing her fingers through her hair. "Also, Tulavan's ship is almost here. Guess what he named it."

Miroray shrugged. "I don't care."

"*The Queen's Tide.*" Kirahnae smirked. "He even painted you standing on the hull."

Miroray's brow arched, like a blade drawn halfway from its sheath. "Did he at least get my jawline right?"

"No. But the hips are flattering."

"Leave it to a man to focus on the *important* things."

Miroray stepped past her toward the mirrored pool at the edge of the chamber. The surface shimmered with ash petals and drifting sunlight. She crouched and dipped her fingers in the water, rubbing them across her collarbone—grounding her breath.

Kirahnae padded closer, watching her sister through the mirror's reflection, as attendants applied coconut oil to Miroray skin—sealing the ink.

"You nervous?" Kirahnae asked.

Her sister didn't answer immediately. Just stared at the water.

Then: "No."

"You're marrying Tulavan."

"*He*, is marrying *me*. I already wear the crown."

Kirahnae hesitated. "Do you love him?"

Miroray smiled faintly. "Is that supposed to matter?"

"I don't know," Kirahnae said. "I thought it did. I thought maybe you... wanted more."

"I want power that *stays* mine, even when the tide changes," Miroray said, standing again.

"I want daughters who inherit a throne with no need to bow to any bloodline but their own. I want to feed the Reef Court so well that not even Eldaraine dares whisper about hunger. And if marrying Tulavan helps me hold it all—then let him call himself king."

Kirahnae blinked. "That's a lot more words than yes." She wished she didn't understand. But she did.

Miroray turned. "Then learn to listen to more than words."

Outside, a wind gusted up the slope from the reef, carrying the scent of spiced meat, boat-tar, and Firewine. It passed over the temple towers and into the bridal chambers, rustling the veils and scattering the last of the flower ash into the pool.

A servant entered, bowed low and announced: "His sails have docked. The groom has arrived."

Miroray nodded. She walked to the ceremonial stand, where her mantle—reefglass-threaded, heavy with flame-dyed panels—hung beside the royal anklet carved from coral bones.

She reached for it.

Not slowly.

Not with hesitation, but with purpose.

There was no room for faltering.

"Dress me," she said. "Then alert the choir."

Kirahnae watched her sister—a storm in coral and dusk light, about to make landfall.

⸻ ✶ ⸻

The deck of the *Queen's Tide* groaned beneath Tulavan's boots as the prow kissed Shan'Talune dock with a practiced nudge. Sailcloth flapped overhead in a wind thick with salt and burning fruit-pitch; every rope creaked like it had a story to tell.

From the high stern, he could see the terraces already beginning to bloom with wedding colors—seafoam silks, pearl-dye banners, and those absurd sun-spun sashes the priestesses insisted on draping over every godsdamned arch.

"Smells like someone overcooked the firefruit again," Tulavan muttered.

Apeck—one foot braced on a coil of mooring rope, the other dangling casually into nothing—took a long pull from a wineskin that had no business being open this early. He smacked his lips and nodded toward the shore.

"Smells like tradition to me. Rotten tradition. With nutmeg."

Tulavan didn't smile, not quite. "You know nutmeg's poisonous in high doses?"

"That would explain your mother's cooking," Apeck said, and grinned with all the charm of a shark that had never apologized for its teeth.

Apeck took another pull from the wineskin, squinting at Tulavan over the rim. "I never thought I'd see you wearing a crown, my friend. And now…" He trailed off, the wine hijacking whatever wisdom had been forming.

Tulavan snorted. "Soon enough. Not that I need a crown to prove anything. I have the fleet. I have my name." He gestured vaguely toward the island, banners snapping in the distance. "This is just ceremony. Vara always did love its pageantry wrapped in palm leaf and spiced meat."

A chorus started singing somewhere inland.

Tulavan smiled wide. "Here we go."

At the foot of the dock, a line of Reef Guard stood in formal posture—bare-chested, arms oiled, spears tipped with reefglass. Behind them, a line of attendants waited with trays of ceremonial offerings: fruit, wine, bracelets of bone and pearl.

Their eyes flicked up at Tulavan, wide and expectant.

He loved this.

They looked at him like a story already written.

Like his crown was already settled, shaped, worn—and ready to be claimed.

He gave them a half-salute and a crooked smile. "I hope one of those trays has fermented courage on it. I've been told I'm getting married today."

One of the women blushed. Another looked down at her feet like they'd just started whispering secrets.

Apeck stumbled down beside him, slapped his shoulder. "Married to a Queen no less. Lucky bastard."

"Lucky?" Tulavan raised a brow. "You know she once broke a man's nose with a ceremonial feast bowl for calling her lovely?"

Apeck grinned, and took another pull from the wineskin. "She rules like she fights—clean, direct, and without warning."

They walked together, led by silent attendants through a winding path of coral-tiled steps and hanging moss. Women scattered petals ahead of them.

"Ever think," Apeck said, "about skipping all this? Just sail off, raid a spice port, shack up with a fisher's daughter named something impractical?"

"Like what—'Sailstra'?"

Apeck beamed. "Or 'Kelpina.' Or 'Mist.' Definitely Mist. She'd be moody and mysterious."

Tulavan smirked. "She'd drown you in your sleep."

"She'd *try*. I'm slippery when wet." His grin held, but his eyes flicked briefly to the horizon—like maybe, just maybe, he'd meant it.

They rounded a corner into the preparation hall—an open-air stone structure shaded by flowering vines and carved archways. Bowls of scented oil burned low along the walls. Attendants—mostly young women, all barefoot and stone-faced—waited with garments, oils, and not a single word between them.

"Split us up, will you?" Tulavan said. "I'll cry less that way."

Apeck shrugged. "Your loss. I was planning to sing."

Tulavan entered a curtained space framed by obsidian columns.

A low stone bench stood in the center, beside it bowls of crushed fruit pulp, copper salves, a brush for sand, and folded ceremonial garb—blue and bone-white, marked with storm sigils and the coral crown glyph.

He sighed and stripped off his tunic. One of the young women approached with a carved ladle and dipped it into the oil bowl. She was newly assigned, quiet, dark-eyed. Her hands trembled as she touched the warm oil to his shoulder.

He caught her glance.

"You're from Kava'Tan, aren't you?"

She blinked. Nodded, almost shamefully.

"Don't be nervous," he said. "I'm not one of the *bad* ones. I only bite if you oil me wrong."

That earned him a stifled laugh from one of the other attendants nearby. The blush was immediate.

He leaned back on the bench as they worked—smoothing the scent of firefruit and lemongrass into his chest and arms, brushing sand from his legs, preparing him for the mask of tradition he'd wear until the crown kissed his head. By the time the ink dried on his brow, he would no longer be a man of the sea. He'd be a man of the throne.

"King," he muttered, tasting the word like wine on his tongue.

"You say that like it's a curse," Apeck's voice cut in from behind the curtain.

Tulavan craned his head. "You're supposed to be in your own chamber."

"Got bored."

"Of what?"

"The oil. The staring. The part where they won't let me bring wine."

There was a brief shuffle of movement. A *gasp*. Then silence.

Tulavan sat up just in time to see two of the attendants step back sharply. One had her hand to her mouth, the other had turned completely away, face burning crimson.

Tulavan narrowed his eyes.

"Apeck—are you *naked*?"

Apeck appeared in the doorway, bare as a reef pearl and entirely unbothered, holding out his arms like a hero returning from war. "What? I thought we were bathing."

"You don't get *completely naked*, you fool."

Apeck blinked. "Why not?"

"It's a wedding, not a salt scrub!"

A third attendant dropped the brush she was holding.

Apeck looked down.

"Oh," he said. "That would explain the lack of soaps."

Tulavan laughed.

Deep and unrepentant.

"Gods, man—put that away before you put someone's eye out!"

The reef bells began to ring—low, rising, then broken at the peak. The *Call of Joining*. Meant to herald unity and invite the gods.

Miroray stood already beneath the *Arch of Tethered Flame*, her silhouette framed in twisting vine-lanterns and reefglass chandeliers, each flame tinted green by the temple's sacred oils. Her gown flowed around her like dusk, stitched from flame-orange silk and salted-thread lace, trimmed with coral beadwork from her mother's wedding crown.

She wore no veil. She wore power.

The sash at her hips was cinched tight in ceremonial knotwork, the silk of her gown—catching the low-angle sun as she stood, already in place.

She stood alone at the top of the coral dais—except for the girl beside her.

Princess Kirahnae stood wrapped in the traditional *waiting gown*—ceremonial and untouched by shame—a pale blue clinging silk that bared one shoulder and trailed behind her in vine-green ribbons. Her hair was braided with thin vines and stormpetal blossoms. At her hip hung a ceremonial dagger, untouched and mostly symbolic—but sharp enough to remind onlookers that *Kaeleen daughters were never just ornaments.*

Miroray scanned the crowd.

To the left—delegates from Saharieth, adorned in net-cord and pearlflecked capes. To the right, the Whisperers from Jasheel's Way, veiled in mist-hued robes and silence.

Directly below—Sea-Clan elders from every outlying isle, rising in rows like sculpted coral, eyes fixed on her with the hungry patience of those who came not to witness, but to *weigh.*

She looked for the *one thing that was missing.*

No black-and-green standards bearing the stag and thorned tree.

No Eldaraine envoys bearing writ or word.

No Avanna.

And not a single godsdamned Eldaraine ship on the horizon.

Her jaw tightened, but the ache beneath her breastbone flared like salt in a wound. Avanna had not even sent a lie to cover the insult.

"Perhaps they were delayed," Kirahnae whispered, eyes still forward.

"Perhaps," Miroray said. Her voice didn't crack.

Her gaze didn't drift. But something in her stance—sovereign and sharp—grew just a hair more still. The kind of stillness that warned of storms.

She had counted on disappointment. But not this particular flavor.

Then, the horns.

Low, long, laced with salt.

From the path below, ascending with pomp and zero shame, came the groom.

Tulavan, High Captain of the Sea Serpent Fleet, walked the aisle not like a man giving himself to anything, but like a conqueror claiming tribute.

His robes were draped over one shoulder, leaving his chest bare and oiled. The crest of the Coral Reef blazed at his belt in polished obsidian.

Tulavan walked with the confidence of a man who'd survived twenty years of storms and come out louder.

Captain Apeck a step behind, smiling to the people gathered like he knew something they did not.

The crowd rose.

Some out of respect.

Some out of reflex.

Tulavan didn't notice the difference. And wouldn't of cared if he had.

He soaked in every glance like wine. Tilted his head toward the musicians with a grin. Bowed to a chieftain from Kava'tan as if the wedding were merely a military alignment dressed in flower petals.

Apeck peeled away before the steps, a brief hand to Tulavan's arm—familiar, unceremonious.

And all the while, Miroray did not move.

She watched him ascend toward her—posture perfect, expression unreadable, gaze a blade honed to ritual sharpness.

Kirahnae leaned in, barely audible. "He thinks he's being crowned." She said it like a joke, but her fingers twisted in her sash.

Miroray smiled. Just slightly.

"He's not wrong," she murmured. "He just doesn't know *whose* crown it is."

A ring of dancers spun barefoot across the polished coral cobbles, their steps measured and ancestral. Each movement coiled and snapped—a tide turning, a blaze unraveling.

A flute cried from a hidden alcove, climbing toward the canopy arches where banners swayed in the breath of the reef wind.

When the music fell silent, belief made space for vows.

Their hands were bound now—Miroray's and Tulavan's—by a cord of thread dyed in the bloodroot of the deep reefs, knotted seven times by the *Tide-Blesser*, from a great shell bowl, the priestess poured sacred brine across their joined palms.

"By tide, flame, and wind," the priestess intoned, her voice rising with each word, "on this day, the bond is made. May it break only when the sea forgets its name."

A roar rose from the Reef Court.

The dancers burst outward, like surf scattering from a rockfall—graceful, chaotic, beautiful in their retreat.

Tulavan stepped forward, raising one hand slick with brine. A servant brought a carved pearl goblet brimming with Firewine, its rim crusted in salt.

He took it.

He raised it.

His voice carried over the music.

"To the sea," he said, clear and unhurried. "To the fire. To Queen Miroray, who agreed to marry me before she knew how often I snore."

Laughter swept the crowd. Gentle. Familiar. Even Miroray smirked—but only slightly.

Tulavan's gaze cut across the gathered—ministers, clan-elders, tidecaller sailors. And spies. Always spies. He let his eyes linger a moment longer, then turned slowly toward the lower slope—toward the harbor where banners of Eldaraine should have been.

"And to Queen Avanna of Eldaraine," he added, his smile turning sharp enough to draw blood. "Who sends her regrets. And none of her ships."

A ripple moved through the guests.

Not laughter. Something thinner. Quieter. Like a tide pulling back before the break.

He sipped.

Then glanced sideways at Miroray. "Some call it a slight," he said. "But I call it freedom. No northern eyes on our dancing. No steel behind their smiles."

Miroray's expression didn't change. But her voice—low, exact—carved clean through the incense and music.

"And no help when the storms come."

She didn't raise her voice.

The words *lingered.* Heavier than the crown.

Tulavan's smirk faltered for just a breath. Then he lifted his goblet again.

"Then we'll dance harder," he said, the firewine burning a little slower on his tongue. "Until the storms forget we're here—or remember too late."

The silence that followed wasn't full.

It was waiting, like something with teeth beneath the tide.

Above them, the stars began to emerge—one by one, faint against the dusk.

Music, looser now, pulsed beneath the canopy from skin-drums and reed-pipes. Servers moved gracefully through the crowd, balancing platters of grilled muskfish, firefruit-glazed fowl, and cups of spiced ash-petal wine. The mingled scents of citrus bark and stormpetal wove through the warm evening breeze.

Miroray's crown had been removed, her ink still fresh, her skin still faintly oiled beneath the ceremony's silk mantle.

Tulavan stood beside her, one hand on a goblet, the other clenched just loosely enough not to look like it wanted to hit something.

"Well," he muttered, lifting the cup toward his lips. "That went smoothly."

"Your toast was nearly tolerable," Miroray replied. "You only insulted one sovereign and alienated half the council."

The music shifted—slower now, more rhythm than melody.

A stringed instrument plucked notes like dripping water, while dancers receded to the courtyard's edges. The tide was changing.

Tulavan and Miroray stepped away from the coral arch, hand-in-hand for ceremony's sake.

They walked a narrow path between guests, stopping here and there to offer a smile, a bow, a half-whispered word of thanks.

By the time they reached the lower terrace, Tulavan's smile had returned and his voice had thickened with charm.

He greeted each island delegation with flair and time-worn familiarity: He drank their wine, praised their trade fleets, kissed three hands and one forehead with perfect timing.

The Varanese nobility watched him work—amused, wary. He was a man let into the house, but they all remembered he was not born there.

Once they passed the veil of sea-lanterns near the marble basin, their hands slipped apart.

The moment they were alone, Tulavan's voice sharpened.

"Still no word from your sister?"

Miroray didn't answer immediately. She stepped to the basin, dipped her fingers into the perfumed water, and watched her reflection ripple apart—fluid, beautiful, unrecognizable. She had expected some kind of message. A sign. Even a lie dressed in green ribbon.

"Avanna is queen of an empire that doesn't understand how to breathe outside its own halls. Late messages are nothing new."

"But no message?" Tulavan's tone darkened. "Not a gift. Not a banner. Not even a ceremonial envoy with gilded boots and ten crates of wine they overpaid for?"

He folded his arms. The silk on his shoulder fluttered, restless.

"That's not forgetfulness. That's intention."

Miroray turned to face him, her expression composed—smooth as moonlight, and just as distant.

"She's my blood. Daughter of Queen Avara Kaeleen. Do not mistake her absence for insult."

"Oh, I don't," he said, voice low and amused. "I mistake it for strategy. I don't mind the game," he said lightly, as if testing the words for balance. "I just need to know what game is being played."

He stepped closer—not touching her, but close enough for the space between them to tighten.

"Your sister sees what this place is becoming—a throne without her permission. A king not of her naming."

Miroray's eyes narrowed—just enough to cut.

"Careful, Tulavan."

"Why?" he asked, his smile more teeth than charm. "You brought me here. You crowned me. You lit the fire."

"I handed you a spark," she said, cold and precise. "Not the hearth. Don't forget the difference."

He looked away, jaw tight. The silence that followed settled between them.

"I deserve to be treated like a king."

"Then act like one."

That stopped him.

Miroray stepped past, her voice quieter—but harder.

"The flame here is old. It does not answer to tide. And in Vara," she added, eyes locking with his, "the woman holds the key to the home."

"So, I'm to smile and nod while your sister acts like we don't exist?"

"You're to remember that without me, you would still be a Sea Captain with charm and no crown. A Tidecaller without a shore."

He said nothing.

And Miroray didn't wait for him to.

She turned, stepped into the veil of blue lanternlight, and vanished into the palace with the grace of a storm choosing not to fall.

Tulavan stayed where she left him, staring after the blue-glow veil. His crown felt heavier than it had minutes ago.

Above on the gift-receiving platform shaded by woven palm-frond parasols, Princess Kirahnae stood tall and radiant, the ceremonial dagger still fastened at her hip.

She bowed to dignitaries with measured grace, accepted offerings with polished thanks, and replied to flattery with dangerous smiles. A reef-lord from Saharieth presented her with a strand of *spirit pearls* harvested during moonfall—rare and luminescent.

Kirahnae accepted it, nodded politely, and murmured, "Very generous. I'll be sure to wear it the next time I swim past your spies."

The lord paled slightly. Bowed twice. Left in a hurry.

Behind her, servants stifled grins.

Apeck navigated through the lively crowd with the confidence of someone who'd weathered enough storms to feel at ease amid ceremony and politics alike. His step was steady—just enough wine warming his blood to ease formalities, but not enough to dull his senses.

He approached Princess Kirahnae near the pavilion, bowing respectfully, a smile genuine and warm.

"Your Radiance," Apeck said with easy charm, eyes alight with sincerity rather than bravado. "May I have the honor of presenting one of my finest crewmen? A young sailor who has already made a name for himself aboard the Sea Serpent Fleet."

Apeck smoothed his sash, suddenly aware of how ceremonial he sounded. Gods help him—he was becoming one of them.

Kirahnae tilted her head slightly, curiosity sparking her expression. She gestured gently with her hand, inviting Apeck to proceed.

"Princess Kirahnae Kaeleen," Apeck continued, stepping aside to reveal the young man who stood respectfully behind him, his bearing proud yet humble. "This is Kaelos, born of Zareth'Kai, swiftest hand aboard the ship and a true master of tides. If he steers a vessel half as well as he manages his manners, he may yet command his own fleet."

Kaelos stepped forward with practiced grace and bowed deeply, his expression earnest.

His hair was twisted into neat braids adorned with shells and sea-glass, marking him unmistakably as an islander.

His eyes flicked up—briefly, measuring the Princess's gaze—before lowering again.

"It's an honor, Princess," Kaelos spoke clearly, his voice steady yet tempered with youthful modesty. "Captain Apeck is generous in his praise, but I am grateful for the opportunity to meet you."

Kirahnae's eyes softened with genuine warmth. "Captain Apeck rarely exaggerates about those who serve with him. If he speaks highly of you, Kaelos, you must indeed be exceptional."

Kaelos inclined his head, color warming his cheeks slightly, "I will strive every day to prove worthy of such words, Princess," he added, the words coming more boldly than he had intended. "Not just for your favor—but for the chance to matter among those who shape the tides."

Kaelos hesitated briefly, then found his voice again, steady despite the subtle flush on his cheeks. "Princess, perhaps I might have the honor of seeing you again once your duties are through?"

Kirahnae's gaze returned, and she gave him the slightest, wordless dip of her chin—a promise made in silence. Apeck gently touched Kaelos' shoulder, indicating it was time to withdraw.

She held his gaze a breath longer than court manners required, then buried the moment behind a diplomat's poise.

"Come, Kaelos," Apeck said lightly, steering him gently from the pavilion. As they walked away, he nudged Kaelos with an encouraging elbow, his voice dropping conspiratorially. "She likes you, lad," Apeck murmured. "Trust me—I've charted these waters."

Kaelos glanced back once more, encouraged, then turned his attention forward, matching Apeck's confident stride as they left Kirahnae to her many awaiting guests.

Miroray sat in her private chamber with the window shutters thrown wide, letting in the salt-thick breeze and the distant rhythm of drums echoing from the palace court.

She didn't hear them. Not really.

A plate of untouched firefruit sat near her elbow, its juices congealing in the carved bowl. She'd dismissed the attendants the moment she stepped through the threshold.

She wasn't angry.

Not exactly—but she was simmering.

Simmering was still heat. Still danger—the kind priests coaxed in braziers before a reckoning.

Tulavan was bold. Too bold. She had expected ambition—welcomed it, even. Fire without fuel was nothing. But fire that forgot where it was lit? That was dangerous.

And yet, it wasn't his words that gnawed at her most. It was Avanna's silence.

No envoy.

No gift.

No letter.

Not even a note politely excusing her absence with some war council or seasonal cough. Miroray had written the invitation herself. Folded it. Sealed it with her own signet. Made sure it passed through proper channels. Watched it leave.

Nothing.

She told herself it had to be strategy. Court theater. A move on the board whose shape hadn't yet been revealed. Avanna was too proud. Too deliberate. She didn't forget.

And yet—it wasn't like her.

Miroray's quill hovered over the fresh vellum before her, the ink already drying at its tip.

To Her Majesty, Queen Avanna of Eldaraine, Eldest Daughter of the Sea-Throne, Lady of the Ironback…

She scratched through the line.

Too formal.

It wasn't the silence that unnerved her. It was the memory of the last silence between them—the kind that left ash no rain could cleanse.

She dipped the quill again, stared at the blank space, then wrote:

Sister—

She stopped.

Miroray frowned, set the quill down, and pressed her fingers to her temple. The headache had been threading behind her eyes since the second toast. The wine hadn't helped. Tulavan's smirk hadn't either.

She glanced toward the corner where the ceremonial brazier still burned. The flame there was steady. Unwavering and loyal.

"If only the rest of them behaved so well," she muttered.

A knock came—soft, measured, and unwelcome.

Miroray didn't answer.

Not yet.

She was waiting. And if silence had a sound, it was the space where a sister's voice should have been.

The knock returned—firmer now, no longer patient.

"Your Highness?" came the voice—tentative. One of the women from the bathing hall. "The hour draws near. The… the *Royal Joining of Stone and Sea* awaits."

Miroray rolled her eyes so hard she felt it in her spine.

"*The Royal Joining of Stone and Sea,*" she muttered.

"Spare me. Just call it what it is."

She leaned back in her chair, glaring at the blank vellum before her like it had personally betrayed her. Her fingers flexed once, then released the quill.

"Enter," she said, already regretting it.

The door opened, and the woman stepped inside, barefoot, her wrap tied in crisp ceremonial knots, skin still damp from the perfume mist.

She held a folded robe across both arms, carefully arranged to show its embroidered edges: coral, tide, flame—traditional symbols of union, none of which Miroray felt inclined to honor tonight.

The woman curtsied low, eyes fixed to the floor with the discipline of someone taught to disappear.

"The attendants are preparing the bath, Your Majesty. Should I lay out the jade combs… or the gold?"

"Neither," Miroray said flatly. "I won't be crowned again for lying on my back."

The woman blinked, eyes flicking up involuntarily before snapping back to the floor.

"As you wish, Majesty."

Miroray rose slowly, brushing past the table, the unstarted letter, and the ache building behind her eyes. Somewhere below, drums thudded again—slower this time. Heavier. She wondered if that was Tulavan's doing. Probably. The man drank like he was trying to drown his own ego.

"If he reeks of firewine," she said, half to herself, "I will drown him in the bath before the gods can bless a single thing."

The attendant wisely said nothing, merely stepping aside to let her queen pass.

Miroray moved with grace, but her expression was carved from stone—queen of flame, of tide, and tonight, of obligation. Every step toward the bath felt like one away from the woman who had once ruled alone.

As she reached the inner archway to the bath chamber, she paused and exhaled through her nose.

"Some dead ancestor cursed me with this tradition," she muttered.

"My queen?" the attendant asked softly.

Miroray waved the question away without looking back.

Steam billowed outward, curling around her shoulders like an unwanted cloak. The air was heavy with flower oils, perfume, and heat.

Two attendants, one male and one female, stood sentinel on either side of the bath, dressed in unadorned white robes woven for this singular rite.

They bowed—deep, reverent, silent. At their sides, low lacquered tables held the instruments of ceremonial service: drying robes, ash-laced soaps, and oils scented with lemongrass and firefruit. Silent stewards of tradition.

Tulavan was already in the water and lounged with the practiced ease of a man who believed the world was lucky to hold him, arm braced on the ledge, half-lidded eyes fixed on the steam rising from the pool. The water slicked his dark skin like oiled bronze, catching candlelight along the ridges of his chest and shoulders. A single droplet clung to his jaw, then fell—slow and deliberate.

Miroray paused. Gods help her, at least it would not be unpleasant. She felt heat pool beneath her skin, unwelcome but undeniable.

He lifted a hand languidly as she entered the chamber, revealing a cup of firefruit wine. His grin was lazy. Faintly smug.

"You're late," he said.

She stopped just inside the arch, arms crossed tight against her chest. Her gaze narrowed at the cup, then the man.

"You've had too much," she said flatly.

Tulavan's grin widened. "Enough to be charming. Not enough to forget my own name."

"Pity," Miroray stated flatly.

She crossed the room slowly, circling the pool without urgency. Each step deliberate. Weighted.

Her hips moved with the rhythm of a body long accustomed to power. The air seemed to tighten around her, thick with steam and expectation.

Tulavan watched her as a man might watch embers banked low—appreciative, reverent, aware they could burn.

Her skin caught the torchlight in gold and rust, curves wrapped in shadow, carved from royal expectation and something fiercer underneath. His grin faltered, just slightly.

"To the Queen of Salt and Flame," he said. "Who scowls better than she kisses." His voice had dropped—smokier now, thick with things unsaid.

She stopped at the edge, looking down at him like a priestess debating whether to throw the offering in—or the offender.

She seriously considered drowning him.

Then thought better of it.

"Tulavan," she said, voice dry. "Let's just get this over with."

He blinked, once. A man trying not to flinch in front of a storm.

Miroray removed her sash and gown with the same precision she might draw a blade—graceful, unhurried, without the courtesy of hesitation. The cloth slid down her hips and pooled at her feet, a quiet surrender to tradition, if not to the man waiting.

She felt Tulavan's gaze follow her, lingering, testing the distance he dared not cross.

She stepped into the bath. Heat kissed her thighs, curled around her, pulled her into its breath. She did not flinch. She had no illusions. This was a crown ceremony, not a wedding night.

Not love. Not want.

But something inevitable.

Ritual.

She crossed the water to him, stopping when only a breath remained between them. This close, the wine on his breath mingled with the scent of her skin—salt and citrus, heat. He said nothing now. There was nothing left clever to say.

Her voice, when it came, was silk spun over steel.

"Lie back, King Consort," she whispered. "Let the sea show you who taught the flame to burn."

And when her hand touched his chest, it wasn't gentle.

It was sea, claiming stone.

CHAPTER FIVE

North of Castellon, the rural hills of Eldaraine lay under a lingering cold—no longer northern-sharp, but damp, grey, and inhospitable. Cloud shadow slid across fallow fields and half-green slopes streaked with old snow and thaw-darkened soil as Rodrik walked the trade road, hood drawn low.

His pace never changed. He neither hastened nor lingered, boots striking the packed, frost-hardened earth in the same measured rhythm whether the road dipped into hollows or climbed open ground. The double-headed axe rode across his back, hidden beneath spare cloth and worn leather, betrayed only by the quiet creak of its bindings. A small satchel hung at his side—food, water, little else.

If questioned, he would give a name common enough to vanish the moment it was heard. Osmund. The lie required no effort. Silence usually did the rest.

By midafternoon, Castellon's towers emerged ahead—distant, pale against the southern sky. Not far from the road, a derelict farmstead sagged into dead grass, its fence swallowed by bramble and neglect.

Rodrik slowed for the first time that day.

He scanned the horizon once, then angled off the road toward the ruins.

One corner of the farmhouse still stood—stone beneath rotted timber. It would do.

He stepped through what had once been the doorway and paused to read the space.

Dust.

Mold.

Old rot.

Daylight cut through the broken roof in narrow shafts, illuminating rusted hooks, a collapsed bench, the warped remains of a bedframe.

In a shadowed corner lay a child's blanket, gnawed and half-buried beneath leaves.

The hearth was choked with damp ash and debris.

Against the far wall sat a low wooden trunk, its lid warped but intact. Rodrik knelt, tested the hinge, then opened it just wide enough to see what remained inside—Eldaran clothing. He inspected the items. A yellowed linen shirt and two wool cloaks, one smaller, for a child perhaps, the other moth-eaten but serviceable. Nothing valuable. Nothing recent. Nothing his size, but would do.

He changed quickly.

The leather jerkin and fur cloak came off. Plainer clothes replaced them—looser, softer, wrong in ways that had nothing to do with fit. He folded his outer layers and tucked them inside, then settled the trunk back into shadow.

When he stepped outside again, the road felt closer.

Castellon nearer.

Rodrik adjusted the unfamiliar weight of borrowed cloth, turned south, and left the farmstead behind.

He stepped out into a light drizzle that clung like sleet and followed a deer trail east. It wound between budding alder and birch, then bent toward a small village settled low along a lake and between two green hills.

Smoke rose in thin ribbons from chimney pots, dissolving into the grey air. A smith's hammer rang somewhere near the center—steady, unhurried. Goats bleated behind a splintered fence. Children's voices carried from the village center, sharp with laughter.

Rodrik slowed his stride and let it show.

He kept his hood half-raised, posture easy, eyes forward. He did not scan roofs or count exits—not overtly. To anyone watching, he was just another road-worn man drifting in ahead of evening.

The borrowed cloak scratched at his neck. Ignoring it and walked on, letting the village close around him, close-packed and cold.

Rodrik's first stop was a cooper's stall at the village edge. The stall itself seemed built more from stubbornness than skill, rough timbers leaning against each other in perpetual argument.

Out front stood a lean, weathered man with knotwood forearms and a deeply furrowed brow, hands marked by years of hard work.

He was absorbed in the meticulous carving of a barrel stave, his attention fixed, his drawknife moving slowly with practiced care.

"Looking for something specific?" the cooper asked without lifting his gaze.

Rodrik approached with a nod of acknowledgment, producing a small ring of iron nails, plain and well-made—useful enough to earn a second glance. "Trade?"

The cooper lifted his head, eyeing Rodrik with guarded interest before grunting approval. "Tarcloth and boiled pitch," he offered, reaching beneath the stall. "Fair trade. You from the hills?"

Rodrik met the cooper's sharp gaze, voice even. "Further."

The cooper smirked faintly, pushing a small wooden box toward Rodrik. "Thought so. You don't smell southern. Lucky you that."

Rodrik tilted his head slightly. "Why's that?"

"Because those who do," the cooper muttered darkly, eyes flickering briefly toward the southern road, "either show up with scrolls or swords—and neither knows a damned thing about barrels."

Rodrik's gaze followed the man's, "Seen a few then."

"Seen them?" the cooper snorted. "Enough to last me." "Had one lordling down here just last month, wanting wine barrels made from trees that only grow near Tarnhollow. As if barrels had bloody preferences." He shook his head bitterly. "Next he'll want barrels carved from stone, just to see how many backs it breaks."

Rodrik chuckled. "You make them?"

The cooper raised an eyebrow. "Oh, aye. Took his coin, sure. Gave him fine barrels, fit for a king they were—straight from the trees behind my shed. If he notices, I'll swear it's the wine that turned sour, not the wood."

Rodrik's smile widened just enough to show teeth. "Brave. Or foolish."

The cooper shrugged, eyes sharp beneath his heavy brow. "Not half so foolish as telling the truth. Especially in these parts."

Rodrik inclined his head slightly, acknowledging the wisdom without comment. He tucked the pitch and cloth into his satchel. "Stay careful, cooper."

"Careful?" the cooper asked dryly, sliding a weary glance toward Rodrik. "Careful's just another word for stayin' alive long enough to know better than most. I'll stick to barrels—wood's honest. It only turns on you when it's meant to."

Rodrik stepped away from the cooper's stall. The man's tone lingered with him—not for its bitterness, but for its certainty.

His next stop brought him to the baker's store, presided over by a robust woman. Her hair, once black, was now streaked with silver and pulled back into a loose braid, with wisps escaping to frame a face weathered by sun and smiles. She kneaded dough with energetic slaps, her thick forearms and apron smudged liberally with flour and honey.

There was a spark in her eyes—a mischief unbent by age, and a sharpness that suggested she missed nothing that happened in the square. She looked up as Rodrik approached, eyes twinkling.

"Gina o' Three Loaves," she declared brightly, her voice thick with the musical lilt of someone raised on streets far from castles—even though her bread tray clearly held only two loaves.

Rodrik eyed the store with a quiet smile. "Three loaves?"

She leaned forward, lowering her voice to a conspiratorial whisper. "Third loaf's in the oven, luv. Keeps 'em 'angin' about a bit longer."

Rodrik gave a soft huff, appreciating her craftiness. "Clever."

She paused mid-knead, looking him up and down with playful boldness. "Cor, yer a sturdy one, ain't ya? 'Andsome, too, fer a wanderer. Got 'ands strong enough for dough, I wager. What's yer name luv?"

Rodrik's lips twitched, a polite smile touching his eyes. "Osmund, and I'm afraid my hands are better suited to eating bread than making it."

Gina clucked her tongue with exaggerated disappointment. "Ah, shame that. Could use a good set o' shoulders 'round 'ere. Dough don't knead itself, ya know. Still, can't complain, eh? Least ya stopped fer a chat."

Rodrik inclined his head slightly, gently steering the conversation. "Ever been to Castellon?"

She snorted loudly, slamming the dough onto the counter again. "Once were enough. Didn't care much fer their fancy wine, nor the blokes, neither. All 'oney in the mouth, but nuffin' behind their eyes, ya get me?"

He leaned forward slightly, curious. "And what about the king—Harald Thornsword?"

Gina paused, floury hands planted firmly on her hips as she considered. " 'Arald? Now there's a proper king fer ya. Fine-lookin' fella, strong jaw, steady eyes. 'E don't flinch, that one." She shook her head, a dry breath of laughter escaping her. "Could be worse, luv. Could be them nobles runnin' things. Now, they flinch plenty—jus' never fer our sakes."

Rodrik nodded thoughtfully. "Honest enough."

Her eyes narrowed playfully, and she wagged a flour-coated finger at him. "Oh, yer a quiet one, ain't ya? Usually means trouble. Good trouble, though, I'm guessin'."

"Or perhaps I'm just tired," Rodrik replied, eyes gentle yet distant.

"Ah, pull the other one, luv," she laughed, slapping the dough down again with cheerful force. "You don't fool ol' Gina. Yer quiet's got stories. Wicked ones, I reckon."

Rodrik allowed himself a faint smile at her good-natured teasing. "I'm afraid I'm only passing through."

She placed a floury hand dramatically over her heart, sighing theatrically. "Oh, tragedy o' me days! An' 'ere I thought I'd found meself a new assistant. What'll I do without them shoulders?"

Rodrik shook his head gently, a faint sound escaping him. "Your bakery might not survive it."

She winked and smiled broadly. "This bakery's tougher'n it looks. Ya get weary o' wanderin', Gina and 'er loaves'll be waitin'—an' not jus' the ones in the oven, ay?" She gave her chest a playful jiggle, grinning. Her good-natured audacity drew a quiet chuckle from him—brief, unguarded, and quickly gone.

Rodrik coughed slightly, amusement flickering in his eyes. "Careful, Gina. You wouldn't want to scare your third loaf out of rising."

She threw her head back in a hearty laugh that echoed through the stall.

Cheeks rosy, she returned to kneading her dough.

Rodrik inclined his head politely, grining despite himself.

He stepped away, her laughter following him into the raw winter air, leaving him with the sense of a village that, despite its troubles, still knew how to smile.

Rodrik continued onward, letting the noise of the square fall back into its own rhythm as he moved deeper into the village.

Not all encounters came with such forthright charm.

A younger man stood leaning against the weathered wood of the stable, scarf hiding half his face, eyes narrowed in suspicion. As Rodrik drew closer, the youth deliberately spat at the ground near Rodrik's boots, watching to see if the insult landed.

"You ask'n too many questions," he muttered darkly, shifting slightly, enough to let Rodrik glimpse the hilt of a knife tucked in his belt.

Rodrik didn't blink, keeping his voice calm but firm. "Just passing through."

"Good," the man retorted coldly, turning back slowly, as if dismissing Rodrik. "Then pass faster."

Rodrik held his gaze a beat longer, forcing the youth to break contact first, grumbling quietly as he returned his attention to the horses.

He had expected discontent at Eldaraine's rural edge—cautious looks, half-swallowed complaints. Instead, civility here felt brittle, held together by habit more than trust.

Rodrik lingered by the village well as dusk crept in, draping the vale in winter twilight.

Around him, the village murmured in low whispers, unsettled as night fell.

Children chased each other, laughter bright and reckless, blind to their parents' anxious glances cast toward the trade road.

A merchant's cart limped along, axle cracked and splintered, swaying with the kind of desperation that marked more than just a single journey.

He stood motionless in the fading light, his borrowed cloak tugged by the cutting evening wind.

He'd seen it before.

Not violence—not yet—but the quiet before it, when people watched the road more than the fields.

Kneeling near the goat pens, he pressed his hand into the dark soil. It was rich and dark, slick with thaw.

The kind that rewarded care. Few here bothered with it. Instead, their eyes watched the path, fearing what would arrive rather than caring for what grew beneath them.

As darkness thickened, he left the village and returned to the farmstead he'd claimed for shelter. The stone walls held against the wind. Inside, the space was quiet.

Known.

Dust stirred lightly as he knelt beside the trunk, the scent of old wood and stale air rising sharp and biting, like a breath long imprisoned.

He opened the trunk. Inside, his folded leathers and traveling gear lay undisturbed from earlier.

One final piece remained.

His fingers closed around the familiar haft of his axe, feeling the leather grip molded by his palm, smooth and faintly warm despite the cold.

He hesitated only a moment, grip tightening. It had been companion, protector—part of him. Now he had to leave it behind.

"You'll wait," he murmured. It was a promise more than a command, meant for the blade as much as himself.

In Eldaraine, only men who wished to be remembered carried such distinctive blades. Bringing it would draw questions he couldn't afford.

Rodrik had no intention of drawing eyes. If any still lived who might recall his face, he preferred they not call alarm.

Instead, he drew the smaller blade from his boot—the bone-handled knife borrowed from Eirik's stores before he left Hravnskot. He tested its edge, thumb sliding along steel, dull but sufficient. Smaller weapon, he thought with grim approval—same purpose. He slid it into his belt, a silent companion, ready if needed.

He closed the trunk carefully, pressing down until it settled into place. With a slow breath, he dragged the broken bench atop it.

He rose to his feet and let his eyes trace the worn stone walls and the child's blanket forgotten in a shadowed corner.

If all went well, he would return.

Stepping into the deepening winter dusk, Rodrik drew the cloak tighter around his shoulders and began his descent toward the heart of Eldaraine.

He followed side roads and half-hidden trails, his path lit only by the faint glow of distant stars and the grey glow of a full moon. His eyes fixed steadily southward, toward Castellon. Toward a city he had never wished to revisit.

"The cracks are not at the walls," he would tell Eirik.

"They're in the nails. And no one is watching them rust."

With those words turning slowly in his thoughts, Rodrik slipped into the gathering night, becoming just another shadow on the path.

The wagons arrived at House Caerlyn's gates just past dawn, the air still cold enough to sting, wheels creaking under heavy loads of grain no one had expected. Thick clouds of pale road-dust and frost rose behind them, settling on guards whose puzzled looks matched those of the wagoneers guiding their tired horses forward.

Lord Quentyn Caerlyn stood on the balcony overlooking the courtyard, his morning tea forgotten in hand, brows knitting into a puzzled scowl. He watched the wagons jostle to a halt, their loads spilling trickles of barley onto the cold, polished cobblestone. Two guards rushed forward from the gatehouse, waving frantically at the drivers.

"What is the meaning of this?" one guard called, his voice high and anxious.

The foremost wagon-driver, a heavyset man with shoulders wide as an ox, pulled off his cap and scratched his head. "Got a delivery for House Caerlyn, I 'ave—straight from Lord Valen down Goldacre way. A dozen wagons, urgent like. Got the scroll wiv the seal an' everythin'."

Lord Caerlyn frowned deeply, placing his cup on the railing, irritation creeping into his normally composed expression. Below, one of the younger guards whispered, "Why here?" Another replied under breath, "'Cause no one else has the silos—or the stomach."

Lord Caerlyn descended swiftly, polished boots clicking on the cold marble stairs as he moved into the courtyard.

The driver, seeing him approach, quickly straightened, clutching a tightly rolled parchment with nervous fingers. "Beggin' yer pardon, m'lord, but—"

"Let me see it," Lord Caerlyn said sharply, holding out his hand.

The driver handed the scroll over quickly, stepping back with visible relief.

Lord Caerlyn broke the red-sealed wax—the unmistakable sigil of House Valen, a weasel entwined around sheaves of grain—and began to read, his scowl deepening with every line.

Lord Quentyn Caerlyn,

Forgive the abruptness of this dispatch. Circumstances necessitate that I store this season's surplus grain within your capable custody. Your silos, I am told, remain the last bastion of reliability—qualities vanishingly rare in these uncertain days.

In recognition of the inconvenience, enclosed you will find terms of compensation generous enough to dispel doubt or discomfort. It is my sincere hope this arrangement serves mutual benefit and further cements the bond between our noble houses.

With Respectful Urgency,

Circus Valen, Lord of Goldacre

Valen's tone was polished to excess—courteous, insistent, just a shade too careful. Of course the grain came here. The others had refused. Or burned their silos. Or been paid to look away.

Lord Caerlyn read slowly, expression unreadable. The words were polished—too even, too deliberate for a message meant to be hurried. He didn't trust the gift, nor the hand that sent it. But for now, he would receive it.

He filed the thought away. One of the estate grounds stewards approached from the stables, the confusion on his face matching his masters.

Quentyn lowered the scroll, disbelief fighting openly with suspicion on his face. He turned sharply toward the steward. "Were we expecting correspondence from Goldacre?"

"No, my lord," the steward replied cautiously. "Nothing beyond the usual tax ledger requests."

Lord Caerlyn turned his sharp gaze on the driver again. "Where is Lord Valen himself? Has he offered no explanation beyond this?"

"Jus' the scroll, m'lord," the driver replied uneasily. "Said we was to drop it off prompt-like, no fuss. All I knows is, 'e said it were urgent—real hush-hush like."

Lord Caerlyn's jaw tightened.

"A dozen wagons is hardly quiet."

The driver shrugged, breath puffing faintly as he spoke, apologetic. "Lord Valen ain't known fer quiet. Or warnin', truth told."

The steward leaned in, voice lowered. "My lord, it is... generous compensation. Far above usual market value."

Quentyn fixed the him with a skeptical stare. "Generosity is not among Lord Circus Valen's many vices."

He stared down at the parchment again, eyes narrowed, as though the words themselves might shift if he watched long enough. "And yet, his seal..."

The steward hesitated. "Perhaps Lord Valen seeks favor or an alliance. Or perhaps he is simply desperate."

Lord Caerlyn's mouth twisted in doubt. "Desperation does not suit him, nor has he reason to court my favor. Valen hasn't spoken my name in three years—not in court, not in whisper. That makes this gesture all the more suspect."

The steward shifted nervously. "Shall we send it back, my lord?"

Quentyn paused.

Tension tightened across his shoulders. Sending it back would insult Valen publicly—accepting it risked entanglement in schemes he could not yet see. Eldaraine's political web was delicate, and Lord Circus Valen was among the most dangerous spiders weaving it. Yet the scroll seemed genuine enough; the handwriting precise, the signature firm, the seal unquestionably authentic. He tapped the parchment softly against his palm, decision grinding behind his composure.

Finally, he sighed.

"Store it in the outer silos for now—but keep it separate. No mixing of Lord Valen's grain with our own. Post double guard at the storage. And watch the wagoners carefully—no whispers, no gossip. Whatever game he is playing, I won't stumble into it blindly."

The grain would settle in the silo before sunset. But what Valen truly wanted—what game he was setting in motion—would take longer to reveal itself.

He turned, voice sharp with suspicion. "Send word to Castellon discreetly. Find out what the Crown knows of this. I'll wager the answer is 'nothing'—and if so, that's the worst news yet."

The steward nodded swiftly, bowing low. "Yes, my lord."

As the wagons rolled onward into the estate, Quentyn returned to his balcony, eyes narrowed in thought, the scroll a cold riddle in his hand.

He strode into his private study, the door slamming behind him with more force than intended, rattling the gilded frames of maps and portraits lining the walls.

The scroll from Lord Circus Valen lay heavy in his grip. He tossed it onto his desk with quiet disdain and stared at it as though it might ignite under scrutiny alone.

He began pacing.

The steady rhythm of his boots marked his frustration across the polished wooden floor. "Circus Valen," he muttered, venom laced beneath his breath. "offering grain and generosity without prompt or persuasion? More believable to see wolves bearing lambs upon their backs."

A quiet knock at the door disturbed his thoughts. "Enter," he snapped.

The door opened smoothly, and Head Steward Edwyn Fallow stepped inside, calm and composed, his graying hair and lined face speaking of experience.

Edwyn's dark gaze drifted to the desk. His thoughtful eyes immediately fell upon the scroll, the seal broken.

"News spreads swiftly, my lord," Edwyn began carefully, watching his lord closely. "The servants whisper of Lord Valen's wagons, heavy-laden with grain."

"Oh yes, and what grain it is," Lord Caerlyn replied bitterly. "A gift or curse, I cannot yet say. But surely a game. Valen plays generosity poorly and subtly worse."

Edwyn extended a hand toward the scroll, eyebrow raised slightly. "If I may, my lord?"

Quentyn handed it over irritably. "Please. Prove to me that insanity is now neatly packaged in parchment and sealed with wax."

Edwyn glanced up, his voice dry. "It wouldn't be the first time."

He read slowly, his careful silence stretching the moments uncomfortably thin. Finally, he looked up, brow furrowed. "It appears genuine."

Quentyn turned away, jaw tightening visibly. *Generosity from Circus Valen,* he thought bitterly, *is as comforting as seeing your name freshly carved into a gravestone. Worse, perhaps—at least with gravestones, intentions were never in doubt.*

"Of course it does!" Lord Caerlyn snapped, then softened slightly at Edwyn's steady patience. "Too genuine. He places grain in our silos, compensation well above reason—yet no prior message, no negotiation. Generosity that rings false is dangerous."

Edwyn nodded gravely. "A fair assessment, my lord. Yet if the scroll and seal are authentic, then he believes himself justified. Could another be involved? Perhaps manipulating him?"

"Valen, manipulated?" Quentyn gave a derisive laugh. "Would that I live to see it. But your point has merit. If not him, then whom?"

The door swung gently open again, this time without a knock. Lady Olivia Caerlyn stepped gracefully inside, her presence immediately steadying the room. Quentyn straightened almost imperceptibly, but Edwyn inclined his head without hesitation.

Her eyes—sharp and intelligent—regarded both men calmly. She took measure of the tension at once.

"Good morning, my lord. Edwyn," she began evenly, folding her hands neatly before her. "I trust there is an explanation for the wagons currently cluttering our courtyard?"

Lord Caerlyn sighed deeply. "Valen. Grain. Generosity. Three words that should not share breath in one sentence."

Olivia adjusted her cuffs with clinical precision, then moved to the desk, eyes narrowing just slightly. She lifted the scroll, reading it quickly but with a practiced eye for detail. "Lord Circus Valen's handwriting, indeed. His mannerisms, phrasing... all impeccably familiar."

"Too familiar," Lord Caerlyn grumbled again.

She looked up, calm and thoughtful. "You presume he sent it."

Quentyn paused, glancing sharply at her. "You suspect forgery?"

Lady Caerlyn considered carefully. "Perhaps. Circus is greedy and corrupt, but seldom careless. This gesture is precisely the sort of bold move he avoids. It draws unwanted attention. Either he is desperate, remarkably foolish, or—"

"Or he is being played," Edwyn finished quietly, eyes narrowing.

Olivia allowed herself the faintest sigh. "A common ailment in Eldaraine, I fear."

"Though if this is forged, my lady, it's masterfully done. Valen's seal alone would fool nearly any eye."

"Any eye," Lady Caerlyn echoed softly, "but ours."

A heavy silence filled the room.

Lord Caerlyn resumed pacing. "If a forgery," he murmured, "it is crafted with deadly skill. It is meant not merely to deceive but to provoke response."

She nodded slowly. "Precisely. Someone hopes we react rashly, publicly accuse Valen, or worse—seek open conflict. Our actions now must be patient. Our spies must move swiftly but silently."

Lord Caerlyn dipped his chin firmly, glancing at Edwyn. "I want eyes in Castellon. And ears at every gathering. Discreetly. Uncover the source of this game."

Edwyn gave a crisp bow. "Our informants are unmatched, my lord. We will find answers."

Olivia stepped forward, placing a gentle hand on Quentyn's arm, her expression sharp yet reassuring. "Be cautious, husband. If another has already moved the pieces, then they've planned for your next move. Assume nothing."

Quentyn covered her hand briefly, drawing a steadying breath. "I will not. But neither will I allow House Caerlyn to become a lever."

Olivia smiled faintly.

Her expression was like tempered steel. "Then let us ensure we are the hands moving the levers, not the lever itself."

She stepped back gracefully, her voice lowering to a whisper edged in quiet confidence. "Let them assume we haven't noticed."

Quentyn agreed solemnly, his resolve firm, even if his unease lingered. He had managed drawn-out conflicts before, but never without knowing who had begun them. He straightened, turning to Edwyn. "Send word quietly to our best people. Find out who truly moves behind this grain shipment. If this is a forgery, find the forger. If Valen is involved, find out how deeply."

Edwyn inclined his head respectfully. "It shall be done."

He exited quietly, leaving husband and wife alone in the heavy silence of the study. Olivia stepped onto the balcony, her gaze drifting down to the wagons below.

"You believe we can untangle this deceit quickly?" Quentyn asked as he joined her.

Olivia adjusted one cuff with meticulous care. "Quickly?" She gave the faintest shake of her head. "No. Whoever set this in motion is careful. Patient. Dangerous." Her eyes flicked briefly toward him. "Perhaps even more so than Lord Valen himself—assuming he is not merely the blade being used."

Quentyn rested his hands on the stone rail. "Flame help us if we misjudge the hand behind it."

"That would be unfortunate," Olivia said mildly. "So we won't."

Together they looked out across the courtyard.

Morning light washed over House Caerlyn in deceptive warmth while servants hurried below, guiding the final wagons toward the iron-bound silos.

"Someone has already moved inside our walls," Quentyn muttered.

"Yes." Olivia's gaze remained fixed on the courtyard. "And they will believe we didn't notice."

Quentyn's jaw tightened.

Below them, Edwyn Fallow directed the unloading with his usual steady efficiency, though even from the balcony the tension in the steward's shoulders was plain.

"We built our reputation on seeing danger before it reached our gates," Quentyn said.

"And yet here it stands," Olivia replied calmly.

A chill breeze tugged at her dark hair.

"Circus Valen is ambitious," she continued, "but he lacks the patience for something this clean. Someone steadier guides him."

Quentyn studied the wagons. "They want to divide us. Strain our trust in Castellon."

"Perhaps," Olivia said. "Or something larger."

Below them the last sacks disappeared into the silos.

The doors closed with a hollow clang that echoed across the courtyard.

Olivia watched them shut.

"They have already gained ground," she said softly. "The question now, my dear husband… is how ruthless we are willing to be."

✶

CHAPTER SIX

The morning sun had just begun to warm Castellon Shield's ancient stone walls, casting amber light through the tall eastern windows—the first hint of warmth, the heat slow to take hold after a long season of cold. In the distance, the Ironback Mountains rose in silent, jagged ranks, their snow-dusted peaks cutting the horizon like a scar. In the fortress's northern wing, courtyards echoed with the muted clash of morning drills, steel on steel, underscored by the low murmur of early councils already at work.

Here lay the Royal House Apartments—quarters reserved by centuries-old decree for the seven Great Houses. They were not indulgences so much as infrastructure: permanent residences that allowed the realm's most powerful families to remain close to the crown without constant travel. Each major house occupied roughly half a tower floor, built around carved stone hearths and deep-set ashwood walls darkened by age rather than ornament. Silk-draped windows stirred faintly in the morning air, the breeze still carrying a winter's edge. Furnishings from the surrounding realms were present, but restrained—signals of status, not displays of excess.

By contrast, the quarters allotted to lesser houses—still politely termed apartments—were little more than elongated guest chambers. Narrow, functional, and sparsely furnished, they resembled respectable inns rather than noble residences. Adequate, certainly. But within Castellon Shield, adequacy was simply the clearest reminder of where one stood. Lady Elara Icewind's apartments faced north, overlooking the tiered royal gardens and, beyond them, the training yard.

From here, the sounds of steel carried faintly on the cool air—distant, constant, and familiar, breath sharpening as it left the lungs—controlled, measured against the cold. This was where she lived when she was not at Icewind Manor—close enough to the crown to matter, never close enough to belong.

Elara sat at her writing table, one hand resting near the inkwell, the other supporting her cheek, sleeves pushed back despite the chill that lingered in the room's shadows. A ledger lay open before her, pages filled with careful notations—harvest yields, livestock births, margins tightened until they squeaked. Her quill hovered over the pages, forgotten.

The hearth crackled softly behind her, steady and contained, but her attention had slipped its leash. Her gaze drifted from the page to the fire, and then beyond it, pulled by memories that never stayed buried for long.

The lakeside lodge came back to her with cruel clarity. It had been the longest days of the year—Midswell holiday—whitewashed stone bright against the edge of Lorne Lake. Her father's pride, her mother's refuge. She and her brothers—Deklan, fearless and loud, and Odin, sharp-eyed and quick—had spent those days in motion, racing barefoot along the pebbled shore, leaping from the old dock until their skin stung and their laughter carried clear across the water. They built rough forts from driftwood, chased dragonflies through the reeds, and collapsed at dusk with mud-streaked arms and aching lungs, convinced the world would never ask more of them than this.

Elara had been twelve. Old enough to recognize happiness. Young enough to trust it.

That morning had begun in laughter—the real kind. The kind that softened her mother's voice and creased her eyes at the corners. Laughter that echoed across the lake as Deklan splashed too hard, as Odin followed with more courage than grace.

Even now, Elara could recall it with painful precision: the clean bite of lake air, the thread of woodsmoke drifting from the lodge, the shock of cold water flung carelessly her way. Her mother's voice, bright and unguarded, had carried across the shore.

A perfect day, she had said.

Mother had gone inside to begin preparations for the evening meal. Perhaps it was a wayward spark, grease turned over carelessly—no one ever knew exactly how it started.

It began with her mother's scream—sharp, animalistic, raw enough to shred the fragile perfection of the morning. The sound ripped Elara abruptly from laughter into terror, freezing her on the lakeshore, cold water dripping from her fingertips. Before she could move, her father's voice thundered through the chaos, desperate and anguished: "Lyanna!"

Elara watched, frozen, as her father charged toward the burning lodge, flames tearing at timber and glass. "Stay back!" he yelled over his shoulder, his voice cracked and urgent, disappearing instantly into the choking darkness.

Deklan was already sprinting forward, features hardened with stubborn bravery, determination propelling him into the billowing smoke without hesitation. "Stay here!" he shouted back, but his voice was already swallowed by the roaring flames.

"Father! Mother!" Elara screamed, her voice splintering in sudden panic, smoke and fear swallowing the morning.

Odin seized her roughly by the arm, dragging her backward toward the safety of the trees. "You heard Father—stay back!" His voice came out ragged, urgent, slicing sharply through her confusion.

Smoke surged from the lodge in dark, choking torrents, blackening the sky and devouring daylight in angry, swirling coils. Flames surged upward, stripping paint from timber and turning cherished memories to ash. Windows that had once reflected clarity shattered outward under the furnace's fury.

For a heartbeat, there was only ringing silence.

Then—through the acrid haze—Elara glimpsed them.

Her father staggered first from the wreckage, his tall frame buckled by coughing spasms, eyes streaming tears of smoke and pain. Clutched desperately in his arms, her mother clung tight, her once-serene face smeared with soot, mouth open in a silent cry of fear.

Behind them, Deklan braced their father's steps, jaw set hard, eyes cutting through the smoke with frantic focus.

Odin released Elara instantly and lunged forward. She reached for him without thinking—too late.

"Stay here!" he shouted, the words nearly drowned out by the roar of the fire. "I have to help them!"

"No!" Elara screamed, panic punching the breath from her chest. She lurched after him, desperate, and her foot caught on something unseen. The ground vanished. She hit hard against roots and stone, pain tearing through her knee as it split open.

She pushed herself up, vision swimming, heart battering her ribs.

Through smoke and tears, she saw her family stagger clear of the flames—almost.

The lodge groaned.

Timbers cracked like bones. The roof buckled inward, collapsing in a thunderous rush of fire, wood, and tile. In an instant, the space where her family had been was gone.

Her scream never reached them.

She crawled forward on hands and knees, nails scraping dirt, voice breaking into hoarse pleas that faded as the heat drove her back. The lodge was a pyre now—no doors, no voices, no way in.

Then arms closed around her.

They were steady. Certain. She fought them for a heartbeat before the strength holding her refused to yield. Whoever it was said nothing—no questions, no comfort offered too soon—only held her until the shaking slowed and the world stopped spinning.

He led her away from the fire without ceremony, shielding her from the worst of the heat, guiding her step by step until the glow dimmed behind them.

He took her home that day.

And he stayed.

Not in her rooms. But close enough to matter.

When whispers curled through halls that were no longer kind, he was there. When blame found its way toward a girl who had survived, he stood between it and her without ever stepping into the light. He never caged her, never softened her. He simply remained—watchful, deliberate, unmovable—until Elara learned to stand on her own, carrying what she had lost without letting it break her.

Rumors followed her relentlessly from that day—whispers that she had lit the blaze herself, a young heir ambitious beyond her years, eager for inheritance even at twelve. They faded with seasons and passing years, but never vanished, clinging like smoke caught in silk.

"I didn't want it," she whispered now to the empty room. "I loved them."

Her voice broke on the last word. Tears came hot and sharp, spilling despite her efforts to dam them. She brushed them away with an irritated swipe, refusing to let grief take full hold.

She missed her mother's voice—soft, melodic, a balm against scraped knees and restless nights.

She missed Deklan's rumbling laughter, steady as distant thunder. Odin's quick grin, always a heartbeat before the lie.

Her breath shuddered once more. Another tear escaped, cold against her skin.

Elara wiped her cheek and drew a slow, steadying breath, forcing the grief back behind walls built over years of silent endurance.

She straightened. Her fingers closed around the quill with deliberate firmness. The ledger lay open before her, waiting.

She would not let their memories be reduced to rumor or ash. She would not become the disappointment others expected. She would not be dismissed as a foolish girl.

Each caréful notation. Each alliance weighed and chosen. Each quiet maneuver. Not ambition—armor.

Elara dipped the quill and returned to her work.

The numbers met her without mercy.

Crop yields had fallen again—not from this year's fields, but from stores running thin after a long Winterfall. Last year's harvest had not stretched as far as it should have. And Lady Wynmere's promised grain had yet to be delivered.

The stable records were worse.

Not a single foal yet confirmed for the coming season.

Not one.

Mares that should have quickened by now had not taken.

The silence of the stables rang louder than any accusation.

Her estate was bleeding coin. Resources draining away like candlewax before dawn.

Elara flipped the ledger pages, scanning detailed notations before pausing at the vassal house reports. Her fingers found the silver ring on her hand, spinning it once, twice, a gesture so familiar it no longer felt conscious.

House Taranth had failed their winter grain quota—again, stores short despite allowances already granted. House Berwyck had delivered barely half their promised elk hides, citing poachers and sickness moving through the herds—claims difficult to disprove and impossible to audit before thaw. House Lyonswark had defaulted entirely on their timber shipment, citing flooded cuts and bandit interference along the winter roads. Each entry was another weight pressing upon her shoulders—failures not dramatic enough to punish outright, yet too consistent to ignore.

"Near enough to bankruptcy," she murmured, her quill hovering above the parchment.

She needed gold. She needed allies. Most critically, she needed leverage.

Her thoughts inevitably returned to Lord Valen. Valen had gold in excess—mountains of it, bought with whispers and schemes.

But align herself with him? The memory of their last encounter twisted her stomach. Valen's oily smile, his hungry, calculating eyes as he'd dared propose a *union* over stewed venison and honeyroot wine. The thought of his hands on her, claiming her as a prize, tightened her throat with revulsion.

No. That path was worse than poverty, worse even than flames. She refused to become just another prize in that bloated parasite's collection. She required power—not charity masquerading as favor. Influence—not pity dressed up as generosity.

A sudden clang from the training yard below broke her concentration. Her head snapped up, eyes narrowing sharply.

Through the tall, silk-draped windows, the yard below was alive with activity, blades flashing like quicksilver in the morning sun. Young nobles and squires sparred fiercely, movements precise and disciplined, each strike measured. Commander Cinquedea barked orders, his voice echoing like distant thunder, punctuated by rhythmic clashes of steel upon steel.

"You there—if I wanted to watch a drunken goose dance, I'd go to the Midharvest Fair! Reset and try not to offend the gods this time!" Cinquedea's voice cut through the yard, mingling with the metallic tang of sweat and effort.

Elara rose from her desk, velvet skirts whispering as she crossed to the window. The training yard pulled at her attention with a gravity she didn't entirely trust.

Her gaze found Prince Baldrik Thornsword almost immediately.

Duck.

Turn.

Strike.

His movements carried an easy grace, but the seams showed—blade dipping a fraction too low, footwork a breath behind where it should be. Youth, not incompetence. Promise still outrunning experience.

Baldrik faltered when a younger squire went down, stopping mid-exchange to haul the boy upright with a muttered word and a steadying hand before turning back to the line.

That, more than the swordplay, caught her attention.

Favor followed him like a second shadow. The Queen watched him closely. The court whispered his name with expectation. He was the heir apparent—for now—his future still malleable, his shape not yet set.

Baldrik broke from the line and moved toward the water buckets, shoulders tense, jaw tight with something training alone wouldn't grind away.

Not exhaustion, Elara decided. Weight.

Something unresolved. Something human.

The thought came uninvited and unwelcome—and she did not push it away.

Flint and tinder, waiting only for a spark.

Perhaps it was time to leave ledgers and balconies behind. Time to step into the yard. Time to let the prince become more than a distant figure framed in stone and sunlight.

Elara's smile, when it came, was faint and thoughtful—calculating.

"A distraction," she murmured, more to herself than the mountains beyond the walls. "Or perhaps… a way out."

Below, steel rang against steel as the yard surged back into motion, sunlight climbing higher, sweat brightening skin even as the air retained a winter bite, echoes carrying between the stone walls as youth, discipline, and ambition collided.

At the yard's center stood Prince Baldrik Thornsword, chest heaving, feet planted wide, eyes narrowed in focus. Opposite him, Samuel Rowleigh grinned, sword held loose but ready, confidence worn like a second skin.

Baldrik lunged, blade cutting upward. Sam deflected cleanly, steel scraping in a bright clash.

"Still slow, Baldrik," Sam said, sliding aside with infuriating ease. He tapped twice—quick, testing strikes Baldrik barely turned. "Trying to impress the ladies in the windows, or just giving them something to talk about?"

Baldrik dodged, boots slipping briefly on packed grit and old frost, then recovered. "Maybe I'm letting you wear yourself out with all that dancing."

Sam laughed, circling. "If dancing wins battles, you should take lessons."

They closed again.

Blades flashed.

Feints. Parries. Ripostes in quick succession. Baldrik fought with grit and drive, but Sam's precision stayed half a breath ahead. Baldrik cursed under his breath as his footing slipped.

A squire at the rail called out, grinning. "Careful, Baldrik! Rowleigh's out for royal blood today!"

Sam spared him a glance. "Only royal pride. Much easier to bruise."

Baldrik surged forward at once.

Turning irritation into force. Sam gave ground—one step, then another—guard opening just a hair too wide, an invitation he knew Baldrik would take, as the prince pressed harder, each strike heavier, more committed.

Cinquedea's voice cracked across the yard. "Is this a fight or a courtship? Thornsword. Rowleigh. Less flirting. More steel."

Baldrik's jaw tightened. He lunged again, blade snapping out, close enough to brush Sam's shoulder.

"Romance?" Baldrik snapped, sweat trickling into his eyes. "I'd sooner court a hungry bear!"

Sam laughed, parrying a blow at his midsection with casual precision. "Ah, but bears don't gossip afterward."

A few eyes tracked the exchange beyond the circle—some amused, some sharp. A veteran knight stood with arms crossed, brow furrowed. Nearby, a young noble scratched notes onto a scrap of parchment, eyes flicking between footwork and grip.

Torin Lyonswark watched in silence. Sun-bleached hair, crooked nose, stance too relaxed for a squire of his ranking. His gaze stayed on Baldrik—not the blade, but the choices behind it.

Baldrik pressed harder. Steel rang as their swords met, locked for a heartbeat.

Breath burned hot between them.

"You talk more than the palace bards," Baldrik muttered.

"Because you give me time to," Sam shot back, twisting free.

Baldrik adjusted.

Shortened his swing.

Planted his feet.

The irritation burned off, leaving focus behind. He advanced—step by deliberate step—driving Sam back with heavier strikes, forcing him to work.

Then Baldrik hooked low, snapping Sam's blade down hard enough that it nearly tore free.

A sharp intake of breath rippled through the onlookers.

Sam stumbled back a step, sweat streaking his grin as he lifted both hands. "All right. That one I felt."

Baldrik exhaled.

A tight smile broke through. "Try standing still next time."

Cinquedea's voice cut across the yard. "Enough. Water. Then back in. And Rowleigh—fight with your sword, not your mouth."

Sam grinned unabashedly. "I'll consider it, Commander."

Baldrik lowered his sword, smiling despite himself, and wiped sweat from his brow. He exhaled heavily, shooting Sam an amused look as the tension bled out of his shoulders.

"Saved by the commander," Sam smirked, slapping Baldrik's shoulder as they moved toward the barrels. "One more minute and you'd have been begging for mercy."

"In your dreams," Baldrik muttered. "And only there."

They broke apart at the water. Baldrik drank deep, savoring the cold shock from water drawn too early from winter wells, then glanced toward the far hedge.

"Back in a moment," he said casually, stepping away. "Bladder's more urgent than duty."

He slipped past the edge of the yard, boots crunching over gravel and fallen petals, and reached the hedgerow beneath the wisteria arbor. No squires. No swordmasters. Just shade, quiet—and relief.

He reached for his belt.

"Your Highness."

Baldrik froze.

Every muscle locked, heat rushing up his spine. He straightened slowly and turned.

Lady Elara Icewind waited beneath the stone archway, ivy framing her like deliberate decoration.

"I hope I'm not interrupting," she said, her tone smooth, eyes bright with restrained amusement.

"Only everything important," Baldrik muttered, hastily adjusting his tunic. "Do you plan your ambushes, or is your timing simply cursed?"

"You'll find, that I don't waste good timing." Elara replied, stepping forward with unhurried grace, fingers brushing the ivy once as if claiming the space

She wore ice-blue velvet edged in silver, practical despite its elegance. Her dark hair was pinned back with a simple silver comb. Nothing excessive. Nothing careless.

Her gaze met his—sharp, assessing, unreadable.

Baldrik swallowed. This was… not the moment he'd expected.

Baldrik cleared his throat, regaining composure. "I'd call this a surprise, but that would imply I didn't anticipate being followed through hedges by politics."

"You're not particularly difficult to track," she noted lightly.

"I was trying to be."

She smiled, unapologetic. "There's a Winter Hearth gathering tonight—one of the Shield's little habits. Fires, wine, stories. Nothing official." She held his gaze a moment longer than necessary. "I would ask that you attend with me. As my escort—if you're willing."

Baldrik studied her carefully, weighing intentions. "And if I refuse?"

"Then I'll attend alone," she said lightly. "Which will be noticed." She tilted her head, studying him. "And you'll spend your evening sweating in leather, training with men twice your size and half your charm. But it appears you enjoy pain."

"I do," Baldrik replied dryly. "Especially when it smiles like a wolf. I'll consider it."

She smiled—briefly, controlled. "That's close enough to yes."

"I said I'd consider it. Besides," He glanced back toward the yard's persistent noise. "I've been told you're dangerous."

"Rumors," she said, eyes steady on his.

She stepped gracefully past him, hands folded in front of her. At the path's turn, she paused and glanced over her shoulder.

"Dress warmly. The fires do their best, but winter still bites."

Then she was gone, leaving him alone in the hedge-shadow, aware—uncomfortably—that he had never held control of the exchange to begin with.

Behind him, swords rang; ahead lay trouble in silver-blue velvet and a clever smile.

Baldrik sighed, looking down at his half-laced tunic. "There had better be good wine."

Above, the sun dipped behind Castellon's towers, long shadows stretching across the training yard.

Prince Baldrik Thornsword returned, tying up his chausses, tunic still half-loose from his garden detour, his thoughts not quite where his feet were.

He rolled his shoulders in an attempt to clear the tension, retrieved a blunted training blade from the rack, and quietly stepped back into the ranks. Around him, sparring matches continued with fierce determination, blades ringing sharply through the yard.

Commander Cinquedea stood at the edge of the yard, arms crossed in stony silence, his narrowed gaze sharper than any shouted reprimand. His displeasure radiated outward, sending ripples of discomfort among the assembled trainees, who straightened beneath his stern vigilance.

Baldrik took his place opposite Samuel of Rowleigh, whose familiar, teasing grin suggested every match was another joke he was eager to share. They began to circle cautiously, each measuring the other anew, blades raised, muscles coiled.

Sam exaggerated his carelessness, shoulders rolling with a looseness that belied practiced skill. His feet dragged slightly in the gravel and half-thawed grit, clearly baiting Baldrik into a rash attack. Baldrik resisted, unwilling to rise to the obvious provocation, yet his earlier distraction lingered in his stance, subtle enough to go unnoticed by most—but not by Sam.

Commander Cinquedea gave a low grunt—more an indifferent gesture than a command. Still, it was all the signal needed to begin.

Sam lunged first, his blade sweeping dramatically wide, telegraphing his movements purposefully.

Baldrik's response was clean and practiced, smoothly deflecting the strike with a precise twist of his wrist, steel glancing off steel in a crisp ring that carried through the yard. They stepped lightly, circling again, boots shuffling and stirring up faint clouds of dust mixed with damp grit and crushed frost where winter thaw had not fully released the ground.

"You look distracted," Sam murmured lightly, his eyes bright with playful curiosity, dancing beneath raised brows. "Did your meeting in the garden go that well?"

Baldrik pivoted swiftly, thrusting sharply toward Sam's ribs. "If you moved you sword half as well as your tongue…" he replied, irritation mingling with dry amusement.

Sam parried easily, but his grin softened just enough to signal he'd noticed more than he was letting on. "Mm," he said. "That bad, then."

They moved again, blades crossing in quick, efficient exchanges. Sam pressed, not hard, but persistent—testing angles, crowding Baldrik's space, forcing him to stay present.

"Careful," Sam added under his breath as their swords locked for a brief, grinding heartbeat. "You fight like someone who's halfway somewhere else."

Baldrik broke the bind with a sharp twist and stepped back, jaw tightening. "I'm here."

Sam didn't argue. He shifted tactics instead, circling wider, drawing Baldrik after him. The bait was obvious now—not carelessness, but concern, wrapped in familiarity.

A feint. A tap against Baldrik's guard. Another retreat.

Sam lowered his voice. "Good, because if you weren't, Cinquedea would've already made an example of you."

As if summoned by the words, the commander's gaze flicked toward them, cold and assessing. Baldrik felt it like a weight between his shoulders and adjusted instinctively, grounding his stance, breathing through the distraction.

Their blades met again—cleaner this time. Baldrik drove forward with renewed focus, forcing Sam back two hard steps.

Satisfaction flashed briefly across Sam's face before he masked it with a grin.

"That's the prince I know," he said aloud. "Try not to lose him before the next swing."

Sam parried neatly, turning aside the strike and forcing Baldrik off-balance, pressing his advantage by ducking beneath Baldrik's hurried counter. "And you dodge more than just blades," he teased, delivering a swift jab that Baldrik barely managed to deflect.

Their blades clashed again—a low arc met by a high parry, followed by a sharp riposte.

Steel rang between their movements, punctuating each sharp word and breath. The trainees around them paused, casting glances at the exchange as the intensity crept beyond friendly sparring.

Sam leaned close as their blades locked, faces inches apart. His whisper carried playful mockery edged with curiosity. "Did she at least kiss you?"

For a heartbeat, Baldrik's grip faltered. Heat touched his ears, quickly smothered beneath narrowed focus.

Baldrik shoved Sam back, driving an elbow into his friend's ribs. "Perhaps you'd prefer to spar with her next?"

Sam laughed, stumbling before regaining his footing. “Flame take me, no—she'd eat me alive. Politics and wolves are your domain, Prince. I'll stick to sparring.”

Baldrik barely suppressed a smile as he sidestepped a low sweep aimed at his legs.

He twisted into a backhanded swing aimed at Sam’s shoulder.

Sam narrowly deflected the blow, immediately spinning into a graceful riposte aimed at Baldrik’s exposed ribs.

Baldrik stumbled, then recovered, frustration sharpening his reflexes. Determination hardened his gaze, pushing aside lingering distraction. He lunged again, blade moving faster, attacks fueled by something deeper than pride.

Sam's eyes widened slightly at the sudden intensity, matching Baldrik's pace, breaths quickening with exertion and exhilaration. Around them, the other trainees stopped entirely, drawn to the rapid exchange—strikes and counterstrikes blending into a fierce, precise contest.

Sweat trickled into Baldrik’s eyes, stinging. He pressed forward, turning irritation into motion. Sam pivoted, barely dodging another thrust, breathing hard, voice strained but still teasing. “Did she wound your pride, or just your dignity?”

Baldrik growled, feinted left, then struck from the right—his blade nearly grazing Sam’s shoulder.

“You're testing my patience Sam.”

“Then perhaps I’m doing something right,” Sam laughed, parrying again—now clearly on the defensive.

Commander Cinquedea’s voice cut across the yard, breaking their concentration. “Five-minutes, water, then switch partners!”

Baldrik lowered his sword and stepped back with a weary breath. Sam, breathing equally hard, grinned brightly, clasping Baldrik briefly on the shoulder. “At least you made it interesting.”

Baldrik managed a reluctant smile, shaking his head slightly as they moved toward the side of the ring. As he wiped sweat from his brow and half-listened to Sam’s teasing, Elara Icewind’s measured smile lingered—unwelcome and persistent.

Baldrik exhaled and lowered his sword as Sam approached, breathing easier, grinning. Together they trudged to a nearby bench, its wood cold beneath their weight, and dropped onto it. Sam produced a flask from under his leather cuirasses and handed it to Baldrik.

“So,” Sam said, elbowing Baldrik. “Did she corner you for a blessing, or was she laying siege one velvet smile at a time?”

Baldrik blinked, nearly choking. "What?"

"Lady Icewind," Sam said. "You and her. Under the arbor. Half the kitchen staff saw. You didn't even attempt to duck."

Baldrik groaned and tipped his head back. "I wasn't cornered. If you must know, she caught me attempting to take a piss."

Sam snorted, nearly dropping the flask. "You were halfway there!"

Baldrik punched Sam on the arm, scowling. "Don't be disgusting, Sam."

Sam chuckled, still amused. Baldrik rubbed his eyes wearily. "If you must know, she invited me to a Winter Hearth gathering. Asked that I attend with her."

"Hardly nothing," Sam replied, leaning in. "That's not nothing at all. That's being seen."

Baldrik exhaled through his nose. "I told her I'd consider it."

"Besides, a prince could do worse than starting his reign beneath a lady's skirts." Sam pretended thoughtfulness.

Baldrik smirked despite himself. "Flames, Sam."

"I'm serious," Sam insisted. "Icewind's dangerous—but the good kind. Knows which fork to use, and how to kill a man with a sentence. What else could a ruler possibly desire?"

Baldrik laughed softly, though it didn't quite reach his eyes.

Sam pressed on. "Imagine the court gossip—you, her, a moonlit terrace—"

"Sam."

"Maybe some tasteful hair-pulling. Her, not you. Probably."

"Sam."

"If caught, you could always claim diplomacy—"

"Enough."

Baldrik's voice was quiet and sharp, slicing through Sam's humor. Sam's smile faltered as he tilted his head, suddenly attentive.

Baldrik set the flask down, gaze steady. "She's not a joke, and neither am I. I don't like being discussed as though I'm deaf—or stupid."

Silence stretched.

Sam cleared his throat, the humor draining from him.

"Fair enough," he conceded quietly. He shifted on the bench, then nodded once, decision made. "If you go, you don't have to go alone. I can stand with you. Keep the worst of the room off your back."

Baldrik was quiet for a moment, eyes on the yard. "*If* I go," he said. "And only if you promise not to embarrass me."

Sam recoiled as if struck. "Me?"

Baldrik answered by punching his shoulder.

They rose and made their way to the water barrels. Sam splashed water onto his face and glanced sidelong at Baldrik.

"You realize she was watching you earlier, right?"

Baldrik stiffened. "She was?" he asked, a touch too quickly.

"Top of the north tower. I nearly froze from her chill."

Baldrik said nothing, though the corner of his mouth twitched slightly. Sam nudged him.

"Bet she likes you sweaty."

"Shut up," Baldrik muttered, face heating in embarrassment that had nothing to do with the afternoon sun.

Before Sam could tease further, Commander Cinquedea's voice cracked through the yard. "Enough pillow talk. Sam, out. Torrin, in."

The grins vanished.

Squire Torrin Lyonswark strode toward Baldrik—lanky and confident, expression set and unreadable. His tunic was marked from earlier bouts, knuckles cracking audibly as he approached.

"You ready, Thornsword?" Torrin called, voice level, eyes fixed on Baldrik. "Or do you need a moment?"

Baldrik said nothing, jaw tightening silently as he stepped forward into the sparring circle.

He flexed his fingers around the hilt of his dulled blade, sweat already beading along his forehead—not from the sun, but from tension coiled tight in his muscles.

The stones and ground beneath their boots radiated heat where the sun reached, but shade still held a winter chill; each breath drew dry air that tasted of dust and cold stone. Around them, trainees pressed closer, murmurs swelling into shouted wagers. The mood charged the air.

Opposite him, Torrin rolled his shoulders once and settled his grip, blade coming up clean and ready. He gave Baldrik a short, formal nod—acknowledgment, courtesy.

Commander Cinquedea raised a calloused hand. "Begin. The mutton is ripe on the vine."

Silence fell. Trainees froze, blades held mid-motion, gazes snapping toward the commander. Eyebrows rose—but nobody dared laugh openly. Cinquedea remained stone-faced, posture unchanged, eyes hard and distant.

Baldrik refocused sharply, snapping his attention back to Torrin. Torrin's expression tightened, focus sharpening as the last traces of humor drained away. He struck first, lunging forward swiftly, testing Baldrik's defenses with quick, sharp jabs.

Baldrik blocked cleanly, blade ringing clear against steel, then sidestepped fluidly, responding instantly with a precise thrust aimed at Torrin's ribs. This wasn't the clumsy exchange from earlier—Baldrik's strikes now were calculated and controlled.

Torrin stepped back, circling warily, eyes narrowing in reluctant appraisal. "You're improving," he admitted grudgingly, tone edged with reluctant respect. His mouth tightened, testing rather than mocking. "Still tense," he added. "You'll tire yourself out."

Baldrik felt irritation flicker within him but refused to rise openly to the taunt. Instead, he held his silence, feinting left before lunging sharply forward, his blade slicing the air with dangerous precision.

Torrin retreated, boots scraping across loose gravel as Baldrik drove him backward. He stumbled slightly, nearly losing his balance, but recovered quickly, his agility keeping him upright amidst a sudden roar of appreciation from the surrounding trainees.

Torrin's expression hardened, focus narrowing. Baldrik pressed forward again, confident in his advantage.

He spun without warning, far quicker than Baldrik anticipated.

His elbow snapped out, catching Baldrik high along the jaw with stunning force.

Pain exploded through Baldrik's head—white-hot and blinding. The world blurred violently around him, sounds muffled into distant echoes. His balance abandoned him completely, and he toppled toward the ground, limbs numb, breath forced from his lungs as he slammed hard into the cold, churned earth, slick with thawed mud.

Above him, voices faded into whispers, colors bleeding together in disorienting swirls. The sky spun slowly, impossibly, tilting and sliding from his grasp. Sound wobbled and receded, mingling with the pounding in his head.

Even as his vision blurred, Baldrik fought for control, forcing clarity back bit by bit. Pride burned hotter than the sun overhead, dragging him through the haze.

Slowly, Baldrik propped himself onto one elbow, breath ragged, ears ringing. The yard had gone silent, trainees frozen in place.

Commander Cinquedea's voice cut through the stillness. "Thornsword. On your feet."

Baldrik grit his teeth, focusing every ounce of willpower on rising. Each movement sent pain flashing through his skull, but his resolve held. He pushed himself upright slowly, limbs trembling, vision gradually sharpening back into clarity.

Across from him, Torrin watched in silence, expression set and unreadable. The yard remained quiet, the previous jovial energy replaced by tense anticipation, every eye fixed on Baldrik.

Baldrik straightened fully.

Moving with deliberate dignity. He lifted his chin defiantly, ignoring the lingering dizziness and the dull ache still throbbing relentlessly through his head.

The blow had stung far beyond pain—it cut at pride, and Baldrik could not let that stand.

He took a shaky step forward, meeting Torrin's gaze unflinchingly. "Again," he said quietly, voice steady despite the tremor in his body. "Unless you're finished."

Torrin hesitated only a heartbeat, then nodded. "As you wish, Prince." His blade came up clean and ready.

Baldrik stepped forward again, his grip tightening on the hilt, eyes fierce. He lunged, swift and purposeful—but Torrin anticipated it perfectly. In one smooth motion, Torrin sidestepped Baldrik's thrust, pivoted, and drove the pommel of his sword into Baldrik's ribs. Pain burst through his chest, staggering him backward as his breath tore free.

Before Baldrik could recover, Torrin shifted his weight and drove in close, shoulder low, catching Baldrik square through the center of his stance. The world tilted once more, the cold-packed ground rushing up with unforgiving force.

He slammed down hard, vision swimming, darkness licking at the edges of consciousness. The light faded—then twisted.

Above, the sky rippled strangely, heat pulsing in slow, disorienting waves—time stretching, sensation unmoored. Within that shimmering haze, a figure appeared, impossibly clear yet distant.

A monk stood robed in crimson and ivory, a sharp collar at his throat, a golden sunburst clasp gleaming at his chest. He stood in a vaulted hall, silent and isolated. In the monk's hands rested the king's crown—held reverently, delicately, as though it might shatter beneath careless touch.

He did not wear it. Instead, he carried it carefully away from an unseen throne, like a sacred relic meant for preservation rather than power.

Baldrik stared, pulse hammering in sudden, inexplicable dread.

Torrin extended a hand, offering a brief, respectful nod. "I'll give you this, Thornsword—you fight like a mountain goat. All charge, no grace."

Baldrik grasped Torrin's hand and was pulled upright, his gaze drifting past Torrin, past the trainees, toward the Citadel Spire rising starkly above Castellon.

Not a seat of conventional power—but the heart of the Flamebound Order, a jagged monument to duty. In that moment, Baldrik felt its presence like a beacon calling him forward, an undeniable pull.

The vision lingered vividly—the monk in crimson and ivory, the crown carefully carried, deliberately preserved but not claimed. Not seized, or worn, guarded with solemn reverence.

A crown that was not his to bear.

Yet that vision pressed against something older, deeper. It felt more like memory than revelation. Not fear or faith—something else entirely, something patient, watchful.

The path ahead seemed suddenly clearer, sharply vivid in his mind.

For the first time in weeks, Baldrik felt sure—certainty settling in his chest, doubts falling quiet.

Across the yard, beneath the shadow of a stone arch, Commander Cinquedea stood motionless, scratching notes onto a slate, his gaze steady and unhurried as he observed every detail.

Later—when the yard emptied and the ring of steel faded— Cinquedea stood alone near the weapon racks. He removed his gloves and tucked them behind his belt. Dust coated his uniform, sweat darkened the stiff collar, yet his posture remained rigid—today's sparring merely prelude.

Twilight settled over Castellon Shield. Cinquedea moved across the yard, snow crunching beneath polished boots, shadows stretching across empty battlements. Through dim corridors lit by flickering sconces, he ascended a narrow staircase, steps worn smooth by generations.

He paused before a heavy oak door, unmarked and severe, its surface scarred by age and use.

He straightened his uniform. Knocked once.

And stepped into Lord Darkoak's chamber.

The north gallery stretched beneath late-afternoon light, high stone walls lined with tactical maps, muster records, and pinned reports. Lord Lanyard Darkoak stood at an alcove, silhouetted by the window as he examined reports spread across a polished table. His posture was rigid, unyielding as the stone around him.

Commander Cinquedea stepped over the threshold, his footfall echoing in the quiet.

"Commander," Lanyard acknowledged without lifting his gaze from the papers.

"My lord."

"Speak." Lanyard's voice was hard, unchanging—like stone grinding against stone.

Cinquedea clasped his hands neatly behind his back. "The prince returned late from his midday break. Distracted. His training suffered."

Lanyard didn't move, his gaze unwavering, fixed on the documents before him.

"During a rest," Cinquedea continued calmly, "he spoke with Samson of Rowleigh. Their conversation turned to Lady Elara Icewind."

Lanyard's head lifted slightly, eyes sharpening—not with interest, but irritation. Elara Icewind again. Persisting. "Go on."

"The boy did not deny meeting her privately in the gardens. Claimed she'd invited him to a gathering. Winter Hearth." Cinquedea paused briefly, his tone measured, neutral. "Rowleigh made crude remarks. The prince appeared…unsettled."

Lanyard's jaw tightened almost imperceptibly. He released a slow breath, the sound thin with restraint.

"You believe this warrants closer attention?" he asked quietly.

Cinquedea inclined his head slightly. "Any other boy, and I'd leave it to idle gossip. But princes can't afford that luxury."

A thin, humorless smile flickered across Lanyard's lips.

"No," he murmured softly. "They certainly cannot."

No formal dismissal was offered, yet Cinquedea gave a sharp nod then turned sharply and exited without further word.

Lanyard remained standing after the commander had departed, his gaze fixed out the window as shadows lengthened across Castellon's stone towers. Silent and motionless, he added one more invisible mark beside the name of Lady Elara Icewind.

Outside, the city stirred, oblivious to the quiet battles waged beneath polished smiles and behind closed doors. The sun dipped lower, clouds gathering on the horizon.

Lanyard Darkoak watched the fading light with narrowed eyes. One hand rested on the table's edge, fingers still. The other tightened into a fist, knuckles whitening with restrained resolve.

Wars were not always fought with steel and blood. Some were waged between lines of ink, murmured in shadowed corners, hidden behind polite masks worn by those who moved unseen pieces across Eldaraine's board.

Lady Elara Icewind was one such piece—an inconvenience that refused to be swept aside. Her house was failing. Her persistence was noted. Whether desperation drove her, or something sharper hid behind that careful smile, he had yet to decide.

Either way, she had drawn his attention.

And attention, once given, was rarely withdrawn.

✶

CHAPTER SEVEN

Beneath an iron-gray sky swollen with snow yet to fall, Prince Baldrik Thornsword left the training yard. His breath steamed faintly in the cold, muscles aching from stiffness and exertion, the bite of late Winterfall gnawing through sweat damp linens beneath his gambeson. The air was brittle rather than heavy, sharp with the promise of snow before dawn.

Near the royal stables, where the dry scents of hay and horseflesh mingled with the smoke of banked braziers, stood his father—King Harald Thornsword. He was silent and still, a sentinel carved from patience and duty.

The King's attention rested on a tall black mare. One broad hand moved over her neck, careful, practiced, murmuring low affections meant for no ears but hers. Baldrik halted without thinking, caught by the sight. His father was rarely gentle where anyone could see it.

For a moment, Baldrik did not know how to approach him. Harald turned as he drew closer, blue-grey eyes sharp but not cruel, reading more than sweat and scraped knuckles. Baldrik slowed, uncertainty flickering despite himself. *What now—another lesson, or another reminder of what I am meant to be?*

"Father," he said, keeping his voice level. "I didn't expect you here."

Harald allowed himself a small, tired smile and continued stroking the mare's neck. She flicked an ear and gave a quiet nicker. "I thought I'd check on your companions," he said. "You always did understand horses better than people."

Baldrik stepped closer, resting a hand against the mare's warm flank, grateful for the heat beneath her coat. "They make sense," he said. "When I ride, everything else goes quiet."

Harald looked at his son.

"It did for me as well, at your age."

He paused, eyes drifting toward the frozen yard beyond the stable doors. "I used to dream of open ground and hard wind. Of outrunning expectations—especially your grandmother's."

"Did she disapprove?" Baldrik asked quietly, sensing the deeper weight of unspoken history behind his father's words.

Harald nodded, measured, his gaze drifting past the stable wall. "She did. Riding was indulgence, she said—beneath the dignity of a future king." His mouth tightened, with familiar restraint. "My mother believed warmth bred weakness. That a king should be carved down to function—nothing soft left to fail."

He looked back at his son then, eyes clear and unyielding. "Queen Edwina ruled by control and cold certainty. Duty was to be borne, not enjoyed."

A deliberate pause settled. "But I am not your grandmother."

Baldrik held his gaze, hearing the boundary in that statement as much as the reassurance.

Harald stepped away from the mare and turned fully toward him. "Walk with me."

They moved along the stable path.

Boots crunched softly over frost-stiff gravel. The cold had crept deeper with the fading light, breath clouding each step. Only when they were clear of the horses did Harald speak again, his tone casual. "Commander Cinquedea tells me your footwork is improving."

Baldrik's mouth twitched. "I believe his exact words were 'slightly less embarrassing.'"

A quiet huff of amusement escaped Harald. "From Cinquedea, that borders on effusive praise."

Baldrik hesitated a fraction too long. "Lady Elara Icewind cornered me during a break," he said at last. "She asked if I would escort her to the Winter Hearth tonight."

Harald did not stop walking, but his attention sharpened. "Cornered," he repeated mildly. "An interesting choice of word."

"She was… direct." Baldrick clarified.

"That, at least, is consistent." Harald smirked.

They moved a few steps in silence, frost grinding beneath their boots.

"You know her reputation."

"I know what people say," Baldrik replied. "But *I* don't know her."

Harald agreed. "Being seen with the right people steadies a prince. Being seen with the wrong ones invites speculation." His tone remained even. "Icewind is not the worst company you could keep. Nor the safest."

Baldrik glanced at him. "Do you think she's suited for me?"

Harald's expression did not change, but something thoughtful moved behind his eyes. "I think she is intelligent. Ambitious. She has endured more than most in this court. Whether she is suited for you is another matter."

"I've not had cause to judge her yet."

"Then tonight would be a good time to learn more about her."

Harald let that settle between them before adding, quieter, "A king cannot afford ignorance—especially of those who seek his company."

They walked a few paces more, the air tightening with cold and unspoken thought.

Harald slowed at last, turning his head just enough. "You're not finished," he said. "There's more."

He let another step pass between them before adding, without looking at him, "Something troubles you. Say it."

Baldrik's shoulders tightened. He stared ahead, jaw set, bracing himself against his own thoughts. After a breath that stung his lungs, he spoke. "I had… something. On the training ground. I don't know what to call it."

Harald stopped.

Baldrik turned to face him. "A vision, maybe. The Flamebound Order. Their temple—a monk and a crown. It wasn't a dream. It felt… solid. Like it mattered." His voice dropped. "Like I was meant to see it."

Harald studied him carefully.

The humor was gone now, replaced by a colder, older focus. "And it came unbidden?"

Baldrik shrugged. "I don't understand it."

Harald exhaled slowly, the sound thin in the Winterfall air. "Your grandmother believed in such moments," he said at last. "She spoke of the Flamebound as watchers—of truths meant to be endured rather than welcomed."

Baldrik's voice lowered, stripped of bravado. "Did you believe her?"

Harald paused, considering his memories. When he answered, his voice was quiet. "She believed enough for an entire court. I was… cautious. Skeptical." A corner of his mouth tightened. "Faith wielded as certainty can be a dangerous thing."

He looked at Baldrik more closely then, as a king might—but also as a father. "But when I look at you now, I see her in your eyes. Not her control. Her hunger. The need to understand rather than obey."

Baldrik drew a breath that shuddered faintly in the cold. "I need to know what this means," he said. "I can't pretend it didn't happen."

Harald inclined his head. "Nor should you."

Silence held for a moment.

Frost creaked faintly under shifting boots.

"And the throne?" Harald asked, his tone even, though the question carried weight enough to bruise. "A king cannot drift. To rule, you must want the crown."

Baldrik stared back at the stable doors, at the dark beyond them. His answer came quietly. "I don't know if I do."

Harald closed his eyes for the briefest moment. When he opened them, the decision was already made. "Then you will find your path," he said. "Follow this—whatever it is. Learn what it asks of you." His voice lowered, steady and certain. "Your mother will not be pleased. This is not the future she has imagined for you."

He met Baldrik's eyes fully now. "But she is not the one who must walk it. I will not bind you out of fear."

Baldrik turned, startled. "Even if it leads away from the throne?"

"Yes."

Harald's reply was immediate, firm. "Eldaraine will survive another uncertainty. I will not have my son rule it as one."

Relief crossed Baldrik's face before he could stop it. "Thank you, father."

Harald placed a hand on his shoulder—solid and grounding. "Remember this," he said. "Visions are lanterns. They show what lies ahead. They do not choose your steps."

His hand tightened, a rare squeeze that carried more weight than any speech.

"Your path is your own, my son," Harald said quietly. "Whether you walk the path of flame or the crown." His gaze flicked toward the darkening yard. "Come. The air is getting cold."

Baldrik nodded, something unspoken settling between them. Together, they turned and walked back toward the stables, their boots crunching in unison on the frozen stone as Castellon Shield rose to meet them.

The lights of the keep burned steadily against the Winterfall gloom.

Storms always came, within and without—but a king did not flee them. He carried the weight and endured.

By the time the doors closed behind him, the cold had followed. It settled in his bones as braziers and tapestry lined stone walls failed to drive it out.

Harald stood behind his desk, fingers splayed across the parchment as if he meant to hold the kingdom still by force of will.

Across from him, Lord Lanyard Darkoak stood with his arms behind his back, posture impeccable, eyes sharp enough to flay deceit.

"What news, old friend?" Harald asked without looking up.

Lanyard began his report, blunt and concise.

"Lord Valen holds too many cards, and he's forgotten the art of silence.

Lord Narcona mistakes proximity for loyalty—he lets the Scorchlands breathe too freely."

Harald grunted, balanced between wry amusement and growing frustration, without lifting his gaze from the map beneath his fingers. "You say that every council session."

"And every session they validate me," Lanyard replied dryly, the faintest crinkle touching the corner of his keen green eyes.

The king straightened slowly.

He met Lanyard's stare evenly. "What did Valen tell the emissaries from Vara this time?"

Lanyard's lips twisted. "That their wine tastes of regret, and their ships smell like fish left too long in the sun."

A faint chuckle escaped Harald, brief relief from the knot tightening between his shoulders. "He's not wrong about their ships."

"Lady Caerlyn has secured lumber rights from House Stennon," Lanyard said. "In exchange for her niece's hand."

Harald's brow lifted. "A niece?"

"Yes," Lanyard replied. "Old enough to be useful. Young enough not to protest."

Harald's amusement flattened. "Stennon has timber, not ambition."

"Which makes them easy to bargain with," Lanyard said. "And dangerous to underestimate."

Harald exhaled through his nose. "We ought to keep a ledger—of every noble who trades blood for leverage."

"We'd run out of parchment before winter's end," Lanyard said evenly.

"Also, House Caerlyn's little spy syndicate spreads too far and whispers too often," Lanyard said, his voice crisp as a blade's edge.

Harald's fingers flexed against the parchment. "Caerlyn's steward has been everywhere of late."

Lanyard inclined his head a fraction. "Edwyn Fallow made inquiry at the Crown's ledger hall regarding a Valen grain contract—wagons delivered to Caerlyn."

Harald's gaze sharpened. "Did the Record Wardens give him an answer."

"They did. He was not satisfied."

"You suspect deceit?"

Lanyard raised a brow. "From Valen?"

Harald conceded with the faintest shift of breath. "I see your point."

"According to the contract," Lanyard continued, "Caerlyn holds Valen's grain while Goldacre repairs its own stores. Temporary stewardship. Signed and sealed."

Harald's jaw tightened. "Have you spoken to Avanna of this?"

"I have."

"Good." Harald's eyes returned to the map. "And Lord Harker? Still ill?"

"Claims sickness keeps him abed," Lanyard said. "Yet he's been spotted hawking dogs in Blackwool Market."

"Perhaps he's training them as messengers," Harald murmured.

"If so, they'd deliver clearer messages than his handwriting," Lanyard said—then fell silent under Harald's gaze.

The king studied him, noting the lines at his eyes and the stiffness in his shoulder—the quiet toll of years and service. "Do you trust any of them, Lanyard?"

A pause. Barely a breath. "Do you, Your Majesty?"

"That," Harald said, "is hardly comforting."

"Then no one."

The pause stretched, familiar and uneasy, until Harald spoke again. "Lady Icewind has taken an interest in Baldrik."

The twitch of Lanyard's jaw was answer enough.

"She has asked him to escort her to the Winter Hearth this evening." Harald's tone was neutral, observational.

Lanyard's expression hardened a fraction.

Harald noticed. "I take it you do not approve?"

"She is dangerous in her charm. Patient. Cunning."

"That sounds almost like praise."

"It wasn't meant as such."

Harald moved to the narrow window slit, gazing down into Castellon's inner yard, where frost clung to stone like a second hide.

"Icewind plays for position, not applause," he said. "I respect that. I do not trust it."

"She understands scarcity," Lanyard added. "Late Winterfall sharpens that instinct. Sooner or later, she'll choose whether to endure—or to cut."

Harald was quiet a moment. "Baldrik doesn't know her."

"Then he should keep his distance."

"No." Harald's voice remained calm. "Let him make up his own mind about her. See whether or not he judges her less harshly than we do, my friend." He glanced back. "She is, after all, not her father."

Lanyard's brow lifted slightly, but he did not argue.

"He is also gauging the Flamebound," Harald said.

Lanyard inclined his head, waiting.

"I will give him room," he continued. "Enough to learn whether this path steadies him—or leads him back to the throne."

"Avanna will oppose it," Lanyard said. "The monks. And Icewind."

"She always does," Harald said. "When she cannot steer the outcome. Nevertheless, I will stand with my son."

Lanyard studied him a moment longer, then bowed his head. "And if he chooses the monks?" Concern lining his words.

Harald let out a breath, "Then the crown will adapt."

"As you wish." Lanyard showed nothing; a pinch of irritation flickered across his face and vanished.

Harald turned fully now. "Elara. Watch her. Not as an enemy—yet."

He reached for his goblet, tasted the wine, and set it aside. "Do you think she intends him harm?"

"She intends advantage," Lanyard said. "And sometimes the difference is academic."

The brazier popped.

"And yet," Harald said, rubbing his beard, "you haven't suggested stripping her of titles or sending her to the Breaks."

Lanyard's mouth thinned. "Ambition doesn't always turn traitor. Sometimes, it becomes useful."

A knock interrupted—a gentle rap, purposeful but patient. Harald ignored it momentarily, his voice lowering. "Is there anything else?"

"Just a rumor, perhaps nothing more. The forge-master's apprentice says he saw Lady Meyra Wynmere with a cloaked stranger by the Metallurgical Academy at dusk."

Harald's hesitation was slight—gone almost as soon as it appeared.

"Probably meaningless," Lanyard conceded.

"Yes, probably nothing." Harald conceded, "If the rumor persists, inform me. Until then—"

Another knock, sharper now, insistent. Before the king could respond, the heavy oak door creaked open without invitation, and Queen Avanna Thornsword entered swiftly. Her presence was immediate, chilling the room like a sudden frost, emerald silk fitted to her frame with the precision of ceremonial steel, her eyes colder still.

"Your Majesty," she greeted Harald with a carefully measured nod, ignoring Darkoak entirely.

Harald straightened subtly, in acknowledgment. "Queen Avanna."

"We must speak," she said crisply. "About the Prince."

Lanyard stepped back at once, retreating to the edge of the room with the smooth economy of a man who knew when his presence sharpened blades. He didn't leave; he simply became furniture.

Avanna waited a heartbeat longer. When Harald did not dismiss his commander, her mouth thinned. "I will not waste time," she said. "Baldrik has been indulged long enough."

He folded his hands across his chest, fingers interlaced, posture calm, immovable. "He has been training since dawn," he replied. "If that is indulgence, it is a strange sort."

"Do not patronize me," Avanna said, stepping closer. The emerald silk murmured against the stone, winter-weighted and immaculate. "He is distracted. Withdrawn. He has been speaking of monks and visions instead of duty."

Lanyard's eyes flicked once—barely—to Harald. Then stillness again.

"Visions are not crimes," Harald said evenly. "Nor is reflection."

She crossed toward the table, resting a hand at its edge—not claiming space outright, but asserting proximity and control masked carefully as concern. "He's drifting. Court studies neglected, letters unanswered, training sporadic at best. The court whispers."

Harald sighed, frustration tinged with exhaustion. "The court always whispers."

She leaned in, voice lowering dangerously. "But the people listen. If they begin to doubt their heir's strength, they will lose faith."

From his place near the window, Lanyard interjected, "Better a hesitant heir than a reckless one."

Avanna's head snapped toward him, her jaw tightening sharply. "This is not your concern, Lord Darkoak."

Lanyard met her stare impassively, refusing to flinch. "With all respect, Your Grace, the heir's preparation is precisely my concern."

Harald lifted a hand. His authority was absolute.

"Enough, both of you. Give us the room, Lord Darkoak."

Lanyard hesitated just a breath, then offered a curt nod before exiting. The heavy door closed behind him.

The atmosphere shifted—less guarded, more volatile.

Harald moved around the table slowly, pausing just out of reach, his gaze searching Avanna's face carefully. "You've always possessed a sharp eye, wife. But sometimes sharpness cuts too deep."

Her stance didn't soften; she held firm, eyes glittering with restrained intensity. "And sometimes waiting leads only to bleeding out."

"He's young," Harald said.

Her tone gleamed with the cold cruelty of polished steel, barely above a whisper yet cutting. "So was Boris."

That name struck Harald like a hammer on heated steel, forcing his eyes momentarily away, memories unbidden and painful. "My father was taken by his ambitions. My son faces something slower, something harder. He must find his own path."

"And if he doesn't?" she demanded quietly, voice edged with a rare hint of vulnerability.

"Then," Harald said carefully, "it will break him."

Avanna drew a slow breath, her composure wavering just slightly. "So you expect him to break?"

Harald's response was gentle yet unyielding. "No. But I know the weight crowns carry. I will not forge my son upon the anvil that cracked my father."

Avanna's lips tightened, and she studied Harald—truly studied him—for the first time in weeks.

Doubt flickered briefly in her eyes, not for the prince, but directed squarely at her husband, the king. For an instant, something seemed poised on her lips—a letter hidden away, a secret she guarded—but she pressed it back down, masked by practiced calm.

"You're too gentle with him," she said finally, voice carefully neutral.

"And you're too harsh," Harald replied.

They stood facing one another, truths suspended between them as the wind brushed at the curtains.

Avanna's voice faltered slightly, her control slipping only a fraction. "I just—I want to be certain he won't fall."

Harald stepped closer, his hand brushing hers—a touch not of command, but presence. "He will choose," Harald said. "And I will trust that choice, even if it leads him away from this."

Avanna's eyes widened sharply, alarm flickering clearly across her guarded features. "Away?" Her voice edged with disbelief and urgency. "Harald, there is no 'away' from this. His only path is the throne. You've seen fit to deny the kingdom—to deny *me*—a second heir. Baldrik is the only option we have."

Harald's expression tightened, irritation simmering just beneath the calm surface of his response.

Before he spoke, another thought surfaced—quiet, persistent, unwelcome. There was another path. Another name. Not Baldrik—not the son Avanna had shaped beneath golden halls and expectation. A colder option, buried beneath layers of secrecy. He exhaled through his nose and forced the thought back down, where it belonged—for now.

He blinked once, steadied himself, and returned to the moment.

"His path will be his own, Avanna," he said, voice low yet unyielding. "This kingdom has endured worse storms; it will not crumble simply because a prince seeks a different road."

Avanna drew back, eyes hard with anger and calculation. The tension settled between them, charged and unresolved. Outside, the wind rattled the shutters. In the hearth, the fire snapped once, sharp and brief.

The Hall of the Shield was quieter at this hour, the torches set high along the stone ribs of the ceiling burning with a steady, practical light. A few retainers lingered near the archways, their voices low, boots echoing in measured passes across the slate.

Prince Baldrik stood near one of the tall windows, fastening the clasp at his cloak, gaze turned outward toward the courtyard where lanterns were already being lit for the evening.

"My prince."

Baldrik did not start; he had heard the approach. "Lord Darkoak."

Lanyard came to stand beside him, not quite shoulder to shoulder. Close enough to be private. Distant enough to be formal.

"I understand you intend to attend the Winter Hearth tonight."

Baldrik's jaw shifted faintly. "I do."

"With Lady Icewind."

"Yes."

Silence stretched between them, taut but controlled.

"You are aware," Lanyard said at last, "that Icewind is not a house one associates with lightly. Particularly not in public. Particularly not now."

Baldrik's expression remained even. "She asked for an escort. I agreed."

"She did not ask idly."

"No," Baldrik conceded. "She did not."

Lanyard's gaze moved briefly toward the length of the hall, confirming they were unobserved. "The Queen would not approve."

Baldrik's eyes flicked back to him. "My father did not discourage it."

"Your father is a king," Lanyard replied evenly. "He must allow you room to choose. The Queen does not think in terms of room. She thinks in terms of precedent."

Baldrik was quiet.

"Icewind has ambition," Lanyard continued. "That is not a crime. But when a prince is seen at her side, it becomes signal. Houses read it. Valen reads it. Caerlyn reads it. The monks would read it too, should word reach them."

Baldrik's brow furrowed. "You believe she seeks to use me."

"I believe she seeks position," Lanyard said. "And position is often purchased with perception."

A servant passed at the far end of the hall. Neither man spoke until the sound of steps faded.

"If I refuse," Baldrik said slowly, "it will be read as insult."

"It will be read as caution," Lanyard corrected. "A prince who cannot be drawn into display is a prince difficult to maneuver."

Baldrik's gaze returned to the window. Lantern light flickered below, gathering warmth where frost still clung to stone.

"And if I go?"

"Then you will be measured," Lanyard said. "By her. By others. By those who prefer you uncertain." He paused. "Ask yourself whether tonight you wish to be measured—or to observe."

Baldrik exhaled through his nose, slow and controlled.

After a moment, he unclasped the cloak.

"I will not attend," he said.

Lanyard inclined his head, approval subtle but unmistakable. "A prudent choice, my prince."

Baldrik's eyes hardened slightly. "Prudence is not the same as fear."

"No," Lanyard agreed. "It is not."

He stepped back, giving the prince space once more. "The Winter Hearth will burn without you."

Baldrik said nothing.

Lanyard bowed lightly and departed, leaving the prince alone in the hall, lantern light rising in the courtyard below.

Winter Hearth firelight pulsed against stone and bare branches, throwing long shadows across the frozen ground.

Someone—thoughtful, or perhaps merely practical—had laid rush mats and crushed gravel over the worst of the ice, the day's thaw locked hard again by night, the cold creeping up through the soles of Elara's boots.

The air smelled of resin and smoke, sharp enough to sting the lungs before settling into something faintly comforting.

The fire was set low and wide, deliberate rather than spectacular. Flames rolled and snapped within a ring of blackened stone, tended by servants who knew better than to hover. Around it, small knots of nobles and retainers had already formed—hands wrapped around cups of spiced wine, warming their insides as much as their spirits. Cloaks were worn open near the heat and drawn tight again when guests drifted back toward the edges of the court.

It was not a formal gathering.

No herald stood watch.

No seating had been assigned.

That, Elara suspected, was precisely why it endured.

Near one of the pillars, a young noble—or perhaps a retainer dressed above his station—worked doggedly at a lute that refused to stay in tune. His fingers slipped, the melody wandered, and more than once he lost the thread entirely. Each failure was met with clapping and laughter, good-natured and loud, voices rising to sing along whether the tune allowed it or not. Someone thumped a heel in time. Someone else shouted a correction that only made things worse.

It had the careless heat of youth—too earnest to be skilled, too pleased with itself to mind.

Elara paused just inside the garden entrance, allowing the firelight to find her before she stepped fully in. Her cloak was winter-weight wool, dark and well cut, clasped high at the throat. Beneath it, she wore nothing that would mark the evening as courtly rather than social.

Instead, she waited.

From where she stood, she could see most of the court at a glance: familiar faces, a few strangers newly arrived at the Shield, guards lingering at the margins. Conversation ebbed and flowed with the flames, laughter threading through it in uneven bursts as the lute tried—and failed—to find its footing. Time passed, marked by the slow burning of logs, the uneven rhythm of clapping hands, and the swell and fade of voices. Cold lingered at the edges of the gathering, but it never quite found a way in.

She kept her gaze loosely fixed on the path beyond the archway.

Every arrival pulled her attention a breath longer than it should have.

He would come, she told herself. Or he would not. Either way, the night would answer.

Footsteps sounded against stone.

Elara straightened, already recognizing the cadence—lighter, quicker, carrying just a touch too much purpose.

Squire Rowleigh emerged from the arch, cloak pulled up, head angled as if he might pass unnoticed along the edge of the gathering. He made it only three steps.

"Sam—" she began, then corrected herself smoothly. "Squire Rowleigh."

Sam froze.

He turned with the careful innocence of a man caught mid-theft. "My lady."

Elara's expression remained pleasant, composed, firelight warming one side of her face while the other stayed in shadow. "Have you seen Prince Baldrik?"

A pause. Brief and honest.

Sam cleared his throat. "No, my lady." He hesitated, then added, "I was to meet him here."

The fire cracked behind them, followed by another round of laughter as the lute faltered again and someone clapped loudly, determined to carry the tune whether it cooperated or not.

Elara inclined her head once, acknowledgment without dismissal.

For a moment, she stood exactly where she was.

The realization came softly.

She had been counting time.

It came with a faint tightening in her chest—not hurt, but annoyance. She did not wait for men. She measured them. That she had marked the passing minutes at all was a miscalculation she did not enjoy discovering in herself.

Of course he would be late. Of course a prince's time was rarely his own. The thought should have settled the matter.

It did not.

Another log shifted in the hearth, sparks climbing and dying in the dark. Nearby, laughter flared and softened, the lute was quiet now, the player gave up trying. Still, the path beyond the arch remained empty.

Silly, she told herself—not for wanting him here, but for mistaking anticipation for strategy. This was a gathering, not a summons. No vows had been made. No promises spoken aloud. She had extended an invitation for advantage, nothing more.

And yet—

She had not asked him here merely for company. Influence moved more easily in gatherings like this, passed hand to hand with wine and warmth, wrapped in proximity. A prince seen at her side would have been…useful. Reassuring. A quiet signal to those watching that House Icewind still stood within the crown's regard.

The irritation cooled into something quieter.

Disappointment, she realized, carried less heat but more weight.

Elara exhaled.

She turned back toward the fire, lifting her hands to the warmth. The fire took them gladly, heat biting at her fingers before easing into something steady. She let herself stand there, just another figure drawn to the fire, cloak open now, posture relaxed by choice rather than comfort.

Across the fire, she caught sight of Squire Rowleigh again—no longer attempting invisibility. He stood half-turned toward a young woman with chestnut hair pulled loose from its pins, her expression animated despite the cold. Anna Stennon, if Elara's memory served. A minor house, sworn to Thornsword, arrived only days earlier.

Sam said something low. The girl laughed, quick and unguarded, and reached out to touch his arm as if it were the most natural thing in the world.

Elara watched for a heartbeat longer than necessary.

Then she looked back to the fire, the heat steady on her palms.

She chose motion over waiting. She stepped into the ring of light, accepted a cup pressed into her hand, and let a smile—real enough—find her face.

If Baldrik would not come, the night would not stall for him. She would be seen, heard, and remembered all the same.

Rodrik approached Morrenfell with a measured, practiced gait, his boots thin from long northern miles. His cloak carried the pale dust of forsaken roads, whispering against the morning light. At his side, the bone handled knife hung—nothing more was necessary. A worn leather satchel rested lightly on his shoulder, overshadowed by the sharper glint in his eyes.

Morrenfell stood without gates or guards at the village edge. A solitary weathered post leaned at the village boundary, its sun-faded notice flapping aimlessly. Rodrik barely glanced at it; the neglect itself spoke clearly enough.

The road twisted into the village, a narrow track crowded by buildings leaning inward, each relying heavily on its neighbor to remain upright. Plaster peeled from walls, revealing rough stone beneath—old wounds left unhealed. Thin smoke rose from chimneys into an uncertain sky, while broken gutters dripped snowmelt onto muddy earth.

The main thoroughfare was uneven, a blend of cobbles and dirt. Merchants moved slowly, arranging their goods with habitual fatigue. A woman stacked crates of pickled fish beneath a leather tarp brittle from years of sun and salt, the brine stinging the air like old wounds reopened, her face lined deeply by hardship.

Rodrik moved unobtrusively among them, observing without drawing attention. He listened carefully, finding more meaning in silence than spoken words. Conversations were subdued, movements cautious. Suspicion and resignation marked every glance, tension beneath their routine.

Morrenfell was old and worn.

Sustained by habit and stubborn resolve.

Rodrik's gaze hardened as he ventured deeper into the village.

He crossed the square, observing two soot-covered boys hauling baskets of charcoal from a blackened smithy, their boots thick with ash from labor.

At the square's heart stood a ruined statue of King Boris Thornsword—now just weathered stone limbs entwined in ivy, and a sword reduced to a blunt, pitted stump. The statue's head lay nearby, mossy and cracked in two, marked by a crude tar-painted moustache.

Rodrik slowed half a step.

No humor in his eyes. He had faced Boris's banners once—from the other side of the mountains. He held frozen ground while Eldaraine pushed north, had watched men bleed out in snow and vanish into drifts because a southern king wanted his borders redrawn. The ruin felt fitting.

Not mockery, but measure. Stone reduced, name forgotten, war paid for in bodies that never received statues of their own.

He did not look again.

Two guards argued heatedly near the well, stabbing fingers at a tax scroll as though accusing it of theft.

"That's clearly a five, you blind ox."

"And you're clearly drunk or daft."

Neither guard gave Rodrik more than a fleeting glance as he passed.

At the square's fringe stood a monastery of the Flamebound Order, its once-grand stone façade cracked, its banner faded nearly beyond recognition. The flamed-sun emblem—barely discernible through layers of grime—fluttered weakly, an echo of forgotten vigilance.

The village had not completely surrendered to ruin, but hope had long since fled. People moved with guarded steps, accustomed to hardship and wary of worse days ahead. Joy had retreated entirely, replaced by the gritty endurance of those who lived each day in Castellon's long shadow.

Adjusting his borrowed cloak, Rodrik continued onward—a unassuming trader with dusty boots and no questions worth answering. The village let him pass without greeting or hindrance, indifferent to his arrival, its struggles unspoken yet evident.

A tavern sign creaked on rusted chains above a battered door at the square's edge. 'The Boar's End,' it proclaimed, the carving depicting only the rear of a boar, polished smooth by years of exposure and crude humor. Rodrik raised a questioning eyebrow and stepped inside.

He paused just long enough for his eyes to adjust. Places like this seldom held warmth—only memories soaked into old wood, and gazes that lingered too long.

Inside, the tavern walls leaned inward, sagging from age. The air lay heavy with sour ale, acrid smoke, and the earthy scent of damp wool. Patrons conversed quietly by the hearth, their voices muffled by shadows.

The hearth on the back wall provided sparse warmth, its flames low and faltering. Above it, a boar's head stared blankly from cracked wood eyes, seeming both confused and betrayed by its incomplete story.

Rodrik moved to an isolated corner, nodding once to the barkeep—a compact woman with sturdy shoulders and the practiced indifference of someone who asked no names and kept no stories.

"What's hot?" Rodrik asked.

"Barley stew with onion," she replied without looking up.

"Ale?"

"Barely,"

Rodrik slid coins across the counter. She eyed them skeptically. "More barley or more onion?"

Rodrik met her stare evenly. "Surprise me."

She regarded him with a look reserved for those who tested her patience, silently daring him to push his luck.

Rodrik took a seat near the hearth, back firmly against the wall. The chair groaned briefly under his weight, then settled. The fire flickered dimly, casting little heat and a smoky glow. He loosened his cloak but kept it wrapped around him.

The ale arrived swiftly—thin, pale, but blessedly warm. He sipped it, appreciative despite its watery taste. Shortly after, the stew appeared: gray, thick, and oddly fragrant, with pungent spices masking its lackluster appearance. Rodrik had eaten worse; he'd once dined on boiled moss in the northern reach—this was almost pleasant by comparison.

At the bar, three men talked loudly over their mugs, laborers by appearance. One had blackened nails from soot; another sported a wool cap so worn it seemed part of his scalp.

"I'm tellin' ye," one said gruffly, "grain's lighter'n usual. Payin' full price, gettin' sacks that're half air."

"Air's free, innit?" responded another sharply . "Count yer blessin's, mate."

"I ain't buyin' air," growled the first. "I'm payin' fer bread, and these sacks wouldn't feed a bairn."

"Might feed a pig's arse. Probably why this dump got its name, eh?"

A burst of rough laughter followed—brief and harsh, a forced sound in the grim room.

"Bet Valen's behind it," the first man muttered darkly. "Always squeezin' us, he is. Wants us grinnin' while we chew sawdust."

The barkeep, polishing a mug with weary indifference, remarked plainly, "Could be worse. Could have rats in them sacks."

"Rats, I can eat," the first man retorted. "Air just makes ye fart polite."

That earned another bark of laughter, but it died faster this time.

A man further down the bar leaned in, voice lowered. "Heard the guards been posted at the well three days now."

"For water?" someone scoffed.

"For order," the man said. "Or what passes for it."

"Funny place to guard," another muttered. "Wells don't run off."

"No," came the reply. "But folk do, when they're thirsty."

Rodrik remained impassive.

Absorbing every word. Grain shortages and inflated costs were common enough, but the bitterness toward Valen hinted at resentments that had been rotting here for years.

Talk shifted to lesser matters—a niece caught stealing bread, cedar tiles lost to wind—but resentment never fully drained away. These weren't fresh complaints.

They were embers kept alive by habit.

Rodrik finished his ale. Now cold, it tasted metallic and stale. Outside, wind rattled the tavern sign—the boar's hindquarters creaking on rusted chains.

As Rodrik reached the last spoonful of barley stew, a chair across from him scraped against the stone floor.

The newcomer was weathered—lean, grey-bearded, his face a map of hardship. A jagged scar ran from his scalp to his brow, disappearing into an empty eye socket. His remaining eye was keen and unblinking.

He gestured at Rodrik's bowl. "Judging, or out-staring it?"

Rodrik didn't smile. "Still deciding."

The old man snorted. "Pretend. Fool your tongue."

He signaled the barkeep with two twisted fingers.

Rodrik observed him in silence, letting the pause work.

"Where from?" the man asked as two steaming bowls arrived. "Don't walk like that without burying kin. Or kingdoms."

"Foot of the mountains," Rodrik said simply.

"Further I'd guess, but no matter." the man eyed him flatly.

They ate in silence, neither pressing nor avoiding conversation, content to see what words surfaced on their own.

The old man jerked his chin toward the street. "See that statue?"

Rodrik nodded without looking up, his eyes still on the stew.

"King Boris Thornsword," the man said, wiping his mouth roughly with the back of his hand. "Now pigeons shit on him, moss claims the rest."

Rodrik's gaze remained steady. "Stone isn't kind. What about the man?"

"Dead." The old man gave a short, dry laugh. "But alive? Took the throne young, barely filling his father's armor. Died fighting northern raiders, or so they say." He snorted. "History's full of lies."

He paused, taking another spoonful of stew. "Boris wasn't much of a ruler at first. But he learned fast. Fought like a storm. Rarely smiled, but we ate well. Raiders learned quickly to avoid our borders."

Rodrik leaned back slightly, considering the man's words. "And now?"

"Now we're left with his shadow." The man tapped the table once for emphasis. "King Harald. Less storm, more stone. Moves only when pushed—then crushes what he touches."

Rodrik's voice lowered. "The Queen?"

"Varanese." The old man's expression hardened; his eye narrowed. "Sharp voice. Sharper eyes. Silk like armor. Never seen her myself, but I know the type."

"And the Prince?"

The old man gave a dismissive snort. "Keeps quiet. Some say he is trying on Flamebound robes, others call him weak. Rarely seen outside the Sheild. Cloistered, vanished—no one knows. No one cares."

Rodrik let the silence stretch; the hearth snapped once. The old man didn't blink, his gaze steady.

Rodrik spoke quietly, almost casually. "Seen anything unusual lately?"

The man scratched at his beard, considering. "Lord Valen's riders came through. No sigils. No words. Paid well. Didn't stay long."

Rodrik said nothing, and stood, placing two coins on the table. "For the stew. And the talk." The old man didn't thank him, continuing to eat, his one good eye tracking Rodrik to the door.

Outside, the wind had shifted. Heavy gray clouds pressed low over Castellon, smothering the towers in mist.

Rodrik paused beneath the tavern sign, the carved boar's backside swaying on its chains.

"Eirik," he murmured, adjusting his cloak. "You were right. This kingdom doesn't need pushing."

He glanced once more at the storm gathering over Castellon.

"It's already leaning."

Rodrik emerged from The Boar's End, tightening his cloak against a biting wind that cut through wool and leather alike. Whispers of unrest rode the gusts through Morrenfell's streets, carrying an undercurrent of frustration.

The old man's words still echoed in his mind, adding clarity to an already troubling puzzle. His eyes roamed across the villagers—faces drawn tight with worry, eyes hollow from sleepless nights, breath ghosting in the cold, shadows flickering at doorways.

The signs were clear: the heavy snows that still clung to shaded ground, Valen's hidden grain, the restless murmurs—they were pieces of something far darker.

The market, Rodrik decided, was the next logical step. Traders gathered there daily, a natural focal point of village discontent. If Valen's manipulations were as deep-rooted as they seemed, evidence would show plainly where trade and tension intersected.

He walked steadily toward the market, boots crunching over frozen mud, alert and observing. Children with muddied faces darted swiftly through narrow alleys, boots soaked and hems stiff with frost; shopkeepers regarded sparse shelves with grim resignation; villagers exchanged brief nods loaded with suspicion. Each observation sharpened his resolve. Morrenfell stood at a precipice, fragile and tense—one misstep from collapse.

Voices rose sharply near the grain merchant's stall, pulling Rodrik from his thoughts. He moved toward the commotion, instinct guiding him toward conflict, where truth most readily surfaced.

Two villagers faced off angrily against a red-faced merchant, their breaths puffing white as they shouted. "You call this grain?" one villager snapped, brandishing a nearly empty sack. "Beggars have heavier bags!"

The merchant, wiry and defensive, raised his hands hurriedly. "Blame Lord Valen, not me. Grain's scarce, shipments shorted for weeks."

An older man with a rough beard jabbed his finger forward. "Easy to blame Lord Valen when your own purse doesn't suffer."

Rodrik approached, voice calm but firm. "Hold. What's behind this?"

The younger villager whirled on him, frustration evident. "Full price for half sacks, moldy bread for our children."

Rodrik's jaw tightened. He recognized that tone—the edge people took when their children cried with nothing left to give.

The older man growled bitterly. "Started in deep winter—stores went bad before we ever saw thaw. Damp crept into the cellars, rot followed. Carrots, cabbage, maize—lost before spring ever had a chance."

"Even wheat and barley," the younger man added, voice heavy with sarcasm. "Turnips, too. Turnips! They survive wars, for flames-sake."

The merchant exhaled heavily, exhaustion weighing his words. "I don't choose to sell rot. Lord Valen's men take the good grain, leave us scraps."

Rodrik studied them quietly, seeing clearly how Valen's grip tightened unseen, squeezing villagers into desperation.

"Lord Valen may squeeze you," the older villager spat at the merchant, "but our families starve first."

Rodrik did not hesitate.

He produced a pouch of coins and set it on the stall, the leather dull and cold from the air. "Here. The grain's on me."

The villagers paused, breath fogging as they weighed pride against necessity. "We don't take charity," the younger one muttered.

"Not charity," Rodrik replied evenly, meeting his gaze. "Consider it overdue justice—or kindness, if you prefer."

The merchant quickly pocketed the coins, nodding urgently. "Take it now, before others do."

As the villagers reluctantly gathered their grain, Rodrik glanced toward Castellon's looming clouds, low and heavy with more cold than snow.

He glanced once toward Castellon's looming clouds, then back to the men. "Keep your stores dry," he said evenly. "And watch who counts them."

The older villager lifted his sack, eyes dark and resigned. "We watch," the older villager said quietly. "That's all we ever do."

Rodrik moved on through the market, boots crunching over frozen ruts, catching snippets of heated disputes—unfair prices, unreliable workmanship. Occasional laughter echoed from children, innocent yet already bearing hardship's marks.

Heading back toward The Boar's End, Rodrik followed the river's edge, its surface skinned with thin ice that broke and reformed along the banks. Near a worn stone bridge, he noticed a beggar hunched beneath ragged cloth, his bowl empty, fingers blue and stiff in the fading light.

"Spare a truth, traveler?" the beggar rasped.

Rodrik paused, curious. "Most beg for coin, not truth."

The beggar chuckled hoarsely, then fell silent, gathering strength. "Coin feeds the belly today. Truth might feed hope tomorrow."

Rodrik crouched to meet his gaze. The beggar's cloak slipped aside, revealing a faded campaign knot burned into the skin at his wrist—old army mark, half-scar, half-brand—and a hand missing two fingers, taken clean years ago. "And what truth do you hunger for?"

The beggar hesitated, breath shallow and uneven. "News. Rumors. The whisper of revolt." Another pause, filled by labored breaths. "Valen's men stir trouble. Harald does nothing. There's talk… hidden meetings… barns and cellars."

Rodrik inclined his head slightly. "Rebellion is dangerous."

"So is starving quietly," the beggar retorted faintly. "We're a breath away from open flames."

Rodrik stood, removed his cloak and draped it over the beggar's shoulders, and tossed a coin into his bowl. "Perhaps it's time someone blows on the embers."

The coin rang too loud in the quiet.

The beggar smiled crookedly, voice steadying briefly. "Careful Stormwalker. You might fan more than intended."

Rodrik stilled.

"How do you know that name?"

"Know of you," the beggar murmured faintly. "Men talk. Stories travel. Storms tend to follow the greying skies." His gaze rose slowly to the darkening sky. "Looks like rain."

"Rain might wash away ash," he said quietly, "but only fire forges anything new."

Rodrik dropped another coin into the bowl. Without another word, he turned away, walking back toward The Boar's End. He cast one last look toward Castellon's towers.

Rodrik returned to The Boar's End as twilight deepened into night, the tavern's door creaking a weary welcome. He stepped inside, enveloped by the sour tang of stale ale mingling with smoke clinging to the rafters, sharpened by the scent of unwashed bodies.

Behind the bar, the barkeep—eternally unimpressed—polished tankards with mechanical precision. Her heavy brows lifted briefly in recognition before settling back into practiced indifference.

A serving woman, slipped through the tavern with practiced ease born from navigating cramped rooms and choosing when to welcome attention and when to ignore it.

Her dress, thin from frequent washings, hugged her frame, worn to draw eyes—and coin—with the confidence of someone who knew how to wield both.

She spotted him, eyes sparking with calculated mischief, and altered her path to intercept him, moving with the sway of someone accustomed to holding a room's attention.

Her voice carried the edge of Morrenfell's streets, playful and knowing. "Evenin', handsome. Ye look like a man who could use somethin' a sight warmer than ale an' hearth tonight."

Rodrik studied her for a moment, a faint smile touching his lips. Her cheeky charm reminded him of Gina Three Loaves—brash, sincere, with eyes that had seen more than they let on. He shook his head gently, offering her a respectful, weary smile. "Tempting as your company might be, lass, rest is all I'm after tonight."

She feigned heartbreak, clutching at her chest, eyes dancing with amusement. "Wound me, ye do," she teased, voice sinking to a playful whisper. "Most men'd kill fer my offer."

Rodrik chuckled, appreciating the theatrics. He pressed a few copper coins into her palm. "For your charm alone," he murmured kindly.

Her eyes widened in surprise before her smile softened, bravado slipping into warmth. "Ye've a good heart fer a man who hides it behind tired eyes," she whispered with gratitude, slipping the coins away discreetly.

Rodrik watched her retreat, her manner snapping back into place as she traded banter with the tavern's patrons. He crossed the worn floorboards toward his modest room near the hearth—the one small luxury the tavern offered. Warmth seeped through the thin, warped door, promising relief from the night's chill.

Once inside, Rodrik lit a sputtering candle and retrieved parchment from his satchel. His charcoal stick hesitated over the page before he began to write.

"Eirik—

I've traveled deep into Eldaraine, and every step reveals a kingdom rotting from within. Villagers starve beneath heavy taxes and spoiled crops, while whispers of revolt fester behind guarded gazes.

The royalty cloister themselves—King Harald remains immovable, a mountain blind to the tremors beneath him. Queen Avanna, Varanese born, appears as sharp and guarded as rumored. Her presence feels like a blade pressed to Harald's back, though I've yet to uncover her true intent.

Prince Baldrik remains elusive; tales describe him as pious or weak, but always distant. The villagers speak little of him, as though he's a ghost rather than their heir.

Lord Valen's hand is unmistakable—stockpiling resources, breeding resentment, preparing for something I have yet to grasp. His agents move quietly, but their footprints are clear.

Every interaction and whispered word confirms your suspicions. Yet, the full shape of this conspiracy eludes me. There's more at play here, hidden beneath ash and silence."

Rodrik paused, his eyes narrowing at the flickering flame. The candle sputtered, casting restless shadows across the unfinished message. He exhaled, set the charcoal aside and folded the parchment.

The rest would reveal itself in time.

—— ✶ ——

CHAPTER EIGHT

The hearth in Alerick's apartment had burned low, throwing thin, uncertain shadows across the stone room on Castellon's lower east side. Shelves lined the stone walls, crowded with half-finished scrolls and neglected tomes. Near the window, a chessboard sat untouched, its pieces frozen where they had been left weeks earlier—a dark jade queen tilted against a fallen pawn.

Alerick sat at his writing desk, shoulders drawn inward beneath the candlelight. His attention had drifted past the clutter of maps and forged documents scattered before him, fixed on something farther away. The room was spare and deliberate, arranged to suggest nothing more than the forgettable life he passed as Faileas, a wandering scholar.

His fingers tapped against the worn oak desktop—steady, unhurried.

"A Flamebound king… a flame never lit."

The words surfaced without invitation. His father's voice, half-remembered, clung to them.

Alerick's gaze moved to the corner shelf. It held little—a ledger, a thin book of court psalms. What he needed to see lay beyond reach, sealed within the Grand Citadel's restricted vaults: Flamebound histories, rites of ash, truths buried by design.

He tried to set the words aside. His jaw tightened instead.

He rose and crossed the room to a worn wooden chest at the foot of the bed. Beneath false panels and folded satchels, he drew out an old monk's robe—coarse, threadbare, taken long ago from a starving pilgrim for warmth.

He turned the fabric in his hands, feeling its roughness.

A thought surfaced: "You want more than the truth. You want what lies beneath it."

No commoner or amateur scribe could seek the Order's records openly. A pilgrim, however—a humble seeker with dust on his boots and patience in his manner—would be admitted.

He crossed to the basin and took up a pair of iron shears, cutting his hair close to the scalp. Strands fell into the basin, one after another. When he finished, he reached for a small jar of pale powder and lightened his brows. The face in the mirror shifted—still his, but easier to overlook.

He donned the robe and pulled the hood forward. His shoulders lowered, his stance softened. The change was subtle, but complete.

He tested the voice once. "The flame burns best when watched, not wielded."

"Kælric, from Westmere. I seek knowledge and clarity."

He studied the reflection in the tarnished mirror. It would pass.

Outside, dusk crept across Castellon. Alerick—now Kælric—looked toward the distant spires of the Grand Citadel, dark against the dimming sky.

The phrase returned once more, quieter than before:

"A Flamebound king… a flame never lit."

He turned away from the window. What lay ahead would not reveal itself freely.

That was fine. He had never relied on permission.

The Blackwood Hills lay hushed at this hour, the world narrowed by cold and darkness. Lanterns burned along the outer road in careful intervals, their light dulled by falling snow. Smoke drifted low from the manor chimneys, held close to the stone as if unwilling to rise.

Lord Circus Valen's estate lay where it always had—imposed upon the land rather than settled into it. Even after previous visits, the place resisted familiarity.

Wealth here was not comfort or beauty; it was dominance. Stone, iron, and ornament existed to remind visitors where they stood, and who owned the ground beneath their feet.

Inside, the halls were warm and watchful. Servants moved with practiced restraint.

Lord Dravik Narcona stood by the hearth, arms folded across his broad chest. His gaze was fixed on the portrait hung prominently above the marble hearth, depicting a family scene that had been carefully altered—two figures scraped away to leave Valen standing alone where others once belonged.

Across the room, Lady Meyra Wynmere occupied a couch chosen less for comfort than assertion. She worked at an orange with a small dagger, peel falling away in controlled, unbroken strips. The motion was unhurried, precise.

She wore a gown cut high at the thigh, silk dark and fluid against her frame—chosen less to provoke than to signal ease where others stiffened.

From somewhere unseen, beyond the ornate chair at the table's head, a voice carried into the room—smooth and acidic, amusement stripped of warmth.

Heavy oak doors groaned open, reluctant hinges announcing Lord Circus Valen's entrance. He swept inside, draped in a crimson-and-black brocade robe threaded with gold, the cut extravagant and unmistakably intentional. A controlled trace of scented oil followed him—clove, overstated and indulgent.

He paused just inside the threshold, surveying the room with the ease of someone who expected it to bend around him. One ringed hand lifted in a mild, dismissive gesture.

"My dear friends," his voice slick with mock regret, "forgive my timing. I've always thought punctuality so terribly common—particularly when delicate matters are on the table."

Lady Wynmere paused her blade briefly against the fruit's skin, eyes flicking toward Valen in dry appraisal. "Ah, Valen—so kind of you to appear. For a moment, I feared we'd have had to begin without your theatrics." Her knife resumed slicing. "Such a terribly dull discussion that would have been."

Valen's lips curled into a slow smile, his gaze glittering with mock injury. "Oh, Meyra, you wound me. Careful—someone might mistake your wit for investment."

Meyra's lips curved into a sly, cutting smile. Her blade whispered delicately through the citrus rind.

"You know, Valen," she began smoothly, voice lightly tinged with intrigue, "on my way here, my coach passed riders heading south—about fifteen or so. No banners, no sigils, and not a hint of house colors." She let the words hang, eyes glittering subtly with suspicion. "Curious. Would you know anything about that?"

Valen paused, lips curling. "Perhaps you see ghosts, Meyra. Or perhaps it's wishful thinking."

He raised his goblet slightly in a silent, mocking salute.

Dravik's brow furrowed. After a moment, he glanced back toward Valen. "Is this your family?"

Valen's smile thinned, but he did not look at the portrait. "Once," he said. "Before they proved inconvenient."

The doors opened quietly, admitting a house servant who stepped forward with ordered grace, eyes respectfully lowered.

"Lords Caerlyn and Durnhart," the servant intoned softly, her voice precise and poised.

Quentyn Caerlyn entered, composed and austere, his gaze sweeping the room in cold appraisal and lingering briefly—with open disdain—on Valen.

Lord Branik Durnhart followed a step behind. He did not meet anyone's eye. His jaw was set tight, shoulders rigid beneath travel-worn wool. The discomfort was not theatrical—it sat in him like debt.

Valen's smile widened, arms spreading in practiced graciousness. "Ah, Lord Caerlyn and Durnhart— pillars of dignity, at last. Perhaps your arrival will lend this discussion the gravity it deserves."

Valen snapped his fingers. "Wine?"

The doors opened; two servants entered with trays of goblets and wine, arranged to Valen's taste.

Following closely, silent as a shadow, Rennic Stride entered the chamber, expression impeccable, posture rigidly precise.

Valen's eyes lit briefly. "Ah, Smudge. How comforting."

Lady Elara Icewind paused at the threshold of Valen's manor, the murmur of voices pressing faintly through the heavy doors. Warmth bled out around the edges, scented with wine and resinous smoke. She did not linger. Hesitating here would be read as weakness.

She stepped inside.

A servant stepped forward at once, a woman in simple, tasteful robes of undyed wool, her movements practiced and precise.

"Lady Elara Icewind," she announced, voice quiet yet carrying cleanly into the hall.

Conversation shifted. Heads turned.

Elara entered beneath the weight of their attention, her expression already settled into something cool and precise. She did not look for Valen—not yet. She let the room take her measure first, as rooms always did.

Of all the houses she might have been forced to court, Valen's was the one she despised most. Not for its politics, but for the man himself. She had not forgotten his offers—lavish, urgent, and all contingent on a price she would not name, much less pay. The way his gaze lingered now was only confirmation that nothing had changed.

Valen noticed her at once. His gaze took her in with an appraising pause—long enough to be deliberate, short enough to pretend courtesy. He leaned back, lips curving.

"Lady Elara," he said, voice easy. "Goldacre improves when you choose to grace it." His eyes flicked, assessing rather than roaming. "You do make restraint look… alluring."

Elara met his look without hurry. Her smile was precise, unwelcoming. One hand rested at her waist, near the dagger's jeweled hilt—not a threat, merely a reminder.

"Valen," she said softly, "you mistake appraisal for interest. An easy error for men who confuse attention with invitation." Her gaze skimmed his robe, cool and dismissive. "Do keep it brief. I'm told tonight values efficiency."

Quentyn Caerlyn cleared his throat, impatience thinly veiled. "If we've quite finished exchanging observations, perhaps we might proceed. Some of us prefer our arrangements swift and effective."

Dravik grunted from the hearth, eyes still on Valen's altered family portrait, not bothering to look toward Caerlyn as he spoke. "Quite. I've breathed enough of Valen's perfumed air."

Meyra sighed, setting her dagger down on the table with exaggerated boredom, citrus peel curling neatly around the blade. She did not look at Valen when she spoke—only at the men who might pretend not to listen. "Indeed. One can only feign interest in trivial insults for so long."

Without another word, Lady Elara drifted toward a seat near the hearth—not at the table's center, but just within its circle—settling where shadow and firelight met. From there she could watch them all without being forced to join any single flank. Lord Circus Valen sat at the head of the long table, where the candlelight caught the gold in his cup and left the rest of him in measured shadow.

Rennic stood a pace behind his right shoulder, silent and unobtrusive. Across from Valen, Quentyn Caerlyn had claimed the opposite end—close enough to contend, far enough to signal parity. Dravik remained nearer the hearth than the table, half-turned toward the room as if ready to rise at a moment's notice.

Durnhart kept to a high-backed chair near the doors, apart from the main arc. Meyra lounged along the table's side, angled rather than square, one leg crossed, present, but beholden to no alignment.

Valen raised his goblet, swirling the rich wine thoughtfully, his gaze sweeping the gathered lords and ladies with deliberate calm. "Friends," he began evenly, "you all know why you're here. Vara has gone silent. Caravans arrive late—or not at all. Prices rise before ships make harbor. The Crown calls it fluctuation." His mouth curved faintly. "I call it negligence."

He let the word settle before continuing. "Trade frays. Supply strains. And when supply strains, loyalty follows. We can pretend this is temporary… or we can decide our houses won't bleed for the court's complacency."

Quentyn leaned forward, fingers steepled, expression sharp. "If the Crown will not steady the markets," he said, voice controlled, "then the markets must steady the Crown. My granaries can be… adjusted. Shipments delayed. Distribution narrowed. Pressure, applied carefully, reminds even kings who feeds their cities."

Valen's gaze flicked to him, mild but attentive, though his fingers stilled against the stem of his goblet. "Adjusted?" he echoed lightly. "I was under the impression your outer silos were… secured."

Caerlyn did not blink. "They are. Storage and scarcity are separate instruments, Valen. I assumed you understood the distinction."

Dravik did not look away from the hearth. "Granaries are patient instruments," he said evenly. "Sometimes too patient. Inspections at the Narcon Gate can become… selective. Escorts reassigned. Caravans delayed. Pressure applied on the road travels faster than hunger."

Meyra's gave drifted towards Dravik. "And our personal shipments?" she asked lightly. "I trust you can keep those dogs from spoiling our contracts." Her tone remained smooth, but her eyes sharpened.

Dravik's gaze shifted to her at last, measuring rather than appeasing. "I control who enters and leaves through the Narconian Gate," he said. "Not what happens once they're past it."

Lady Meyra subtly rolled her eyes, picking up the dagger and idly slicing another curl from the citrus. "Force is loud," she said lightly. "Rumors, whispers—that's how you erode trust. A few careful words in the right ears, and Harald's allies will begin questioning every move."

Valen did not chuckle. He studied Meyra over the rim of his goblet, then inclined his head once toward Dravik—subtle, affirming. "Pressure," he said calmly, "must be applied from more than one direction." His eyes moved between them without preference. "Fear, hunger, doubt—each holds its own power. Each has its place."

Lady Elara Icewind, seated near the hearth, spoke softly yet firmly. "All fine enough, but we overlook something crucial. Harald's court itself must fracture. I'll ensure Castellon's court has ample reasons to quarrel among themselves—distracted nobles rarely guard their king effectively."

Dravik's voice remained level, though his weight shifted forward as if testing the space between them. "Squabbling royals alone won't steady a realm, Lady Icewind—not without muscle to remind them what matters."

"And muscle without strategy is merely thuggery," Quentyn shot back coldly, without glancing at Durnhart. "Perhaps discipline your Cliff Wardens first, Dravik, before presuming to lecture others."

Valen raised his hand gently, silencing them. "Our disagreements are useful," Valen said calmly. "Applied correctly, they leave the Crown reacting instead of ruling. Starvation unsettles. Fear spreads. Suspicion divides."

No one voiced agreement. Dravik's jaw set. Caerlyn's fingers tightened once against the tabletop. Durnhart did not move at all.

He cleared his throat once, the sound rough. "There is a difference between weakening a crown… and starving Highfield or Greystone Circle to prove a point."

Caerlyn looked briefly to Valen. Dravik did not. Meyra's dagger resumed its slow spiral. No one answered him directly.

Valen's gaze settled on Durnhart, assessing without warmth. He did not answer at once. The silence stretched just long enough to make the hearth crackle loud in the pause. "Sacrifice," he said at last, voice mild, "is rarely evenly distributed."

Valen raised his goblet once more. "Use your strengths wisely. Pressure applied correctly has a way of clarifying loyalties."

The chamber door creaked open, and the young servant announced in a calm voice, "Lord Gil Lesserin."

Gil entered without hurry, offering a restrained bow to the room before taking in its arrangement with a single measured sweep of his eyes. "My lords. My ladies." His tone was even. "I was informed my presence was required."

Quentyn Caerlyn's eyes flashed sharply, voice clipped with irritation. "Valen, why is Lesserin here? Did you invite him? He's from a minor house under my jurisdiction—not a voice in this council."

Valen did not smile. He regarded Caerlyn steadily, expression neutral, as though noting a predictable reaction. "Consider it my whim, Quentyn. Even minor voices can hold… unexpected promise."

Quentyn stared coldly, suspicion deepening, clearly unsatisfied. His hand flattened against the table as if staking ground. No one spoke.

Gil inclined his head once and chose a seat near the door—not as retreat, but vantage—hands folding loosely before him, expression unreadable.

Lady Meyra glanced sidelong at Gil, her eyes coolly appraising, a faint smirk touching her lips.

"And what exactly does the boy lord contribute," she asked, "aside from questionable fashion and anxious apologies?"

"I summoned him and he answered," Valen said.

Gil did not rise to the bait. "I came because the summons bore Lord Valen's seal," he said calmly. "I serve House Caerlyn—"

"No one has insinuated—that you have chosen otherwise?" Valen interrupted gently, almost indulgently.

He let the question linger just long enough.

Quentyn's stare shifted—first to Gil, then to Valen. Sharp and assessing.

"No such claim has been made," Valen added. "Only an observation."

Quentyn tightened his jaw, but did not look at Gil again.

Valen cleared his throat and straightened, the moment already spent. "Time grows short. Shall we outline our plans?"

Quentyn inclined his head. "Distribution can be… recalibrated. Certain contracts delayed. Surplus redirected to private holding until stability returns. Castellon will feel the tightening—but not collapse."

Dravik gave a curt nod. "Patrol patterns can shift. Certain routes may find themselves… less observed than others. Delays have a way of encouraging cooperation."

Meyra lifted her glass, stained berry-dark at the rim, and offered a casual smirk. "I suppose now's as good a time as any. Weeks ago, I had a man intercepting Firewine orders from Vara. Disrupt the trade. Shift demand my way."

Dravik raised a brow but said nothing. Valen's expression did not change, though Rennic's attention sharpened.

Meyra took a slow sip and added, more sourly, "Naturally, the man's a dolt. A handsome one, but useless as a broken funnel. He started intercepting everything. Not just merchant ledgers. Letters. Reports. Even a few addressed to the Queen, I think."

Dravik leaned forward, voice low. "Have you any idea what this might look like? To Vara? To the Queen? Cutting off communication with the Sea-Queens? Vara won't take that lightly. If they suspect—"

Valen interrupted him, voice smooth as winter silk, not looking at Dravik as he did so. "No. This delightful little blunder might serve us better than any design. Let them think Castellon has gone deaf to Vara's cries. Or worse—arrogant."

He lifted his glass, eyes cold and calculating. "Don't correct the simpleton."

Meyra tilted her head, uncertain. "Excuse me?"

"In fact," Valen said, "cut him off entirely. Sever the chain."

Valen shifted slightly in his chair, two fingers tapping once against the stem of his goblet—a small, deliberate signal—his gaze still fixed ahead.

Rennic stepped to stand beside Valen, "How does the fool deliver the intercepted pieces?"

Meyra exhaled through her nose. "He drops them in an empty Firewine barrel. Behind the Iron Cup tavern. My steward collects the barrel, delivers it to the vineyard for sorting."

Rennic spoke with his usual precision, voice cool and surgical. "Stop retrieving it."

Meyra's expression tightened; for the first time that evening, she looked directly at Valen. "What, just let the letters pile up?"

"No barrel," Rennic replied evenly. "No message drop. No proof. He'll stand in an alley waiting for a collection that never comes. Eventually, someone will ask why."

"And what will that prove?" Meyra asked setting her dagger down, the citrus now entirely peeled.

"Deniability." Rennic said flatly.

Valen raised his glass. "To incompetence."

The words hung in the air. No one laughed. Into that quiet, Elara leaned forward slightly, her voice soft yet firm. "I'll seek the Prince's favor. Capturing Baldrik's ear might offer leverage from within."

That drew attention. Caerlyn's gaze shifted toward her. Dravik's expression did not change.

Meyra leaned forward slightly, her eyes sparkling with subtle intrigue.

"Elara," she said, mischief curling at the edge of her smile, "if you're truly set on captivating a prince, perhaps you might benefit from something a bit more… provocative." Her gaze swept appraisingly over Elara's elegant but conservative attire. "I have several gowns far more suited to such endeavors—one in particular that's guaranteed to show enough leg to stir even royal blood."

Color bloomed in Elara's cheeks before she could stop it. Her lips parted briefly in genuine surprise before she quickly composed her expression into dignified calm.

She offered Meyra a polite yet resolute smile. "Your generosity is appreciated, Meyra, but I believe subtlety serves me best. Still," she added softly, her eyes coolly meeting Meyra's teasing stare, "I'll keep your offer in mind, should circumstances… change."

Meyra chuckled warmly, clearly amused, her eyes gleaming with genuine respect. "As you wish, Elara. Just remember—subtlety often leaves opportunities untouched. Though in your case," she added lightly, "I suspect patience may prove just as effective."

Valen observed the exchange in silence, eyes narrowing fractionally—not at Meyra, but at Elara. He lifted his goblet, not in toast but acknowledgment. "Yes Elara, one should not waist their assets," he said evenly. "Keeping the Prince's hands occupied could be beneficial."

Elara did not raise her glass, her smile untouched by kindness. "Not every opportunity is meant to be touched."

Muted laughter and cautious nods around the table signaled the gathering's reluctant conclusion. As each conspirator stood, smoothing attire and offering measured farewells, Lord Lesserin spoke without raising his voice. "There is a vulnerability in the southern ledger routes—"

Quentyn's response was swift and cold, slicing through Gil's hopeful silence. "No, Lesserin. No one does."

Valen turned his attention to Gil, expression unreadable. "Come now, Gil. You weren't invited for your wisdom." A brief pause. "Merely to remind others what happens when enthusiasm outruns judgment."

Gil's expression did not change. Only his eyes cooled a shade. For the briefest moment, his gaze shifted—not to Caerlyn, but to Valen. Then he rose without haste, inclined his head once more to the room, and departed in silence.

Lady Meyra watched him go, smiling faintly. "Valen, you truly are a veritable ass."

Valen inclined his head a fraction in acknowledgment, offering no reply.

As the conspirators filed from the chamber, exchanging cautious farewells, Meyra waited until the others were distracted before she touched Elara's sleeve.

"Walk with me."

They took only a few steps, just far enough that voices became texture instead of meaning.

Meyra did not waste time.

"The grain will never reach Icewind Manor."

Elara stilled. "Delayed?"

"No." Meyra's mouth tightened. "Taken, bandits from the Breaks—organized ones. They killed the drivers and left the bodies where the road bends. The carts and the grain are gone."

For a moment, Elara said nothing. Her gaze shifted briefly across the chamber—toward the hearth, toward Dravik—before returning to Meyra. When she spoke, her voice was even.

"Is there another shipment?"

Meyra shook her head. "My stores are already thin. I stretched them to send what I did. I can't risk another loss without failing my own quotas."

Elara exhaled slowly, the sound barely audible.

"It seems misfortune is the only thing granted freely."

"I am sorry," Meyra said. And she meant it. "Truly."

Elara met her eyes, disappointment clear but contained.

"Thank you for trying."

Meyra squeezed her hand once before stepping away, already reclaiming her public face. She crossed the chamber with measured ease, her attention returning to the broader room even as its shape subtly changed.

At the other side of the room Lord Caerlyn watched until the others drifted from earshot. Then he stepped closer to Valen, voice lowered to a quiet, cautious murmur.

"Your grain is secure, Valen. The outer silos are filled nearly to bursting, and guards have been posted, as you requested."

Valen regarded him steadily, swirling the wine once before setting the goblet aside untouched. "As I requested?" he repeated mildly. "I don't recall requesting storage."

Caerlyn's jaw tightened a fraction. "You expressed concern over market volatility. I offered a solution."

"A solution," Valen echoed, voice smooth. "Generous."

He let the word rest between them without committing to it.

Caerlyn waited—perhaps for mention of terms, coin, acknowledgment. None came.

A tense moment passed before Caerlyn inclined his head stiffly and turned away, each step measured, irritation shadowing his movements.

Valen watched him depart without expression, attention already shifting.

The moment the chamber door closed behind the last guest, servants moved swiftly, silent yet hurried, gathering empty goblets and clearing away half-eaten delicacies. Valen lounged back in his ornate chair, swirling the remnants of wine thoughtfully. Rennic stood nearby, watching impassively as the room was restored to its immaculate state.

"What do you think, Smudge?" Valen asked quietly, voice stripped of pretense.

Rennic considered briefly, eyes sharp and calculating. "Quentyn believes himself cautious, yet he's transparently anxious. He dislikes being kept waiting—especially when he believes he's owed something."

Valen nodded slowly, eyes narrowing. "Agreed. And Meyra?"

"Formidable," Rennic replied evenly. "She's as likely to cut us as anyone else, given reason or advantage. Useful, if carefully handled."

"And Lady Elara?" Valen asked, his tone neutral.

Rennic's lips twitched slightly, barely perceptible. "Driven more by desperation than ambition, perhaps more dangerous for it. She'll move cautiously but decisively."

Valen drained his goblet, setting it down gently. "Then we'll watch her closely. And the boy, Lesserin?"

Rennic allowed himself a brief, humorless smile. "Embarrassed pride makes men reckless. Lesserin feels slighted and will seek ways to prove he's more than mere entertainment. Keep him close—his next mistake might prove useful."

Valen inclined his head once. "Indeed. And Elara—unfortunate about her estate," he said, gaze lingering on the ledger before him. "That blight in her stores spread faster than expected. A pity she declined my offer."

"Shame indeed," Rennic echoed, his tone flat as slate.

Valen's gaze drifted to the fire. "She was warned. Assistance was offered. On generous terms."

Rennic adjusted his cuffs. "Pride is expensive."

"Especially for someone as young as her," Valen replied mildly. "Scarcity has a way of clarifying priorities."

He closed the ledger with deliberate care.

"Then our plans proceed carefully," Valen continued. "Keep eyes open, Smudge. Tonight's friends have a habit of becoming tomorrow's liabilities."

Rennic inclined his head once before continuing. "The coin placed with the Scorchland bands is paying dividends."

Valen did not look up. "Go on."

"They've been careful. Quiet. No patterns that can be traced. Trade along the Murkhar Road has suffered." Rennic paused. "Several winter shipments never reached their destinations."

Valen considered. "Good. Shortages spread faster than blame. Ensure Shade gets an extra purse."

Rennic added a line to his ledger next to Shade's name. Then looked up.

"There's more," Rennic said. "The raids have bred hesitation. Merchants reroute, delay, or sell early rather than risk the roads." He hesitated, then added, "Lord Narcona will order his southern patrols thinned. A blind eye, by his own words."

Valen finally glanced up, a hint of amusement touching his mouth. "That will loosen the whole weave."

"With the southern routes left open," Rennic continued, "the pressure bleeds north. Free village caravans hesitate, the Murkhar Coast road clogs, and what does move travels in smaller, dearer lots. Some losses were… specific."

Valen's brow lifted a fraction. "Coincidental, I assume."

"Entirely," Rennic said.

"A shame," Valen replied lightly. He reopened the ledger, turning a page. "Uncertainty can be so… convenient when properly encouraged."

Rennic's mouth twitched once. "And when the quotas come due?"

Valen's smile thinned. "Then Elara will have a choice. She may come to me seeking relief… or she may watch her lands absorbed, debt by debt, into steadier hands."

He dipped his quill and began to write. "Either way, the Crown is paid."

Rennic did not move immediately. "Durnhart?"

Valen's quill paused only a heartbeat. "Uneasy."

"With Harald?"

"With us." Valen resumed writing. "His holdings sit too close to the burn line. Highfield feeds half his pride. Greystone Circle feeds the rest."

Rennic inclined his head. "Shall I place eyes?"

"Quiet ones," Valen replied. "He dislikes the taste of this table. Men who grow uncomfortable sometimes remember they once had spines."

Rennic gave a single nod. "I'll see to it."

In the heart of Castellon's great forge, the fire roared, casting molten light across stone and iron. King Harald Thornsword stood alone at its core, stripped of royal finery, clad in the simple garments of a smith. His powerful figure was starkly illuminated by the furnace's glow, sweat tracing rivulets through soot and grime, a testament to honest labor.

Each strike of Harald's hammer rang through the chamber. The ritual did not still his thoughts. The metal glowed under his hammer.

Aulfis. The name echoed persistently between hammer strikes, bringing both hope and uncertainty. Harald considered the boy, his blood yet untouched by royal politics, strong and unspoiled. It would enrage Avanna, undoubtedly, yet Harald trusted her practicality to eventually see reason.

He paused, studying his warped reflection in the blade. Would they embrace a son raised outside courtly walls?

He returned to the work, striking with deliberate care. This was not only a sword he was shaping. Aulfis would be carefully introduced, his legitimacy crafted through deeds and carefully chosen narratives.

Yet, beneath the calculated reasoning, a shadow of doubt lingered—Baldrik. Harald's heart twisted painfully at the thought of his younger son, whose choices had led him toward a different path. Would Baldrik understand the necessity, forgive Harald's choice?

His thoughts then turned to Maralei—Mara, as only he had known her. Her absence was a constant ache, a wound time refused to heal fully. He struck the steel more lightly, remembering the steadiness in her eyes.

"You should see him, Mara," Harald whispered. "I will ensure he is worthy of your love, of our love."

With fierce resolve, Harald finished the blade, inspecting its intricate patterns woven through gleaming steel. Resilient and balanced—a gift worthy of the son whose existence he had too long denied openly. It was not meant only for battle, but as a promise.

Harald stepped from the forge into the night, bearing both the crown of kingship and a fragile spark of hope.

High atop the rugged cliffs that marked the south-western edge of Eldaraine, the town of Seabarrow clung to the sheer stone like barnacles to a shipwreck.

Carved from salt-weathered rock, the settlement stood resolute against wind and wave. Narrow cobbled streets twisted between squat stone houses, each bearing scars from the ocean's rage—moss-stained walls, cracked plaster, and weathered shutters creaking in the gusts.

Above it all, perched defiantly at the highest point, stood Wynmere Manor, ancestral seat of House Wynmere. It was a fortress masquerading as elegance, its spires sharp and dark against the storm clouds, its walls formidable yet meticulously adorned with intricately carved stonework.

Within the manor, Lady Meyra Wynmere stood in her sitting room, gazing out through a grand floor-to-ceiling window that dominated the chamber. The expansive glass afforded her an unrivaled view of the Cold Sea, now a boiling cauldron of slate-grey fury capped with foaming white crests. Waves crashed violently against the cliffs below, their force shuddering through the stone beneath her feet.

The sea offered no mirror to her thoughts. It was simply there—violent, indifferent, predictable in its brutality.

Her figure stood outlined against the stormlight, framed by violet silk curtains embroidered with the white heron of her house—wings spread in defiance of the tempest.

Meyra's eyes watched the horizon without expectation, measuring distance rather than seeking answers. Her hand rested against the windowpane only long enough to feel its cold, then dropped away.

A subtle shift in the shadows at the room's entrance pulled her from contemplation.

She did not turn immediately, letting the pause test his patience, or perhaps her own composure.

"Alerick," she finally said, her voice rich with quiet authority and edged in velvet steel, "you move quietly, even here, amidst stone and storm. Most men would not make it past my guards so easily."

Alerick stepped forward, with fluid, unassuming confidence. His features were plain, forgettable by design, but Meyra found herself studying him closely, searching for something deeper beneath that practiced neutrality. He inclined his head respectfully, though his gaze never settled.

"Your guards see what they expect to see, Lady Wynmere," he replied calmly, a faint smile barely touching his lips. "A messenger here, a courier there—no one ever questions what's ordinary. Perhaps your house should train them to expect the extraordinary."

Meyra turned now, fully facing him, the edges of her mouth curving upward in mild appreciation. "Perhaps I already have. You stand before me, after all." The warmth vanished as quickly as it came. "With the storms, I expected you to be late, yet here you are—on time, as promised. I trust you understand the discretion required by what I am about to ask of you."

"Discretion is why I'm here," Alerick assured.

"The coastal roads were kind enough—maintained, at least. Mud, ruts, and storms do their best, but three days from Castellon would break lesser men. Speed carries cost."

"Then you understand it must be precise, untraceable, and utterly tasteless," she continued, voice dropping to a near whisper as though the sea itself might overhear. "Nothing to betray its presence until it is far too late." Her eyes held his firmly, unyielding and bold. "I need a poison capable of silencing a queen."

Alerick's gaze remained steady, only the faintest shift in his stance indicating he heard her clearly. Outside, the wind pressed against the stonework, a low, constant presence.

"Silencing is a flexible term, my lady," Alerick offered softly, a faint smirk touching his lips. "Do you wish the queen dead, invalid, or perhaps... simply mad? Pick your poison."

Meyra's eyes narrowed slightly, her expression a mix of irritation and grudging respect.

"Death is crude, Alerick, and frankly beneath me. No, I require subtlety. I want her alive, but doubting everything—her surroundings, her confidants, even her own mind. She must question reality itself."

Alerick considered this carefully. "Such an elixir exists. Difficult to acquire, costly to procure, but I know where to find it."

"Coin is not my concern," Meyra dismissed smoothly, a flick of her wrist emphasizing the insignificance of expense. "Only time. How soon?"

"I can have it soon enough," Alerick assured, his gaze sharpening slightly, his voice lower.

Meyra's gaze narrowed the decision made. "Once you have the poison, see that it reaches Castellon directly. I trust your hands to deliver it more swiftly and securely than any other. Time, Alerick, is a luxury we no longer have."

Alerick inclined his head in immediate understanding. "If I don't need to return here," he said evenly, "I save time and risk. From Seabarrow to Edgewatch by carriage, then fifty hard miles on horseback through the Scorchlands, and north to Castellon again—ten days, if the roads hold and the storms don't worsen."

"Then see it done," she replied firmly.

He paused.

"Naturally, I'll require travel expenses."

Without hesitation, Meyra crossed to a small iron-banded chest resting on a narrow table near the window. She opened it, retrieved a small pouch, and tossed it toward him with casual precision. "This should cover your travels, Shadow."

Alerick caught the pouch deftly, weighing it lightly in his hand but not bothering to count. He bowed, pocketed it, and slipped silently from the room.

Meyra turned back to the window and lifted her wine. The sea continued its work without her attention.

Lord Lanyard Darkoak stood at the balcony's edge, a statue in shadow, watching the flickering torchlight dance across the worn wooden stage below. The theater remained popular by day, its stage alive with actors and laughter. By night, it was empty but for torchlight, blades and the scrape of boots. Lord Darkoak had secured its use quietly. Nothing about the arrangement invited questions.

Commander Cinquedea circled his younger opponent without hurry, boots whispering over the boards. His blade flicked in small, testing motions—never committing, never idle.

Opposite him stood Aulfis Brightoak, tall and lean, shoulders loose, balance settled. He moved with a confidence that went beyond training—too precise for a man his age, too controlled for something learned quickly. Aulfis grinned lightly, blade poised, matching Cinquedea's steps.

"Come now, Commander," Aulfis teased gently, his voice matching his movements. "You're not going soft on me, are you?"

Cinquedea barked a short laugh. "Soft?" He rolled his shoulder, blade dipping an inch. "Boy, if I were soft you wouldn't be bleeding. Swing your damn sword."

Steel met steel with a sharp crack. Cinquedea pressed forward, forcing ground. Aulfis gave it—then took it back with a quick sidestep that opened Cinquedea's flank. Cinquedea adjusted instantly, blade snapping up just in time, the exchange breaking as quickly as it formed.

"You've been practicing," Cinquedea growled approvingly, blade scraping along Aulfis's guard as he pivoted away.

"You told me not to waste my free time," Aulfis retorted lightly, eyes glinting with amusement. "Apparently, I've learned to listen."

"Miracles never cease," Cinquedea barked back, leaping forward aggressively, their swords locking with a snarl of steel. Cinquedea leaned in, breath sharp with garlic, and growled through gritted teeth, "Next thing, you'll tell me you've learned table manners."

Aulfis laughed, ducking beneath the commander's sweeping strike and turning into a deft riposte. "Careful, Commander. Keep talking like that, and I'll start thinking you're fond of me."

"Fond? I'd sooner cuddle a scorpion," Cinquedea roared, driving Aulfis back step by step. "You're too damn cocky."

Cinquedea feinted left, blade flashing, but Aulfis anticipated, deflecting effortlessly and pivoting sharply. Using the commander's momentum against him, he sent Cinquedea stumbling briefly off-balance.

"Not bad," Cinquedea growled, swiftly regaining his footing, eyes glinting with renewed determination. "You're finally learning to read moves, not just bodies."

Aulfis offered a quick, focused nod, his breathing steady. "You taught me swords lie, but shoulders rarely do."

Aulfis pressed in, closing the distance until their guards ground together. For a breath they were chest to chest, steel snarling between them.

"Confidence is earned, Commander," he said quietly, voice tight with effort. "And paid for dearly—you've made sure I remember that."

He twisted, blade snapping up in a precise, unexpected move that Cinquedea barely deflected, stumbling back as Aulfis's sword lightly touched the commander's throat.

Cinquedea's free hand rose at once, fingers brushing his neck. He glanced down at them—red, thin, undeniable—then looked back up.

"Earned indeed," Cinquedea admitted grudgingly, stepping back, sweat tracing stark lines through the grime on his forehead. "Well done, pup. Seems I finally taught you something useful."

"You've taught me plenty, Commander," Aulfis said earnestly, nodding with sincere respect. "Though mostly how to creatively insult an opponent."

Cinquedea barked out a loud laugh, shaking his head ruefully. "And you're the finest student I've had in that art, I'll give you that." For a moment, only heavy breaths and the fading echoes of clashing steel filled the space.

Lanyard broke in with a call to cease, his voice calm yet commanding. "That's enough. Commander, thank you for your service. Remember, you still have squires to train."

Cinquedea grunted, nodding sharply. "Don't remind me," he muttered.

He paused briefly at the edge of the stage, turning back just enough for his gruff voice to carry clearly. "Keep this up, pup, and soon you'll be the one training cocky brats who think they know it all." His mouth tightened briefly—approval, given sparingly. Without waiting for a reply, he stepped from the stage, leaving his words hanging as he went.

Aulfis took a steady breath, set his sword aside, and drank deeply from a waterskin. Lanyard waited until Cinquedea had left before he descended from the balcony, approaching Aulfis with unhurried steps.

"Your skills have improved considerably," Lanyard observed, his tone cool and measured.

"Thank you," Aulfis replied, genuine respect evident in his voice. "I've had excellent guidance."

Lanyard inclined his head a fraction. "Take tomorrow off from training. Spend the day in the market. Rest and gather your thoughts."

Aulfis blinked in surprise but nodded gratefully. "Thank you, my lord. May I ask what's next?"

"You'll begin new training the following day," Lanyard informed him evenly. "Master Junfolda has arrived from Aynaraq. He specializes in hand-to-hand combat."

"Master Junfolda?" Aulfis echoed, intrigued.

"Yes," Lanyard confirmed firmly. "Be prompt, respectful, and pay close attention. Also—do not neglect your political lessons. Mastery of combat is only half the battle."

Lanyard paused.

"This next trainer is different. He won't care how well you strike or how fast you move. He'll watch what you do when you're tired, frustrated, or alone. Learn from him."

Aulfis nodded a few times, then hesitated. "Hand to hand," he said. "After all this." He glanced back toward the darkened stage. "Why now?"

Lanyard's eyes followed his look, then returned to him. "Because blades end fights," he said. "Men don't."

Aulfis picked up his water skin, then stopped. "Is Cinquedea done with me?"

Lanyard turned away. "No. He's done shaping you. Rest. Tomorrow is a reward, not a retreat."

Aulfis smiled, setting the water skin down. "I understand, my lord."

"Good," Lanyard said quietly, turning away. "Rest well, Aulfis. You'll need your strength."

———— ✶ ————

CHAPTER NINE

Night settled slowly over the lowlands as Winterfall loosened its grip by degrees rather than mercy. The day's last light bled out along the horizon, leaving the riverbanks damp and chill, the ground soft with meltwater and mud. Mist clung low to the marsh and treeline alike, drifting in slow curls that blurred distance.

Ashbriar crouched where forest and marsh gave way to the river road. Charcoal kilns squatted along the edge of the trees, their stone mouths black with ash. Fish racks stood empty for the night, ropes creaking softly. Beyond them, boar pens pressed against rough palisades, the animals restless in the cold.

The river bent hard here. Barges could go no farther south without risking the falls downstream, making Ashbriar an end of line for trade—where cargo was broken down, stored, or sent on by road. Charcoal, fish, cured meat. Nothing glamorous. Everything necessary.

Ashbriar belonged to no House.

That fact kept it free. It also left it exposed.

Most of the village had turned inward for the night. Lamps burned low behind shutters. Life narrowed to hearths and breath and the small comforts that made damp nights bearable.

Then the horses came.

Hooves found the softer ground by the riverbank and made little sound. Shapes emerged from the mist—riders two abreast, cloaked dark, moving with practiced restraint. No banners. No colors. Just leather, steel kept close, and the discipline of men who did not expect resistance.

Ashbriar noticed.

Shutters tightened. Fires dimmed. People stepped into the street anyway, drawn out by the shared understanding that hiding would not help. Fear moved faster than sense, pulling the village together beneath the lanterns.

The riders reined in as one at the edge of the square.

Their leader dismounted and stepped forward and did not hurry. His boots sank slightly into the mud and lifted free again, unbothered. He took in the kilns, the sheds, the river road—not with interest, but assessment.

"I am looking for your mayor, bring him out," he said.

He did not raise his voice. He did not explain.

Confusion rippled through the crowd, faces turning, searching. Someone spoke the mayor's name aloud. Someone else shook their head. The mayor of Ashbriar did not appear.

The moment stretched as the villagers waited, eyes fixed on the riders.

Irritation flickered across the leader's face—brief, sharp, gone.

He did not repeat himself.

Instead, he lifted one gloved hand and pointed.

The man he chose stood near the edge of the crowd, a step behind his family. He was broad-shouldered, thick through the arms, still wearing a work coat smeared with soot and fish-scale shine. One of his children clutched at his leg. His wife shook her head, once, in disbelief.

Two riders moved immediately, seizing the man by the arms and dragged him forward. He stumbled, boots slipping in the mud, until a hard shove sent him down. He landed on his hands and knees, palms sinking into the wet earth.

The crowd pressed in without meaning to, breath held, bodies drawn by the certainty that this was the moment everything tipped. The leader stopped a pace from the man in the mud and looked down at him, not with anger, not even with interest.

"Please," the man said, the word breaking as it left him. He looked back toward his family, then up at the rider. "Whatever you think I've done—"

"It doesn't matter," the leader said. "You will deliver a message to Castellon."

Hope flared—brief, desperate, unmistakable.

The leader drew his blade.

The motion was smooth. Economical. The kind practiced until it required no thought at all. Steel slid forward and drove cleanly through the man's chest, straight and sure.

The sound he made was small.

The blade was withdrawn as easily as it had entered. The man collapsed forward into the mud, face slack, eyes already empty.

The leader stepped back, blade angled down, blood darkening the earth at his feet.

"That," he said, his voice carrying easily, "is the message."

The crowd stood frozen, breath held, the world narrowed to the body in the mud and the blade that had ended him. His wife made a sound that was not a scream so much as a tearing—raw and wordless. One of the children lunged forward before being hauled back, small hands clawing at empty air.

The leader did not look at them.

He wiped his blade on the dead man's coat with a brief, practiced motion and slid it away. Then he turned back toward his horse.

"Your village will be the message," he said.

He mounted.

"Burn it."

The order broke the moment.

Torches flared as if the word itself had lit them. Riders split off in practiced pairs, firebrands thrust into thatch and timber, pitch flung hard against doors and sheds. Flames caught fast in the damp-dark night, smoke boiling up thick and choking.

Panic tore through the square.

People scattered—some toward the river, some into alleys, some nowhere at all. Shouts collapsed into screams. The boar pens erupted in noise as animals slammed against their rails.

A few of the riders drew bows.

They did not aim carefully. They did not need to.

The first arrow dropped a man running toward the kilns. He went down hard and did not rise.

The second struck a woman at the edge of the crowd, spinning her sideways into the dirt.

The third found a figure already stumbling, finishing what fear had started.

Another broke from the crowd, instead of fleeing, he rushed a rider with a woodcutter's axe in his hands—wild, desperate, already screaming.

A bowstring snapped. The arrow punched through him mid-stride and drove him hard into the mud.

But the charge was enough.

The rider's horse shied at the sudden movement, slipping in the churned earth. The man cursed as the animal went down, throwing him clear into the muck before scrambling back to its feet.

At the far edge of the square, where the firelight thinned and the river mist still clung, a man broke from the chaos with purpose. He did not shout. He did not look back.

He ran hard for the livery sheds, boots slipping once before he caught himself. A half-wild mare screamed as he tore her loose, fingers shaking as he hauled himself onto her back.

An arrow hissed past him and vanished into the dark.

He drove his heels in and rode west—away from the river, away from the falls, toward Emberfist—leaning low as the night swallowed him.

The riders split.

No battle cry.

No charge.

Just motion—precise, measured.

Intent, sharpened to a point.

Ashbriar would burn before dawn.

Darkness lay heavy over Goldacre Manor, pressed close and airless. River mist clung to the windows, dulling distance and swallowing the grounds beyond the lantern light.

Valen's study carried citrus and old polish—carefully maintained, faintly sour beneath it.

Lord Circus Valen reclined across a couch of lavish crimson brocade, tunic unbuttoned enough to offend, a gold-tipped boot resting insolently upon a lion's head stool carved in lifelike snarl.

A decanter perspired on the sideboard next to a plate of shriveled figs and an abandoned pear, browning at the edges. Valen's eyes were cold, distant, fixed upon a parchment in his hands as if trying to decipher the heart of an enemy.

Rennic Stride stood three paces away, posture exact. He held a folded report in one hand and a narrow leather ledger in the other, ink stained thumb marking a page. His gaze rested on a knot in the floorboard, not deferential, simply fixed. Every few breaths, he adjusted the cuff of one glove by a fraction—an unconscious correction.

"No names?" Valen finally asked, voice idle yet edged like freshly honed steel.

"No names," Rennic replied, tone clipped and clinical. "No crests. No colors. But disciplined—efficient. Your instructions were followed precisely."

Valen's lips twitched subtly, caught between amusement and irritation. "Efficiency in others bores me, Smudge. Originality is what I admire." He placed the parchment down beside the plate, fingers flicking as though to discard a piece of soiled linen. "And originality is precisely what this lacks."

Rennic's brow rose fractionally. "Perhaps next time we might instruct them to juggle torches as they ride, my lord. The mayor would find it memorably original."

Valen's gaze sharpened momentarily before easing into a dry smirk. "Careful, Smudge. Wit is only charming when it does not come at my expense."

"Then I assure you, my lord, it was intended entirely at their expense." Smudge's voice remained neutral, the faintest trace of humor ghosting beneath.

Valen shifted on the couch, eyes narrowing faintly as he considered. "Send something appropriately mournful—grain, assurances, a gentle lie. Double the shipment price, Smudge."

Rennic's gaze flickered briefly upward, precise, calculating. "Bread grows dear when served alongside grief. And grief, as always, is good for business."

Valen raised his goblet, swirling the bruise-colored wine slowly. "Precisely. Fear, loss, and hunger—these three are always profitable. Especially when combined." He drank deeply, savoring the bitter undertones. "Bread tastes sweeter once you've watched your neighbor's house burn."

Rennic did not answer at once. He lowered his eyes to the ledger in his hand and turned a page with care, the scrape of quill on paper briefly filling the room.

Valen, observing Rennic's silence, set the goblet down with a dull thud. "Something troubles you, Smudge?"

"Curiosity, perhaps," Rennic allowed evenly. "Your actions grow bolder. One wonders—are you pushing too far, too openly? Ashbriar was more direct than your usual style."

Valen's smile curled, sharp and unpleasant. "Two birds, one flame, you might say." He allowed himself a brief, satisfied pause, savoring the implications. "Openly, Rennic? No, never openly. The open wound gets bandaged, tended to. It's the hidden infection that festers, unseen until too late. Ashbriar served multiple purposes. A bold stroke, perhaps, but necessary. Trust my methods—they have yet to fail us."

"Indeed," Rennic said smoothly, tone polite but subtly edged. "Though some might argue the line between boldness and folly is thinner than parchment."

Valen's gaze drifted toward the hearth, voice softer yet more dangerous. "She should have known better."

Rennic paused at the threshold, turning slightly. "The mayor's daughter?"

Valen didn't look up. "She could have enjoyed a few pleasurable nights, some fine wine. Instead, she laughed—openly. At me." His lips drew back in a bitter snarl. "Jokes cost dearly when told at my expense. This wasn't merely a message to the Mayor. This was a reminder to the realm that my patience has limits."

"An expensive lesson," Rennic agreed mildly, adding, "though perhaps cheaper than juggling torches on horseback."

Valen chuckled, devoid of warmth. "Precisely, Smudge. Expensive lessons are the only ones people truly learn."

Rennic bowed his head slightly, acknowledging the sentiment.

As he turned to leave, Rennic brushed two fingers against the threshold trim—three quick taps, measured and silent. The gesture, habitual and unspoken, had worn a pale groove into the wood over years, like a superstition too old to question and too precise to forget.

He left without another word.

The sun dipped behind the western towers of Castellon Shield, casting a thin wash of gold across the upper terraces of the royal gardens. Queen Avanna walked alone along the trimmed stone paths, her pale green silk gown brushing the ground with a steady insistence. She wore no crown, no brooch, no sigil of house or kingdom—only ivory lace gloves, her hands folded more from habit than grace.

The garden bloomed with things that did not belong together. Winter Roses from the western bays, white as fresh snows. Frost-blossoms from Hravnskot, pale and unyielding.

Salt-thorn hedges whose bitter blossoms grew only in ground long scarred by old violence.

Avanna passed without lifting her eyes, her thoughts moving in careful spirals. Baldrik's silence. Harald's growing distance. Whispers at court slipping from her grasp. She had long believed herself the hidden hand behind Eldaraine's tapestry. Now the threads felt loose, misaligned, resistant to her touch.

She paused beside a rose bush crossbred from Eldaraine soil and Varanese rootstock, when in bloom, the petals were variegated in white and vivid crimson. Near by, the Cross-blossoms were in full bloom. One flower fuller than the rest, trembling slightly in the evening breeze. Avanna reached out, fingertips hovering just above the blossom.

A breath caught nearby, sharp enough to break her focus.

Hidden beneath petals, a thorn pricked precisely through silk and lace, drawing forth a single, elegant bead of red. She withdrew her hand slowly, staring briefly at the scarlet dot blooming against ivory lace. Real beauty draws blood, she remembered her mother saying—perfume and lies can only go so far.

Behind her, the breeze stirred again—sudden.

Near the fountain colonnade, where jasmine climbed marble pillars and scent mingled gently with the murmuring of water, Avanna slowed and stopped within the shadows. Ahead, two young women in embroidered cloaks moved along the path, voices low but confident in their privacy.

"The prince entered the Citadel again this morning," one said in a low voice, edged with curiosity.

"Again?" the other replied, younger and hesitant. "I thought only the dying visited the Flame so often."

"Quiet," the first warned. "Walls have ears here. Dangerous words have a way of reaching dangerous ears."

The women's steps receded from earshot, but Avanna remained still, tension settling in her chest. Baldrik's visits troubled her more deeply than she admitted, even to herself. She had fought fiercely for every piece of her life—her crown, her family, her place here. But Baldrik's choices now seemed beyond her grasp, hidden behind veils she could not lift.

"Your Majesty?"

The voice behind her belonged to Serai, a trusted runner in Lord Darkoak's household, reliable for discreet errands and the mother of Lana, Avanna's own chamber maiden. Avanna turned, managing a faint, practiced smile.

"Serai. You startled me."

Serai lowered her eyes respectfully. "Forgive me, my Queen. Lord Darkoak has sent word; he wishes to speak with you at your earliest convenience."

Avanna's expression softened slightly, though unease threaded her response. "Yes, of course. Did he say what this concerns?"

Serai hesitated briefly, clearly uncomfortable, but knowing better than to withhold information. "He did not say directly, Your Majesty. But I overheard him speaking to Commander Cinquedea. They mentioned concerns about the prince's frequent visits to the Citadel. Lord Darkoak believes it requires immediate attention."

Avanna released a resigned breath. "Yes, of course," she said. After a brief pause, she gathered herself. "You have something else?" she prompted gently.

Serai raised cautious eyes. "It's only that—there are whispers among the staff. The prince seems troubled, distant. The whispers say he carries a burden, heavier than he can manage alone."

Avanna's heart tightened, but she forced calm into her voice. "And what do you think, Serai?"

The woman met her gaze squarely. "I think he's alone in it," she said. "And people don't carry things well when no one else knows the weight exists."

Avanna inclined her head. "Thank you. You may go."

Serai returned the nod—measured, respectful—and departed without another word, her posture straight, steps unhurried.

Left alone again, Avanna's gaze returned to the frost-blossoms. A breath of wind loosened three petals, and they fell at her feet.

She spoke into the gathering dusk, a plea lost to the space between monks and grief:

"Where is your head, my son? Where is your heart?"

The hall toward the upper chambers lay cool and shadowed. Avanna moved through it with measured steps, already weighing what Lord Darkoak would say—and what he would not.

Lord Lanyard Darkoak stood before a portrait of King Boris Thornsword, Harald's father, painted in bold strokes that captured the old king's strength and quiet dignity. Darkoak's expression was thoughtful, reflective, as he studied the familiar face.

"Your Majesty," he turned as Avanna approached, bowing his head respectfully. "Thank you for coming so swiftly."

She inclined her head and stepped closer, joining him before the portrait. "You admired him greatly, did you not?"

Lanyard inclined his head, a faint softening at the edges of his stern expression. "I served as his sword for many years. He was strong and decisive. The kingdom held together under his rule."

"I never had the chance to know him," Avanna said. "But I've heard many speak fondly of his reign."

"As they should," Lanyard replied. "He understood the heavy weight of the crown, the isolation it can bring." He paused, turning to Avanna with careful deliberation. "It is partly why I asked to speak with you. Commander Cinquedea has brought troubling news about Prince Baldrik."

A chill settled in Avanna's chest. "His visits to the Citadel?"

Lanyard nodded slowly. "Yes, that and more. It seems Lady Elara Icewind has reached out to him during one of his visits to the gardens. Nothing serious, not yet. But Elara's presence rarely brings comfort—or coincidence."

Avanna tightened her fingers beneath the lace of her gloves. "What would you have me do?"

Lanyard's voice remained even. "Speak plainly with Baldrik. Understand what draws him to the Citadel—and ensure he sees clearly the intentions of those around him. Especially Elara."

Avanna straightened. "His visits trouble me as well, but it's not only that. His interest in his studies wanes daily, his mind always elsewhere. I worry deeply about his preparedness."

Lanyard's brows knit thoughtfully. "Commander Cinquedea shares similar concerns. Baldrik has shown flashes of brilliance, but his consistency is lacking. He's distracted, preoccupied—traits dangerous in a future king."

"And now Lady Elara." Avanna's voice tightened slightly. "I admit, she's pleasant enough, intelligent and charismatic even, but her ambitions are hardly subtle. She finds herself in precarious circumstances, her estate hanging by a thread. It's possible she seeks to leverage Baldrik's heart or his influence to her advantage."

Lanyard inclined his head. "That is my concern. She is clever—perhaps too clever. Circumstance has a way of sharpening people into tools, and tools do not choose where they are used."

Avanna drew a slow breath and straightened. "Then I will speak plainly with Baldrik. He must understand the pressures around him—and who applies them."

Lanyard inclined his head in return. "You are not alone, Your Majesty. Do not forget that."

On the lower east side of Castellon, Alerick stood on a narrow half-balcony above the market, watching the city work.

Below him, carts pressed through the crowd while guards drifted in loose patterns that suggested presence more than vigilance. Smoke from a small brazier curled past his shoulder, carrying the faintest hint of sea salt and citrus.

With practiced indifference, Alerick released another letter into the waiting flame. The wax seal flared, curled, and collapsed into ash. The scent confirmed what he already knew—Varanese.

Lady Meyra Wynmere's doing.

She had set a street errand boy to collecting correspondence tied to the Firewine trade. The boy could not read. He brought her everything bound for the Vara Islands.

Alerick caught him in the act a week earlier. Rather than slit the boy's throat, he pressed him into a private arrangement: the letters would pass through Alerick's hands first. He kept only what he wished to understand.

Miroray again.

Invitation after invitation, grievances softened into courtesy, sincerity pressed too thin to survive the journey. Good faith, misdirected—fed to the flame and erased before it could do harm. Not one of them had reached the eyes they sought.

He considered, briefly, how Miroray might react if she learned the truth. The thought led nowhere useful.

Alerick watched as the flames took her latest words, ink collapsing into ash.

His fingers flexed once at his side, then stilled.

Alerick dipped a practiced hand into the worn leather satchel once more, fingertips dancing lightly over crisp parchment edges before selecting the next victim. He drew forth a scroll embossed with the crest of House Caerlyn—a nine tailed fox over a full moon.

He unfurled the scroll and read it through, habit demanding attention even when the contents were already known.

"Lord Valen—

It is imperative that we revisit our current arrangement. The grain alone raises dangerous questions, yet your continued refusal to halt shipments borders on recklessness. If you fail to respond swiftly and decisively—"

He didn't bother finishing. The letter's tone had already twisted—confusion souring swiftly into alarm, carefully chosen courtesies fraying at their edges. Panic did not blur motives. It clarified them.

House Caerlyn—proud, confident in its grasp upon the kingdom's precious grain—was only now awakening to the colder truth: every shipment, every wagon they had received had arrived at Alerick's quiet urging, delivered by couriers he selected, bearing scrolls forged in Lord Valen's name. False seals, whispered suggestions, ambition-clouded ears. No accords made. No bargains struck. Only illusions wrapped in wax.

It was warfare without steel, betrayal without traitors named. Power undermined without banners or blood.

One scroll remained in his satchel.

Alerick didn't consign this one to the flames.

Instead, he unrolled the parchment with care, keeping the vellum smooth, the wax undisturbed. Elara had warned him not to read it. She had trusted him to obey. But trust was brittle, and instinct had always served him better than restraint.

The words cut sharper than he expected. Not merely accounts of grain and wagons, but accusations laid bare—*"useless royalty," "paper-forged nobility,"* and darker still, *"the crumbling heart of Castellon."*

Forged in Lord Caerlyn's hand but signed in Valen's own, it was a seed of doubt carefully planted.

Alerick re-rolled the scroll and held it just above the heat, long enough for smoke to darken the wax. Then he withdrew it and watched the seal cool and harden.

This scroll was not meant for the flames.

This scroll was to be delivered to the Storm itself.

The questions had narrowed. He understood why Elara had asked for Rodrik, just as he understood the risks she pretended did not exist.

And he could not be certain they would endure if the storm came again in force.

Alerick's gaze drifted back toward the crowded marketplace—and as if answering the thought, the storm stepped into view.

Rodrik.

The man moved carefully, wrapped in threadbare commoner's cloth, yet his gait betrayed him. No humble farmer moved with such fluid, dangerous confidence; no common thief studied corners while marking exits with such care. Rodrik wore caution like armor, but even that could not hide the steel beneath.

Rodrik paused before the Iron Cup—a squat, grime-streaked tavern squeezed awkwardly between a cobbler's cluttered stall and a butcher's permanently shuttered window. Its wooden sign hung askew, paint long faded to an iron-gray memory. The windows were thick with grime, fogged by decades of ale and old breath.

With one last wary glance, he stepped inside.

"That one," Alerick said. "He'll feel it soon enough. That scroll carries teeth."

A creak behind him froze him mid-thought. He tilted his head slightly, listening for any further sound. Nothing but wind moving through cracked shutters. Or perhaps the landlady again, creeping upward for conversation—or something else.

She'd knocked once the week before, leaving a steaming bowl of stew on his doorstep. Said he looked thin—as if secrets weighed nothing at all.

"You don't eat, Faileas," she'd said once, arms folded, gaze narrowed in that strange blend of suspicion and warmth. "You just watch. Like a cat waiting on a ghost."

"I prefer ghosts to critics," he'd answered, with a sideways grin and closed the door with a nod that almost meant thanks.

Below, Castellon pulsed with its nightly rhythm. Guards shifted posts beneath torchlight. Merchants packed crates with the stubborn pace of men racing coin. And inside the Iron Cup, nestled in the city's deeper bones, a man from the mountains sat down to gather truths like kindling before a storm.

Alerick turned from the rail, scroll in hand, and stepped back inside.

He had many clients to attend to. Few worth listening to.

Tomorrow, perhaps, the scroll would drift into the Northman's path.

Not like fire or ink.

Like hunger.

Rodrik drew the borrowed cloak tighter around his shoulders as he stepped through the gates of Castellon Shield. Smoke hung low in the twilight, softening the city's edges without hiding its weight. Lanterns guttered as they were lit, casting amber pools that did little to warm the stone.

He paused just inside the portcullis. His breathing remained steady, but an old, bitter taste surfaced all the same. The press of people closed around him—faces tired, guarded, intent on getting home or finding cover in taverns before full dark. Though his clothes marked him as common enough, Rodrik felt the glances slide across him and move on.

Anonymity had always served him.

Old habits held—measuring distance, tracking movement, noting hands that lingered too long near blades. Memory tugged at him, but he did not indulge it. The dead did not need him looking back.

Ten years had passed since he last walked these streets. Ten winters since war had burned through Castellon and left it standing, changed in ways stone could not show. The city remembered that season differently than the north did. What had been valor to some had been survival to others, and defeat wore many names depending on where a man stood when the walls shook.

Though familiar, Castellon felt hostile to Rodrik, as if the stones remembered him and disapproved of his return.

The avenue ahead carried the day's last business. Vendors called out what remained unsold. Carts creaked past one another. Guards walked their routes with practiced boredom. Children ran where they were not meant to, laughing as if the city were harmless, while mothers hurried them along with one eye always searching for trouble.

His destination was the lower east side, where Castellon's grace decayed into shadow and anonymity was more than convenience—it was survival. Here, alleys narrowed, walls leaned close, and candles burned low behind boarded windows. The air carried woodsmoke, stale ale, and something older beneath it.

The Iron Cup sat wedged uncomfortably between a cobbler's cluttered stall and the lifeless, shuttered front of what had once been a butcher's shop. Its sign creaked in the breeze, paint flaking down to iron-gray. Rodrik halted briefly, his eyes scanning swiftly yet methodically, marking exits and recalling how complacency had once cost lives. Finding nothing immediately amiss, he pushed open the tavern door and let the warmth and murmur of voices close around him.

Shadows moved across battered tables and weathered faces. Patrons clustered in cautious groups, eyes lifted briefly as he entered, quickly categorizing and dismissing him as one more traveler come to lose himself.

Rodrik chose a seat in the far corner, back pressed securely against stone, away from the weak glow of the hearth.

A barmaid approached his table, wiping her hands anxiously on a frayed apron. She was a plain woman, her features worn, rouge applied too thick to hide the fatigue beneath.

"Wot'll it be, traveler?" she asked with a practiced smile and a rough-edged accent.

"Ale," Rodrik answered, eyes briefly meeting hers. "Nothing fancy."

Her smile broadened, all dark yellow teeth, at least the ones that remained.. "Ain't got nuffin' fancy 'ere anyway," she drawled, her grin widening beneath the rouge. "But our ale's still better'n the lot wot drink it."

Rodrik managed a polite nod. "I'll take your word for it."

She chuckled, though the sound was hollow.

"Wise choice, guv." She turned away and moved back through the dim tavern, her awkward gait carrying her toward more receptive customers.

Rodrik settled deeper into his chair, his attention sliding back to the ebb and flow of conversation around him.

Rodrik had not come seeking pleasure, nor rest.

He had come to listen—to watch, to measure what lay beneath words, and to trace the movements of a city edging toward unrest.

——— ✶ ———

The sun hung high yet gentle, casting long, golden beams through the ornate spires of the Grand Citadel. Shadows stretched like careful fingers across the sacred courtyards of Castellon, where the Flamebound Order kept their silent vigil—vaulted halls steeped in incense, reverberating softly with whispered prayers older than memory.

The path to the inner sanctum was deliberate.

Prince Baldrik walked alone. Not unguarded—merely unaccompanied. He bore no herald, no attendant. His boots made measured clicks on stone polished smooth by centuries of reverent passage.

His cloak draped askew across one shoulder, half-unfastened, betraying the subtle unease he fought to conceal. His expression was that of a boy donning a man's solemnity—jaw set too firmly, shoulders a fraction too rigid.

The Grand Citadel consumed sound, absorbing every whisper and footfall. The vaulted halls—ribs of pale stone etched with veins of flame-kissed gold—pressed its weight deeply into the bones of all who entered.

Torchlight wove gently across carved columns bearing likenesses of monks now lost to memory, folded into the singular blaze of the Flame: hollow eyes, parted lips, hands extended, forever cradling fire.

Pillars loomed in ordered ranks, their surfaces darkened by age and smoke. Baldrik passed through without slowing, eyes forward, the weight of the Citadel pressing in as the space gradually narrowed beyond the great chamber.

As he advanced, fewer eyes marked his progress. The Citadel emptied around him—stone walls thickening, murmurs thinning until they vanished..

Two robed attendants nodded respectfully as he passed the outer cloister. Their bows were directed not at the prince, but at the eternal flame burning steadily in the shrine behind him..

Each step drew him deeper into the Citadel's depths.

Baldrik did not hesitate.

He knew this path. He had walked it as a child, escorted dutifully to solstice rites, mourning days, and once alone—his first hunt, blood not yet dry upon his boots.

The Sanctum of Flame bore little resemblance to the grand chapel above.

Here, flame spoke louder than sermon ever could. The chamber was circular and domed, ringed by smokeless braziers. Frescoes curved across the walls, illustrating myths of the Flame's aspects: the Mother Ash, the Consuming Hand, the Watcher Without Voice.

At the center, upon a dais of cracked obsidian knelt a figure garbed in ash-white and ember-red—fabric plain yet flowing, hood lowered across his shoulders, revealing no sigils or clasps. A charcoal cloth bound his arms at the elbows, concealing their purpose. He waited, still as judgment itself.

As Baldrik entered, the figure rose with graceful deliberation.

The man appeared neither old nor young. His face was lean and pale, cheekbones stark, his hands precisely folded. His eyes held neither hunger nor warmth—only weight.

Baldrik inclined his head, respectful yet cautious. His eyes narrowed slightly, curiosity surfacing. "I don't recall seeing you here before."

"I am Kælric, from Westmere," the man replied evenly, voice carrying clearly. "I walk a pilgrimage—seeking knowledge and clarity."

Baldrik studied him briefly: the man's closely shorn hair revealed a head shaped by discipline, and his eyebrows, lightly dusted to a pale hue, gave his face an austere, almost ethereal quality.

He offered a courteous nod. "Welcome to Castellon, though clarity may be scarce—like everything else these days." His tone was dry, unadorned.

Kælric gave a single, calm nod. His voice was low and measured. "The Flame receive you, son of Thornsword."

Baldrik stepped forward, his eyes drawn briefly to the spiraled ceiling where stone vanished into shadow. He gestured upward faintly and remarked, "You know… I always thought the spire here was compensating. Perhaps the architect had his own shortcomings."

His words went unanswered. Kælric offered neither smile nor rebuke, merely regarded him with patient weight..

Baldrik cleared his throat awkwardly. "Seems reverence isn't renowned for humor."

The priest inclined his head subtly. "How may I assist you, my Prince?"

They sat opposite one another, the dais between them cool beneath their hands. A basin of softly glowing coals rested at its center, the faint crackle filling the space between breaths.

Baldrik leaned forward, his voice lowered. "I had a vision, perhaps a dream—I'm uncertain. But it was clear, vivid."

He paused thoughtfully.

"There was a monk unlike any I've known. Robed in crimson and ivory, a sharp collar around his throat, clasped with a golden sunburst. He stood within a hall like this—older, perhaps grander—and he held the king's crown."

Kælric's expression remained unchanged.

"He neither wore it nor seized it. He carried it gently, as something fragile and sacred—not his, yet his responsibility. He moved away from the throne deliberately, carefully."

A pause stretched between them, the embers' glow the only movement.

Baldrik leaned back. "Perhaps he wasn't claiming the crown. Perhaps he was carrying it… until it found the right head."

Kælric's eyes did not leave the coals. "And on whose head, Prince Baldrik, does it belong? Or is it something you mean to set down… and let another lift?"

Baldrik held his gaze. "Not on mine."

He said it without bravado. The words landed—and Kælric let them sit there, unanswered, as if weighing whether they would hold.

Kælric nudged a coal with the iron, sending a brief scatter of sparks upward. "There are roads that do not lead to thrones," he said. "They narrow as they go… until there is only what you cannot set down."

Baldrik's breath eased. "The Order."

A single nod. "The Order burns away what is not needed. Names. Claims. Comforts." His gaze flicked, measuring. "Tell me, then—what do you surrender first?"

Baldrik let out a quiet breath that might have been a laugh. "Everything. Let it all burn. I choose this."

A beat. Then he grinned, certainty edging his face. "Let the Flame take the prince. When do I get my own robes?"

A pause, thin as a blade. "Robes help the fire along. They are not the fire."

Kælric watched him—long enough to make the silence a question. A faint, almost-private smile touched nothing but the corner of his mouth. "Choice is easy at the mouth of a path. Anyone can put on robes and call it choosing." He rose. "Walking with that choice is what proves you are not merely dressed for it." His voice cooled a fraction. "Or it will prove that you were never meant to wear the robes at all. We shall speak again."

He inclined his head—no deeper than courtesy, no shallower than respect.

Baldrik stood, brushing a hand over his tunic. "I should go. Miss another lesson and my mother will have me strung from the walls." A faint, crooked smile. "Varanese memory is a dangerous thing."

Kælric did not return it. "Walk carefully, Your Highness. Ash remembers what men try to leave behind."

Baldrik turned and left the way he came. Kælric moved to a nearby sconce, where ash had settled beneath the flame. With precise fingers, he traced the symbol of the Flamed sun into the pale ash—ringed by fire, threaded with a subtle spiral. His fingers lingered over the emblem, hovering thoughtfully.

Then, with a deliberate sweep of his hand, he cleared the symbol away, leaving no trace behind except disturbed ash settling back into anonymity.

He murmured, "A Flamebound king… a flame never lit."

His eyes returned to the departing Prince.

✶

CHAPTER TEN

The storm hadn't broken yet, but circled above like a living predator—listening, waiting. Wind clawed at the vine-wrapped towers of Flamegrove Palace, tugging at emerald banners. Far below, waves shattered against coral cliffs, their rhythm too precise to be mere chaos.

In the highest chamber of the obsidian wing, King Consort Tulavan stood barefoot on storm-polished stone, framed by towering panes of stormglass. His arms rested rigidly behind his back, hands clasped, spine straight as the spear he once carried into battle—before the throne had turned muscle into burden, valor into muted ceremony.

The air reeked faintly of brine and ozone—salt and threat. Home and insult. He'd fought storms louder than this stillness. Storms at least had the decency to scream their intentions. But this—this stillness—felt like surrender. And he'd never learned how to greet surrender without drawing a blade.

Behind him, upon a table of black glass and ivory driftwood, lay numerous recent scrolls and missives from across the realms—parchment crisp, wax seals pristine. Reports from distant outposts. Trade letters stamped in Eldaraine wax. Even a formal plea from the Flamebound, urging Vara to abandon old gods for new flames—all expected, all carefully read and thoughtfully considered.

To fall silent now—after Vara had opened its harbors and sent a Queen to stand beside a Thornsword—felt like lines being cut. The kind you only notice when the helm stops answering.

Yet amid this steady stream of communication, one silence loomed larger than all the rest: there had been no word from Eldaraine's royal house. The last message bearing the thorned tree and stag—sent by Queen Avanna herself—had arrived a season ago. Since then, nothing. No inquiry. No courtesy. No reply.

"They ignore us," Tulavan said finally, his voice edged with the tension of a tide about to break. "Or perhaps they choose to forget."

Queen Miroray reclined nearby, legs folded gracefully beneath her on a cushion of reef-dyed silk, a forgotten comb resting idly in her lap. Her unbound hair shimmered like captive sunlight, flame-gold curls salted and tangled by the wind. Her eyes, sharp with guarded thought, fixed firmly upon the darkening horizon.

"Avanna is not careless," Miroray said, voice steady but laced with subtle caution. "If she's silent, it's deliberate. Like a tide pulling back before the crush."

Tulavan didn't turn. His jaw worked, the muscle shifting beneath skin bronzed by salt and heat. "Then it's an insult. Or a distraction."

He exhaled slowly, nostrils flaring. "Does it matter which?"

Miroray's gaze shifted briefly toward open sea. "She wrote me—twice. Last Midswell. Since then… nothing."

"She didn't come to the wedding," he said bitterly. "No wine, no coin, not even a puffed-up envoy with his hollow smiles and polished boots."

"No."

"She sent nothing," he said, naming it as if it were a blade, sharp and deadly.

"Yes," Miroray rose smoothly, silk rippling around her like liquid twilight. "And silence holds power only when wielded deliberately."

Tulavan turned at last, obsidian beneath him scattering fractured green and gold reflections. "Then we'll break it—like a hull through kelp."

Miroray studied him carefully, measuring wind against tide. "You've moved the fleet?"

"I've begun preparations." His gaze didn't waver. "We'll call it a goodwill voyage. For the banners, at least."

Miroray's brow arched skeptically. "How many warships does your goodwill require, Tulavan?"

"Twenty."

She tilted her head slightly. "Twenty? That's not goodwill. That's a threat dressed for court."

"It will give notice. And make them look twice."

"Oh, they will," she said. "Right before they string their bows."

Silence held as Tulavan sipped his wine before speaking again.

"I'll be on the lead ship," Tulavan stated firmly.

Miroray's eyes widened slightly—not in surprise, but in sharp assessment. "You've decided this without my counsel?"

He met her gaze, the defiance in his eyes tempered by respect. "Yes. And I assumed you would approve."

She said nothing for a long moment, fingers trailing over the edge of her sash. The wind caught her hair, lifting it like a banner.

She held his gaze the silence itself becoming a quiet assertion of her authority. "I do. And I will sail with you—not because you would think to command it, but because Vara speaks with my voice."

He nodded, acknowledging the subtle rebuke with restrained grace. "I want Eldaraine to see our strength."

Miroray smiled sharply, poised and commanding. "Then let them look. Let them stare until they're blind to what creeps in behind."

Tulavan stepped into the heart of the chamber. A gust rattled the high vents, carrying scents of salt and jungle bloom. The chamber felt tighter for it.

"We sail in the morning," he said, firm. "Half a season. No longer."

"And Kirahnae will rule in our stead," Miroray stated without hesitation.

He didn't answer right away. His hand brushed the reef-glass edge of the war table, as if weighing resistance with his fingertips.

"She's sixteen," he reminded her.

"She's Varanese," Miroray replied, already moving toward the staircase, confidence unwavering. "We are forged young and tested hard. And she is my sister, heir to the Reefglass Crown. She will lead as I would—with wisdom and strength, guided by the elders. Besides, you yourself said it would only be half a season."

"She's young. Inexperienced."

"So was I," Miroray paused on the top step, voice calm yet edged sharply like coral. "The first time I wore the Reefglass Crown. Unlike you, she listens before she speaks."

Tulavan gave a short, bitter laugh. "Listening isn't always a virtue."

"No," Miroray agreed. "But it's the reason we'll return to a palace—and not to silence and ash."

Tulavan turned back toward the sea, where fractured reflections danced across restless waters.

"She'll do fine," Miroray said. "And if she stumbles… Veluna and Na'shivar stand behind her. Every elder watches her every breath."

"That should reassure me?"

"It should."

"It doesn't."

"Then save your worry for the sea," Miroray brushed past him, her tone final. "The land answers to me."

Tulavan returned to the table, fingertips tracing the edges of Eldaraine's most recent scroll.

"I fear something is wrong," Miroray's gaze drifted to the horizon as if answers waited beyond sight. "It is unlike Avanna. We must discover why she's chosen silence—and ensure it isn't being imposed upon her."

Tulavan looked up, eyes meeting hers with unwavering resolve. He exhaled through his nose. "Then we sail for Eldaraine. And drag truth from the depths—or bring a storm to whoever dared silence a queen."

The early morning sun shone hot over a harbor alive with preparations—ropes tightening, sails unfurling like storm clouds. Tulavan stood at the edge of the docks, arms crossed, surveying his gathered fleet as though daring the sea itself to protest. Beside him, Captain Apeck of the Sea Serpent Fleet, leaned in casual defiance, one boot on a mooring post, sipping something dangerously alcoholic from a flask and smiling like he already knew the punchline to a joke nobody else had heard.

"Twenty ships," Apeck said too chipper for morning, eyes scanning the decks with practiced indifference. "You know, usually when you want to make friends, you send flowers. Maybe some nice fruit."

Tulavan gave a half-snort, not bothering to turn. "Last I checked, Eldaraine wasn't interested in bouquets."

Apeck shrugged loosely, raising his flask in mock salute. "And here I thought the problem was they weren't interested in you."

Tulavan's lips twitched in a half-smile. "Careful, friend. Sound like that again, and I'll have you swim along the Queen's Tide until barnacles crust your belly."

"Ah, but then who'd remind you that chasing after northern approval is as useful as pissing into the tide?" Apeck grinned, taking another lazy swig. "You'd miss me after the first lonely night."

Tulavan turned fully now, giving his oldest friend a flat stare. "Miss you? The man whose solution to every diplomatic crisis involves nudity or wine?"

"Worked so far," Apeck retorted cheerfully.

"Because I keep saving your ass."

Apeck chuckled, lowering the flask. His gaze steadied, serious beneath the teasing surface. "And I'll keep following after you when you chase storms. I've watched your back since we were idiots learning the sea together. I figure it's habit by now."

Tulavan looked away for a moment, the weight of history pressing between them. Then he met Apeck's eyes, a rare moment of sincerity easing his features.

"I wouldn't sail into this without you, old friend."

Apeck's eyes glinted mischievously again. "Of course not. You'd be bored stiff without my sparkling charm."

Tulavan scoffed, shaking his head. "Charm. Right. Is that what they're calling drunken stupidity these days?"

"You're mistaking drunkenness for genius again," Apeck retorted, feigning hurt. "Common error. Both involve a lot of falling down."

Tulavan clapped a hand firmly onto Apeck's shoulder, half-warning, half-affection. "Just keep your clothes on this time. I don't need Eldaraine thinking we've brought a sea-monster."

Apeck laughed, a rich bark of genuine amusement, nudging Tulavan playfully with his elbow. "No promises, Captain. After all, nothing says goodwill like giving their spies something to talk about."

Their laughter carried through the harbor, clear and unguarded.

Miroray moved swiftly through corridors of obsidian and reef-stone, her steps purposeful yet graceful, her gown trailing behind her. The halls breathed with salt air and incense, ancient coral holding the weight of each step like memory pressed into sand. Beside her, Princess Kirahnae struggled to match her sister's pace, youthful bravado edged faintly with uncertainty. Miroray did not glance back, her stride as unwavering as her tone in council.

"I'm ready," Kirahnae said firmly, her voice colored by more assurance than she felt. Her gaze was bold, defiance flickering behind eyes as bright as reef fire.

Miroray paused at a high archway, sea winds tugging at their gowns like tidehands trying to lead them back to shore. She turned, studying her sister closely, weighing confidence against the subtle tremble Kirahnae fought to conceal.

"You'll have Veluna at your side. She's guided queens since before either of us could walk. Listen to her wisdom."

Kirahnae tilted her chin defiantly, a stubborn glint returning to her eyes. "I can lead, Miroray. I'm Varanese—I understand our ways."

Miroray steadied herself and said, "Understanding is not the same as ruling, Kira. You'll feel alone—but remember, you're not."

Kirahnae drew a breath, gathering strength. "And protection?"

"Commander Na'shivar stays," Miroray affirmed. "The island guard trusts him—his spear and loyalty are yours."

Kirahnae exhaled slowly, shoulders easing fractionally. "Good. I prefer his honesty."

Miroray smiled faintly. "So do I. Elders will watch, weigh your choices. Some will test you. Show them the iron beneath your silk."

Kirahnae nodded slowly, determination flaring. "And if I fail?"

Miroray leaned closer, voice dropping to a fierce hush. "Then fail boldly. Make even failure fear your name."

Kirahnae straightened, the weight of her sister's faith steadying her. "I'll make you proud."

"You already have." Miroray embraced her briefly—tight, fierce, conveying everything words could not. As she drew back, their eyes met. Neither looked away.

Miroray turned back toward the waiting ships below, but halted suddenly, glancing sharply at Kirahnae.

"Do not forget about the fish harvest at Vael'Sura." Miroray's voice turned quickly practical, worry creeping back in. "And the clans at Kava'tan still expect words of salt in every blessing—"

"Miroray." Kirahnae reached out, catching her sister's wrist gently, interrupting the flood of anxious instructions. "You've told me all of this—three times today, and twice yesterday."

Miroray blinked slowly, irritation warring briefly with affection. "Have I?"

Kirahnae gave her sister a soft, knowing smile. "Every detail. Twice. Possibly three times."

Miroray sighed, shoulders slumping just slightly. "It's only because…"

"Because it matters," Kirahnae finished gently. "I know. Truly. But I have this. And if I don't, Veluna does. And the elders."

Miroray studied her for a long moment. Then she nodded.

"Good," she said. "That's enough."

Kirahnae straightened, shoulders squaring without prompting.

Miroray stepped in and embraced her again—brief, fierce, uncompromising. When she drew back, she smoothed an unruly curl from Kirahnae's brow, then let her hand fall.

"Rule while I'm gone," Miroray said. "Not as my sister. As Queen."

She paused, just long enough to meet Kirahnae's eyes.

Kirahnae swallowed, then lifted her chin. "I will."

"Half a season, little sister. We will celebrate Midswell together, I promise."

"Be careful," Kirahnae said, the words catching despite her effort to keep them steady. "Eldaraine isn't Vara. And when you see Avanna—"

"And when I see Avanna, I'll tell her you miss her."

"Miroray?" Kirahnae's voice barely rose above breath. "I love you."

Miroray held her gaze for a long moment.

"I know," she said. "I love you too."

With a final look, she descended toward the ships below, each step measured, deliberate, already carrying the weight of what waited beyond the horizon.

Kirahnae remained at the top of the coral staircase, shoulders squared, chin lifted.

As Miroray disappeared into the press of sails and salt air, Kirahnae let out a slow breath.

"Safe journey, sister."

Cold rain traced the stone of Castellon, the warmth of an early thaw turning snow to runoff beneath the eaves, the last light of dusk fading from the high windows. In Prince Baldrik's upper chambers, candlelight flickered across a narrow desk and the bare floor beyond. In the hearth, a single log smoldered, fire biting inward as ash gathered beneath it.

Baldrik sat cross-legged on a thick rug, the tome resting open in his lap. Pages lay half-turned, half-forgotten, the parchment rough beneath his fingers. His eyes slipped over the lines without holding—but the margins stayed sharp, crowded with a disciplined hand, angular and precise.

"Temper the fire. Let it refine, not consume."

Not scripture—stern, deliberate. His gaze lingered on the inked script longer than the text itself, returning to it again and again, as if repetition alone might yield something the words refused to give.

Baldrik exhaled and pressed his knuckles to his temple. The chamber felt close. He glanced toward the hearth; the fire hissed, a brief spit of sparks collapsing into ash.

Outside, the rain intensified slightly, against the old castle walls.

Three knocks sounded against the heavy oak door—deliberate, more announcement than request.

Baldrik did not respond.

A second knock followed almost immediately.

"All right," he said at last, irritation edging through the quiet. He shifted, planting a hand on the floor as he rose. The tome slipped from his lap, striking stone with a dull thud as he stood. "I'm coming."

Baldrik reached the door and pulled it open.

Lady Elara Icewind stood just outside, already angled forward as if she had expected it to open sooner. For half a breath, neither of them spoke.

His brows lifted—barely. Surprise, not displeasure. He cleared his throat once, as if catching himself a beat late.

"My lady," he said, then hesitated, glancing down the corridor behind her. Empty. Still, his hand remained on the door, knuckles tightening as if measuring who might be passing.

Elara took the pause as permission.

She stepped inside without waiting to be asked, posture composed, confidence riding close to impropriety. Her gown was darker than her usual palette, the neckline cut low enough to challenge good sense nearly defying it.

Baldrik shifted aside to give her room, stepping back to let her pass. Out of habit more than intent, he pushed the door closed behind her, the latch settling with a final click. His fingers brushed the wood again before he let his hand fall.

Only then did he look at her properly.

Not at the dress. Not where she had hoped his eyes might stray. At her face—searching, curious, faintly guarded.

"I wasn't aware I was receiving company," he said, polite but honest. "Is something wrong?"

"You stood me up," she said, her tone carefully balanced between mild reproof and gentle curiosity. "The Winter Hearth? I invited you."

His mouth twitched, just barely. "Oh, I couldn't find my good gloves."

"Your gloves?" Elara echoed, her face showing doubt.

He glanced away, then back again, the humor thinning. He exhaled and said, "Truth is, I hesitated."

She moved further in, steps soft on stone, deliberate. Her presence shifting the rhythm of the chamber. She had expected deflection—but not distance.

"I didn't take you for thoughtless," she said.

"I wasn't thoughtless," he said. "I was cautious." A beat. "And—if I'm being honest—out of my depth."

She lifted a brow, eyes glinting briefly in the candlelight. "Out of your depth?" She shook her head once. "I meant the invite as a friendship—"

"I know," he said. "And I wanted to go. But being seen beside you—there, like that—would have raised questions I wouldn't know how to answer."

She paused, reassessing, the practiced response she'd prepared slipping sideways. "You were afraid of the wrong eyes," she said.

"That," he said after a beat, "and the fact that my mother and Lord Darkoak would not have approved of the pairing."

Elara blinked. The answer was too honest, too unpolished. A laugh escaped her before she could stop it, surprised and genuine.

"Pairing. Interesting choice of words. But you're not wrong," she said, smiling openly now.

Baldrik picked up the open tome from the floor where he had been sitting and closed it carefully, setting it on a nearby table—not hidden, not offered. The gesture was deliberate, unadorned.

"What were you reading when I knocked?" she asked, glancing curiously at the heavy tome.

"Flamebound texts," he admitted casually, a faint reluctance shading his voice.

She tilted her head slightly, a playful challenge lighting her eyes. "You're not considering becoming a monk, are you?"

He smiled faintly, deflecting her teasing easily. "Nothing so drastic. Just interested in their philosophy."

"Ah," she murmured softly, stepping closer. Her voice dropped to a softer note, playful yet probing. "And here I thought you were about to give up the crown for a life of contemplation."

"Not yet," he replied dryly. "I prefer my contemplation in smaller doses, preferably with wine."

"When I first saw you training," she said, "you were just another boy with a sword. Standing here now, you're… more than that."

"I've seen you in court, heard the things people say," he said. "Until the other day, we'd never spoken. Court's loud. It's hard to tell who anyone is in it. Until recently I only heard the rumors."

He shrugged, once. "You're not what I expected either," he said.

"Oh, how so?" Elara genuinely curious. "What exactly is it you see in me, my Prince?"

Baldrik didn't answer at once. He studied her as if the question deserved it.

"You notice things," he said at last. "Not just what's said—what's avoided. You keep count." A faint, crooked smile touched his mouth. "Most people don't like being seen that clearly. You don't seem to mind it. Or you hide it well."

Her smile held, but something in it tightened.

"You don't break, not where others would. You bend, you adjust… but you don't break." His tone softened, just a fraction. "I think that's rare. And… a little terrifying."

Something flickered—unexpected, and she couldn't quite name it.

He added, "House Icewind matters to you more than anything else."

Now the narrowing of her eyes was deliberate, measured.

"And you?" she asked lightly.

He met her gaze, steady, without heat. "I'm… useful to that. And I'm not blind enough to pretend otherwise." A beat, then the ghost of that same crooked smile. "Though I suspect you'd prefer I said something about your eyes first."

Her composure slipped a fraction before she caught it.

"Is honesty always this charming for you?" she asked, recovering behind a sharper edge.

"Honesty isn't charm," he said, just as gently. "It's just… easier to trust."

Elara studied him carefully, her expression shifting from playful allure toward something more measured.

"Most men prefer charm," she murmured, softer now, genuine despite herself. "They like pretty words and easy smiles."

"Boring," he replied simply, holding her gaze steady. "Words are cheap. Smiles even more so."

She tilted her head slightly, considering him anew. Her voice lowered, carrying genuine interest rather than scripted allure. "Then what impresses you, Prince Baldrik?"

He thought for a moment too long. "I don't know," he said finally. "People who don't dance around what they mean."

Elara searched his face for deception—and found none. The calm steadiness unsettled her more than charm would have.

"Disappointed?"

"No," she said, meeting his eyes openly for the first time, her practiced charm replaced entirely by sincerity. "Just...surprised." She paused, just a heartbeat—but it was long enough for her to realize she'd stopped pretending.

Elara studied him—really studied him. She saw no deception or malice. She didn't see the boy from the training yard. She saw a young man, a young prince, honesty in his eyes.

The fire popped behind them, underscoring the pause.

Baldrik shifted, weight settling unevenly, the silence breaking him first. When he spoke, he hadn't meant to say anything at all.

"Do you ride?"

She blinked, thrown. "Horses?"

"No," he said, flat as stone. "Ducks."

The laugh that escaped her was quick and genuine, gone almost as soon as she realized it had slipped free. "Yes, I ride. I keep a small stable at what's left of the Icewind estate. We still provide for the Crown—last I checked."

Baldrik nodded, gaze dropping for a moment to the book on the side table, then lifting again. For an instant he looked less like a prince and more like a boy weighing whether to ask something he hadn't practiced.

"Silly question," he muttered. Then, after a breath he didn't quite manage to hide, "Would you… like to go riding? Just us. Somewhere quieter."

Elara studied him—not the offer itself, but the plain honesty beneath it. The absence of expectation. The lack of game.

"I'd like that," she said.

He nodded, then looked away, unsettled by how plainly his vulnerability had shown.

"I should go. Goodnight, Prince Baldrik," she said again—gentler this time.

"Baldrik's fine," he replied, eyes drifting back to the hearth as it cracked, sparks lifting and fading.

She lingered a heartbeat at the door. "Then goodnight, Baldrik."

She turned down the hall, composure settling over her shoulders like silk returned to its fold. Three steps in, she slowed.

She slowed after three steps. That had not gone to plan. She had come to snare his attention, not leave with her own in disarray.

Farther down the corridor, tucked into the shadow of an archway, Lord Lanyard Darkoak leaned against the stone, arms folded.

His gaze lingered on her retreating form. Assessing.

Only when she was gone did he shift, mouth tightening briefly before he stepped back into the shadows, leaving the corridor empty again.

The gardens outside Castellon Shield were trimmed with almost excessive care, orderly flower beds precise and symmetrical. So close to First Word Celebration, even the gardens seemed to wait. Faileas stood beneath the drooping branches of a willow, positioned where paths converged but sightlines failed—private without appearing so.

He had chosen this spot deliberately—a gentle haven that contrasted sharply with the subtle shadows of intrigue in which he thrived. Moments later, Serai emerged along the narrow path. Her expression was guarded, her pace measured, eyes already assessing angles and exits. Her dark eyes immediately sought him, narrowing thoughtfully.

"Faileas," she greeted, cautious but controlled, her gaze sweeping the garden before fixing on him. "Your note was rather vague. Should I be worried?"

Faileas inclined his head respectfully, his voice smooth as polished stone. "Not at all, Serai. Merely cautious. These gardens have ears as well as blooms."

She smiled faintly, an edge of skepticism still evident. "Then let's be brief. What do you need from me?"

He produced a small vial from his sleeve and held it where she could see—but not take. The glass was plain and unmarked. "An elixir," he said. "Entirely harmless. It will help ease the queen's moods, calm her anxieties."

Serai did not reach for it. "I've never seen the queen lose control," Serai said.

Faileas's smile was mild, understanding. "She wouldn't. Openly. Royal pride seldom allows for such confessions. But her strain has not gone unnoticed by those closest to her. This is merely a small kindness—one drop per bottle of wine. Simple, discreet, effective."

Serai hesitated, clearly uneasy. Her lips parted, then pressed together again. The mention of the queen's wine had shifted something colder behind her eyes. "Why Lana," Serai asked.

Faileas's expression softened. "Because she is trusted, and she is unnoticed—two essential qualities. A queen's troubles should never become gossip, Serai. Lana's gentle touch ensures it never will."

Serai crossed her arms, wavering slightly. "This is no simple request. If someone were to misunderstand…"

"They won't," Faileas said. "The vial is unlabeled, the substance odorless, tasteless. Lana herself need not know precisely why—only that it's a kindness. I would never place either of you in harm's path."

Serai exhaled slowly, meeting his steady gaze. "You're asking me to risk the queen," Serai said.

"I am," Faileas acknowledged, holding her gaze. "But trust, dear Serai, is the currency we both trade in. Allow me to spend a little now, and repay generously when the time comes."

She studied him in silence, weighing posture, breath, the spaces between his words. At last, she took the vial carefully, holding it lightly in her palm.

"One drop per bottle," she confirmed, almost to herself.

"Precisely," Faileas agreed, offering a reassuring nod. "A calmer queen is a safer queen. For you. For Lana. For the kingdom."

Serai tucked the vial safely away, her gaze still wary but resolved. "Very well. Lana will handle it with care. But Faileas—"

"I understand," he said, meeting her eyes firmly. "No harm will come of it. Not from the vial."

She regarded him, a sigh escaping her lips. "I hope your word is as good as you say."

"Better," Faileas promised, as she turned to leave, he produced two silver coins and pressed them into her hand. "For errands," he said. "Nothing more." Serai hesitated, then closed her fingers around them.

He watched her disappear down the garden path, coins safely tucked away. Whatever warmth had surfaced was gone almost before it registered, leaving only the work of calculation.

Away from the Shield, tucked into the lower quarters of Castellon, the Iron Cup stank of smoke, sweat, and wet wool. Every table groaned—beneath elbows, stained plates, or men trying to drown their troubles in sour ale. Near the hearth, a bard with thinning hair and less talent strummed a mournful ballad about a fisherman's widow. No one listened.

Rodrik sat in a shadowed corner, nursing a tankard of Ale that tasted like it had been wrung from a moldy tavern cloth.

He took a sip, grimaced.

"This isn't ale," he muttered. "This is what happens when water loses a fight."

A tavern wench passed, hips swaying like she was paid to pretend she still cared. She stopped beside him, leaning just close enough for him to catch the lilac perfume—cheap, and doing a poor job of masking the scent of boiled onions.

"Care for another, handsome?" she purred, fingers tracing the rim of his cup. "Or something with a bit more… warmth?"

Rodrik gave her a look—flat as a lake under frost.

"Only thing less appealing than your offer is this ale," he said. "Try the bard. He looks lonely."

She blinked—offended, confused. Then shrugged, muttered something about northern manners, and moved on without another glance.

He returned to brooding. The firelight danced on his empty plate. Outside, the wind scraped at the shutters—like it wanted in on the secrets. Winterfall was losing its grip, and it was going out fighting.

In a corner, a thin man counted copper coins one by one, each clink landing heavy, when he ran out of coin, he scooped them back up and counted again, as if he was trying to convince himself he had more in his hand than the previous count.

A shadow dropped into the seat across the table. Uninvited.

Rodrik didn't flinch. But his hand shifted to the knife handle in his belt—his pulse quickened just slightly, muscles coiled like wire, ready.

The man was cloaked, his face half-lit by the fire. Sharp lines. Emerald-green eyes. Rings that shimmered just enough to make a man distrust him instantly.

"Rodrik Stormviðr," the man said. "Your reputation walks louder than your footsteps."

"You've got five seconds to vanish, shadow," Rodrik said. "Or I decorate this table with your teeth."

The man smiled. "Charming."

He slid a silk tied scroll across the table. "This is for you."

Rodrik didn't touch it. "Who are you?"

"Alerick."

"That supposed to mean something to me?"

"Depends who you ask," Alerick said. "To you? Just the messenger. But *she* knew you were coming. And that I was to greet you when you arrived. So I have."

Rodrik's jaw flexed. "Who's 'she'?"

"Not your concern," Alerick said, with not so much as a blink.

Rodrik's hand twitched—closer to the knife.

"But," Alerick continued, "she's not your enemy. Neither am I. Open the scroll."

Rodrik eyed the scroll. "What is it?"

"A gift," Alerick said, like it cost him nothing.

Rodrik's jaw tightened. He picked up the scroll, and untied the thread then unrolled it—slow, deliberate.

He read in silence.

Then again—slower this time.

At the bottom of the scroll was a seal, the wax was deep red. The sigil—a cunning weasel entwined around sheaves of grain. And a signature, heavy-handed. Impatient. Like the man who scrawled it across the velum.

–Lord Circus Valen.

When he finally looked up, the casual menace was gone.

What replaced it wasn't fear. It was calculation.

He let the silence thicken—measured, careful. Men died for less clarity than this.

Rodrik did not know the scrolls originator, Lord Caerlyn, but Circus Valen. That name he knew. That name—was a debt unpaid.

"So," Rodrik said, voice dry. "The south's eating itself. Anyone with eyes can see that. It has Valen's name on it. And it stinks worse than your cologne."

"You flatter me. I don't wear any."

"Figures."

Rodrik scanned the scroll again.

Treason, tied up with a bow.

Enough to hang ten men—if there were ten men left in the capital worth trusting.

"Scroll's real?"

"Tied with silk and sealed with gold," Alerick said. "But yes—real. As real as the rot it describes. Valen's not just crooked. He's cutting deals behind the king's back. Grain to House Caerlyn. Coin to the wrong nobles. Talk of 'new blood.' You think Castellon's walls are strong? They're held up by gossip and wishful thinking."

Rodrik let silence settle, soft as ash. "Why give it to me?"

Alerick's tone shifted—just slightly.

"Because you're not just a scout. You're Eirik's blade. You're not hunting rumors. You're weighing weakness. Measuring the spine of this realm."

Rodrik rolled the scroll—slowly. Methodically. Like it might cut

His fingers stilled on the scroll.

"What do you want?"

Alerick leaned in, voice low.

"I want the kingdom intact. Banner colors don't interest me, or which corpse gets planted beneath the throne to make it happen."

Rodrik smirked. "So, you're a patriot."

"I'm a realist," Alerick said. "There's a difference."

Rodrik tapped the scroll against the table.

"If I believe this—and that's a tall 'if'—what am I supposed to do with it?"

"You go north."

Rodrik snorted. "I just came from there."

"I know. Hravnskot. But I mean *further.* Over the Boulderfists. Into the true north."

Rodrik arched a brow. "To what—rally the spirits of the snow?"

Alerick didn't smile this time. His voice cooled.

"There are people there. Old blood. The Northmen. They don't fly banners. They don't kneel to crowns. But they remember debt. And honor. And how to make war without gold."

Rodrik's brow lowered—just slightly, his mouth curled faintly. "I know the Nuvareki. They trade with Hravnskot, and on their own terms."

He leaned forward, eyes narrowing thoughtfully. "But what makes you think they'd speak with me? They're not known for welcoming outsiders—even northern ones."

Alerick's voice dropped—just above the crackle of firelight.

"Because you are the Stormwalker."

Rodrik said nothing, his fingers stilled on the table, jaw tightening at the name, as his stare held, steady as iron.

Alerick's eyes caught the firelight, glinting with quiet intensity.

"Go north. Find Arqviqta Vika Sullunavk."

"I know of her." Rodrik's eyes narrowed thoughtfully, studying the man before him. "Why should I meet with her?"

"To make allies," Alerick answered without hesitation. "Strengthen the north. Then show that strength clearly to Eldaraine—to King Harald himself."

Rodrik focused his gaze, suspicion edging his voice. "Whose idea is this, truly? I doubt it's yours, shadow."

Alerick smiled faintly—openly admitting the truth without a trace of discomfort.

"My employer sees advantage in northern tensions. A modest disturbance, a rumor of unity among your people. Nothing more."

Rodrik's eyes darkened. "I've had war. I'm not longing for it again."

"Not a war," Alerick clarified smoothly. "A distraction. Just enough noise on the mountain to force Castellon's eyes north. She gains time and space unnoticed—and your people gain strength, unity, respect."

Rodrik studied him skeptically. "And if Harald doesn't blink? If a distraction becomes a war?"

Alerick met his gaze squarely. "Then don't let it. Go north, shore up your allies, strengthen your defenses. Give Castellon pause. You don't want war, you want security—make them believe a united north is too costly to provoke."

Rodrik exhaled slowly, "And your employer? What does she gain?"

"Time," Alerick said quietly.

Rodrik's gaze dropped to the scroll again. Just for a moment. His thumb brushed the lower edge where the red wax seal had been pressed—Lord Valen's mark, clean and unmistakable.

Rodrik's expression hardened, his voice dropping into a rough, decisive growl. "I'll go north—but if blades come out, it'll be because there's no other choice and on my terms. Not because you or your employer say so."

Alerick shrugged slightly, voice calm and indifferent. "Peace or war—it's leverage either way. Just make sure the north is loud enough to draw King Harald's attention."

Rodrik tucked the scroll away, eyes cold with warning. His fingers lingered a moment longer than necessary—then curled into fists beneath the table. "If this is a game…"

"You'll kill me," Alerick finished for him, unfazed. "Probably slowly. Come now, Stormviðr, you're not the first person to threaten me."

Rodrik didn't smile. "You're either mad," he said, "or exactly what this realm deserves."

"Maybe both," Alerick said, rising with a quiet clink of rings. "Good luck, Stormviðr. The north is going to like you."

Alerick stood next to the table, offering a final nod before turning and walking steadily out of the pub, his departure as quiet and deliberate as his arrival.

Rodrik watched him leave, the Iron Cup closing in around the space he'd vacated. He was no stranger to tension—he wore it like a blade, familiar and sharp—but this sat heavier. Not fear. Weight.

A strengthened north mattered. Not to spill blood—but to stand hard enough that the south thought twice before raising banners again.

Rodrik climbed the creaking stairs to his rented room above the tavern's noise. The oak door shut behind him with a final thud.

He sat, drew the half-written parchment closer, and dipped his quill. The candle guttered. He waited for the words to settle, then wrote to Chieftain Eirik.

"I have finished in Eldaraine—I will return to Hravnskot. But I go first to Qilauriq, to seek out Arqviqta Vika Sallunavk. Allies will be our strength, unity our shield. I will send word again upon my arrival. Until then, stay watchful.

—R"

Rodrik folded the parchment and pressed the seal. The wax spread gray beneath his thumb.

He held the letter a moment longer than necessary, then slid it into his pack.

The north would rise united—or it would fall divided. And some debts would not be left unanswered. Whatever followed would be answered on his feet, not in ink.

Three days had passed since Rodrik left Castellon behind. Alerick's words still rang in his ears; the scent of the Iron Cup clung to his clothes; the taste of truth lingered, bitter.

The road north had been quiet. Frost clung to the fields in stubborn patches, and the trees lining the old trade route had not yet shaken free of winter's memory. Rodrik traveled without urgency, but not without purpose. Each step carried him closer to the old life he had once buried—and to the man he had tried to leave behind.

On the morning of the third day, as sunlight broke pale and thin across the horizon, he crested a familiar rise. Below lay the same village he'd passed through on his first descent into Eldaraine.

The village hadn't changed. Not in any way that mattered.

Same lopsided signs. Same patchy roofs clinging stubbornly to rafters. Same dogs half-barking at nothing in particular. Smoke curled from chimneys as if time had simply circled back on itself.

Rodrik walked into it with the road still clinging to his boots. The wind here came from the north now—colder, sharper, full of unfinished sentences.

He headed straight for the bakery—if it could still be called that. It was really just a crooked lean-to tacked onto the front of a clay-walled house, with a slate chimney that coughed more than it breathed.

Gina Three Loafs was already at her shop, propping open the crooked shutters with the heel of her palm when she spotted him.

Rodrik's mouth twitched at the corner—a rare, brief echo of fondness he didn't bother to hide.

"Oi! There's me big 'andsome stranger!" she called, voice bright as ever. "Come back 'cause ya missed me bread, or me loaves?"

Rodrik let the ghost of a smile crease his face. "Could be both," he replied simply, lifting a hand in greeting.

Gina stood in the doorway of her shop, arms braced against the frame, apron already dusted with flour. The sleeves of her dress were rolled past her elbows, and a streak of dough marked one cheek like a badge of mischief.

"Still got that charm," Rodrik added, pausing at the threshold.

"An' you still smell like a man wot's fought the wind an' lost," she grinned. "Come in then. Long road ahead, I reckon?"

He nodded, his voice measured. "Farther north yet. Need provisions before the trail grows lean."

"Ya came to the right woman, luv."

Inside, the little shop was warm, filled with the scent of fresh crust and sweet spices. She waved him toward the counter where two loaves—crisp, dark, and still steaming—waited on a wooden board.

Rodrik selected both. "These'll do."

“A man o' good taste,” she said, then reached beneath the counter and produced a cloth bundle. The scent hit him instantly—sticky fruit and browned sugar.

“Pastries?” he asked plainly, raising a skeptical eyebrow.

“Fresh batch, luv. Ripe fig an' spiced 'oney. Lil' somethin' for the long climb.”

Rodrik shook his head slightly. “The bread is enough.”

“Nonsense,” Gina said firmly, wrapping three pastries into a linen square despite his protest. “Can’t 'ave ya starvin' out there on that long road.”

She leaned closer, voice lowering despite the cheer. “Picked a fine day t’return, didn’t ya? King’s lads came through ’fore dawn. Drank half the well dry an’ grumbled it weren’t wine.”

Rodrik glanced once toward the banners. “Trouble?”

“Not yet,” she said. “But folk don’t fancy soldiers this far north. They don’t stay polite long, ya get me?”

Gina added the small bundle of pastries despite his protest.

“For the road.” She said.

Rodrik met her eyes. “If they give you trouble—”

She snorted softly. “Oh don’tcha worry now. I’ll outlast ’em. Always do.”

“No charge,” she added, voice softenin'. “Jus' so long as ya come back an' visit ol' Gina—an' tell me if ya find any nobles worth the trouble along the way.” She winked.

Rodrik looked at her, and for a moment the long road, the silence, the blood yet to be spilled—none of it reached him.

Rodrik gave a brief nod, his voice sure. “You have my word.”

“Good,” she smiled, already reachin' for another round o' dough. “Now off wiv ya, before I bake somefink else ya pretend not ta want.”

He tipped his head in thanks, stepping out into the morning sun with warm bread in one arm. As he walked away, Rodrik hoped that if he returned with war, Gina Three Loafs and her bakery would be overlooked by its harsh gaze.

The path beyond the village sloped gently northward, curling through frostbitten grass and bramble-laced fence lines. Rodrik walked on, boots crunching over the rutted track where frost lingered in the shadows—familiar enough now to walk with his thoughts elsewhere.

It wasn't far—less than an hour before he saw it again: a lonely rise overlooking the narrow streambed, and atop it, the abandoned homestead.

He approached with the caution of memory, not fear. The door still hung loose on rusted iron hinges, bloated by years of rot.

Moss had crept further up the stone foundation, threaded through cracks like veins of green in gray flesh. Rainwater dripped steadily from the sagging thatch, marking time with soft, rhythmic taps.

Rodrik ducked beneath the crooked lintel, stepping into the hollow dark of memory. The air smelled of dust and wood gone soft with time. Nothing stirred but the faint hum of wind threading through broken boards.

He crossed to the far wall and dragged the broken bench aside, revealing the wooden trunk beneath. Dust rose like old breath as he pried the lid open, hinges groaning in protest. Inside, everything was as he left it—folded neatly, purposefully sealed away. His past, waiting for him. Beneath layers of oilcloth lay the old tunic—storm-gray and wolf-trimmed—and beneath that, his axe.

The grip was worn smooth by time and use. The twin blades were clean, oiled, and sharp as memory.

He drew it from its wrappings, fingers curling around the leather—familiar, weathered smooth by years of callused hands. It felt like shaking hands with an old friend—one who knew all his secrets, and asked no questions.

The axe wasn't just a weapon. It was a legacy etched in iron, handed down not through blood, but through survival.

Every scratch told a tale.

Rodrik set the bread and pastries aside carefully, his movements deliberate and respectful. He slipped the traveling cloak from his shoulders. Stripped down to his linen and pulled on the old tunic. It slipped over his shoulders as if no time had passed. He inhaled deeply, the leather scented with ash and pine. It settled comfortably, effortlessly, a second skin that fit as naturally as breathing.

He slung the axe across his back with practiced ease, the bindings instinctive.

A breath escaped him.

Not relief. Not regret.

Readiness.

Outside, the wind had shifted, carrying with it the icy breath of distant mountains.

Rodrik stood at the threshold, his gaze fixed north. Eldaraine lay behind him—heavy with decay, its corruption as subtle as rust gnawing at iron. He knew the rot well. It had a name now. And names could be cut out—if a man was willing to draw steel.

Ahead stretched a long road—winding, uncertain. His path led into the heart of the Tuhkralin Tundra, to the stark lands of the Nuvareki. Their truths were clear and unforgiving, and Rodrik trusted that. Eldaraine twisted itself beneath veiled intentions, but among the Nuvareki, words cut clean as northern ice.

He took a steadying breath, stepping from the ruins into the crisp mountain air, feeling it sweep away lingering doubts like dead leaves. The familiar heft of the axe at his back spoke more clearly than any vow. This time, he would not glance backward.

There was no longer any need to hide.

PART II

CHAPTER ELEVEN

Morning had risen clear over the western hills, and behind Castellon Shield, the royal stables stirred to life. Dust danced in the angled light, and grooms moved quickly, speaking low—royal horses didn't care for loud voices.

Baldrik waited by the east stall, dressed in plain riding leathers, a sword strapped to his belt—not the ceremonial one. The real one. The grooms knew better than to ask why he was there again.

He hated waiting—it gave thoughts time to surface, and this morning, they were louder than usual.

He stroked the neck of a dapple-gray mare, her ears flicking at the sound of footsteps behind him.

"You're early," Elara said, stepping through the stable doors. She was dressed simply—riding blouse, fitted breeches, her long cloak clasped in silver at her throat. A saddlebag hung over one shoulder.

"I said 'morning.' You thought I meant court morning. I meant real morning," Baldrik replied, glancing back. "The sun's up. You're already late."

She rolled her eyes. "You're charming when you pretend to be humble. Just enough to make me wonder if there's a real man buried somewhere beneath the prince."

"I'm charming when I'm asleep. The rest of the day's hit or miss."

Her horse was already saddled beside his—cream coat, silver mane. As usual. Noble, temperamental. Fitting.

Elara dropped the saddlebag into her mount's satchel and patted the horse's flank, checking the straps with practiced familiarity. "I brought lunch."

Baldrik raised a brow. "Did you cook it?"

"Would that be a problem?"

"Only if you poisoned it. Then I'd know you really were falling for me."

She gave him a playful glare, then swung up into the saddle—only afterward realizing she'd smiled before she meant to.

He mounted without fanfare. Together, they rode out past the city's western edge, into the low hills where wild lavender grew and the grass swayed in the morning breeze—a route both horses seemed to know without guidance.

It wasn't a fast ride—nor slow. The kind of ride that didn't need a destination, only time.

They rode for some time through gentle hills, where early spring grass brushed against leather boots, lavender scent mingling with the metallic tang of rain not yet given leave to fall.

Baldrik kept the pace unhurried, content to let the quiet stretch.

"I hated these rides as a child," he said eventually. "Too quiet. Too clean. No one to yell at."

Elara glanced over. "And now?"

He smirked. "I think I hate them less."

"High praise."

He shrugged. "We princes measure in small mercies." Baldrik

hesitated a moment, his gaze distant as memory overtook him. "My father used to take me riding when I was young. He'd often bring my cousin along."

Elara looked at him curiously. "Cousin?" she asked, her voice carefully neutral.

He nodded slowly. "I think so, maybe. Though I haven't seen him since I was a boy. He was older—I don't even remember his name. One day my mother met us as we returned; she was furious at my father about something. After that, it was only ever the two of us."

"And you haven't seen him since?" she asked gently.

"No," he admitted. "Strange. I hadn't remembered him until now."

They rode on for some time, each lost in their own thoughts.

They passed a crooked tree; its branches twisted like the fingers of an old man. Beyond it, a copse opened to reveal a shallow stream and a flat patch of sun-warmed stone.

Elara slowed her horse and swung down with practiced ease. Baldrik followed without needing to be signaled, already reaching for his reins as if the pause had been agreed upon long before it happened.

She opened one of her saddle bags and pulled out a cloth-wrapped bundle and a dark glass bottle, movements unhurried, familiar.

"Peace offering," she said, holding the bottle aloft—tone light, ritual in the words whether she meant it or not.

He raised a brow. "We were fighting?"

"Not yet."

She uncorked the bottle with a pop. The scent of fruit and spice drifted into the air.

Baldrik blinked. "That smells like money."

"Firewine. From Vara."

"You brought a fortune to a picnic."

"I brought the right wine to the right company."

He took the bottle, eyed it like it might explode, then drank. A breeze stirred the grass, cool against the warmth of the Firewine. It burned sweet—then bitter.

"Not bad," he said.

"That's all I get?"

"I'm trying not to sound impressed."

"Failing," she teased, sipping from the bottle.

He didn't argue.

They talked more, lighter this time, the conversation drifting the way it tended to on these rides. She asked about his childhood. He dodged. He asked about hers. She dodged better.

"Tell me," she said at last, "do you ever think about it?"

Baldrik frowned. "Think about what?"

"The crown."

He looked away toward the water, jaw tightening, as if weighing whether to answer at all.

Then he looked at her—not smiling now.

"I think about what it takes," he said.

"And?"

"And I don't know if I have it. Or want it."

Elara tilted her head. "You say that like you're choosing between titles."

"I'm choosing between futures," he said.

A pause.

She opened her mouth to press—but he cut in first, gently.

"I've been reading the Flamebound texts," he said casually. "Kælric gave me a few. Thought I could use the discipline." He hesitated. "The texts don't preach," Baldrik added after a breath. "They press."

Elara blinked. "Religious discipline?" She sounded curious, not surprised.

He shrugged. "Call it academic curiosity. It's not all prayers and penance. Some of it's about purpose. Balance. What burns and what purifies."

She studied him.

"You're not the boy I expected." She said it lightly—then realized she meant it more than she intended.

"I'm not sure I am either," he said. "But I'm trying to figure it out."

The words weren't defensive. They weren't jokes.

She looked away, caught off guard by his earnestness.

"We should head back," he said, sensing the shift in her mood with the ease of someone who had learned when to speak—and when not to. He rose smoothly, offering her a hand.

The ride back was quieter, each lost in their own thoughts. The horses took the rise without urging until they crested the last hill overlooking a small village nestled among barley fields.

Baldrik's brow furrowed, eyes narrowing.

Something was off—movement that didn't belong.

People moved with purpose through the muddied streets—turning corners, doubling back, scanning doorways and field edges. Concern, not panic—but wrong all the same.

Then came the sound of raised voices—calling a name, distant but clear, carried on the wind.

Baldrik spurred his horse forward. "Come."

Elara followed close behind, her cloak snapping as the tension below seemed to pull them in.

"What happened?" Baldrik called, pulling up near a cluster of villagers gathered at the well.

A woman turned toward him, eyes wide—panic there, sharp and immediate.

"My daughter!" she gasped, her voice breaking. "She's gone—wandered off this morning, into the woods near Blackstone Ravine. We can't find her. Flames, we've searched everywhere!"

"Sylvie!" she called again, the name catching in her throat as if it hurt to say. "My little Sylvie…"

Baldrik dismounted at once, his gaze steady. "Sylvie, is it? How old is she?"

Elara said nothing. Her eyes followed him—concern, certainly, and something else she did not name.

"Just seven," the woman sobbed, clutching her apron. "Please, Your Highness, she's all I have."

He turned quickly, eyes scanning the faces around him with the ease of someone used to being obeyed outside the court. "We'll find her. Gather torches and ropes. Form small groups and spread out. Stay within shouting distance. Check every ditch, every thicket."

The villagers hesitated, uncertain. Baldrik's voice hardened, not with anger but authority. "Now!"

They scattered into action, buoyed by his command. Baldrik turned swiftly to Elara. "Stay here. Organize the village center. Keep everyone calm and ready in case we need supplies or help."

Elara raised an eyebrow, mouth tightening with resolve. "I can help search." She already knew he would say no.

"No," Baldrik said firmly, already striding toward the edge of the village. He paused, glancing back at her, his expression softening just slightly—an unguarded flicker she'd begun to recognize on these rides. "I need you here, Elara. You can do this better than I can."

She hesitated, then gave a brisk nod. "Be careful."

Baldrik's lips curled in a quick, reassuring smile. "Always am."

He took the lead, villagers falling into groups behind him as they moved swiftly toward the tree line. Meltwater still darkened the earth beneath their boots, and the low sun of early Bloomrise stretched long, restless shadows across the ground. Elara watched him go, something tightening low in her chest—unsettling, uninvited.

She saw the man beneath the crown—not the boy she'd once assumed she could maneuver, but a man who moved others without force and carried responsibility as if it had always been his to bear.

She clenched her fists, then turned to meet the expectant faces that looked to her for guidance. "Fetch blankets, food, and fresh water," she called, her voice steadying. "We must be ready when they return with Sylvie. Hurry now."

As the villagers hurried to follow her instructions, Elara drew a deep breath, watching Baldrik disappear into the growing shadows, feeling the weight of something she had not planned for—and did not immediately reject.

Turning her attention back to the anguished mother, Elara approached and took the woman's trembling hands in both of her own—a gesture practiced, steady, learned over years of necessity rather than kindness. "He'll find her," she said, steady and clear. "Prince Baldrik won't return without Sylvie."

The woman looked up at Elara, eyes rimmed red with tears, desperation clinging to every word. "But she's so small, my lady. The woods—they're vast, and night's coming soon."

Elara squeezed her hands once, firm. "Listen to me," she said. "Where was she last seen?"

The mother swallowed hard. "By the barley rows," she said. "Near the old marker stone."

Elara nodded. "Good. Stay here," she said, already turning. "Someone keep her with the lanterns. Don't let her follow—she'll only slow him."

Baldrik moved swiftly through the woods, villagers fanning out on either side, torches flaring against damp bark and new growth, their light catching on fresh buds and slick roots alike. "Sylvie!" Baldrik called loudly, his voice clear and firm, echoing among the thick trunks and dense underbrush. "Sylvie, can you hear me?"

The villagers followed suit, their voices weaving through the trees, a chorus of anxious hope carried through damp leaves and budding branches. They pressed forward, methodically searching every shadowed hollow, every twisted cluster of roots and vines.

Baldrik paused briefly at the edge of a narrow trail, crouching low to inspect faint impressions in the softened earth, still dark with meltwater. Small footprints. Fresh.

"This way!" he called, waving the villagers to follow. They moved quickly, urgency sharpening their movements as the fading daylight pressed them forward.

"Sylvie!" Baldrik's voice rose again, strong and reassuring, echoing through the deepening twilight. "We're coming, Sylvie! Just hold on!"

Ahead, the darkness of Blackstone Ravine loomed beneath towering cliffs, where winter runoff still ran unseen. Baldrik felt a chill ripple through him—not from fear, but from the sudden, narrowing focus that came whenever someone else's life depended on him.

Baldrik took a steadying breath and stepped toward the darkened ravine.

Inside the ravine, towering walls of dark stone rose on either side, cloaking the path in shadow. Damp moss clung to the stone where new growth fought for purchase. A cool, damp chill hung in the air, the kind that lingered long after winter had officially loosened its grip. Small stones skittered beneath boots, echoing against the stone.

Baldrik slowed as a faint sound reached him—a small, broken sob, nearly lost beneath the rush of water and wind.

"Sylvie?" he called, pitching his voice clear.

A small, frightened voice echoed faintly back, trembling in desperation. "I'm here! I'm stuck, help me, please!"

"Stay where you are, Sylvie!" Baldrik shouted firmly, his pulse racing with relief and resolve. He turned swiftly to the villagers behind him, urgency sharpening his expression—but not his voice. "Over here! She's down here—hurry!"

He moved quickly but carefully toward the sound. Villagers gathered close, torches pushing back the dark. Hope surged, sharp and sudden.

Baldrik reached the edge of a narrow crevasse and knelt, lowering himself so he wasn't towering over the shadows below. Sylvie looked up at him, her small face smudged with dirt, a shallow cut on her forehead that looked worse than it was. She trembled slightly, eyes wide with relief and lingering fear.

"Are you hurt, Sylvie?" he called, keeping his voice steady. "Can you move?"

"My ankle hurts," she sniffled, voice wavering slightly. "I can move, but I can't climb out."

Baldrik nodded. "My name's Baldrik, Sylvie," he said. "I'm here with the villagers. We're going to get you out and take you back to your mother. Just stay calm, alright?" He shifted slightly as he spoke, the torchlight catching the edge of a signet ring on his hand—noticed by no one who mattered. "Rope," he said, extending his hand behind him without breaking eye contact with the frightened child, already trusting someone would answer.

A villager stepped forward swiftly, uncoiling a length of sturdy rope and passing it to Baldrik. He took it, testing its strength with a sharp tug before handing it to another man standing beside him.

"Tie this around your waist," he instructed. "Lower it down slowly, and carefully. We don't want to startle her."

"Yes, Your Highness," the villager responded quickly, securing the rope and carefully beginning to lower it into the crevasse.

Baldrik knelt at the edge, settling into stillness so Sylvie could see his face clearly, unhurried, solid. "Sylvie, listen carefully," he said in a calm, reassuring voice. "Grab onto the rope tightly with your hands and walk your feet against the side as we pull you up. Understand?"

Sylvie nodded bravely, though fear still shone in her wide eyes. "I'll try."

"Good," Baldrik said. "Hold on tight. We've got you."

The rope reached her, and Sylvie gripped it firmly, small knuckles white with determination. "I'm ready," she called up shakily.

"Pull gently," Baldrik instructed the villagers, rising to his feet and gripping the rope alongside them. Together, they carefully began to draw Sylvie upward, the girl's feet scrabbling gently against the damp stone as she slowly ascended, the rope firm in practiced hands.

"Just a little further, Sylvie," Baldrik called. "Keep holding tight."

With a final gentle heave, Sylvie emerged over the edge of the crevasse, and Baldrik reached out at once, grasping her firmly beneath the arms and drawing her onto solid ground with practiced care.

He knelt again, inspecting her briefly, movements calm and economical. The shallow cut on her forehead had stopped bleeding. Aside from dirt, scrapes and a tender ankle, she appeared unharmed.

"You gave your village quite a scare," he said lightly. "But you're safe now."

Sylvie wrapped her arms around his neck without hesitation. "Thank you," she whispered. She leaned back slightly, eyes wide with awe. "You're really the Prince?"

Baldrik chuckled and nodded. "I am."

Sylvie glanced down at herself, then back up at him. "I'm all dirty."

Baldrik smiled once and lifted her into his arms as if it were the most natural thing in the world.

"Hold tight, little star," he said. "Let's get you to your mother. She must be terribly worried."

Sylvie nestled gratefully against him, a small sigh escaping her as the villagers closed in around them, anxious faces loosening as the group turned back toward the village.

Elara stood at the village center, the villagers' anxious murmurs pressing in around her like surf. She exhaled slowly, only then realizing she'd been holding her breath. She had kept the villagers busy and ordered, but her gaze kept drifting to the shadowed tree line.

The glow of torches appeared first, flickering in the growing dusk, followed by figures emerging from the woods. Relief hit her hard as Baldrik emerged from the trees with Sylvie safe in his arms.

A cheer broke loose, sudden and loud, washing fear out of the square. Elara watched, transfixed, as Sylvie's mother broke from the crowd, running swiftly toward Baldrik and her daughter, tears of relief streaming openly down her face.

"Sylvie! My darling Sylvie!" the mother cried, reaching eagerly toward her child.

Baldrik lowered Sylvie into her mother's arms and stepped back without ceremony, already yielding the moment back to where it belonged. The mother clutched her daughter fiercely, sobbing, pressing kisses against the little girl's dirt-smudged face.

"Oh, my brave little girl, thank the Flame you're safe!" she whispered.

Sylvie nestled close, smiling despite her exhaustion and relief, eyes glowing with trust and adoration as she glanced back at Baldrik.

Elara found herself watching Baldrik as villagers gathered around him, thanking him, touching his arm, speaking all at once—as if they trusted him without needing to be told to. There was something altered in how he stood—no performance, no hesitation—only ease.

He smiled at each villager, accepting their gratitude with steady composure, answering where needed, listening where it mattered. His eyes were bright, sincere—more open than she had expected. Something in her tightened at the sight of it, sharp and inconvenient.

Baldrik looked up, catching Elara's gaze through the joyful chaos. His eyes softened, a small, genuine smile touching his lips—unguarded. Her heart kicked once, sharp and unwelcome, and she forced herself to hold his gaze as if nothing had changed—because it shouldn't have.

She drew a slow, calming breath, forcing composure back into her expression. This was a complication—unexpected and unwelcome, and therefore dangerous. She looked away, too late, aware that whatever she'd just seen could not be unseen.

Elara swallowed, aware the careful lines she'd drawn for herself were no longer holding.

Sylvie nestled against her mother, a small smile brightening her dirt-smudged face as she turned, eyes wide with wonder. "Mama, he saved me—just like the princes in the old stories!" she said, casting a glowing look up at Baldrik.

"He called me 'little star', Mama. I like him."

Her mother laughed through her tears, cradling Sylvie close. "Yes, my sweet. A real prince indeed."

Elara stepped forward through the villagers, a small smile touching her lips as she approached. Sylvie looked up, curious eyes studying her.

"Hello, Sylvie," Elara greeted warmly, crouching slightly to meet the child's gaze. "I'm Elara."

Sylvie's eyes sparkled with innocent curiosity. "Are you going to marry the prince?"

Caught slightly off guard, Elara chuckled, her cheeks coloring faintly. "I don't know about that," she admitted, shooting a playful glance toward Baldrik.

Baldrik's face reddened, and he cleared his throat, embarrassed but taking it in stride.

The villagers around them laughed warmly, sharing smiles and nods as Baldrik and Elara exchanged amused glances. They said their goodbyes amidst waves and grateful farewells, then moved toward their waiting horses.

They mounted and turned back toward Castellon, the village fading behind them into twilight. They rode in silence for a time, each with their own thoughts. A breeze stirred, brushing their cheeks, carrying with it a trace of the village's laughter into the cooling air.

After a while, Elara spoke. "What you did back there," she said, careful and measured. "It mattered."

Baldrik glanced at her, resolve etched into his face, like a promise left unspoken. "It wasn't duty," he replied. "It was just what people should do."

Elara inclined her head, saying no more, and they rode on in silence.

Upon reaching Castellon, they returned their horses to the stable hands, walking slowly toward the castle entrance. At the door, Elara paused and turned to face him. She looked at him—really looked—then stepped closer and pressed a brief kiss to his cheek.

"Thank you for today."

She hesitated just a heartbeat longer, then added, "We should go in; the council meeting will be starting soon."

Baldrik shook his head slightly, a gentle, thoughtful smile touching his lips. "I won't be attending. I think I'll go for a walk instead. Goodnight, Elara."

Before she could respond, he turned and moved away, leaving her standing there. Elara watched him go for a moment. The warmth of the moment lingered—too much so. It had gone well. Far too well. The thought tightened something in her chest.

She turned and hurried inside, already rebuilding walls she had never meant to test.

The lamps had been lit in Castellon Shield, burning warmly and casting long, steady shadows across the King's study. King Harald Avahn Thornsword stood at the edge of the table, staring down at his kingdom like a warden taking measure of a realm already straining.

The map stretched across the oak, pinned at the corners with iron weights. Candlelight bled gold over its inked rivers, catching on tooth-edge mountain ranges.

Every marked road and river told a story he had no time to reread.

The Ironfists cut the kingdom like a scar. Beyond them, Hravnskot brooded. The border here was theoretical—no more real than the promises the council made behind each other's backs. It wasn't the mountains that kept them apart.

It was the people beyond them—and what they were willing to cross for.

Beyond Hravnskot—past the Boulderfist mountain range—ice and the Northmen.

He traced the Ironback Mountains with a callused fingertip, resting it just above a sketched ridge. His eyes slid east to the newer ink—Aynaraq—where the Keshin Barrier ran like a blunt stitch along the frontier. Reports were thin. Stone held, for now. Walls always failed after men did.

Bandits in the south. Raiders bold enough to torch Ashbriar's outer farms. The silence from the Mayor since the fire gnawed at him—uncertainty he found harder to stomach than outright betrayal.

Either he'd fled or been flayed—both possibilities unsettled him.

His mouth twisted grimly. "Borders don't hold—steel does," he said under his breath to no one, the words striking the silence like a hammer on cooled iron. "Cutting our grain lines and torching fields… Rats are getting teeth. And someone's feeding them."

A knock tapped his chamber door.

"Enter," he said, not looking up.

The door creaked, and a boy stepped in. Gangly arms, ceremonial livery too big at the shoulders. The royal crest of King Thornsword sat crooked on his chest.

"Your Grace," the page said, voice barely above a breath, "the council waits in the great hall. All but Lady Icewind, who has been delayed. And… Lord Valen sent his steward. Sir Rennic Stride."

The page hesitated, uncertain if he'd chosen the right title for Lord Valen's man.

Harald didn't move. His gaze lingered on the stretch of wild, unlabeled terrain north of the Boulderfist Mountains.

"Of course he did," he said under his breath. "Lord Valen hasn't left Goldacre in years. I doubt he still remembers how a horse smells."

The boy hesitated, clearly puzzled by the King's humor.

"And Stride—how charming. Nothing like beginning a council with ink and blood on your boots."

The boy stared back, not understanding.

Harald waved a hand, then paused. "And the prince? Where is he?"

"After his ride with Lady Icewind, Your Grace, he was seen walking toward the Grand Citadel."

Harald's brow furrowed, just slightly. The boy was always walking toward something these days. Always looking.

The king grunted—whether with approval or concern, even he didn't seem sure.

"Run along," Harald said. "Tell Lord Darkoak I'll be along presently. Let Rennic polish something while he waits."

"Yes, Your Grace."

The boy bowed low, stumbled once, and backed out the door like it might bite him.

Alone again, Harald exhaled through his nose and leaned forward, both fists braced against the table's edge. His knuckles brushed the southern coast of the map.

If it's Valen feeding the fire, we'll smell the rot soon enough. And if it's someone worse…

He left the thought unfinished.

He stood, his crimson-lined robes falling into place with practiced weight, and turned toward the door.

He didn't take the map with him. He didn't need to.

It was already burned into his mind.

Beyond the King's study, where strategy lingered like smoke on steel, the tone shifted. Ceremony crept in like perfume—faint at first, then stifling.

The great council hall loomed vast, its vaulted ceiling lost in shadow and old smoke.

Stone pillars, thick as watchtowers, rose to meet it—each carved with the deeds of kings who had never suffered through nobles' bickering.

Lord Lanyard Darkoak stood silently to the side, sharp eyes tracking the nobles seated around the council table. Lord Branik Durnhart sat rigidly, eyes flickering with barely restrained impatience. Lord Caerlyn's jaw was tight, fists half-clenched atop the oak.

Lord Narcona sat stoic and irritated, cracking his knuckles once—sharp and deliberate—before falling still again.

Lady Wynmere had chosen a gown notably daring for court—shoulders and neckline exposed far beyond current fashion, a choice that drew a subtle frown from Lord Darkoak. Stride lounged in Lord Valen's seat, smug and unconcerned.

The doors opened quietly once more, drawing Lanyard's attention.

Lady Elara Icewind stepped swiftly into the hall, her cheeks faintly flushed from the lingering chill of her recent ride. She had changed from her riding attire, now dressed impeccably in shades of ice-blue silk trimmed with silver threads. Her eyes briefly met Lanyard's, cool yet challenging, as she took her seat without apology.

King Harald entered the room, his presence drawing the hall's attention as he moved silently but purposefully toward the head of the table.

The long council table stretched like a spine through the center of the hall, crafted from alternating slats of iron and northern oak. The iron had been worked in the great forge of Castellon, strong and dark, while the oak was sourced from the ancient trees on the Thornsword estate lands, smoothed by years of use and scarred by countless arguments.

Candlelight flickered along bright-plated helms and caught the gleam of signet rings. Guards lined the walls, stiff as statues, but their eyes never stopped moving.

The scent in the air was familiar: melted wax, parchment, old wood, and the faint bite of sweat beneath silk.

King Harald sat at the head of the table. The weight of his crown was more than gold.

The murmurs died the moment he leaned forward.

Lords and ladies looked on with caution and calculation.

His gaze lingered a moment on Lady Icewind—not long enough to be a challenge, but enough to remind.

He did not smile.

Lord Darkoak spoke first.

His dark leather chased with silver, caught the light like storm clouds. His voice was gravel smoothed by discipline.

"Your Grace," he began, "your brother brings word from the northern edge. Scouts report movement across the high passes. Clans gathering in numbers too large for mere trade or kin-feast. Hravnskot is stirring."

At the mention of Hravnskot, Elara's eyes flickered briefly downward, her breath catching just long enough to feel it. The reaction was gone almost at once—smoothed away before anyone could name it.

Some exchanged glances. Others tried to pretend they hadn't.

Lady Elara leaned forward, her elbow propped with the careless grace of the young and sharp.

"Hravnskot has never crossed the mountains," she said, voice lilting like snow over steel. "They snarl in winter and retreat in spring. Why should this year be any different?"

Lanyard's eyes turned to her—slow, like a blade being drawn.

"You speak as if you've faced them, Lady Elara," he said evenly. "Yet you forget, they crossed the Ironfists ten years ago. Perhaps your memory falters; you were, after all, merely a child—decorated in silks, not steel."

Elara's gaze sharpened instantly, cold and brittle. Her voice cut through the chamber like frost splitting stone.

"My memory, Lord Darkoak, is perfectly intact. I was twelve, yes—and my family died in the fires that war brought to our lands." She did not raise her voice. "I merely meant they haven't crossed since. I've not forgotten a single moment of it."

Her eyes never left his.

"And I do know my history. It was King Boris who first crossed the mountains into Hravnskot — and you were at his side when he did. Perhaps it is your memory that falters, not mine."

He didn't raise his voice nor did he retreat.

"The north does not pace in circles like the nobles gathered here," he said, tone even and unyielding. "They do not trade whispers over wine or slip knives between smiles at feasts. They train. They hunt. They bleed. And when they gather in numbers, it is not to dance—it is to march."

For a moment, his gaze held hers—flat, assessing, entirely without apology, lips curling into a smug, humorless grin.

Elara said nothing, but her cheek twitched. Her fingers found the ring on her hand, spinning it slowly.

Lord Darkoak turned back to the table, as if she were already settled business, letting the silence linger just long enough to underline his satisfaction before continuing.

"Lord Narcona reports that raids have intensified in the southern reaches along the shelf, posing threats to our outlying villages and trade routes. Edgewatch continues to struggle—its outer walls barely mended, and its Cliff Wardens strained thin. Assistance may be necessary if they're to recover before the thaw exposes new weaknesses."

He paused, glancing down at his notes before continuing, irritation barely masked. "On a less urgent note, Castellon soldiers have been filing rather tedious reports regarding their greave straps. Apparently, they've developed an alarming tendency to loosen unexpectedly, much to the irritation of our captains."

Harald cleared his throat, sharp.

"Your counsel is heard, Lord Darkoak," he said. "And not dismissed. We will reinforce the watchtowers at Frostmere and Arrowhall. Send a contingent to bolster Lord Narcona's Cliff Wardens at Edgewatch. But no one draws steel without my command. The realm can't afford a war of shadows."

Dravik shifted in his seat. "We've posted added patrols, Your Grace. The raiders are... opportunists. Nomads from the edge of the Breaks. I welcome your help in this matter, your Grace."

He let that settle. A few lords shifted uncomfortably in their seats—one cleared his throat but said nothing. Then Harald turned to the table.

"Now," he said. "To the matter of supply. Alvis?"

Alvis Thornswood, narrow-faced and already scowling, leaned forward with the confidence of someone used to being heard—and the temper of a man deeply displeased.

"My rangers have received no horses from House Icewind since last Bloomrise—nearly a year now," he said. "We were promised six for the coast patrol."

Elara didn't flinch. "And I was promised coastal timber from Stonewatch in exchange. What I received was a shipment of soggy firewood and a note saying the rest had 'suffered water damage.'"

Alvis scoffed. "We lost two supply barges in a storm."

"And I lost two colts to a bog," Elara said. "But you don't see me sending you the bones."

The table twitched with barely concealed smirks.

Rennic leaned back nonchalantly, fixing Elara with a lazy, accusing glance. "Speaking of accounting, Lady Icewind, your ledgers seem remarkably… optimistic. Perhaps overly so… unless the merchant traders now accept your '*charms*' in place of coin."

Elara straightened immediately, her voice calm but firm. "My ledgers accurately reflect the state of my estate, Rennic. Perhaps your confusion stems from unfamiliarity with honest accounting."

Lady Wynmere shifted forward slightly, offering Elara a subtle glance of reassurance. "Indeed, I've reviewed Lady Icewind's accounts myself. They're impeccable, as always."

Harald raised a hand. "Enough."

Silence followed. Sharp, uneasy silence.

Finally, Lady Wynmere coughed lightly. "And what of the grain? We've had reports of hoarding—of shortages spreading east."

All eyes turned.

Rennic, seated at Lord Valen's usual place, smiled thinly. "Goldacre will simply increase its shipments. Our stores run deep, and the kingdom is in need."

Anger painted Quentyn's cheeks crimson. "Then why are half those shipments ending up in my silos? I never requested them. I never agreed to store them. And yet the wagons keep coming."

Stride's smile remained serene. "Lord Caerlyn, perhaps you forget—it was you who asked Lord Valen to hold those shipments, to better control market prices. Valen graciously complied."

Quentyn snapped back, his voice rising with indignation. "That's a damned lie! Valen requested those silos be filled, claiming overstock that needed urgent storage. This was his arrangement, not mine."

Rennic's demeanor stayed calm, almost amused. "Your confusion is understandable, Lord Caerlyn. Agreements blur when responsibilities multiply."

Quentyn stood abruptly, knuckles white against the edge of the table. "I remember clearly. Valen's lies are as transparent as his motives."

Rennic said nothing. His smile did not falter, though something behind it took note.

Lord Durnhart stood suddenly, the legs of his chair scraping back like drawn steel. His face—flushed, rigid—held none of the restraint that had framed his entrance.

"If this council won't name treason when it stares it in the teeth," he said, voice cutting, "then it is no longer a council. It is a stage. And we are fools playing parts written by liars."

The silence that followed was not shock. It was recognition.

His cloak snapped behind him, boots striking stone like war drums. Not one noble moved to intercept his retreat—only their eyes dared follow, wide with unspoken fear.

But they watched.

Hard.

Measured.

Weighed.

The guards at the doors opened them without word or gesture. His footsteps echoed long after they'd shut again.

Harald didn't watch him leave. The words lingered, undeniably true.

The sound of his boots was enough—measured, unflinching. Branik meant it. That was what troubled them. Not the exit, but the conviction.

And now—

There it was.

The shuffle. That brittle pause. That brittle pause where a dozen nobles sat very still, hoping someone else would speak first. Afraid of being next. Afraid of being wrong. Afraid of being seen.

He might have laughed if the stakes were smaller.

Instead, he let the moment steep.

Let them feel the tremors beneath their careful facades, wondering whether he would hold the foundations steady—or let it all crumble.

Truth was, he was surprised it had taken this long. Years of rotted trade pacts, smugglers in noble garb, whispers traded for coin—and only now, only when a single voice shouted treason in their faces, did the rest flinch like gut-stabbed pigs.

He let his gaze drift across the table. Not one of them met it.

Good, he thought. *Let them look down. Let them feel the weight. Then maybe, finally, they'll be ready to listen.*

No one moved.

Harald remained seated. His fingers steepled before him on the table. His face was unreadable.

Somewhere near the middle of the table, Lord Narcona cleared his throat and looked to speak—then thought better of it. A rustle of silk as someone shifted, a cough that was more nervous than sick.

Even Rennic didn't smile now.

So many polished faces. So many names inherited, not earned.

Finally, King Harald lifted his gaze.

"Lanyard," he said evenly, "Bring me ledgers. Manifests. Every contract—authentic or forged—from Valen's house to Caerlyn's silos. Every name: clerks, merchants, wagon owners."

Quentyn flinched at the order. He sighed, as if he could exhale the problem away.

He looked at Stride—Rennic the Smudge. The man wore his master's arrogance like a second skin. Harald could see it in the way he folded his hands, the way he let silence do the insulting. A snake sent to guard the henhouse, and half the fools at the table welcomed him with wine and flattery.

And Valen… Valen didn't even bother to come.

But it was Lord Branik Durnhart who caught him. His voice, like a drawn blade, rang louder than the iron bell in Frostmere Tower.

There was fire in that one. Not always aimed well—but real. And rare.

He had stood when the rest swallowed their tongues.

That matters, Harald thought. *Flame help me, I'll need fewer cowards and more like him before this is done.*

Lanyard didn't move. "You'll have them."

Harald's eyes scanned the room again. He let the quiet return—not heavy, but surgical. And in that quiet, something coiled behind his expression. Not anger or defeat.

Strategy.

Then, slowly, he rose like a smith stepping back from the anvil—slow, deliberate, the work not done but cooling.

He looked once more to where Lord Durnhart had vanished. "Anyone wishing to leave may do so now. If you stay, you will remember why you're here."

No one moved.

Turning his back on them he walked from the chamber, his cloak brushing the flagstones. He didn't look over his shoulder.

Behind him, the nobles watched his back the way men watched smoke on the horizon.

They remained seated, knowing tradition dictated they would only rise after the King had departed the chamber.

"Lanyard," Harald said, his tone low, crisp as a drawn blade. "A word."

They walked together beneath the vaulted colonnade outside the council hall. The flicker of torches cast long shadows between the pillars, and servants knew better than to linger when the king spoke in lowered tones.

"He's not wrong," he said under his breath. "Branik—he just said it before I wanted him to."

Lanyard kept his pace steady. "You expected the table to crack."

"I expected it to rot. Cracking is progress."

A moment passed between them.

"I want eyes in Goldacre," Harald continued, "Not just on Valen. On the men who whisper near him. Who dines with him. Who he loans coin to."

Lanyard gave a slight nod. "Consider it already set in motion."

"And if you find ledger hands with shaky fingers—"

"They'll never write again."

Harald exhaled through his nose. "Good."

They turned at the next pillar without speaking.

"How's the boy?" Harald asked.

Lanyard didn't need clarification.

"Sharper," he said. "He's quick with the blade now. His training with Master Junfolda is improving. Less so with diplomacy—but he listens when it counts. And he's asking better questions."

Harald nodded, still not looking at him.

"He may have to," he said quietly. "If Baldrik chooses the path of flame."

It wasn't scorn. Just resignation, worn smooth by years of use.

"I won't stop him," he added. "Baldrik's made his choice clear, even if he hasn't said it aloud. I'll not chain him to a throne he'd rather spit on."

Lanyard said nothing.

Harald's voice lowered.

"But if the crown needs a different head… I'll not be unprepared."

Another pause.

"And Elara?" he asked.

Lanyard followed his gaze.

Lady Elara Icewind stood at the far end of the corridor, half turned in conversation with a page, her cloak catching the light like frost trimmed in silk.

"She's clever," Lanyard said. "And dangerous. But not careless. Not yet."

Harald's eyes narrowed. "I've let this go on long enough—her and Baldrik. She's growing too comfortable with proximity."

"She knows how to play the game," Lanyard replied.

"And she enjoys it," the king added. "That's what worries me."

Harald stopped at the next alcove.

"See how far she's willing to push back. But don't start the fire unless you mean to finish it."

Lanyard inclined his head.

"With your leave, Your Grace."

Harald didn't nod. He just walked away, cloak whispering against stone.

And Lanyard—the king's sword—turned to intercept the frost-veiled ambition waiting at the end of the hall.

Just beyond, the corridor stood quiet—save for the fading murmur of nobles lingering behind closed doors. Night had fallen, leaving the hallways dim and cool, the stone holding the day's last breath. What little light remained came from polished marble. The day fully spent, and shadows grown still.

Lady Elara Icewind stepped lightly from the hall, expression calm, her pace unhurried. Her dress rippled with each step; a slow procession of ice-blue silk trimmed in gray fox.

She didn't see him until he moved.

"Lady Elara."

The voice stopped her like a hand to the throat.

Lord Lanyard Darkoak stepped silently from the shadows pooled between two pillars, as if the darkness itself had summoned him forth. The torchlight caught his sigil ring and the edge of his steel-gray tabard.

"Lord Darkoak," she said smoothly, turning to face him. "You should be more careful where you linger. Someone might mistake you for a shade haunting these halls."

"Better a ghost than a fool."

She raised a brow. "Was that meant for me?"

His boots echoed once as he stepped closer—measured, never rushed. His voice lowered.

"His Majesty grows… troubled by your proximity to the prince."

Elara didn't blink. "Proximity? We're acquainted. He invited me for a ride. Are courtiers no longer allowed to spend time together?"

"Courtiers… has it come to that, then."

He stood close now, not enough to touch, but enough to loom.

"You speak to him in gardens. You linger outside his chambers. He smiles more than he should. These things do not go unnoticed."

She held his gaze, irritation flickering like sparks beneath her careful composure. "Is it treason now to be well-regarded?"

"It's dangerous to be too *needed*," he said, voice like iron under cloth. "Especially by a prince who should be focused on duty, not distraction."

"You believe I distract him?"

"I believe you play a game whose rules you don't fully understand."

That struck.

Her smile thinned. "Perhaps it's the game that fears being played."

He stepped closer still, voice now a whisper of threat.

"Be very careful, Elara. You are not his equal. You are not his kin. And you are not trusted."

Her lips parted slightly, but no retort came.

"I deliver this warning," he said, voice steady, "because the King requested it—and because the realm can ill afford another fracture. Should I need to deliver another, the message will not require words."

He turned, cloak swirling.

Elara stood motionless, pulse hammering loud in her ears.

Then, drawing herself tall with icy composure, she turned sharply and walked away, shoulders set in unyielding defiance.

But in her chest, something twisted—not fear, but white-hot fury born of insult and wounded pride.

Behind her, Lord Darkoak paused at the corridor's end. He didn't watch her go.

She would disregard the warning—he was certain of it. And when she did, he would ensure the King saw clearly how dangerously this distraction could grow.

Outside, beyond the threats of court corridors, another confrontation waited—cut from darker cloth.

The heavy doors of the council hall groaned shut behind him.

Rennic didn't rush. He walked with the lazy confidence of a man who knew exactly where his boot would land. Torchlight bled across the steps of Castellon Shield, catching the edges of stone and steel as he descended toward the courtyard.

He was halfway down when a voice stopped him cold.

"Stride."

Rennic turned.

Lord Caerlyn stood at the top of the stair, not shouting—just focused. His cloak whipped behind him, his expression granite.

"Leaving so soon?" Quentyn asked.

Rennic tilted his head. "I assumed the performance was over."

Quentyn descended one step, frustration tightening his jaw. "You think this is theater?"

"I think it's many things," Rennic said. "Some staged. Some tragic. And some merely peasants' fodder and blood."

Quentyn descended another step.

"You've dumped three shipments of grain in my silos," Quentyn said. "Unrequested. Unpaid. And publicly. The merchants think I'm hoarding. The townsfolk think I'm bleeding them."

Rennic smiled faintly, his voice smooth and unruffled. "House Valen supports the realm. Stability is our business."

"Don't pretend ignorance," Quentyn went on. "My house steward reviewed the contract your master sent with that grain. Edwyn Fallow's seal validated it. Terms. Storage. Compensation."

He held Rennic's gaze. "So either Valen believes my house too dull to read what it signs—or someone expects me to swallow the insult quietly."

Quentyn's expression hardened. "Valen owes my house for storage. I expect payment."

Rennic felt a flicker of confusion—and buried it.

He turned fully now, still three steps below.

But when he spoke, it was as if he stood above him.

"I've been told, with age comes forgetfulness—perhaps your memory isn't as reliable as you believe."

Quentyn's voice dropped to ice.

"I won't waste my guards protecting Valen's grain. Let the looters take it. Let the rats chew it clean. That's not my loss."

Rennic gave a dry chuckle. "Spoken like a man who builds fences after the wolves are already inside."

Quentyn narrowed his eyes.

"A lesson," Rennic added smoothly, "you should've learned from the folk of Tarnhollow… I would think."

The wind caught between them—sharp and brittle.

Quentyn stepped down again. "If I'm accused of mismanaging it, I'll open the doors myself and show them your seal on every sack. The crown can seize the lot of it for all I care."

Rennic didn't blink. "You always this generous with your enemies?"

"I'm just making room," Quentyn said. "For the ones who still matter."

Rennic studied him. As if punctuating the tension, one torch sputtered, snapping from its mount to die against the stone.

"You're braver than the rest," he said.

"I'm angrier than the rest," Quentyn replied.

Rennic stepped up one stair, closing the distance.

"Careful, my lord. Keep walking this path, and you'll find yourself very alone."

"If alone means not swinging from the gallows beside Circus and his lapdog, I'll take alone," Quentyn said.

Rennic's smile faded to something colder.

"We'll see."

Quentyn turned without answering, boots striking hard against stone as he climbed.

Rennic waited until he was gone, then flexed his ink-stained fingers and descended into the dark. He was already considering whose ear needed his whispers next—and what words would twist them best.

Dawn broke cold and colorless over the southeastern port city of Eastmere.

The sky was torn in shades of lilac and silver, clouds dragging low and swollen with rain. Mist pressed against the rooftops like gauze pulled too tight, hiding what the morning dared to show. The scent of salt, coal ash, and netting clung to every eave. Harbor bells tolled with a slow, hollow rhythm—three times, then silence. Then again. Not the toll of market or fog. This was a call older than commerce.

Captain Denric Hallam stood on the east tower of the inner watch, his gloved hand tight on the cold brass of the spyglass. Wind stirred the salt-crusted fur of his collar.

"Twenty," he muttered. "Two moving to dock. Eighteen… holding formation."

His second officer shifted beside him, squinting against the fog. "War colors?"

"Not yet. But look at their hulls—goddess spare us…bone-rimmed bows. Jungle bark armor. Sharktooth pennants. Eastern latticework on the sternplate."

He stepped back, voice steady. "That's no merchant fleet."

A beat. The glass clicked shut.

"That's *Vara*."

The word fell like iron on wet cloth.

Below, the garrison roused. Boots struck stone. Orders were barked. Steel unshuttered in quiet efficiency. Eastmere had seen war before. The Iron Bay Raids. The pirate sacking of Redwater Port. But no one in living memory had seen twenty Varanese warships glide in without so much as a gull's cry.

Denric kept watching. Waiting.

Only when the lead vessel—a long, sinuous vessel of dark lacquer and silent oars—unfurled a pale green banner, trimmed in vine-thread and bearing the twin sigils of the Emerald Flame and Sapphire Throne, did he allow himself a breath.

"Envoy colors," he said grimly. "Not invasion. But Flame save us. They brought royalty."

The ships coasted into the harbor like reef beasts on the hunt—silent, sleek, dangerous in stillness. The two lead vessels moored with uncanny precision, anchors lowered without splash, sails furled with ritual grace. No shouting. No signals. The crews moved like they were carved from tradition.

Queen Miroray Kaeleen stepped ashore first, barefoot as Varanese rite demanded.

Her cloak coiled around her ankles, pale fabric brushing the stone. A braid of obsidian and reef-pearl circled her brow; her violet-blue eyes scanned the dock with unflinching calm, as if measuring the worth of every stone, every man, and finding both wanting.

Behind her came King Consort Tulavan, taller and broader, clad in deep-reef green silk with brass fastenings shaped like coiled wave-serpents. The serpent-blade at his side curved with a predatory grace. His eyes, pale and cold, flicked over the assembled soldiers with assessing contempt.

Miroray stepped forward without pause, though a faint twitch of discomfort passed her features as a gust of wind slipped beneath her sea-lace cloak. Her bare toes curled reflexively against the damp stone.

Tulavan leaned in with a smirk that could slice rope. "Should've let me bring the furs, wife," he murmured just loud enough. "You forget—spring in Eldaraine is still winter to island blood."

She didn't answer, but the glance she shot him said plainly: *You'll die of heat before I show weakness to these men.*

"Summon your port captain," she said to the nearest officer. "And a fast horse. You'll send word to Castellon Shield immediately. Tell Queen Avanna this: her sister has arrived—and does not care for locked gates."

The officer's mouth opened, then pressed shut with nothing to say.

Before he could find words again, Tulavan stepped up beside Miroray. His tone was dry, voice pitched to carry.

"Tell your commander this isn't an invasion," he said. "If it were, your banners would be ash and your gates salt."

That landed.

Miroray turned her head slowly. Her smile was elegant. And lethal.

"King Consort," she said with sweet venom, "perhaps save the fire-breathing for council. Some of us prefer tea to war."

Tulavan gave a slow, unapologetic grin. "Didn't say war. Said ash."

Miroray's gaze returned to the captain without missing a beat.

"Where's your hospitality?" she asked, stepping past him. "I should like tea. And perhaps a full report on your watchtower blind spots."

Behind her, the Varanese delegation moved ashore with silent efficiency. Soldiers in sand-hued silk and armored coral plated leathers fell into tight, disciplined ranks. Not a word spoken. Not a step out of place.

The silence of war. Dressed as diplomacy.

And Westmere held its breath.

A flustered Captain Denric Hallam finally arrived, helm under arm, sweat already prickling his collar. "Your Grace—Your Graces. Apologies for the alarm. We were… not expecting royal visitors from the south."

"Clearly," Miroray said, sweeping past him with a slow, lethal grace. "The welcome has been… enthusiastic."

Denric coughed. "How long do Your Graces intend to stay?"

"A days' rest," said Tulavan. "Then we depart."

"We," corrected Miroray, "will proceed to Castellon Shield with a guard of seven. The rest will remain anchored off the coast. Out of courtesy."

"To remind Eldaraine we still exist," Tulavan added.

Denric bowed stiffly. "Of course. Arrangements will be made for lodging, fresh mounts, and—"

"A proper bath," Miroray cut in. "Not the sort that reeks of stable sweat and apology. And hot."

As crates of provisions were offloaded and the sun lifted from the waterline, the city of Eastmere began to shift from panic to uncertain awe.

And the Queen of the Flamegrove walked its stone streets, already charting the pulse of a kingdom that had, for far too long, stopped writing back.

Their private quarters in the Port Captain's estate were hardly regal. The floors creaked, the walls sweated salt, and the view overlooked only gull shit and tangled nets.

Tulavan stood at the shuttered window, arms crossed, the scent of boiled cabbage already wrinkling his nose.

"This is a storage loft," he muttered. "A drafty one. I've seen better rooms offered to smugglers."

Miroray was removing her earrings, slowly, methodically, in front of a cracked mirror. "That would explain your comfort."

He turned. "I've crossed half a sea for your sister, and now I'm left to dry in a fishing town with rotting curtains and a bed made for peasants."

"You're not here for comfort, Tulavan. You're here because Castellon went silent." She set the earrings down, each with a soft *clink*. "And because I chose to accompany you."

He scoffed. "You chose? I am *king*."

"No," she said, turning to him now, voice honed. "You are only king *because* I married you. Because a dead queen four dynasties ago thought it looked tidy to have a man beside the flame. Not *in* it."

Tulavan's jaw clenched.

Miroray's eyes flashed like a reef just before it draws blood. "No, Tulavan. Remember this, every hour of every day, I am the Queen of the Flamegrove. *You* are the man who speaks second. If at all."

He didn't move.

She stepped closer, inexorable. "You wear my crown. You sail under my flag. And right now, you will remember *why* we came."

He said nothing.

Miroray's voice softened, but it didn't lose its edge. "Something is wrong. Avanna wouldn't vanish. Not without word. Not to me. If this is a message, I'm here to hear it. If it's a warning, I'm here to see it. And if it's a trap…"

She reached up and smoothed the fabric near his collar, fingers grazing the serpent-clasp at his throat like a silent reminder of who placed it there.

"…you'll have your chance to be useful."

Tulavan studied her face, the lines of it carved not from age but pressure. Eventually, he gave a slow, bitter smile.

"You always were good at making kings feel small."

"I don't need you small," she said, stepping back. "I need you sharp."

He tilted his head. "Then you'd better stop dulling me with fishgut and gull shit."

Miroray turned away, gaze falling to the city beyond the window. "Then act like a blade," she murmured. "Not a blunted boast."

The tension between them settled—familiar and heavy.

Below, the streets of Eastmere stirred. Guards changed. Provisions moved. The wind shifted, salt-heavy. Flags cracked against their masts in the breeze, and the first chill of Eldaraine's spring crept under the doorframe.

Tulavan sniffed. "Gods, it's colder than it looks."

He crossed the room, rummaging through a travel chest until he produced a fur-lined mantle—stormwolf pelt, thick and fine. He laid it over the foot of the bed, then turned to Miroray.

"For the queen," he said, voice reluctant. "Before your toes freeze off and the realm is left with me instead."

Miroray arched a brow, dry amusement flickering there. "A sudden concern for toes? Or just an excuse to play dress servant?"

Tulavan offered a crooked smile. "I know my place."

She regarded him for a long, unreadable moment. Then—"Good. Let's hope Eldaraine remembers theirs."

Outside, Eastmere readied itself for guests the continent had not expected.

And for truths no one had asked to hear.

CHAPTER TWELVE

Evening light stretched long across the garden steps of the Grand Citadel, bathing ancient stone in muted gold and shadow, the lingering daylight of mid Bloomrise slow to release its hold. The carved Ash-Wardens along the stair bore the softened features of age and touch, their expressions worn smooth by centuries of passing hands. Baldrik took the steps two at a time, cloak half-buttoned, boots scuffing stone hollowed by time. The air here smelled unmistakably of Bloomrise—wet bark, crushed new leaves, and damp stone warmed by the fading sun.

He moved with an ease he rarely carried at court. The ride beyond the city walls still lingered in his muscles, the unguarded laughter, the reckless freedom of a few stolen hours where he was not prince or heir—only a boy allowed to breathe.

Elara Icewind came unbidden to his thoughts. Just Elara. The name settled warmly in his chest, equal parts comfort and complication. He did not linger on it—could not, not here—but neither did he banish it. Some truths followed you even into quiet places.

He reached the vine-wrapped archway at the garden's edge, where the Citadel gave way to the Flamebound's inner court. The space was deliberately plain—stone, earth, and carefully tended growth meant to calm rather than impress. Sycamore and oak stood along the perimeter, their leaves whispering. At the center rose the consecrated flame-elm, old as the order itself, its roots thick and exposed, gripping the soil with patient certainty. The air here felt warmer—not with indulgence, but with steadiness, as though the world had slowed to match a measured breath.

Kælric sat on a low stone bench, hands folded, posture unyielding without stiffness. His gaze tracked the slow sway of leaves rather than the path, as if he had known Baldrik would arrive before the sound of boots reached him.

"You're late," Kælric said, not looking at him.

Baldrik grinned anyway, because this place let him. "If I'm always late, does it still count as late?"

Kælric didn't answer.

Baldrik settled onto the opposite bench, elbows resting casually on his knees. For a long breath, neither spoke. The mild wind moved through the court in slow breaths. Somewhere above, a bell marked the hour, distant and unconcerned.

"You're missing council again," Kælric said.

"I wasn't summoned."

"You haven't needed to be."

Baldrik looked away. "They don't miss me."

"They should."

Baldrik rubbed the back of his neck. "I don't belong there."

"You do. You just do not like what it asks of you."

Baldrik exhaled through his nose.

"There's nothing in that room but rot and ritual—Valen's lapdog snapping at shadows, Caerlyn sighing like the world owes him comfort, my father pretending the kingdom isn't burning around him."

"Flame cleanses. Ash rebuilds — if the fire is chosen."

Baldrik's brows drew together in a thoughtful frown. "You think I mean to add to the fire?"

"I think you want to step clear before it collapses onto you."

Baldrik leaned back, letting the stone hold him. His gaze drifted toward the lengthening sky.

"Elara asked about the crown," he said.

"And?"

"I changed the subject."

Kælric did not move.

"I spoke of you instead," Baldrik admitted. "Told her I've been reading the texts."

"And?"

"She didn't press."

"And?"

Baldrik sighed, admitting reluctantly. "She smiled," he said. "Like she understood something I didn't."

Kælric turned just enough to look at him. "And did she?"

"I don't know," Baldrik confessed.

"You care for her."

Baldrik smiled wryly—defenses rising, though his tone softened. "I'm not yet so far gone as to admit that openly to a Flamebound."

"Good. That means you're paying attention."

Silence settled between them.

"Is it wrong," Baldrik asked, "to want something beyond duty?"

"No. It's wrong to lie to yourself about it."

Baldrik nodded slowly, plucked a leaf from the bench, and twirled it between his fingers before letting it drift to the ground.

"Your father was born to the throne. That does not mean you were. Or perhaps you were not born to it at all, but meant to walk toward it. The Flame does not measure worth by inheritance."

"But one of us will be disappointed," Baldrik said.

"That's the nature of paths. Some are lit. Some you choose in the dark. Some are laid on you whether you step or not."

Baldrik lifted his gaze to the flame-elm, watching its branches move against the deepening twilight. "Do you believe the Flame has a purpose for me?" he asked.

"The Flame answers nothing for those who stop asking."

"And if I say I wish to serve it?" Baldrik challenged.

"I'd ask why," Kælric returned simply.

Baldrik fell silent, the truth hovering between them, unspoken yet clearly understood.

In the distance, the bells began to toll. Baldrik did not rise.

Kælric's faint smile returned, understanding and gentle. "Still not going?"

"I already know what they'll say," Baldrik said, certainty settling in his chest. "More importantly, I know what they won't."

The wind moved through the leaves above, setting the flame-elm's branches whispering. The garden returned to stillness.

East of Hillmere, the drawing room at Goldacre Manor—ancestral seat of House Valen—reeked of roasted garlic, oiled leather, and a syrupy perfume that struggled to mask something deeper—something rotten beneath velvet draperies.

A fire burned in a blackstone hearth, more for comfort than need, throwing wavering shadows across the grotesque lion's skull mounted above the mantle. Above it hung an ancient dagger, rune-scarred and menacing, now shamefully reduced to holding garlands of brittle bay leaves. Lord Circus Valen sprawled carelessly in a plush chair, his ample frame loosely contained within lavish clothing only partially fastened.

He idly swirled wine in a fat goblet, grease glistening upon his fingertips as he lazily summoned a servant closer. The servant—slight, quiet, and well-trained—approached with measured steps, eyes respectfully lowered.

"Bring wine," Valen drawled, eyes fixed elsewhere, bored yet commanding. "And none of that swill from Wynmere. Fetch an amber, one from my cellar."

The servant bowed gracefully and withdrew quickly, her movements composed and precise.

Valen chuckled softly and turned toward his guest, Shade, who sat opposite, posture tight, eyes calculating. To Valen's left and just behind,

Rennic stood as a casual observer, watching, measuring the man's gait and bearing.

Shade was weathered by sun and wind, skin darkened to burnt copper, arms inked elaborately in serpentine coils and arcane symbols. His sleeveless jerkin revealed lean, sinewy muscle honed by relentless violence. He carried himself like a blade—curved, silent, and honed for killing.

"Lost two near Rivermere," Shade reported, his voice rough and thick with a sharp twang. "One had royal marks. Likely Eldaran guard. Burnt the bugger, no trace left."

Valen wiped grease from his thumb with casual disdain. "Did the fool talk?"

"Nah," Shade muttered with a rough grin. "Bloody bastard fought like a sandskulk with its leg caught. Took Marten's eye 'fore we dropped 'em."

Valen smirked, amused by the image. "Remind me to send Marten something suitable. Perhaps a chicken's eye. Something fittingly useless, yet decorative."

Rennic remained by the fire, gloved hands clasped behind his back.

Shade produced a weathered map from his satchel, creased and dotted with dried blood, placing it carefully onto the low table between them. "Marked all the ambushes. Wagons torched, goods buggered. No one walked away—just like ya said."

Valen glanced disinterestedly at the map, pushing it toward Rennic without further acknowledgment. Rennic unfolded it meticulously, eyes tracing each marked location with practiced scrutiny, noting patterns Valen would not bother to see.

"Minimal risk?" Valen queried, biting into another greasy leg of fowl.

Shade shrugged casually. "One a'them monks tried blessin' the dead as he carked it. Otherwise? Quiet."

"Excellent," Valen murmured between bites. "Keep the outer roads barren, and the prices climb. Even nobles become beggars when hunger pinches their bellies."

Shade leaned forward, eyes gleaming expectantly. "Ya promised gold."

"And you'll have it," Valen said, snapping his fingers sharply.

The slight servant woman stepped forward with elegant composure, her movements careful and rehearsed, as though she'd been warned not to spill a single drop. She placed a heavy lockbox reverently before Rennic, then stepped back.

He unlocked the box, methodically counting out three bulging pouches of coin, tossing one toward the Scorchlander, who caught it deftly while his attention shifted toward the servant. Rennic's gaze moved to Shade, then to the servant woman—just long enough to register the shift in the air, then back to counting.

"No king's mint?" Shade questioned, testing its weight.

"Pure silverweight," Rennic replied. "Cleaned, pressed. Use it where heads don't matter."

Shade nodded, satisfied, tying the pouch securely at his belt. "I'll hit 'em again next moonrise."

"Lovely," Valen drawled, raising his goblet lazily. "Bring something more creative next time. A noble's finger, perhaps. A bard's tongue. Or a monk's precious dignity."

Shade chuckled softly. "Ya got a poet's heart, Valen."

"I have a poet's tongue," Valen corrected, sipping his wine. "But a butcher's hands. We harvest our due."

Shade's eyes slid toward the servant and lingered, measuring far longer than courtesy allowed. She stood still, eyes lowered, waiting. He cleared his throat with exaggerated casualness.

"Been a bloody long ride from The Breaks," Shade began, tone oozing faux courtesy, eyes flickering to the servant and back to Valen. "Might borrow a bit o' comfort for the night."

Valen's expression sharpened instantly. "Even vultures, Shade, should mind what carcass they pick. My servants are not tavern whores. Find your comfort elsewhere."

Rennic silently stepped past Shade, smoothly opening the door with pointed finality.

Shade huffed irritably, the insult landing like a slap, but he rose without further protest. He didn't offer a nod and strode out, boots heavy against the polished floor.

Valen watched him leave with contempt, swirling his wine once before setting the cup aside. The door closed softly behind Shade.

The hearth crackled behind him as Rennic marked new targets with practiced precision.

Valen's gaze returned to the servant, assessing function rather than form.

"You. Wine," he commanded silkily, his tone light and dangerous. "Move swiftly—or I may reconsider my generosity."

She bowed and moved at once. Valen chuckled softly, watching her go.

She crossed the chamber to the sideboard and returned with a fresh bottle, refilling Valen's cup without a word. Valen's attention drifted from imagined pleasures to more immediate hungers.

"Have him followed, make sure he returns to The Breaks."

Rennic nodded and vanished without a sound.

Valen sipped his wine.

"Flame have it, how delightful a kingdom teetering on ruin can be," he mused. "Only then do the rats remember how to feast—and where the marrow runs richest."

It was late in Castellon, the air softened even as the palace held the day's warmth. The royal apartments had gone quiet—too quiet for sleep, not quiet enough for peace.

In the narrow servant's corridor just outside Queen Avanna's chambers, Lana stood frozen, the vial trembling faintly in her fingers. Her breath came in shallow, nervous whispers as she carefully tilted the tiny glass container, letting one drop—just one—fall silently into the queen's third wine bottle. Her eyes widened briefly at the silent ripple. Quickly, she tucked the vial deep into the modest folds of her servant's robes, heart pounding against the thin linen. Two drops already tonight, and whatever calming effects her mother had promised clearly weren't working. Lana swallowed hard, fear tightening her throat. She prayed the queen wouldn't call for this third bottle—and that no one would discover what she'd done.

Within the chamber, the wine had dulled the edges of Queen Avanna's thoughts—but tonight it seemed crisper somehow, the drink pulling darker currents to the surface. Her thoughts sharpened strangely, more desperate, more jagged.

She sat alone in a chamber built for kings and queens who trusted each other. The fire had sunk low, its blue flame casting a restless glow across marble floors and carelessly strewn fabrics—too carelessly, for early Bloomrise nights that no longer demanded such heat. A fur-lined cloak lay draped across a chaise. One slipper, just one, had fallen near the foot of the lacquered desk—as if it had tried to run and failed.

The first bottle was empty. The second stood nearby—uncorked, half-drained. The goblet beside them was dark at the rim, stained like bruised lips.

A letter lay on the desk. Folded. Unfolded. Folded again. The parchment curled at the corners, ink fading to dust—but the words remained. Too legible to forget.

"Harald—The world is colder when you leave me. Colder than the frost in the hills. I don't care for her name, or her crown. Only that you come back with warmth still in you..."

She traced the script again, the faded ink feeling ancient—too ancient to be recent. Whose warmth was Harald carrying that had cooled long before her?

"More wine," she muttered.

No one answered.

She blinked, twice. Then louder: "More wine. Now."

A pause. Then the soft shuffle of small feet beyond the chamber doors.

Avanna's focus snagged as the servant entered. Too young—no, that wasn't right. Or perhaps it was. The shape of the moment refused to settle.

Her name slipped away the instant Avanna reached for it. Lira? Lena? Something small and forgettable. It irritated her, the way unimportant things sometimes did when her thoughts were already fraying.

Lana walked with hands clasped tight before her, the hem of her linen nightdress whispering over the stone. Barefoot, as palace rules demanded at night. Careful. Quiet. Trying very hard not to exist.

"You called, Your Grace?"

"Don't flutter. Pour."

Lana hesitated—but only for a moment—then crossed to the side table and lifted the second bottle. She poured with care, steady despite the tension curling her shoulders. The wine sang as it filled the goblet—one of those delicate little court sounds that made Avanna want to scream.

She took the goblet and drained half in a single breath.

"Do you know what betrayal smells like?" she asked, not looking up.

"I… I don't think I do, Majesty."

"It smells like ink. Good ink. Expensive. The kind they save for laws and secrets. It clings to collars. Lingers on cuffs."

She swirled the wine, watching it lap the sides like slow blood.

"Too many late nights," she murmured. "He leaves the room colder than he entered. That's not love. That's rot."

Lana didn't respond. She stood there, still as prayer.

Avanna raised her eyes—slow. Deliberate.

"Do you know what else is rotting?" she asked. "The Crown. Because my son wants to trade it for robes and ritual."

The girl's hands tightened on the bottle. Her knuckles turned white—silent punctuation to the queen's words.

"Maybe he needs incentive," Avanna murmured. "Something to anchor him."

She looked at the handmaid, then. Really looked—and the moment skewed.

"You have a pretty face," Avanna said, as if assessing a painting. "That can be useful."

The handmaid swallowed. "Your Grace—"

"How old are you?"

"I… I'll be twelve mid Sunswell, Majesty."

"Too young," Avanna said at once. Relief followed irritation, then tangled with something darker she did not like. Her gaze drifted, unfocused, as if the room had shifted a step to the side. "No. That won't do."

She stood. The movement was elegant by habit, unsteady beneath it. The floor seemed to tilt and then correct itself.

Avanna took a step closer, then stopped herself. "Maybe if…" Her hand lifted as if to indicate posture, then fell back to her side. "Stand straighter," she said instead. "Eyes forward. Say nothing unless spoken to."

She frowned, the thought unraveling even as it formed. "No—forget that."

The handmaid did not move. Her breath hitched, shallow and fast.

Avanna blinked—slowly—and a shadow of realization crept across her face like dusk falling on glass.

"Go," she rasped sharply, sudden shame flushing beneath the wine's heat. "Before this room convinces me of nonsense."

The handmaid curtsied. Then turned and hurried out, bare feet a hush on stone.

Alone again, Avanna sank into her chair. The goblet trembled in her grip—then she drained it dry.

The letter waited on the desk—patient, damning.

She picked it up again.

Read it once more.

"Only that you come back with warmth still in you…"

Her sister used to say—"Trim the sail before the storm"—an old Varanese maxim spoken in shipyards and war councils alike. Trim the excess before the wind finds it. Lighten the vessel before it drags you under.

But now, it meant something else.

She looked into the fire. The blue flame curled low, quiet.

Harald had lost his fire. Whatever warmth he had left burned elsewhere—politics, secrets, quiet meetings with Lord Lanyard, cloaked in duties she was never invited to.

And Baldrik… her son couldn't see the throne for the altar in front of it. Dreaming of robes and ritual. Of vanishing into quiet philosophy, hiding from duty in meaningless contemplation.

She needed him to want the crown. No—she needed him to believe he wanted it. Belief was enough. Belief could be staged.

Influence. Guilt. Pressure. Ceremony. Reason had failed. If reason failed, then structure—subtle or otherwise—would have to suffice. She would close every other path until the crown was the only thing left standing.

And if Harald had to fall for that to happen, it would be a mercy. A necessary correction.

"Trim the sail."

Her grip on the letter tightened. The hearth cracked. Spit. Sparks flared, then fell.

She stared into the flame without blinking. Like it might answer.

"I can do it," she whispered. "If no one else will… then it must be me."

She folded the letter with precise care, though her fingers trembled. Then tossed it into the flames. As it burned, a face entered her thoughts. A pretty face. A familiar face.

Elara Icewind. The name burned in her thoughts, a spark where discipline should have been. That girl had no idea what she was touching—no understanding of crowns, or sacrifice, or consequence. She poured herself another goblet, watching the wine darken the silver rim.

A plan took shape—not desire, not appetite, but theater: vows recited, hands clasped for the realm, a queen beside a king in name and necessity alone. The crown did not require love. It required alignment.

I was young once too, Avanna thought, lifting the goblet. Youth was wasted on those who did not understand what it cost. The wine spread warmth through her chest, loosening the tight coil of thought. She was too old for softness, too young for release, old enough to be judged and young enough still to be required. She drank again, deeper this time, savoring the way the wine numbed her bitterness even as it fueled her resolve.

She rose and crossed the room to the mirror, each step practiced, the wavering beneath them carefully ignored. Her reflection gazed back, eyes too bright, mouth set too hard. Power clung to her posture. Control did not. She drank again, draining the cup, then poured another without hesitation.

"Yes," she whispered to her reflection, the word brittle rather than fierce. Her thoughts churned, snagging and tearing on themselves, wine and darker things blurring their edges. Certainty slipped through her fingers even as she reached for it.

Harald had turned from her—she felt that truth like a bruise. Or perhaps he had not. The thought twisted, reformed, hardened again. Either way, she stood alone with the weight of a crown that would not stop pressing.

She stared at herself in the mirror, at the familiar face now rendered slightly wrong by the glass, the drink, and the certainty hardening behind her eyes. For a moment she lifted her hand, as if to smooth some imagined flaw, then let it fall. The woman staring back looked tired. Frightened. Determined in a way that felt more like fear than resolve.

It had to be her. If she did not hold the realm together, it would come apart. No one else understood the weight. No one else would act. She believed that now with absolute clarity. Belief settled where reason no longer could, smooth and immovable.

"I can do this," she said. "I have to."

The goblet trembled faintly as she lowered it. Wine spilled over the rim, staining the desk like a careless wound.

"Leif," she called, her voice steady only by habit.

The chamber door opened, and the guard entered, closing it again with practiced silence.

Avanna stood with her back to him, shoulders tight, one hand braced against the desk. Another bottle sat uncorked beside the candle, its flame guttering in the scented air.

"You came," she said. "That matters."

He inclined his head, saying nothing.

She turned slightly, enough that he could see her profile now—not the queen in full, but the woman beneath the crown, weary and resolute. She was careful not to invite closeness. She did not face him fully.

"I've been thinking about loyalty," she continued, her voice softer now, threaded with fatigue she did not bother to mask. "About who remains when others falter." She exhaled, a small, controlled sound. "You have always stayed." She let the truth of it hang.

Leif's jaw tightened. He did not look away.

"When the time comes," she said, gently, as if confiding rather than commanding, "I will need certainty. Not from the council. Not from men who weigh their oaths like coin."

She finally turned to him then.

"I will need you," she said simply—not as a request, but as a conclusion already reached. "I will need your hand."

The silence stretched. Leif drew a slow breath, as though steadying himself.

"You have it," he said. "All of it."

Avanna studied him for a heartbeat longer than necessary. Something like relief passed over her face—quick, almost imperceptible.

"That is what I hoped," she said. "That is what the crown requires."

"Yes, Your Grace," he answered without hesitation.

The certainty in his voice steadied her. Some of the tightness left her shoulders. She lifted her chin, dismissing him with a small, precise gesture.

"Go. Be ready."

He bowed and withdrew, the door sealing behind him.

Alone again, Avanna lifted the goblet, sipping the wine. Her hand shook this time, just enough to betray her.

She watched the liquid swirl, dark and glossy, and for an instant her face reflected back—older than she remembered, worn thin by grief and fear.

The crown still weighed on her brow, invisible but crushing.

She closed her eyes, clutching the goblet to her chest, and for the briefest moment she looked not like a queen at all, but like a woman drowning beneath her crown.

CHAPTER THIRTEEN

Hidden beneath the grandeur of Castellon Shield, far removed from gilded halls and tapestry-covered walls, lay the servants' corridors—a maze of narrow arches, soot-dulled masonry, and lanterns whose weak flames flickered against blackened stone. Dust motes drifted through crooked beams of torchlight, the air thick with centuries of secrets the palace above chose to forget.

It was here Prince Harald waited, leaning against the cool stone wall, arms folded across a chest still clad in worn riding leathers. His gloves, tucked casually behind his belt, carried the faint scent of horses and the open fields. A fresh scar, earned from a careless swing in the training yard, traced a thin line along his jaw—something he made no effort to hide. Harald's posture was deceptively relaxed, masking the tension in his chest.

Footsteps echoed faintly—deliberate, familiar.

She appeared around the corner, moving without a candle, comfortable in shadows that parted for her like familiar friends.

Maralei.

Barefoot as always, her dark curls spilled in loose waves around her shoulders, framing a face that wore a defiant beauty. Her simple linen gown hugged her waist, modest yet unable to hide the grace in every step. She approached without hurry, as if the corridor belonged to her—and in this small, stolen way, it did.

Harald straightened, his features softening despite himself. His heart betrayed him, quickening at her mere presence. "You always make me wait."

She lifted her chin, eyes bright with subtle defiance. "I always make you earn it."

He smiled faintly, helpless against her charm. She stepped closer, into his space.

Her delicate hands rose, fingertips lightly tracing the fresh scar along his jaw. The insignia stitched into his leathers—new, not yet worn soft—did not escape her notice. "You promised you'd be careful." Concern threaded her words. "They don't give men command of the Ironfist Forces to keep them safe." Her nose crinkled in mischief, light briefly outshining the heaviness in her gaze. "And you smell like horses again. Were you actually riding, or is it merely your convenient excuse to steal away?"

Harald chuckled softly, warmth briefly chasing away his tension. "A bit of both, perhaps. My father allows me that small rebellion—probably because it irritates my mother to no end. She despises horses, calls them filthy beasts unfit for royalty. But he understands it brings me peace."

"I promised not to die," Harald corrected, affection he struggled to conceal. "Careful is something different entirely."

She pressed her forehead against his chest, eyes closed as she listened to his steady heartbeat, reassurance drawn from its constant rhythm. "The Hravnskot are not known for their mercy," she said. "They don't break easily—and they don't forgive."

The pause between them held more than either would say.

Finally, she looked up, her eyes bright with unshed tears. "They will find out eventually."

Harald cupped her face, his thumbs brushing her cheeks with a care he showed no one else. "Then let them find out."

"You don't truly mean that," she said, though her eyes betrayed a desperate hope.

"I mean every word." His voice held fervor, unwavering. "I've stood in those grand chambers," he said, "listened to men who speak of power like it's breath itself. It all feels hollow. But here—" His hand tightened at her waist, not possessive, just afraid. "Here, I feel real. I'd take that over a crown."

Her throat tightened visibly, emotion threatening to break free. "And if they banish me from the palace?"

"Then I would follow."

"You would be king," she protested weakly. "You wouldn't have that freedom."

"I would follow you," he insisted, forehead pressed firmly to hers. "Always."

Her voice fractured, fierce beneath the vulnerability. "You won't have a choice."

"Mara, you've made me forget the blood that binds me—made me dream of a life I was never meant to imagine. I don't know if that's a gift or a cruelty."

She answered him with a kiss—lingering, desperate, carrying the unspoken weight of a farewell neither of them would name.

When she pulled away, tears glistened on her cheeks. "Perhaps it is both."

They stood without speaking, the weight between them saying more than either dared speak.

"I want to give you something," she said at last, fingers tightening around the cord.

"You owe me nothing," he said, but she silenced him with a gentle touch.

"Let me." From the folds of her gown, she withdrew a simple cord—a necklace made of knotted black string adorned with shells and a single polished sea-green glass bead, worn smooth by time and tide.

"My mother gave it to me before I left the islands," she explained. Her voice trembled with meaning. "She said, 'Wear this to remember where you came from. Give it away when you find someone who makes you wish to stay.'"

She placed the necklace into his open palm, closing his fingers around it.

When she turned to leave, he didn't follow—that was their rule. He never walked her back, never risked discovery by leaving together.

Yet tonight, for the first time, that rule felt profoundly wrong.

"Mara—" His voice cracked, revealing the depth of his heart.

She paused at the corridor's edge, turning back slowly to look at him.

"I love you," he said simply, raw honesty laid bare.

She met his gaze, steady despite the sorrow in her eyes. "I know. And that's why I'm afraid."

Then she vanished, leaving behind only echoes of her presence.

For a long moment, Prince Harald remained where he stood, the necklace clenched in his hand—light as nothing, heavy as a promise he did not yet know he would break.

The chamber fell into an oppressive silence as Harald stood motionless beside the still form of his father. King Boris Thornsword, once as unyielding and fierce as the fortress he commanded, lay beneath blankets damp with the chill of death. Harald's breath came shallow, hesitant, as though his lungs had forgotten how to draw air. Loss settled in his chest, sharp and unrelenting.

At the far side of the chamber, Prince Alvis stood straight-backed despite the wetness on his face, his jaw set as if daring grief to show itself further.

Outside the window, dusk claimed the sky, pulling the last light away. Candles flickered weakly, their pale flames battling the encroaching dark.

The room stank of sick-sweet herbs, sweat, and something deeper, more primal—the scent of death had marked the air, an invader that would linger long after the corpse had been carried away.

Queen Edwina Thornsword swept into the doorway, her silhouette framed in candlelight—familiar, and already distant.

Her gaze flicked once to Alvis. "Enough. Leave us."

Alvis did not argue. He bowed his head once, sharply, and withdrew at once, his composure unbroken as he passed into the corridor. Edwina's sable gown looked carved from cold ambition—not grief, her gaze as sharp as a vulture spotting carrion. She glanced over her shoulder at her son, her voice honed by years of bitter victories.

"Harald, stop this nonsense. The court awaits."

Harald stared down at his father's unmoving figure, anger and disbelief warring within him. He felt again like a child—lost, resentful, stripped of choice. "He has barely drawn his last breath," he whispered harshly, bitterness etched into every syllable. "They can wait."

Edwina stepped fully into the room, her skirts whispering like knives against the cold stone. "They won't wait, nor will I allow it," she said, her voice dripping disdain. "A king must show strength—not sentiment. Weakness—grief—is blood in the water. Do you understand, boy?"

His fists tightened at his sides, knuckles pale as bone. "Let them circle, then. Let them see me bleed."

Her eyes narrowed, icy. "They will see more than your blood, Harald. They'll see opportunity. You will not disgrace this house because you lack the stomach to rule."

He raised his eyes slowly, meeting his mother's stare. "Do you feel nothing?"

Edwina drew a careful breath. Her lips curved, not into a smile, but something harder. "Ambition built this kingdom, Harald. It forged your father's legacy and will forge yours. There is no place for empathy. Your father understood that. Now it is your turn."

Without waiting for his response, she turned abruptly, vanishing into the corridor. Her footsteps echoed sharply, a reminder that she would always move first, leaving him alone with grief.

He reached out slowly, his fingers touching the cold, rough hand of the man who'd taught him everything. Memories surged, raw and painful—the weight of Boris's hand on his shoulder after his first hunt, the sharp rebuke following a careless swing of the sword, the rare, quiet nod of approval earned after battles hard-won. All those moments now felt small beneath death—and his mother.

A sound at the doorway drew him from his thoughts. He turned sharply, instinct and grief tangled in reflex.

"Forgive me, Your Highness," said Mara, slipping into the chamber barefoot. Lamplight caught her features, the sorrow in her eyes unmistakable. "Forgive me… I know this is neither the place nor the time, but I couldn't stay away."

His guard fell instantly, replaced by something softer, infinitely more dangerous. "Mara…" His voice cracked, revealing vulnerability he could ill afford. "You shouldn't be here. If my mother sees you—"

She hesitated, then crossed to him. "I belong where you need me. Even as a servant."

He grasped her hand, needing the warmth, the proof of life. "My father is gone. And my mother speaks only of crowns and thrones. Power is her only love, and she'll crush anything in its way. Even us."

Mara's eyes dropped to the necklace around Harald's neck—a simple cord of knotted black string adorned with shells and a single bead of sea-green glass. Her fingers brushed the glass, a smile touching her lips despite the room. "You kept it."

He closed his eyes briefly, savoring her gentle touch on the token of their bond. "Of course I did. It's all I have of you when you're not near."

Her eyes flicked up to meet his, and something deeper, troubled, clouded her gaze. "Harald, there's something else you must know. Something important."

He held his breath, sensing the shift in her tone. "Tell me."

She hesitated briefly, her voice trembling but steady. "I'm with child."

The words struck like a blow. Joy and terror all at once. He stared at her, eyes wide, heart hammering painfully within his chest. "Are you certain?"

Mara nodded slowly, her eyes glistening with unshed tears. "I wanted to wait, to find the right moment. But there may never be one."

He reached for her, drawing her into his embrace, pressing his forehead to hers. "We must be cautious. My mother—"

"I know," she said, clutching his tunic as if it could shield them both from the world. "I understand what it means. But it changes nothing. I will protect our child with everything I am."

He tightened his hold on her, determination taking root within him. "And I will protect you both."

Mara withdrew gently, eyes bright with love and sorrow. "They wait for you. The throne waits. But know you are not alone."

She withdrew, silent as she had come, leaving him beside his father's body, no longer only a son—but a man with something to lose.

With a final glance at the king who had shaped him, Harald drew himself up straight. As he stepped into the corridor, candlelight catching his profile, the servants lining the hall saw not a boy mourning his father, but a king born from loss, haunted by love, and burdened by secrets he could never claim.

Only two days had passed since the King's death, yet the queen's solar breathed serenity, a calm utterly at odds with the turmoil in Harald's chest. Perched in the high eastern tower, sunlight poured through latticework windows, pooling gold upon polished tile. The perfume of almond and jasmine drifted upward from the orchards below—cloying.

Harald despised the room. It was too pristine, too poised—a mirror of the woman who ruled it. He stood stiffly near the window, cloak draped across one shoulder, the royal sash still unfamiliar. A delicate mourning circlet rested on his brow, an intruder's thing rather than his own.

Queen Edwina sat behind her writing desk, her figure draped in mourning black, each line of her posture crisp with precision. Her slender hands worked methodically, melting wax and sealing letters, as though nothing beyond the desk required her attention.

"Why summon me here?" Harald asked. "The council awaits within the hour."

"And you will attend," Edwina replied, not glancing up. "You will speak only the words I've provided you. Nothing more."

He drew a steady breath and swallowed the impulse to argue.

Not today. Not here.

She pressed the final letter closed with meticulous precision, then leaned back slightly, eyes narrowing as she measured him.

"I've had troubling news, Harald." Her voice remained calm. "It seems you've been frequenting the servant corridors. A certain handmaid—Maralei, is it?—has not been sleeping where she ought."

Harald said nothing.

Edwina rose and crossed the room, every step measured, her gaze assessing him the way generals assessed terrain. "Do you think I didn't notice, my son? You carry your father's bearing—but your heart, that weak, vulnerable heart, betrays you."

"She's done nothing wrong," Harald answered coldly. "She's more honorable than most nobles you'll ever favor."

Her smile was thin. "I'm sure she is charming. Exotic—Varanese, I'm told. Pretty in the way servant girls can be until they're reminded of their station."

He felt his hands curl into fists, knuckles whitening. "She carries my child."

Edwina stopped. Then her eyes narrowed, satisfaction flickering there. "I know."

The air grew brittle. Harald stared, disbelief battling dread. "You knew, and you said nothing?"

Edwina let out a soft, humorless breath. "Because it does not matter. It never did."

"I love her," Harald said. "I intend to marry her."

Her expression did not change. "You will do no such foolish thing. You are king now. She isn't fit even to clean your boots."

Anger rose, sharp and uncontrolled. "You married beneath *your* station, mother."

Her voice hardened. "I married a warrior who seized his throne and stained the stones with blood to secure it. I married strength. You, my son, risk your kingdom for a momentary indulgence."

Harald stepped forward, meeting her challenge head-on. "She's no indulgence."

"No," Edwina agreed, her voice quiet. "She's worse—a weakness. And weaknesses are removed."

"Removed?"

"Not harmed," Edwina clarified. "Dismissed. Her service ends tonight. She will be escorted from Castellon under guard and sent beyond the Narcon Gate If she resists, the guards have orders that cannot be reversed."

"You cannot do this."

She met his gaze. "I already have."

He stepped closer, his voice harsh, incredulous. "You expect me to wed some court-bred noble girl, to smile in court and pretend she—Maralei—never existed?"

Edwina regarded him as if he were speaking from ignorance. "I expect you to marry a queen worthy of your name—worthy of this throne. One who strengthens the realm rather than disgracing it. One who will produce heirs suited to their station."

Harald stared at her, the silence thickening into something bitter and irreversible. His voice was low, tight. "I will never forgive you."

"You don't need to," she replied, unshaken, turning back to her desk and dipping her pen into ink once more. "You merely need to rule."

He lingered a moment longer, taking in the hard lines of her profile. Then he walked away, his heart hardening, burdened not only by grief but by duty.

As he left, the door closed behind him with a hollow echo. Inside the solar, Queen Edwina returned to her letters, her hand steady.

Late that same night, the small antechamber outside the king's new quarters lay dim and cold. A dying fire guttered in the hearth. Beyond the narrow window, fog swallowed the mountainside, cutting Castellon off from the world.

King Harald paced the cramped space, his boots scuffing against rushes that had long since lost their freshness. The cold barely registered against the tension in his chest. His fingers clenched and unclenched at his sides.

The heavy door opened, hinges creaking. Lord Lanyard Darkoak entered without flourish and closed it behind him. The scent of steel, leather, and cold rain followed.

"You summoned." His eyes assessed Harald. "You look like hell."

"I am," Harald replied, pausing in his pacing.

Lanyard remained unmoving.

He stopped and faced the older man. "I called for you, Lanyard, because you still serve my father's ideals. Loyalty before ambition. You're the only man I trust with this."

Lanyard raised an eyebrow slightly, something akin to respect flickering briefly across his guarded expression. "High praise," Lanyard said.

Harald drew a slow breath, steadying himself. "My mother has banished Maralei from the palace. She carries my child, and I was powerless to prevent it."

Lanyard watched him. "The servant girl—Maralei—is with child?" he asked.

Harald nodded. "Yes. I intended to marry her. I still do, whatever the consequences. But my mother has cast her out without coin or cloak, abandoned to the night and whatever dangers may find her."

"Your mother is ruthless," Lanyard said. "She fears weakness more than anything."

"I am not weak," Harald said. "But neither will I become heartless. A king who abandons his own blood abandons the crown with it."

Lanyard regarded Harald. "Your mother expects you to crumble under sentiment, to be ruled by passion."

"Passion is not weakness," Harald replied. "I will not abandon the woman I love, nor the child who will carry my blood." He stepped forward. "You swore allegiance to my father. Now you answer to me."

Lanyard held his gaze, then inclined his head. "What would you have me do, Your Majesty?"

"Keep her safe," Harald said. "Hide her and the child. Use what you need—gold, men, silence. See it done."

Lanyard considered, then nodded. "There's a village not too far from Castellon. Quiet. Overlooked. She will be protected."

Harald's features relaxed slightly, gratitude briefly softening his expression. "You'll handle this personally?"

"She will arrive unseen and remain hidden," Lanyard said.

Harald hesitated. "If my mother's spies find her?"

"They will not interfere."

Harald held his gaze. "I trust you, Lanyard. No one else can know."

"You have my vow. My loyalty lies with the Crown—and the man who now wears it."

Harald let out a slow breath. "Thank you."

Harald reached slowly beneath his cloak, drawing forth a small, carefully wrapped object. He unfolded the cloth to reveal a simple necklace—a cord of knotted black string adorned with shells and a single polished bead of sea-green glass, worn smooth by anxious touches.

"Give this to her," Harald said. "Tell her I'm sorry. And tell her I could not follow."

Lanyard took the necklace, its weight heavier than it looked. He met Harald's gaze. "She will receive your words, Your Majesty."

Lanyard turned to leave, pausing at the threshold only long enough to incline his head. Then he was gone, his footsteps fading into the corridor, leaving Harald alone with the dying fire.

It was the first day of Bloomrise, and the Grand Hall of Castellon Shield was dressed in full regalia for First Word—the celebration marking the turning of the year. The hall gleamed like polished armor, candlelight casting golden hues across stone walls freshly cleansed of grief, though Harald swore he could still see shadows of sorrow hidden within their cracks.

Now twenty-three, he wore a crown that weighed upon him, a reminder of duty rather than honor. The young prince he had been was gone.

The hall buzzed with whispers, laughter muted beneath the glittering chandeliers. Nobles gathered—lords, ladies, ambassadors—drawn to witness the forging of an alliance born from necessity, carefully orchestrated by a queen whose ambition held no room for sentiment.

The doors swung open.

"Announcing the delegation of the Kingdom of Vara," the steward's voice pierced the murmuring court. "Queen Avara Kaeleen Keeper of the Sho-Line, Lady of the Flamegrove, Ruler of the Vara Archipelago. Princess Miroray Kaeleen and Her Royal Highness Princess Avanna Kaeleen of the Flamegrove."

Heads turned sharply. Silence spread like frost.

They entered with regal poise, led by Queen Avarra.

She was tall, her bronze-brown skin catching the torchlight. There was nothing soft in the way she moved—every step deliberate, controlled. She did not look to the court as she entered; the court looked to her.

Behind her came her daughters.

Miroray, barely fifteen, held her chin high, her steps measured and practiced. Beside her, Avanna, nineteen, carried herself with astonishing composure—her frame draped in a gown of deep emerald, embroidered with silver thread. Her youth was undeniable, yet she bore the dignity of one well acquainted with duty.

Harald's jaw tightened at the sight of her, discomfort twisting into resentment toward the web his mother had spun.

Queen Edwina rose, her smile precise, her voice clear and unyielding, leaving no doubt who held control. "Welcome, Queen Avarra, Princess Avanna, Princess Miroray. Your presence strengthens bonds that shall secure peace and prosperity."

Avarra inclined her head respectfully, her voice clear and steady. "Your hospitality honors our kingdom, Your Majesty. May our alliance be one of lasting strength."

"Indeed," Edwina responded smoothly. "Strength is forged early, tempered over years. Tonight marks the first step of many." Her eyes slid to Harald, a silent command, precise and absolute.

He drew a slow breath and stepped forward. "Queen Avarra. Princess Avanna, Princess Miroray," he addressed them formally, his voice steady "The Kingdom of Eldaraine welcomes you with open arms. Your journey has been long, but let your hearts find warmth and hospitality within these halls." His gaze briefly met Avanna's "Tonight, your presence marks the beginning of unity between our two realms."

Polite applause followed, dutiful and without warmth.

The banquet commenced—pheasant glazed in honey, fresh river trout adorned with herbs—each dish a symbol of lavish distraction Harald barely touched. He watched as his mother navigated the room, every word and gesture guiding her audience toward her desired outcome, her presence commanding, cold, and undeniably triumphant.

At last, Queen Edwina stood at the top of the dias, her goblet gleaming under candlelight.

"My lords and ladies, tonight is more than feasting. Tonight, we lay foundations for unity. Prince Harald, come forward."

Harald stood. He looked toward Avanna, who met his eyes calmly, yet he saw the flicker of apprehension behind her brave facade.

She did not want this. He saw it in the set of her shoulders, in the careful stillness she held. Refusal meant turmoil—exactly as Edwina had calculated.

Harald let the silence hang. When he finally spoke, his voice was low and dignified.

"There are moments when a man becomes king through necessity, not joy. Today is such a day." His eyes flicked briefly toward his mother, a subtle but unmistakable accusation. He turned to Avanna, his expression grave but kind. "Princess Avanna, you come as a bridge between our realms. Not for love, but for the realm. Do you understand this?"

Avanna raised her head, eyes clear and relaxed despite the gravity. "I understand it well, Your Highness. My life has been shaped by duty since my first breath."

He held her gaze a moment longer. "Then we face this path as allies."

She walked forward, strong and resolute, and placed her hand lightly upon his extended palm. "I shall stand beside you," she said. "Not as your shadow, but as your equal in purpose."

Harald nodded solemnly, careful not to diminish her dignity by smiling falsely. There was no joy here, only solemn acknowledgment of mutual sacrifice.

Behind them, Queen Edwina lifted her goblet, her expression satisfied.

"To unity," she proclaimed.

"To unity." The court murmured dutifully, their applause polite.

Harald glanced at Avanna, seeing a young woman forced into the weight of rule. The bond forged today was political—and permanent.

Avanna held his gaze, understanding what stood between them, her posture unwavering. In her eyes, he saw resolve. That would have to be enough.

Emberfield lay beside the slow moving River Ostyn, tucked beneath dense woodland—a village forgotten on purpose. Muddy paths twisted through sagging cottages and weary taverns, roofs bowed under years of rain, walls greyed by neglect. Whispers lingered long after voices fell.

Into this place came Maralei, a newborn pressed to her chest. Wrapped in worn cloth, eyes sharpened by grief, she carried a southern accent the villagers never placed. They named her quickly—the Widow, the Witch, the Broken One—and let the truth rot where it lay.

Emberfield offered Mara no mercy. Her days began before dawn, feet raw from wet grass and riverbanks, fingers stiff with cold as she gathered herbs no one else wanted. She sold them for coppers and suspicion. By night, she stitched by candlelight while her son slept nearby—clean, fed, untouched by the village's hunger. Everything narrowed to him.

Villagers mocked her openly, yet came to her in secret, begging for fortunes. She gave them half-truths and soft lies—hope shaped to fit their fear.

One summer morning, Mara moved through the market, skirts damp, hair unbound. Stallholders followed her passing with eyes narrowed and wary.

At Old Ferren's fish stall, Mara paused. "Still perch, Ferren?" she asked, her voice edged with mockery.

Ferren gave a rough snort, eyeing her skeptically. "Fresher than those tall tales of yours, Mara."

By the well, washerwomen scrubbed linen, voices low and sharp.

"She was at it again," one hissed. "Last night. Even louder this time."

"About her boy again?" another scoffed, not bothering to keep her voice down.

"Aye," confirmed the first, voice grave. "Crowns, kings, fate—like a tavern minstrel, spinning yarns to scare children."

"Touched in the head," a third sneered, plunging her washcloth back into the bucket. "Or worse, dangerous. Lies like hers breed trouble."

Mara moved on, hearing everything. She pushed into the Copper Stag, its warped door protesting.

The barkeep barely glanced up. "Coin or more ghost stories today, Mara?"

Mara crossed to three farmhands by the hearth.

"My son," she began, her voice low and steady, "dreams of iron and flame. He sees stone towers crowned in fire, lands crying out for him."

One farmhand raised a skeptical eyebrow, smirking openly. "Is that right? And I dream I'm rich—but I ain't waking up in no lord's bed, am I?"

She stepped closer. "Mock as you please. The mark he bears is real—a crown, burned into him by fate. One day, you'll kneel and remember this moment."

Their laughter rang hollow, bravado thinly veiling sudden discomfort. Mara turned and slipped back into the street, their jeers following her.

She knew what they thought: madwoman, liar, danger. But her son bore a mark—nothing more than a birth-scar—but she had shaped it into prophecy. If she spoke it often enough, it might keep him alive.

Far from Emberfield, within Castellon Shield, Lanyard Darkoak read a single line scratched onto cheap parchment:

She's speaking. Loudly.

He burned it.

Coin had been sent when the king allowed it. Visits had been arranged when they could be hidden. This, though—this could not be bought or softened. When the last ash fell, Lanyard turned away, already calculating how much blood silence might cost.

The mist lay thick across the river flats. Dawn brought no relief—only a flat grey light that swallowed Emberfield whole.

No songbirds greeted the morning. No barking hounds echoed from distant farms. Even the trees stood rigid, unwilling witnesses.

Lord Lanyard Darkoak rode into the village's edge alone, his horse's hooves muffled against damp earth, his cloak dark with mist. He wore the smell of leather and pine, his face unreadable beneath the shadow of his hood. When he dismounted, he did not bother securing his mount. Loyalty or instinct would hold the beast—or it would not.

He paused before the cottage. The building leaned slightly west, its shutter hanging loose. Mud encroached on the stone threshold. No smoke curled from the chimney, no life stirred within.

Yet still he hesitated, standing at the door.

One knock.

Silence replied.

Lanyard opened the door and stepped into stale warmth that clung like worn grief. Herbs, now brittle, hung forgotten from the ceiling beams. A kettle sat cold and untouched. A child's wooden horse perched atop the windowsill, one eye skillfully carved, the other left incomplete, lost perhaps in a distraction or disappointment.

And in the corner, beneath a coarse wool blanket, the boy slept. Aulfis—ten years now—curled in sleep, unaware. Dark curls plastered to his forehead, fingers twitching in the last scraps of dream, a fresh bruise purpling on his elbow.

Lanyard moved past him like a ghost.

He had visited often through the years, never welcomed yet never refused. His presence marked only by the boots left by the hearth, bread upon the table, a discreet pouch of silver when taxes became too pressing. The boy had accepted these kindnesses without question, never asking their reason.

But another man visited too, more rarely, hidden beneath the moon's slender crescent. To Aulfis, he was simply Harry—a shadowed figure his mother named as his father.

Now Lanyard stood before the next room's door, fingers brushing the wood, hesitating a heartbeat before stepping through.

Maralei waited within, seated rigidly, hands folded so tightly her knuckles had gone white. The beauty of her face had waned, yet her dignity trembled beneath fear. Her gaze locked on Lanyard, knowing full well the reason for his presence.

"You came." Her voice shook despite her effort at control.

"You spoke." It was not an accusation. It was already a verdict.

She looked away. "I didn't mean to." She swallowed. "They wouldn't stop questioning. They suspected already, so I… I tried to deflect. But I said too much. I'm sorry."

Lanyard said nothing.

Maralei's eyes welled, her voice desperate. "I didn't want this. Please understand, my lord. I want to see him grow. To see him safe. I made a mistake. A foolish, selfish mistake."

"I know," Lanyard said. "But you gave them enough. They will not stop at you."

"Is there no other way? Please, let me take him far from here. I'll disappear. I'll vanish. I swear it."

He shook his head once. "You already swore once. Promises are fragile things."

She stared at him, hope crumbling into despair. Her voice, when she found it again, was broken. "Please, not now. Give me time—a little longer with him. Just enough to tell him goodbye."

"He must not see," Lanyard said. "It must be clean."

Maralei stood slowly, shoulders trembling. Her breathing steadied with effort. "He won't understand."

"He will, one day," Lanyard said. "He'll learn why it had to be done."

She turned. Her breath caught once, then steadied. As she moved, the necklace she had once given Harald caught the faint morning light, the sea-green glass bead shining briefly with quiet defiance. "Promise me—he'll know who I was. That I loved him fiercely."

"I promise," Lanyard said, drawing his blade. "He will remember you."

She drew a final shuddering breath, closing her eyes tightly. "Tell Harald… I'm sorry. Forgive me."

"I will."

She drew a final breath and did not step back.

Lanyard held her gaze. For a moment neither of them moved.

"I will make it quick," he said.

She nodded once, trembling.

He moved forward and pulled her into him, one hand at her shoulder, the other finding its mark beneath her ribs. The blade entered cleanly.

Her breath left her in a small, broken sound. She did not struggle. She held to him until her weight gave way.

He lowered her to the floor himself.

Lanyard knelt only long enough to close her eyes. His mouth moved, but no sound came. Rising, he cleaned his blade and sheathed it. His gaze fell to the necklace tangled at her throat. He removed it carefully, fingers lingering over the sea-green glass bead before closing his hand around it.

Turning to leave, Lanyard noticed a letter lying unfinished on the table nearby. He lifted it, eyes scanning Mara's delicate handwriting:

"Harald— The world is colder when you leave me. Colder than the frost in the hills. I don't care for her name, or her crown. Only that you come back with warmth still in you. He speaks of you, our son. We are waiting for your warmth to return. Eternal Love, Mara"

Lanyard folded the letter and placed it inside his coat.

In the other room, Aulfis sat awake, eyes clouded with confusion and lingering dreams.

"Lord Lanyard?" he asked, voice thick with sleep.

"Yes."

"Where's my mother?"

Lanyard crouched, meeting the child's questioning gaze. "She's gone," Lanyard said. The words tasted like rust.

The boy blinked, confusion warring with growing fear. "Gone?"

"A man came," Lanyard said. He chose the lie. "A robber, desperate and cruel. She stood her ground, Aulfis. She fought for you. Remember that—your mother fought fiercely, She fought for you."

Aulfis' small face twisted in silent anguish, yet tears did not come—not yet. "She always said she'd fight."

Lanyard's voice was low and steady. "She did."

"Did she hurt him?"

"She made him bleed," Lanyard said, his voice thick with a pain far deeper than the boy could yet understand.

"Where will I go?" Aulfis finally asked, voice trembling.

"With me."

"Why?"

Lanyard regarded him solemnly. "Because she asked it of me. And because I gave my word."

Aulfis stared long and searchingly, then rose shakily to his feet, barefoot and uncertain. Without another question, he allowed Lanyard to help him into his boots.

Together they stepped out into the mist.

That night, the cottage burned. Villagers called it robbery and saw only a stranger riding from town at dawn, questions unasked and unanswered.

After that, Lanyard Darkoak never looked at a child without remembering what mercy had cost.

The early morning sun spilled through the high windows, pooling across the stone floor of Lanyard Darkoak's apartments. The chambers were sparse and functional. Thick tapestries muted sound. A fire burned low in the hearth against the chill of the old stone.

Lanyard stood framed by the window's light, watching the city stir. His silhouette cut a figure of command, tall and rigid, his posture impeccable despite the passing years. The faint lines around his eyes and mouth spoke not of age alone, but of burdens carried unseen.

Behind him, seated near the fire, Aulfis rubbed a whetstone methodically along the edge of a short training blade. Each stroke measured, a rhythm learned long ago from the man who stood nearby.

"Again," Lanyard said.

"'Keep your guard up. Control your breathing,'" Aulfis recited dutifully, not pausing in his task.

"And?"

"'Your enemy never cares about your comfort. Make sure discomfort is familiar, an ally rather than distraction.'"

Lanyard nodded. "Good."

Aulfis glanced upward, a grin breaking across his face. "I've memorized your lessons better than most men twice my age."

"Lessons remembered in calm are easily forgotten in chaos." Lanyard turned to face him fully, eyes sharp and assessing.

Aulfis set the whetstone aside, rising fluidly, stretching briefly to ease the stiffness from his limbs. At twenty, he was no longer the uncertain boy once taken under Lanyard's wing.

Time and training had forged him into something far stronger—a man tempered by discipline, with shoulders broad from drills, hands calloused and quick from combat.

Yet still, beneath the strength lay a restless edge, a silent question neither man dared voice openly.

"Master Junfolda says I've improved," Aulfis remarked, rolling his shoulders, already convinced. "Yesterday, he showed me how to strike an opponent's joints and pressure points. Quick moves—like stepping sideways, turning swiftly to twist an enemy's wrist, or using their momentum against them. He has me practicing forms that mimic the movements of animals. There's one like a crane—balanced and precise, and another that resembles a serpent—swift and shifting."

"Daelchi praises sparingly," Lanyard observed dryly. "If he compliments you, be wary—he's either about to demonstrate a painful lesson or expects you to fail spectacularly."

Aulfis laughed, confident. "He reminds me of someone else I know."

"Indeed," Lanyard said, a small, rare smile pulling briefly at his lips. "Pay close attention to Master Junfolda. Soon enough, we will blend his teachings with your swordsmanship—two arts forged into one."

The silence that followed held comfortably, each man contemplating quietly. Lanyard studied Aulfis carefully, memories flickering behind his unreadable eyes—the boy he'd been, the mother he'd lost, the secret he'd unknowingly carried. Aulfis caught the look, tilting his head slightly in unspoken question.

"You have questions," Lanyard stated, not bothering with pretense.

"I always have questions." Aulfis shrugged lightly. "But you taught me answers come only when ready. I can wait."

"Patience is rare in your generation."

"Blame my teacher," Aulfis quipped smoothly. "He taught me well."

Lanyard's expression shifted, a flicker of pride beneath his composed mask. "Perhaps too well."

Lanyard stepped away from the window and crossed to a small cedar chest atop a sturdy oak table. He lifted the lid and retrieved a necklace—a single bead of polished sea-green glass and small shells strung on knotted black cord. He stood a moment, the memory in his eyes unguarded.

He turned back toward Aulfis and held the necklace out. "This belonged to your mother. Do you remember it?"

Aulfis's brows lifted—surprised, but not shaken. "Yes. She wore it every day. I remember it clearly."

Lanyard placed the necklace into Aulfis's waiting palm. "She would have wanted you to have it." His gaze softened. "Remember her—not only as she was, but who she hoped you'd become."

Aulfis held the necklace, gaze fixed on the familiar object. "Thank you. I will honor it—and her memory."

Lanyard returned to the window, his gaze distant. Aulfis watched him, sensing what remained unspoken between them.

"You know," Aulfis said at last, casual and unguarded, "you're the only man I've never heard lie."

Lanyard's jaw tightened. He did not look at Aulfis. "Then you've been listening poorly," he said—and the old lie burned its way back down his throat.

A moment passed before Lanyard spoke again. "Master Junfolda has requested I grant you a rest day. Go to the market, or walk the gardens. Reflect on your teachings."

Aulfis pushed away from the hearth, heading toward the door. "Same hour tomorrow?"

"Earlier," Lanyard said.

Then he turned back toward the window. "Aulfis."

The boy—no, the man—paused at the door, waiting in silence.

"She made sure you'd live. Whatever else you carry, carry that too."

Aulfis nodded once and slipped through the door.

It shut behind him, leaving Lanyard alone. The city sprawled beneath him—bright, indifferent, and unmoved by what he had done to keep it standing.

CHAPTER FOURTEEN

Castellon was quieter at night, damp air threading its alleys. Faileas walked it like an old song remembered in a dream, boots brushing cold damp from the cobbles with each calculated step. No scroll this time. No forged lies tucked under his cloak. Only his face hidden behind a name.

The lamps flickered along the eastern spines of the merchant quarter, where butcher shops met abandoned breweries and forgotten storehouses. Faint whorls of smoke curled up from chimneys.

Faileas—no, Alerick beneath the smile and scholar's lean—moved like someone both known and invisible. The persona fit snug tonight: the quiet scribe, the half-joke of Castellon's court. A man who bowed too easily, smiled too politely, and was always where he didn't belong. Perfect.

He adjusted his folio—empty save for a folded cloth and a small vial of resin that gave off a lemony scent, faint enough to suggest recent travel. One more illusion. One more layer.

The streets narrowed as he neared the Shield. Castellon's eastern rise curved upward, framing the royal quarter like a dagger's hilt—shining, ceremonial, and meant for blood. The lower windows of noble towers were already shuttered against the night air, but high above, a pale glow seeped through velvet-draped balconies and drawn silks.

Faileas' gaze followed one such window.

There were still a few eyes in the dark, and he'd taught most of them how to see.

He passed a pair of guards near the edge of the Shield—young, bored, one slightly drunk. Neither noticed him.

Or rather, they noticed what they were meant to: a harmless figure in travel-worn muted leather, slipping past with the fluid anonymity of a scribe two days late.

And no one had stopped him.

By the time he reached the western stair that led to the Shield's inner terrace, the night had deepened. Fog crawled up the stone like a starving thing. Alerick climbed, bootfalls muffled, posture shifting with each landing—less Faileas now, more shadow.

When he reached the upper hall, he paused.

The apartment's balcony window stood closed—unlocked and unwatched.

The chamber was steeped in warmth, broken only by the low lick of fire in the hearth and the faint rustle of velvet as Lady Elara Icewind studied her reflection. The mirror offered back a woman armored in midnight blue, her nightgown as fluid as shadow, her gaze harder than the steel sheathed beneath it. Around her, opulence pressed close—tapestry-lined walls stitched with gold thread, and a scent of sandalwood and myrrh thick in the air.

Behind her, the handmaiden's hands worked as they finished lacing the gown. She was young, sharp-boned and alert, her posture precise, her eyes quick and assessing even as her hands worked.

"Elara," came a voice from the darkened balcony.

The girl stilled. Elara did not.

Alerick stepped through the parted curtains with an easy, unhurried confidence. His cloak shifted softly behind him. Pale eyes glinted with the kind of mischief that ruined dynasties.

"It is done," he murmured.

Elara lifted two fingers. The handmaiden stepped back, inclined her head in a clean, practiced curtsey.

"Yes, mistress."

She turned and left without haste, the latch clicking shut behind her like a punctuation mark.

"The scroll with Valen's seal—now sits in Stormviðr's hands. He read it twice—first like a warrior, then like a man trying not to believe what he already knows."

She turned toward the fire. "And you think he'll go?"

"He already has." He stepped into the light, his palm grazing the edge of a low shelf. "Whatever that man believes in, it's not Eldaraine. If the Northmen are half as proud as the legends, he'll seek them. He'll warn them. Maybe he'll even lead them."

"Lead them?" Elara echoed.

"You wanted distraction. Nuvareki crossing Frostmere will provide it."

"As long as it only distracts, we do not want a war."

Alerick rolled one shoulder in a loose shrug, gaze drifting toward the fire as if the outcome were a matter of weather.

Elara's expression shifted. "One more crack in the marble…"

She moved toward the hearth, trailing silk and the scent of myrrh, stopping only when the flames bathed her in amber. "And the others?"

Alerick strolled forward, unhurried. "The dissenters in Hillmere and Blackgrove grow restless. With the right push—coin, whispers, the promise of old grievances repaid—they'll be gnawing at the king's ankles before he notices the floorboards have gone soft."

Elara's gaze sharpened slightly. "And the grain shipment to House Caerlyn?"

"Arranged as agreed," he replied. "False shipping orders filed in three different ledgers. Two clerks paid, one threatened. No trail that leads to you." His tone remained cool, as if it cost nothing to engineer distrust between nobles. "Even Lady Olivia's garden-variety spies are convinced."

She held out a small pouch. He accepted it with a slight bow of the head, turning it once in his fingers as if measuring more than its weight. Then he placed it gently back into her palm.

"Keep it," he said quietly. "Your house has greater need of coin than I do."

Elara's fingers closed around the pouch, but she did not lower her hand. "You earned it."

"So did you," he replied.

"It was agreed." Her tone did not sharpen, but it hardened.

"And I am revising the agreement."

For a moment, they simply regarded one another—the coin resting between them like a dare.

At last, she drew the pouch back to her side table. "Very well," she said. "But do not mistake prudence for charity."

Alerick inclined his head slightly. "I never do."

"And what of their honor? The Hravnskot. Will it bend when pressed, or break and turn back on us?"

"It bends if you speak their tongue. Not the words, but the rhythm. They respect strength wrapped in truth. Or a good lie told without flinching."

"You sound almost fond of them."

One brow lifted in faint amusement. "I spent a year in their hunting camps. Once danced shirtless in a storm to earn a clan leader's trust. I regret nothing—except the mead. Flames, the mead."

She almost smiled again. Almost.

Her voice cooled. "You're certain they'll follow *him*?"

Alerick met her gaze, unblinking. "Rodrik Stormviðr is no southern noble. They know his name. His blood ties him to the wilds beyond the mountains, and his scars speak louder than titles. If he tells them Eldaraine is dying, they'll believe it. If he calls them to war…" He tilted his head slightly. "They'll sharpen their axes."

Elara didn't respond at once. The fire crackled. Then: "We must be careful. Their savagery is a blade, yes—but one that rarely waits for a hand to wield it."

Alerick chuckled. "The Storm doesn't want war. Neither do we. But he'll choose his path. We prepare for whichever one he takes."

Elara gave a sharp dip of her chin, deliberate as a dagger drawn. Then she dismissed him—not with a word, but a glance.

Alerick bowed. "Until next time," he said, already stepping backward into the curtains.

Elara's voice followed. "I'll keep the embers warm."

He vanished like smoke, and the fire crackled louder in his absence. Elara stared into the dancing light, her thoughts a blur of tactics and threads, of oaths unspoken and crowns unworn.

Then, a soft knock at the door.

Her spine stiffened, but it wasn't fear. It was restraint. She moved across the chamber with deliberate grace and opened the door.

Prince Baldrik stood there, cloak sprinkled with rain, cheeks flushed from the evening air. His hair was damp at the temples, his hands behind his back. And his eyes—those bright, foolish, honest eyes—searched her face like they were starving.

"I brought these," he said, holding out a small bouquet. White, fragile things with petals like fallen snow. The thorns had been carefully stripped.

Elara took them without looking down. "Winter roses," she said quietly. "These are out of season."

"From the royal gardens," Baldrik said at once. "My mother's collection. She keeps them in protected beds."

Elara's mouth curved, just barely. "Brave. But you shouldn't have."

She stepped aside.

He entered, nervous in the way only the unseasoned and the newly powerful could be.

For a heartbeat, neither of them moved. Then Elara reached for him—once, decisively—and the rest of the world narrowed to breath and closeness and the soft fall of silk as the door shut behind them.

The world beyond the chamber did not return for some time.

The fire had burned low. Shadows moved slow and soft across the chamber walls, amber light brushing the curve of her shoulder where the velvet coverlet had slipped. She sat propped against the headboard, the blanket draped loosely across her hips.

Her hair was unpinned, falling forward in a soft veil over her chest, a careless elegance that left everything and nothing to the imagination. Her fingers traced lazy circles on the rim of her wine cup. The roses he'd brought lay wilting on the writing table, untouched since they'd fallen there.

Baldrik lay beside her, one arm flung over his eyes, the other curled loosely over his chest. His chest rose and fell in the slow rhythm of contentment, not yet sleep.

"You're quiet," she said.

He shifted slightly. "Trying not to ruin it."

"Ruin what?"

"This," he said, voice barely above a whisper. "You. Me. The world before the real world comes knocking."

Elara didn't answer. She watched the fire a moment longer, then set the cup aside. Her thoughts wandered corridors untouched by coin or consequence. Not plans. Not profit. Not the careful curve of whispers she'd set in motion. Just him.

The way he reached for her like she was something worth holding, not hiding. The way his fingers had shaken at first, then steadied—not out of lust, but reverence.

She turned toward him slowly and lay down, drawing the coverlet over both of them.

"You think too much," she murmured, laying her head on his chest.

He smiled without opening his eyes. "That's what the Order says."

She traced his collarbone with her fingertips, slow and knowing. "They're not wrong."

A beat passed. Then: "Will you still be kind when I disappoint you?"

He opened his eyes now, brows drawn. "Why would you?"

She didn't answer right away. Instead, she kissed the center of his chest, right where his heartbeat pulsed against her lips.

He wrapped his arms around her and pulled her close. "I don't want to be king," he whispered. "Not really."

"I know," she said softly.

He rested his chin on her hair. "But I might have to be."

She said nothing at first. Her hand rested flat against his ribs, feeling the steady rise and fall beneath her palm. She wanted to believe there was still time. Time to twist the tide. Time to change which crown would find his brow. Or whether either of them could survive what followed.

She tilted her face upward, eyes playful in the fire's glow. "So am I to marry you now?" she teased softly, echoing the innocent question of the lost little Sylvie.

Baldrik's lips twitched into a mischievous smile, eyes twinkling with exaggerated thoughtfulness. "I am still considering it. It may be too soon to—"

Elara gasped, feigning indignation, and playfully pounded her fists against his chest. "You arrogant—"

Laughing warmly, he caught her wrists, pulling her close until her playful protests melted away in the heat of his kiss. Her breath tangled in her throat, pulse fluttering beneath his touch.

Breaking the kiss gently, Baldrik rested his forehead against hers, his voice tender, earnest, and filled with quiet certainty. "I love you, Elara."

Right there, right then, Elara did not want to be anywhere else. The feeling was exquisite—and it terrified her, sharp and bright as a blade held too close to the heart.

The coals sighed low in the hearth.

Neither moved.

And outside, Castellon slept beneath a sky thick with stars and the hush of spring wind.

The candlelight danced unevenly across the stone walls of the royal bed chamber, throwing shadows across the chamber walls. Queen Avanna's fingers worked with strange rhythm, drawing her needle through dusk-colored velvet. She was no longer sure what she had meant to embroider—some garden bloom or family crest, perhaps—but the design twisted now into shapes she didn't recall starting.

Beside her, a silver tray held a half filled goblet. The wine had already done its work. It always did, subtly. Softening. Distorting. A warmth in her chest that felt like clarity but coiled with shadows just beneath it. A restless sensation crawled under her skin, whispering suspicions she didn't want to hear—about Elara, about Harald, about herself. Reality felt thin, sharp enough to cut if she leaned too hard.

Across the chamber, King Harald stood over his war table, posture carved from stone, eyes fixed on the western coast, where parchment edges curled from heat. He hadn't spoken since she'd started needling the silence.

"They look too comfortable—Elara and Baldrik." Avanna said. Her voice was even, soft, yet brittle.

Harald didn't answer immediately. His fingers hovered briefly over a carved marker, a momentary hesitation betraying a flicker of uncertainty beneath his serene exterior. Then he moved it inland, toward Westmere's vulnerable grain roads.

"She's dangerous," Avanna went on, her tone now sharp with a heat she couldn't explain. "You saw her. That smile. Like a cat who's found the warmest spot in the castle. And plans to piss on it."

Only the scrape of stone on wood answered her, Harald moving another marker.

She let the embroidery drop into her lap.

"What of our son?" Her voice cut, each syllable honed. "Is he to lead our armies? Or retreat into riddles and parables like a cloistered philosopher?"

Harald's brow furrowed. "He is young." His voice was firm, tinged with weariness.

"Eighteen is old enough to bleed," she snapped. Her fingers had curled without realizing it—nails digging into her own palm, pain grounding her momentarily against the paranoia spinning at the edge of her thoughts. "Your father took the throne at fourteen. Baldrik has already survived blades, politics, scandal. What more would you have him endure before he's ready?"

He turned then, face partly caught in shadow, lines deeper around the eyes than she remembered. For a heartbeat, the mask slipped, revealing quiet vulnerability. "He is not my father."

"No," she said coldly. "He's softer. And softer things break faster."

The silence that followed wasn't peace—it was distance.

She stood, moving toward him across the stone floor with a regal, calculated grace. Yet something in her gait stuttered. A half-step falter she disguised with a turn. Her breath caught, jaw tightening—not with rage, but with restraint, like something held back too long.

"He is slipping away from us, Harald," she said. "From me. From duty. From the throne."

Harald exhaled, long and slow, placing both hands flat against the top of the table. The candlelight caught the silver threading through his hair—hair she'd once braided herself, before these talks turned cold and her fingers shook too much for ceremonial graces. He steadied himself with visible effort, the tension in his shoulders a reminder of the burdens he bore silently.

"He wants to join the Order," he said quietly, each word weighed carefully.

Avanna scoffed, bitter and low. "A boy's fantasy. Give him a sword and a crown and he'll feel wise enough."

"It's not a fantasy," Harald replied. "It's a discipline. A way of thought."

"From where?" she hissed, stepping forward. Her head swam, dizziness clawing at the edges of her vision, words tangling on her tongue. She forced the accusation out, venomously clear. "Books and silence—or her?"

Her voice cracked like a whip, and for a breath, neither of them spoke. Her temples throbbed. The chamber pressed in, thick with memory. His face blurred, distant.

"I will not forbid him," Harald said with quiet strength. "He must choose his own path."

"No," Avanna said, "You're giving up."

"I'm letting him grow," Harald countered, and the subtle vulnerability in his voice was clear now. "I cannot rule his heart, Avanna."

"You're handing him to her."

Her hands trembled now, one still clutching the embroidery needle like a forgotten weapon.

"And if he falls into her arms and out of your reach," she continued, "you'll sit here, folding maps while the realm burns."

Harald's jaw shifted, but he kept his voice steady. "You think I'm blind to ambition. I'm not. I know what Elara is. But our son—our son is still shaping himself. If we crush him now, we forge a tyrant."

"And if we wait too long?" Avanna asked. "We forge a ghost."

She turned from him, moving to the high arched window, palms pressed flat to the chill stone sill. She leaned her forehead briefly to the glass. Outside, the towers of Castellon Shield stood vigilant under the pale spring sky, wind stirring the upper banners in restless fits.

Behind her, Harald's voice came quietly, resolute yet burdened.

"We shall see."

She didn't turn.

Her hand twitched once against the stone. A tightness curled behind her eyes—not quite tears, not quite pain. She closed them, breathing slow, trying to anchor herself against the restless whispers echoing louder inside her head.

Somewhere in her, something stirred.

She didn't know if it was worry.

Or war.

But she did know this: Baldrik would not be allowed to vanish into firelight and fables. Not while she still drew breath. Not while the crown still had claims to make and histories to invoke. If his path would not bend to duty, then she would give him reason to return to it—through obligation, through protection, through a future only she could secure.

The queen exhaled slowly, her reflection faint against the glass. Let Elara play her little games.

Avanna did not play games, and she would not lose her son.

★

The Castellon market was alive with energy, vibrant and bustling beneath a bright spring sun. Aulfis moved leisurely, his natural charm drawing subtle, appreciative glances from women young and old alike. His easy-going presence and easy grin created a ripple of goodwill as he greeted vendors and shoppers alike.

Yet beneath his carefree demeanor lay Lord Darkoak's disciplined warnings: *Do not reveal your true heritage, nor your relation to me.* His story was carefully maintained—simple, humble, and utterly believable.

Pausing near a cloth merchant's stall, his attention was captured by a heated dispute. A young woman, dressed plainly in commoner's attire, was locked in a fierce negotiation with a stubborn merchant. Her back was rigid, her face flushed with indignation. The merchant scowled, dismissively flicking his fingers at the neatly folded silk garments spread before him.

Drawn by the edge in her voice, Aulfis stepped closer, catching fragments of their conversation.

"These gowns are fine quality," she insisted firmly, voice steady despite obvious frustration. "Your offer is an insult."

The merchant sneered. "Fine quality or not, these are clearly worn. I'm being generous as it is."

Aulfis cleared his throat, stepping up beside her with an easy, disarming expression. "Pardon the intrusion, but perhaps I might assist?"

Both merchant and young woman turned swiftly. Her eyes widened slightly in alarm, cheeks flushing deeper as she recognized him glancing toward the intimate silk garments.

"I'm considering a purchase myself," Aulfis declared smoothly, feigning serious interest as he reached for one of the garments. He held it up carefully, then hesitated, realizing exactly what he'd grasped—a delicate silk nightgown. He caught the briefest flash of mortification cross the young woman's face and straightened, smoothing his expression with practiced ease.

"Remarkable craftsmanship!" he announced loudly, deliberately ignoring his own discomfort. He turned it gently in his hands as though inspecting a rare treasure. "Why, on Vara they'd pay two gold easily for such luxury. Perhaps even Queen Miroray herself would desire this."

The merchant's eyes narrowed, greed replacing skepticism. "Two gold? You're exaggerating."

"Not at all," Aulfis assured him. "They prize such delicate artistry greatly in the islands. I might just make the lady an offer myself."

The merchant's expression shifted quickly from suspicion to alarm. "Wait now," he protested sharply. "I was negotiating first! I'll pay you thirty silver—that's double my original offer!"

The young woman paused, carefully masking her embarrassment, glancing between them before nodding. "Agreed."

With a quiet breath, she reclaimed the nightgown from Aulfis, folding it neatly before placing it back with the others. Then, voice hushed, she met his gaze—lingering embarrassment tempered by reluctant gratitude.

"Thank you."

"Aulfis," he offered, keeping his expression respectful.

She studied him briefly, a faint, wry curve touching her lips. "Elara."

"A pleasure, Elara," Aulfis replied. "I'll walk with you," Aulfis said easily, already angling his body to match her direction. "Make sure no other merchants try their luck."

Elara hesitated. Her eyes flicked once to his hand, then away. "That won't be necessary," she said politely. "I can manage."

Aulfis remained unbothered. "I don't doubt it. Still—markets are easier with company."

He offered no pressure beyond that, just the quiet certainty of someone used to being agreed with.

Elara inclined her head after a brief pause. "Very well. Briefly."

Together they moved through the crowd. The earlier awkwardness softened, though it did not vanish entirely. Elara laughed once at something he said, then caught herself, her gaze sliding past him rather than meeting his.

They strolled past stalls overflowing with vibrant fabrics, polished trinkets, and the aroma of bread and spiced wine, the air rich with the mingled scents and sounds of city life.

Elara paused frequently, eyes brightening at a glittering necklace or a finely embroidered scarf, though she never lingered long enough to encourage the merchants' hopeful entreaties. Aulfis matched her pace easily, drawn to her laughter and the quiet curiosity that flickered in her eyes.

Eventually, they stopped before a woodcrafter's stall nestled among other artisans. Elara examined a finely carved box, fingers tracing its intricate patterns, appreciation evident in her thoughtful expression.

Aulfis reached absently for a small wooden horse among other carved toys. The polished wood felt smooth beneath his fingertips, the craftsmanship delicate yet sturdy. He stared down at the toy, suddenly silent.

A memory tugged—fragile and scattered. A gift. A voice.

The weight of it in smaller hands. Laughter in a sunlit place he no longer knew how to name.

His breath caught, and for a flicker of a moment, the market sounds dulled into static.

Elara's voice drew him back. "Are you alright?"

He blinked, forcing the memory back behind a soft smile. "Yes. Just... lost for a moment."

"Something meaningful?"

He shook his head lightly, already stepping back. "No. Nothing that matters now."

She regarded him, sensing more beneath the surface but choosing not to press. She offered a polite nod, the kind given when one knows better than to ask more.

They continued their walk, conversation drifting toward lighter subjects—ceramics, jewelry, spices. Aulfis purchased two fresh pastries, handing one to her with a grin.

Beyond the final row of stalls lay the Castellon Gardens, lush and quiet. They wandered down winding paths among rose beds and fountains, the city's noise replaced by birdsong and the trickle of water.

Elara sighed. "I've always loved it here."

"It's beautiful," Aulfis said. "Thank you, Elara. This has been a rare delight."

"It was… refreshing," she said.

They walked in silence, unspoken awareness between them. When the sun dipped behind Castellon's towers, casting golden light through the trees, Elara sighed.

"I must return," she said softly.

Aulfis nodded. "So must I."

They moved slowly toward the garden's edge. At the gate, they paused beneath rustling leaves.

"Well," Aulfis said, "I suppose this is where we part."

"Yes," she replied. "Thank you again, Aulfis. Today was... unexpected."

"They usually come when you're not trying for them. Will I see you again?" he asked.

She hesitated. "Perhaps," she said, and did not meet his eyes. Then added, "Perhaps. In the market. Or the gardens."

With a polite bow Aulfis said. "I hope so."

She turned, and he watched her slip away. She started to glance back, then seemed to think better of it, her smile fading as she disappeared into the crowd.

And for the first time in weeks, he didn't think of Darkoak's rules.

He thought of her.

And how inconvenient that was.

CHAPTER FIFTEEN

The war room in Castellon Shield was high-walled and still. Firelight from the hearth dragged shadows across banners and stone kings long past. The air smelled of ink, parchment, old wool, and cold steel.

King Harald Thornsword stood at the central table, sleeves rolled, knuckles stained with ink, the edge of a compass turning slowly between his fingers. He leaned forward like a man in a forge—not crafting weapons this time, but trying to temper a kingdom on the edge of fracture.

"You know," he muttered, eyes still on the map, "I may be the best swordmaker the realm's ever seen. I can fold steel a hundred times, temper it to sing on strike—but no matter how sharp I make it, I can't stop it being pointed the wrong way once it leaves my hand."

Across from him, Lord Lanyard Darkoak raised a single brow. "Modesty suits you, Your Majesty. Like lace on a hammer."

Harald smirked without humor. "Your honesty is cutting."

He looked up. "Which is one reason I keep you around. Otherwise, I'd have replaced you with someone prettier."

Lanyard didn't blink. "A prettier one might kiss your ass better, but she wouldn't keep it attached."

There was a pause as the jest dried into fact.

"Queen Miroray of Vara is due in Castellon within the week. She's already landed at Eastmere—unbidden. Twenty ships. No warning. No request for audience. The Queen and I have no idea why she comes. See that the streets are cleaned, banners raised, the full courtesy shown. Avanna's sister expects precision."

"I understand. I will see to it at once."

Lanyard turned to leave, but Harald's next words nailed him in place.

"Next order of business—secrets."

The chamber door made no sound—but they both heard it.

Alerick stepped through without a sound. He moved without hurry, dressed in slate-gray linen—no armor, no insignia, not even a blade. Just a man-shaped question wrapped in fabric. The half-smile on his face was the kind usually seen before someone pulled a coin from your ear… or a dagger from your ribs.

Lanyard didn't hide his distaste. "*You.*" The word landed like spit on hot steel.

Harald didn't flinch. "He's not here to stab anyone."

"Shame," Lanyard muttered, folding his arms. "It's what he's good at."

"I pay him for knowledge, not blood." Harald's voice was even, but the unspoken '*this time*' carried enough weight to bend the air.

Alerick approached the map table with the unbothered gait of someone who'd already left three back exits mapped in his head. He didn't bow so much as incline, a gesture laced with indifference.

"Where would Your Majesty like me to start?"

Harald didn't hesitate. "Valen."

Alerick's fingers brushed across the edge of the table. "He's rerouting grain through Caerlyn's eastern silos. Dummy manifests. False shortages. In truth, he's hoarding—twice the crown's quota, if not more. Enough to drive panic in three cities if released in pieces."

Harald's jaw tensed, slow like a grindstone turning on stubborn steel.

"Ashbriar?"

Alerick tilted his head. "Not rebel fire. Paid mercenaries—expensive ones, efficient, clean. Left behind coin trails and bodies missing their boots. Valen's handwriting is all over it. Not literal, of course, but figurative fingerprints? Everywhere."

"And the southern roads?"

"Deliberately targeted. Trade routes cut with surgical precision—enough to disrupt, not enough to ignite rebellion. Delays, raids, scattered reports. All too clean. No one's that efficient by accident. Not even nomads. Word is he's been working with Lord Narcona—nothing formal, no signed contract, but coordination all the same. Valen's likely bleeding both ends of the ledger—chaos up front, coin in the back."

Lanyard's brow creased. "So why hasn't he made a move?"

Alerick smiled faintly, and the room seemed to darken a little, though the fire hadn't dimmed. "Because he's still stacking the board. He hasn't flipped it yet. He's waiting until he's sure no one else can play."

The silence stretched. Weighty. Grim.

Then Lanyard, without looking away from Alerick, asked, "And Lady Elara?"

Alerick extended his hand, palm up.

Lanyard reached into his coat and dropped a coin pouch into it. The sound of silver was brief, but distinct.

Alerick bounced it once, weighing. "She's attached herself to the would-be king by design," he said. "The visits have grown regular. Evenings. Always unannounced. Never through the front hall. He's enamored. She's… considering him."

Harald's eyes narrowed slightly.

"She wants stability," Alerick added. "But she's learned the crown doesn't offer it. Only proximity to power. She's placing her bets on the heir apparent. And she may have wagered more than her title."

Lanyard's gaze narrowed. "You mean she's compromised?"

Alerick gave a sly smile, then let it fall. "I mean she's calculating. And for the moment... winning."

"Continue," Harald said.

"Her estate is a snowdrift in the sun. Failed crops. Drought-stricken foals. Debt up to the rafters. Kept standing by timing, favors, and just enough polish to delay scrutiny. And the run of it—" he paused, choosing the word carefully, "—feels almost too convenient. Bad luck has been especially cruel as of late."

Lanyard's eyes didn't leave Alerick. "Bad luck doesn't usually arrive on schedule. You suspect interference?"

Alerick's shoulders lifted a fraction—barely a shrug. "I suspect patterns. I haven't been asked to look closer. Yet."

"So, she wants the crown instead," Harald murmured, voice low but edged.

"Her original interest in Baldrik wasn't love true," Alerick said. "It was survival. Leverage. That hasn't vanished—but it's no longer the only motive. She's quieter. Less performative. When she's with him, she isn't watching the room the way she used to."

Lanyard stared across the table. "You sure of that?"

"I know obsession," Alerick said. "And I know treason. If she's playing him now, it's the most convincing long con I've ever seen—and it gains her nothing she didn't already want. Draw your own conclusions."

Harald exhaled slowly, the breath of a man who's seen too many sparks catch where no one meant them to. "That'll be all."

Alerick bowed, this time with something closer to respect. He stepped back and left the chamber.

The latch clicked.

Lanyard's voice followed. "We're sitting on a heap of dry tinder. Whatever Alerick believes, Elara Icewind remains a calculated risk. People like her don't stop being dangerous—they just change the rules they play by."

Harald didn't look up from the map. "Let's just make sure no one strikes the match."

The fire snapped again, soft and dry.

Harald leaned over the map, one hand tracing its frayed edges, the other rubbing the tension from his jaw.

"How do we deal with Valen?" he asked finally. "Arrest him? Assassinate him?"

Lanyard didn't answer immediately. His silence had the weight of something sharpened behind the tongue.

"To arrest him would be asking for a fight," he said at last. "His militia is loyal. Paid well. Trained better than they ought to be. We'd win—but it'd look like a civil war dressed in noble silk. The court would panic. Minor lords would start digging trenches just in case."

"And assassination?" Harald pressed, eyes narrowing, voice edged with fatigue. He leaned forward, palms braced against the table.

Lanyard's response was immediate, flat, and resolute. "Effective," he admitted, "but beneath you. More importantly, without Valen to hold their leash, his men turn into wolves—angry and unbound. Rage like theirs doesn't vanish; it spills. Into taverns. Into towns. Into innocents."

Harald's jaw tightened visibly, muscles working beneath the rough stubble of his cheeks. "So, we simply leave him be?" The question carried the heavy frustration of a king caught between honor and survival.

"No," Lanyard admitted, shaking his head deliberately. "But we don't prod him to draw his sword prematurely. We bide our time—watch, listen. Learn what he's truly planning. And if external threats rise…" His voice lowered, silk over steel. "You might still need those wolves, if not their master's leash."

Harald remained still as the fire murmured in the hearth. Finally, with a slow exhale of resolve, he reached decisively for a clean sheet of parchment.

"Then we take the grain," he declared.

Lanyard's eyes narrowed, curious but approving. "How?"

"We confiscate what he's hoarded," Harald said. "And deliver it where it was meant to go. I'll pen the order myself—tonight. Post it quietly before dawn. Let the sun rise with Valen's empty silos and filled bellies across the countryside."

With deliberate strokes, Harald began scribbling the decree, the ink dark and bold against fresh parchment.

He spoke while writing. "I want House Valen watched. And Caerlyn too. Who and what goes in and out, grain, coin, Nobles. Not quiet, make sure he sees them. I want a patrol stationed at the northern passes to Hravnskot. Subtle—just a presence. Same on the Scorchland border patrolling the Narconian Shelf. I don't expect trouble there, but it's time to start covering our ass. Too many open doors."

Lanyard stepped forward and pointed to the map. "Captain Balwick and five of his plainsmen for Valen. They know how to vanish where there's no shadow. Hravnskot—foot patrols, three rotating units from Stonewatch, and Greyhearth. Scorchlands… light cavalry. No more than twelve. Take hardened men from Emberfast—ones who can eat scorpions and stand their ground on bare shale. I'll inform Lord Dravik. We'll set resupply caches here and here." He tapped two well junctions. "Light stocks. No central supply. Easy to burn if needed."

Harald squinted at the map. "You trust Balwick?"

"I trust that he hates being wrong. Close enough."

Harald huffed.

"Send an auditor to Icewind Manor," he continued, not looking up, the quill scratching emphatically. "Quietly. Bring Lady Elara's ledgers directly to me. We'll see just how far she's stretched the truth."

Lanyard nodded slowly, a small flicker of approval passing briefly across his usually inscrutable face.

But Harald wasn't finished. "Ashbriar burned under Valen's shadow—his spite and his coin. But it will rise again beneath mine. Dispatch tradesmen and supplies at first light. Fund it openly, directly from royal coffers. Send a contingent of the King's Guard—have them post the crown's banners."

Lanyard allowed himself the barest shadow of a smile—respect etched in subtle relief. "Very good, Your Majesty."

The king handed Lanyard the writ. "Set it in motion."

He looked at him then, eyes sharp beneath the heavy crownless brow. "You've always been the sword, Lanyard," he said. "But even a sword answers to the hand that sets it to work."

Lanyard lowered his head slightly, recognizing both the trust and the weight in Harald's words. With a deep nod, he turned toward the door.

"One last thing, my friend," Harald called.

Lanyard halted, hand on the iron-bound oak, head tilted slightly in expectation.

"Prepare Aulfis to meet with me tomorrow evening," the king instructed, lowering his voice. "We three have something important to discuss. And I have a gift for him."

Lanyard did not inquire further—his trust implicit, his curiosity carefully masked. "As you wish, my king."

Then the door whispered shut behind him, leaving Harald alone. The fire dimmed, untended, until only embers glowed, and shadows coiled restlessly across the stone walls. Somewhere beyond those walls, a watch horn sounded—routine, distant, and sharp in the night.

The chamber beneath Goldacre smelled of damp ash, old blood, and scorched iron.

Lord Circus Valen stood at the long worktable with his sleeves rolled back, rings removed and set with meticulous care on a folded velvet cloth. Before him lay three ledgers, their spines cracked, pages spread and weighted with iron paperweights cast in the shape of lions. Each margin was crowded with notes in Valen's own hand—tall, slanted script, precise and merciless.

Lord Perrin Halveric of Avahnmere knelt on the stone floor nearby. A minor lord, barely noble enough to matter, important enough to be useful. His wrists were bound behind him with a silk scarf—deep crimson, Valen's colors—knotted neatly, almost tenderly.

"You miscounted," Valen said mildly, without looking up. He drew a bone-handled stylus down a column of figures, the tip pausing where ink had been scraped thin and reapplied. "Here. And here. And again, just before the winter levy."

Halveric swallowed. "My lord, I—"

Valen tapped the page once with the stylus. Not hard. Just enough to stop the sound.

"I didn't ask why," Valen said. "I asked where the grain went."

Halveric's breath hitched. "I followed the instruction exactly. The surplus was redirected to—"

"To whom?" Valen cut in, still calm.

A pause. Too long.

Valen exhaled, slow and controlled. Annoyance flickered—not at the theft, but at the hesitation. He reached to the brazier beside the table and lifted a small iron signet with a pair of tongs, its face glowing dull red.

"Answer quickly," Valen said. "This room is meant for efficiency."

Halveric broke.

"The wagons were redirected to House Caerlyn," he said, words tumbling now. "I swear it, my lord. The order bore your seal. Your hand. I would not have dared otherwise."

Valen lifted his gaze from the page for the first time.

"My seal," he repeated.

"Yes," Halveric said hoarsely. "Wax and signature. I saw it myself."

Silence settled, heavier than before.

Valen studied him for a long moment, not as a man studies a liar, but as a merchant studies a damaged ledger. Something tight settled there—annoyance deferred, not dismissed.

"Whether forged or misread, the loss is yours," Valen said. "You will deliver triple your expected quota until every missing measure is accounted for. Coin if you must. Blood if you fail."

Halveric sagged in relief that tasted like ruin.

Valen addressed the guards who had brought Lord Halveric in.

"Return him to his house," Valen said. "He has work to do."

Before the guard had gotten the minor lord to his feet, the door opened without announcement.

Rennic Stride stepped through the doorway and stopped just inside it. His coat was damp from travel, mud clinging to his boots and marking the immaculate floor. He neither bowed nor apologized. He stopped just inside the doorway, steady and assessing.

"My lord," Rennic stated evenly, voice coolly polite yet edged with urgency. "You'll want to hear this."

Valen straightened slightly, irritation coiled and contained. The guards took Lord Halveric past Rennic, the man never looking up.

Valen's gaze was thin and sharp as a blade's edge. He took a measured sip of his wine before speaking, deceptively soft.

"Tell me, Smudge," he said, silkily dangerous, eyes narrowing, "just how many years has it been since someone dared to open *that* door without my explicit permission?"

Rennic said nothing. His expression neutral.

Valen took a measured breath through his nose. "Speak."

Rennic reached calmly into his coat, producing a tightly rolled parchment. "Royal decree. Grain stores confiscated at dawn."

Valen's smile returned, colder and sharper, slicing away the mask of casual amusement. "Confiscated? On whose authority?"

Rennic handed him the scroll, ink-smudged fingers deftly precise. "King Harald's. Signed and sealed."

With a flick of his wrist, Valen unrolled the parchment, eyes moving swiftly across each line. The humor bled away from his expression like warmth from winter breath.

"And?" Valen asked, controlled, edged with barely restrained fury.

"Two patrol units stationed openly on the outer estate roads. Royal livery. No attempt at subtlety."

Valen lingered on the parchment, repeating the decree's final words under his breath with icy disdain. "To ensure fair distribution of resources in accordance with royal edict… How politely he's chosen to piss on my boots."

He allowed the scroll to drop from his fingertips, ignoring it as it landed near his feet.

Rennic folded his arms, a casual gesture that nonetheless brimmed with quiet menace. "He intends to choke us without ever unsheathing his blade."

Valen turned slowly toward the hearth, the gesture careless and deliberate all at once. The golden light cast unsettling shadows across his features. His fingers brushed thoughtfully across his jawline. "How many towns depended on those grain stores?"

"Five," Rennic replied succinctly. "Six when the river Oystan floods."

Valen nodded, calculations already moving behind his cold, dark expression. "Send riders immediately to Emberfield, and another to the Tarnhallow. Remind them exactly whose wagons kept their stomachs from growling last winter."

Rennic hesitated just slightly, his voice lowering a shade. "They'll know this decree came directly from the king. Are you sure they'll side with you?"

Valen's smile thinned to a blade's edge. "Men tend to side with the one who holds the leash of their hunger. Or at least, the one who once did—and very well might again."

He moved back to the table and poured himself another measure of wine, dark and heavy, swirling it once before setting the bottle aside.

"Have our militia increase their drills. Twice daily, at dawn and dusk. No fanfare, no banners. If questioned, they're simply preparing for possible border maneuvers."

Rennic inclined his head, adjusting the angle of the candle nearest him by precisely two finger-widths.

"And the royal guards who are already watching?"

Valen chuckled, a wicked gleam in his expression. "Let them watch, Smudge. Let them have stories to whisper back to Harald. Let the king believe himself clever and decisive. Let him have his little victories."

He raised his goblet toward the hearth, watching the flames dance and twist as though sharing his amusement and contempt.

"A man who strikes first," Valen said, eyes on the fire, "must ensure he delivers the killing blow. Anything less is noise."

He gestured once toward the discarded scroll laying on the floor. "This decree is noise."

Rennic remained silent, his expression carefully neutral but thoughtful and calculating.

Valen sipped, savoring the rich bitterness. His smile widened, darkly satisfied.

"If Harald wants obedience," he murmured, each word sharp and precise, "he'll quickly learn I have trained dogs of my own."

He drained the goblet, the final drop falling like blood. "And they bite."

Icewind Manor still shimmered with elegance—on the surface.

Sunlight slanted through stained glass, catching on polished banisters and velvet drapery. Beneath the luster, the cracks showed: a hearth burning low, a warped painting, side halls left bare—pedestals empty, tapestry hooks ghosting the stone.

Lady Elara descended the staircase like nothing was amiss.

She wore silver-gray with a fur-lined collar, her dark hair in waves that framed her face with deliberate effortlessness. Her smile was relaxed. Her steps precise.

In the parlor, a man stood stiffly by the window—a royal auditor, cloaked in the neutral browns of Castellon's finance sector, spectacles perched low on his long, thin nose. He did not bow.

"My lady."

Elara greeted him with a warmth so polished it gleamed. "I trust your journey from Castellon was not overly tedious. Please, do sit. Tea?"

"No, thank you," he said, already pulling out his ledger, charcoal stick and quill. Laying them out precisely on the table before him.

They worked through the books for some time.

The auditor's fingers moved with practiced ease, flipping pages, underlining figures, marking inconsistencies with taps of with the charcoal stick. He raised no accusations—just questions.

"Elk birthrates here declined by half over the last two years?"

"The herds suffered frostbite. A cruel spring."

"Interesting. And the stud accounts—your personal records indicate twenty-seven viable sires last season. Yet the regional breeder's registry only lists nine."

"A clerical delay," she said smoothly. "You know how breeders are. Always late with their signatures."

The man didn't look up. He simply wrote a small note. In ink.

Elara crossed her legs, fingers tightening around her teacup.

She watched him, aware of each subtle twitch, each slight furrowing of his brow as he scanned line after line. The silence lengthened.

"Grain yields in your western fields have notably decreased this year," he remarked dryly, turning another page.

"Unseasonably heavy rains," Elara responded, her voice light yet firm. "The farmers did their best, but the fields were too waterlogged."

The auditor paused briefly, adjusting his spectacles and peering over the rims. "Curious. Neighboring estates reported only minimal disruptions."

"Localized storms," Elara countered quickly. "Nature can be remarkably fickle."

He offered no reaction and returned his attention to the ledger. Another note, longer this time, recorded in the margins.

Elara's grip on her teacup tightened further. She took a delicate sip, the tea tasting bitter despite the honey she'd stirred in earlier.

"Wine exports?" the auditor inquired abruptly. "Your accounts suggest increased sales, yet the tax records don't correspond."

Elara leaned forward slightly, her eyes fixed keenly on his face. "You must understand, Castellon bureaucracy tends to lag behind the real-world pace of business. All proper tariffs and taxes were paid in full. Your sector likely hasn't caught up."

"Perhaps," he said flatly, scratching another meticulous note. "Though it is unusual for discrepancies to be quite so… consistent."

He flipped another page, brows rising marginally as his finger traced the figures. "And your textile profits from last quarter—there's an entry here regarding a significant shipment to a merchant at Highstone Manor. Lady Durnhart, I presume?"

Elara hesitated only a breath, her tone perfectly neutral. "House Durnhart is a longstanding client, reliable with payments, if not always punctual."

"Quite," the auditor responded dryly, marking yet another note. "Reliability seems a rare commodity these days."

Elara allowed herself a small, carefully controlled smile. "Indeed, it does."

The auditor closed the ledger gently but purposefully, meeting her gaze directly. "And the books for your minor house vassals? I'd like to review those as well."

Elara nodded with calm precision, masking the brief flicker of concern. "Of course. I anticipated as much." She rose smoothly, retrieving a smaller, leather-bound ledger from a nearby shelf and placing it into his outstretched hand.

He flipped it open, scanning the pages with meticulous care. "House Taranth's grain quota appears unmet again, House Berwyck claims poaching reduced their elk hide yield, and House Lyonswark has defaulted on timber shipments entirely?"

"All true," Elara affirmed coolly. "Unfortunate but out of my direct control. I've done my best to maintain discipline."

He narrowed his gaze slightly. "Yet their records indicate your estate provided them leniency regarding quotas and penalties."

"Temporary measures, only," Elara explained smoothly. "They are loyal houses. I extend courtesy where possible, ensuring long-term stability."

The fire popped, sparks rising and dying in the air. Elara's breath remained even and controlled. She watched the auditor scribble numbers, ink scratching across parchment like nails tapping at her composure.

The scrutiny was relentless. Page after page closed off the time she had counted on—the months she had needed, the margin she had built this entire precarious balance upon. She knew exactly which columns would draw his eye. Which figures she had trimmed too cleanly. Which allowances had been stretched past comfort.

She had expected the audit. Not the timing.

Her gaze drifted to the window, sunlight filtering through the clear glass, illuminating the gardens of Icewind Manor washed in muted greens and blooms. The estate lay deceptively serene beneath a warm Bloomrise sky, the trees swaying in the mild breeze. Yet inside, tension thickened the air, choking the warmth from the room.

Queen Avanna. This bore her unmistakable scent—authority exercised through procedure, pressure applied without spectacle. Whether suspicion or spite drove it no longer mattered.

She set the teacup down with deliberate care.

The audit concluded abruptly, devoid of fanfare or finality.

The auditor rose stiffly, gathering the ledgers with practiced precision. He did not look at Elara as he stacked them, aligning the corners with exacting care.

"The Crown will require these for further inspection," he said, tone neutral, procedural. "They will be reviewed in Castellon."

He gave a short, clipped nod. "A courier will return them with any further inquiries."

Elara's response was silk-wrapped steel. "And if I have questions?"

He paused.

"Then you may submit them to the royal clerk."

Without another word, he turned on his heel and left, footsteps echoing like hollow promises down the stone corridor.

Elara sat motionless for a long moment. The fire in the hearth sputtered low, the room growing colder as if the walls themselves had absorbed the auditor's chill.

Her gaze fell to the empty space on her desk where the ledger had rested moments before. The absence felt louder than any accusation. She remained still.

The realization settled in with clinical clarity.

She had miscalculated.

Time—what little of it she'd believed she possessed—was gone.

Pressure built behind her ribs, tight and airless. Her jaw locked until it ached. For one unguarded heartbeat, her vision blurred.

A tear slipped free before she could stop it. She brushed it away at once, jaw tightening harder, composure sealing back into place as if the fracture had never shown at all.

She exhaled once, already recalculating.

Whatever had begun here was already in motion.

The stone was already rolling. What mattered now was where it would strike.

CHAPTER SIXTEEN

Kaelrik sat on the stone bench beneath the ancient flame-elm. Its branches stirred faintly overhead, restless despite the calm. His gaze rested on Baldrik, attentive, unhurried. Baldrik paced nearby, his steps slow but unsettled, as if movement alone might banish the weight pressing on his chest.

"Why do you struggle, Baldrik?" Kaelrik asked, his voice low and even.

Baldrik halted, frustration etched across his face. The boy in him flickered behind his stormy green eyes. "Because I don't know my path. I see choices... but none feel true. How do I choose when they all feel wrong?"

Kaelrik gave a faint, knowing smile. "Your turmoil stems from grasping—grasping at outcomes, at certainty. Longing and fear have a way of crowding the mind. They make everything look distorted."

"But if I let go of both, what remains? What pushes someone forward?" Baldrik challenged, voice rising with youth's defiance.

"Intent," Kaelrik said after a pause. "Not what you want, and not what you fear. It's what remains when both fall quiet."

Baldrik frowned. "That sounds... poetic. But how do I know what that intent is?"

"You already do," Kaelrik said, leaning forward, the faintest tilt of his head. "It lives in the still places, beneath the noise. Not in what you want, but what you are. Some paths spend their lives learning how to listen for what remains."

Baldrik shook his head. "And if I never find that stillness? What if the storm never calms?"

Kaelrik smiled again, patience and kindness in his demeanor. "Storms spend themselves," Kaelrik said. "But first, you must learn what in you is storm… and what remains when it passes. One is noise. The other endures."

A breeze stirred the hem of Baldrik's tunic. He shifted on his feet, uncertain, but listening.

Silence fell between them. Baldrik's breathing slowed. He sat beside Kaelrik, the restless edge in him easing into thought.

"The crown weighs heavily on my thoughts," Baldrik admitted, his voice low with reluctant vulnerability, the burden of obligation evident in his tone.

Kaelrik nodded knowingly. "You speak of the crown as if it decides who you are," Kaelrik said. "But consider this—the crown itself holds no power; it is merely metal and jewels. Its true weight comes from the meaning others place upon it. Let go of that weight, and the crown becomes neither burden nor prize, merely a path you may choose or leave."

Baldrik's gaze lifted slowly to the ancient flame-elm above them, its branches dancing gently in the soft breeze. "The Flamebound Order teaches detachment from all worldly things. How can I embrace a path that seems so opposed to everything I've been raised to value?"

Kaelrik's reply was gentle yet firm, delivered with composed clarity. "Detachment isn't rejection," Kaelrik said. "It is not rejection but acceptance—acceptance of the impermanent nature of things. It is understanding that joy and sorrow, victory and defeat, life and death, are all passing shadows upon the wall of existence. By loosening your hold on these, you experience life in its full beauty, neither clinging nor fleeing."

Baldrik looked away briefly, processing the monk's wisdom. "I fear disappointing others, Kaelrik. My father, my mother, the kingdom, Elara—they want me to be something I'm not sure I am."

Kaelrik's voice softened, filled with compassion. "People will always tell you who you should be," he said quietly. "Your duty is not to become what others project, but to uncover and honor who you already are. If you live authentically, others may follow or may turn away—but you will remain at peace."

Baldrik exhaled slowly, the tension in him shifting rather than easing. "And how will I recognize when I've found it?"

Kaelrik's expression remained neutral. "When your choice remains steady even under resistance—when doubt does not move it and fear does not bend it—you will know. Purpose does not shout, Baldrik. It withstands."

The garden fell still again, broken only by the soft stir of leaves and the distant toll of temple bells. Baldrik sat in reflection, Kaelrik's words resonating deeper than before. A dangerous awareness stirred within the storm that had long haunted him.

At length, Baldrik rose slowly, offering a respectful nod toward Kaelrik. "Thank you," he murmured, voice hushed but steady. "You've given me much to consider."

Kaelrik inclined his head. "The answers are yours to find, I only help you see what questions to ask."

Baldrik lingered for a heartbeat longer, then turned and walked from the courtyard, his footsteps soft against the stone path. Soon, even that sound faded, leaving only the whisper of leaves.

Kaelrik sat a moment more, allowing silence to return fully around him. When Baldrik had gone, he rose without haste and turned toward the Citadel's inner doors. He moved through the corridors as if each step had been taken before, unhurried, each turn taken without hesitation.

He made for a narrow door leading down into the Citadel's lower chambers—the heart of the Flamebound's histories. Texts, scrolls, and fragile parchments lay stored here, preserved across centuries for the monks alone. Beyond the threshold, Kaelrik began his descent into the dark.

The narrow spiral staircase stretched down into the earth, each stone step smoothed by generations of monks. Kaelrik's fingertips brushed the wall as he moved, anchoring himself in the cool dark. The air grew heavier—thick with dust, wax, and the scent of parchment long undisturbed.

He descended with quiet purpose. Something long-settled had been disturbed. Baldrik's uncertainty had stirred something beneath Kaelrik's practiced calm, and he descended now not as teacher, but as seeker.

There might be answers in the depths— or only older questions. And Kaelrik, ever the watcher behind the lantern, stepped willingly into the dark.

As he passed a shadowed archway, the flame of his candle faltered—just once—though no draft touched his skin. Kaelrik slowed. He stepped back pausing before a wooden bookcase, studying it in silence. The shelves were thick with neglect, but the air felt wrong here—subtly hollow. He shifted a stack of brittle scrolls aside and traced the mortar lines with his fingertips. There—along the edge—hairline seams, nearly indistinguishable from the surrounding stone. Not age. Deliberate. He pressed gently, and a worn wooden door gave beneath his hand.

It swung open soundlessly beneath his cautious push, revealing a modest alcove dimly illuminated by the candle he carried.

Inside, shelves of forgotten texts lined the walls, but Kaelrik's attention fixed immediately on the pedestal at the chamber's center. Resting atop a pale linen cloth—thinned and nearly translucent—was a crown carved from dark, timeworn wood, devoid of gold or jewels. Its surface, dulled to gray, bore the faint etching of a sunburst encircled by flame, intertwined with a spiral. Its edges were smoothed by use, not ceremony.

Kaelrik approached but did not touch it. His gaze traced the uneven glyphs worked into the linen beneath—old script, worn thin by time.

A thought formed—and he refused to follow it. His fingertips hovered just above the crown, as if something in it remembered being worn.

He withdrew a step, breath slow, shoulders steady. The air felt altered—thicker, perhaps from long-sealed dust, or from his own sharpened awareness. He remained there, listening to what he would not yet name.

He closed the door and turned away, carrying the thought with him—not as understanding, but as intent.

Outside the Citadel, the night was still, the quiet pressing in a way Baldrik could not entirely shake. The city slept beneath a waxing moon, and the gardens along the southern walls glistened with dew and silence.

Lady Elara waited at the base of the steps, draped in a cloak of pale gray that caught the light like silk on water. She looked up as he approached, and her smile was softer than he expected.

"Finished communing with ghosts?" she asked.

Baldrik smirked. "They listen better than the court."

She offered her arm. "Walk with me, then. Before they start whispering too loudly."

They strolled through the hedge-laced paths of the royal gardens, past roses and silverleaf, the fountains murmuring softly nearby.

"I wasn't sure you'd come," Elara said.

"I wasn't sure you'd be waiting," Baldrik murmured, a small smile tugging at the edge of his mouth.

A silence passed, warm and close.

"You spend too much time in the Citadel," she said, half-teasing. "Soon you'll be fasting and growing a beard."

He glanced at her. "Would you still love me if I did?"

She didn't answer right away. A flush rose, traitorous and faint, just high on her cheeks before she could will it down. For half a breath, her mask slipped.

Then—cool again, collected. "I didn't say I loved you."

"You didn't say you didn't."

That earned him a slow, sidelong glance. "Flirting like a monk—now that's a novelty. Is that allowed?"

He stopped walking, turning to face her, his expression earnest, youthful vulnerability flickering in his eyes. "I'm not supposed to do a lot of things."

She watched him, her gaze searching. "You're not seriously considering it, are you? Joining the Order?"

His answer came slower than she liked.

"I've been thinking about what kind of king I'd make. And who I'd become."

Elara gave a quiet laugh—too quickly. "You'd be fine. You're brave. Handsome. And if not the wisest, at least well-advised."

"I'm not sure that's enough."

She sobered, her voice cooling. "You'd turn down the crown? For incense and riddles?"

He looked away, his voice softer, uncertain.

"Would you stay, if I did?"

Elara paused, her voice low, almost tender. "Do you truly think I'm here for your crown, Baldrik?"

He shook his head slowly, uncertainty still evident. "I don't know what anyone wants anymore. Least of all myself."

Elara stepped closer, her fingertips brushing his cheek, her gaze holding his with quiet intensity. "Maybe it's not about knowing what you want, Baldrik. Perhaps it's about knowing who you are, and who you're willing to be—for yourself, not for anyone else."

He reached up, covering her hand gently with his own. "And if who I am isn't who they need?"

She offered a faint smile, her voice gentle but resolute. "Then they'll learn to need the person you are. As I have."

His heart quickened at her words, his youthful uncertainty mingling with burgeoning hope. "And who do you think that person is?"

Elara leaned in. "Someone brave enough to question everything, strong enough to find answers, and genuine enough to capture a heart."

A slow smile spread across his face, and he squeezed her hand gently, drawing her a fraction closer. "Even a heart as guarded as yours?"

She let out a breath of laughter. "Especially mine."

Baldrik leaned in, his voice low, uncertain yet filled with quiet determination. "Then perhaps there's one thing I'm certain of."

"And what is that?"

"Right now, at this moment, there's nowhere else I'd rather be."

Before she could reply, a new voice tore through the night.

"Baldrik!"

They turned sharply, their intimacy shattered.

Queen Avanna descended the garden path in a slow, uneven stride. Her hair was loose and tangled, her gown crooked at one sleeve. The sharp scent of Firewine preceded her, mingling with the fragrance of nightroses like an unwelcome intruder. Her eyes burned with unsteady fury—yet when they fixed on Baldrik, they sharpened with startling clarity, the grace she once wore now fractured.

“Mother,” Baldrik said cautiously, stepping forward, concern shadowing his youthful features. “What are you—”

“Is this your new hobby?” Avanna snapped, her voice raw and uneven. “Hiding out here… whispering things you think I can’t hear. Whispering—” She faltered, the word tangling on her tongue. “—whispering promises while the kingdom rots beneath your idle feet.”

Elara stood frozen, her mouth parting slightly as the color drained from her face. For a heartbeat, her steady mask faltered.

Avanna pointed a trembling, accusatory finger at her. “You don’t think I see you, Mara?” The name slipped out before she could catch it.

“Mara?” Baldrik echoed, confusion cutting through his anger.

Avanna blinked, a visible hitch in her breath. “Elara. You think I don’t know what you are?” Her voice dropped, thick and slurred. “A harlot… ash on your hands.”

Baldrik’s voice rose sharply, edged with protective instinct. “Enough, Mother.”

But Avanna’s gaze was unfocused, her fury blind and unchecked. Her accusations tumbled out like stones hurled with careless cruelty. “Sleeping your way toward the crown,” she said, almost conversational now, the words slipping out crooked. “Did you learn that before—” she stopped, swallowing hard, then forced it out, “—before the fire?”

Elara drew in a sharp breath, as if the air itself had turned against her. For a moment, her composure wavered, raw vulnerability flickering beneath the moon’s unforgiving gaze.

“Mother!” Baldrik shouted, genuine alarm surging through him. His concern was no longer just for decorum; he feared deeply for his mother's state of mind.

Avanna’s voice cracked, her words becoming fragmented and desperate, a distorted echo of herself. “Do you think I’d let you sit beside my son?” Her voice fractured. “Wear our name like something you took?”

“Please,” Baldrik pleaded, stepping closer, his hands raised as if approaching a frightened animal. “Stop this, Mother. You’re not well.”

“You will be king,” Avanna said—and for a heartbeat she sounded entirely certain. Then her voice broke sharply, echoing through the gardens and shattering the fragile peace of the night. “And sooner than you may like!”

Elara took a faltering step backward. Her eyes widened.

Avanna swayed, catching herself against a marble bird bath, setting it rocking on its pedestal, chest heaving, one hand visibly trembling at her side. The empty Firewine bottle had long since slipped from her fingers, lying forgotten in the grass, glinting beneath the pale moonlight

Baldrik rushed forward, grasping his mother's unsteady arms gently yet firmly. "Mother, please—come inside. Rest. This isn't you."

Avanna turned hollow eyes upon her son, her voice now barely a whisper, haunted and distant. "Who else could it be?" she murmured, the fight suddenly drained from her voice, leaving behind only confusion and profound despair. "Who else could it possibly be?"

Baldrik looked to Elara, his eyes pleading silently for understanding and patience, even as dread pooled heavily in his heart.

Avanna tore herself free of his hands, drawing upright by sheer will.

"I will not," she said, each word deliberate, "allow a family-killing arsonist… a parasite with a painted smile… to put her claws in my son."

Elara's lips moved, but no sound came.

Baldrik looked between them, helpless, furious, heart breaking in his chest.

The queen turned and stormed back up the path, barefoot, limping slightly, her pride dragging behind her like a torn train.

And in the garden, Elara stood, her face pale, wet with tears she didn't remember beginning to shed.

Baldrik stepped toward her. She didn't move.

The moon glinted on the white petals around them.

The night had been silver, once. Now it tasted of ash.

Baldrik reached for her hand. "Elara… I… I'm sorry. I—"

She shook her head, barely.

"No—no, I must go." Her voice wavered; a whisper wrapped in grief. "Baldrik… I—"

But the word caught in her throat like a thorn. She turned before it could finish, cloak fluttering behind her as she walked back the way they'd come.

She was gone. Again.

Baldrik stood alone, fists clenched, his heart roaring in his chest.

His mother's madness.

Elara's silence.

The Crown.

He stared up at the moon, still full and serene, and wondered how it could look down on this mess with such calm indifference.

"Flames," he muttered. "What the hell just happened?"

The silence of the garden stretched painfully long, broken only by his labored breathing. The sound of footsteps behind him pulled him from his turmoil. He spun around, wary and tense.

Samuel of Rowleigh stepped into the moonlight, Anna Cogswell close beside him, green eyes wide above her freckled cheeks as she lingered at Sam's side, unsure whether to step closer or give space. "Baldrik," Sam said carefully, glancing back toward the path. "We heard shouting. Are you alright?"

"My mother… she's not herself, Sam."

Anna reached out hesitantly, sympathy etched in her gentle expression. "We saw her leave. She seemed… upset."

Baldrik raked a hand through his hair, head bowed. "She said things… horrible things about Elara. Things that weren't true."

Sam stepped closer, his usual playful demeanor replaced with rare seriousness. "Baldrik, she's your mother, but that doesn't mean she's always right. Fear or grief—whatever's happening to her—doesn't justify hurting people who care about you."

"How can I fix this, Sam?" Baldrik whispered, his voice cracking. "How do I protect them both?"

Sam glanced briefly at Anna, who shook her head slowly. Sam took a breath. "I don't have any answers," he said quietly. "I wish I did."

Anna stepped forward softly, her voice low. "Elara will need time," she said. "And your mother… I don't know."

Baldrik searched his friends' faces, seeing genuine care reflected back at him. He nodded slowly, the tension in his chest easing slightly. "I'm afraid I might fail them."

"You won't," Sam said, placing a reassuring hand on Baldrik's shoulder. "And if you stumble, you've got friends right here to catch you."

Baldrik drew a slow breath and straightened.

"Thank you," he turned specifically toward Anna, a gentle smile briefly lifting his weary expression. "Your counsel is always sound, Anna."

"Always here when you need it."

Baldrik glanced sidelong at Sam, a faint flicker of humor sparking despite the heaviness still lingering in his eyes. "Anna, if you ever decide to trade up, I happen to know a bard who still has most of his teeth."

Sam snorted, rolling his eyes with exaggerated offense. "Careful, Baldrik. Bards may have most of their teeth, but they tend to lose fingers around jealous swordsmen."

The laughter was weak, strained by the weight of the evening, but it was enough to momentarily soften the tension around them—even if it could not erase the shadows entirely.

With a final glance toward the darkened path where Elara had vanished, Baldrik turned toward the Shield, following the path his mother had walked, his head aching and his heart still heavy.

Behind him, the quiet drip of a fountain and the rustle of leaves overhead followed him.

Queen Avanna sat alone in the royal solar as evening bled into night. A thin, trembling hand raised the goblet to her lips, the wine burning sweetly as it went down, dulling the edges of the world.

Her thoughts slipped between reason and fear, never settling in either.

"Elara" she hissed.

Her mind snagged on the name, turning it over until it soured. It carried jealousy, fear, and something sharper beneath. Her pulse quickened, heat rising behind her ribs.

"She seeks to poison him," she whispered. "Her smiles. Her patience. Little hooks in my son's heart."

Baldrik, her beloved, her precious boy. Her son, her future.

"Mine, mine, mine."

She clutched the goblet tighter, knuckles bone-white, lips thinning to a bloodless line.

Her gaze drifted to the window. Outside, branches scraped against the glass, dark and restless in the wind.

"She'll ruin everything," Avanna said. "She'll hollow him out."

She stared into the fire, her thoughts turning dark.

"A simple accident. An unfortunate tragedy."

She said it softly, as if persuasion might make it true. "No one would suspect me. No one would blame me."

Her mouth curved, thin and tight. "A fall from her horse. Wet stone. Simple."

Yet even as she spun scenarios, doubts gnawed fiercely at her logic.

"No. Not enough."

Her thoughts edged darker.

"Poison."

She laughed once, sharp and brittle, then pushed herself to her feet, pacing the room, bare soles whispering over cold stone.

Yet, the cruel laughter faded abruptly into silence, leaving her trembling. Clarity flickered briefly, a distant echo of sanity pleading desperately through the haze.

"What am I doing?" she whispered.

Her gaze darted to the corner of the room—as if expecting someone to answer.

Her heart faltered, fear and horror briefly flickering behind her eyes. The Firewine dulled the thought before it could take hold.

"Survival." She hissed defiantly. "You are protecting him. Protecting your son."

She straightened, breath steadying. Avanna stepped closer to the window, palm pressed to the cool glass. Her reflection stared back, pale and intent.

Anything, she thought, with chilling finality. "Anything for my son."

"She'll be removed," the queen decided firmly, her thoughts echoing with icy precision. "Quietly. Elegantly. No scandal."

The words settled, firming her resolve. She paced, fingers brushing the polished wood as her thoughts aligned.

"A hold-up, perhaps. A roadside robbery gone wrong. Yes. Simple. Southern roads swarmed with deserters, smugglers. Easy enough to believe."

She turned sharply, her silken robe whispering in the silence, the faint scent of wine and sweat clinging to her skin.

"Or perhaps… maybe she simply disappeared. Vanished. Leaving behind nothing but questions and whispers. A carefully penned letter left behind, inked in sorrowful resignation, claiming exile in the distant Scorchlands."

That would keep tongues wagging and eyes searching—murmurs thick with scandal.

But then—

"No," Avanna said aloud, the word snapping the thought in half.

She stopped abruptly, eyes narrowing into slits, her chest tightening with cold certainty. Such a disappearance left hope. And hope was a dangerous thing, capable of driving even the most cautious man to madness. She knew Baldrik. He would look for her. He would never stop.

The goblet was back in her hand without conscious thought, fingers tapping rhythmically, once, twice, three times against its golden rim. Each tap seemed to echo louder, ringing hollowly in her ears.

A botched robbery then. Brutally obvious. Violently tragic. Irrevocably final.

A cold smile curved her lips, stark and resolute. "Yes," she murmured. "That would do."

She would require someone skilled. Someone who moved unseen, like smoke and shadow. Someone with bloodless hands and a silent tongue. Discreet. Untraceable. She had heard whispers in the court, murmurs in darkened corridors, fearful awe in whispered names.

A player of secrets. Prince of Shadows.

"But what is his name?" Avanna muttered, irritation sharpening her voice.

Then it came to her, slowly, with the soft clarity of a blade sliding from a velvet sheath.

"Alerick."

She stood, pacing slowly at the edge of the firelight, her shadow flickering and twisting across the stone walls like an unsettling specter. Thoughts raced, stumbling over themselves, frantic yet impossibly clear.

"He will need a queen," Avanna said, pacing at the edge of the firelight. "Baldrik—my son, the future of Eldaraine—cannot rule alone."

Her mouth tightened. "Not some low-brow servant girl. Not another of Harald's sentimental mistakes."

She exhaled sharply. "He requires someone sharp. Educated. Noble. Someone who understands power and does not flinch from it."

Her steps slowed.

"Someone who will not abandon him," she said quietly.

Someone like me.

Avanna let out a brittle laugh, the sound echoing too long in the silence. She did not know whether to sneer at the absurdity or admire the simplicity of it.

"Miroray?" she scoffed quietly, dismissing her sister's name with a contemptuous wave. "She wouldn't leave her precious islands even if the seas ran dry and burned to salt. Coral thrones and seashell crowns," she mocked, shaking her head. "Even as a child, she thought pearls made her a princess."

And Kirahnae. The thought was dismissed even faster. Too young, too naïve. Still amused by court masks, giggles hidden behind coral necklaces. Still a child, playing at nobility.

Her pacing slowed, feet dragging slow and heavy, her heartbeat loud and pounding in the oppressive quiet.

The thought returned, unbidden but insistent.

Someone like me.

Avanna halted completely, her breath catching sharply in her chest. Her reflection danced eerily in the dim light, half-hidden in shadow, half-revealed in flame—a fractured image of a queen unraveling.

Her mind offered the thought again, quieter now, almost reasonable.

Who else could protect him? Who else would guard the throne as fiercely as a mother guards her child?

Avanna's hands clenched tightly, nails biting into her palms, the pain grounding her briefly, starkly.

Her breath trembled as she raised a hand to her face, fingertips brushing skin grown pale and drawn.

"Am I mad?" she whispered hoarsely to the empty room, eyes fever-bright.

The question hung there, unanswered. After a moment, she shook her head, jaw tightening.

"No," she said aloud. "I am awake."

She poured another glass of Firewine, its dark surface catching the candlelight.

"Royal blood preserved itself," she murmured. "It always has."

She paced slowly as she spoke, the words gaining shape as she gave them voice. "It was not scandal then. It was strength. Continuity. The crown protected by blood and by law."

Her voice dropped. "What does it matter… if the realm endures?"

The words steadied her more than the wine. The logic was cold, but it was sound. Or close enough.

"Bloodline. Heir." She said each word carefully, as if weighing them.

A handmaiden, perhaps. A merchant's daughter. Someone young enough, pliable enough. That could be arranged later—later, when the throne was secure.

Her fingers tightened around the glass. She drew in a sharp breath and turned away.

"No," she said firmly. "Not yet."

For now, there were immediate steps to take. Delays to engineer. Paths to narrow. Choices to remove until only one remained.

She drained the glass, the Firewine burning down her throat and settling heavy in her belly.

She crossed to the mirror, studying her reflection in the candlelight. The woman who stared back looked tired—but resolute. Hard lines drawn where softness once lived.

"This is not about desire," Avanna said quietly. "It is about necessity." She regarded herself with clinical appraisal.

She straightened her bodice, smoothing the fabric with practiced care. The gestures were habitual, precise—armor rather than invitation.

"He will not be given the choice," she said calmly.

CHAPTER SEVENTEEN

Lady Elara Icewind's silk gown whispered against the sun-warmed stones as she stepped from her modest carriage into the bustling merchant caravan. The air was thick with the scents of leather, exotic spices, and aged fabrics. Her hand trembled ever so slightly as it clutched the small satchel filled with pieces of a life once grander, richer, and far less uncertain.

The merchant, Rellan—a squat man with shrewd eyes and fingers perpetually stained with ink—leaned heavily against a barrel of dark ale, his smile practiced and unreadable. His gaze roved over Elara's fine features, appraising her with the casual disregard of a man accustomed to holding all the cards.

"Lady Icewind," he began smoothly, his voice low and brimming with mock courtesy, "it's an honor to do business with such distinguished company."

Her lips tightened into a thin line. She inclined her head slightly, a concession born of necessity rather than respect. "I trust your prices remain fair, Master Rellan. House Icewind expects nothing less."

"Fair?" Rellan chuckled dryly, pushing away from the barrel. "Prices, my lady, depend greatly on the need of the seller and the whim of the buyer. So—what treasures have you today?"

She unfolded the satchel carefully, revealing its contents with a precise, practiced dignity. Each piece she laid upon the merchant's table felt like surrendering something that would never be reclaimed.

First, a delicate necklace, sapphires set in silver—her mother's favorite, gleaming like trapped ocean light.

Then bracelets, rings, and finally, neatly folded silk gowns, exquisitely embroidered with silver thread, garments that whispered of a gentler life she had once known.

Rellan's fingers brushed lightly over each piece, his eyes calculating with the detached focus of a man measuring weight, rarity, and resale rather than sentiment. "Lovely. Truly lovely. But sapphires—blue isn't selling well these days. And silk?" He shook his head regretfully. "This close to summer, linen fetches a far better price. Silk is for ladies who don't need to worry about heat."

Elara stiffened, her voice edged with steel beneath the silk. "I assure you, Master Rellan, my silks carry more value than your common linen. Sell them to traders heading north. You'll triple your return."

He leaned back, feigning consideration, fingers steepled against his lips. "Perhaps. But the roads north grow dangerous, my lady. Traders move cautiously when bandits start prowling. And cautious traders pay cautious coin."

"Then your offer?" she pressed, eyes sharp.

Rellan met her gaze, the corners of his mouth curling knowingly. "Seventy silvers—for all."

Shock surged like lightning beneath her composure, swiftly smothered. "Seventy? You jest. The necklace alone is worth twice that."

He spread his hands, helplessly innocent. "Markets, my lady, are crueler than bandits. Seventy is generous. I would offer less, if I could."

Anger sparked bright behind her calm mask, each heartbeat ringing with defiance. She forced the tremor from her voice, leaving only ice. "You mistake desperation for ignorance. Eighty-five, or I seek out your rivals."

Rellan smiled indulgently, leaning forward conspiratorially. "Eighty. And not a copper more. Consider this charity—House Icewind has my sympathies."

Elara swallowed hard, pride warring fiercely against necessity. Her hands clenched beneath her cloak, knuckles white with quiet fury.

Yet she nodded slowly, allowing him the satisfaction of perceived victory, even as her thoughts raced toward the debt owed, and the work yet to be done. Pride could wait. Survival could not.

"Done," she said softly, voice tight but unbroken.

Rellan chuckled as he counted the silver into her outstretched palm, each coin a cold reminder of her precarious hold on dignity.

"Pleasure as always, Lady Icewind. May your next visit bring cooler tidings."

She turned without response, coins heavy in her palm, each step away from the merchant's caravan another quiet surrender she refused to acknowledge. She walked with her head high, silk skirts brushing defiantly against the sun-warmed dust, even as her heart twisted in shame and bitter resolve.

She slowed only once, just long enough to tuck the coins deeper into her cloak and steady her breathing. The clink of silver faded, the noise of the caravan dulling behind her as distance and resolve did their work. Only then did her thoughts inevitably turn—to Baldrik.

The prince had declared his love. Not once, but multiple times, each confession steeped in quiet sincerity, free of the practiced charm so common in the Castellon court. His words had almost undone her carefully crafted defenses. *Almost.*

He could try to help. He would try. That was his nature. But asking it of him would drag him into the same mire tightening around her house. The crown would not bend because he cared. It would harden.

Elara slowed.

Had her plan shifted without her noticing? Had the board changed beneath her hands? This was no longer merely maneuvering for survival.

It was something far more dangerous.

Because she loved him.

The admission settled in her chest, heavy and bright all at once. Flame help her, she truly loved him. And just as swiftly, Queen Avanna's face rose unbidden in her mind—sharp with fury, eyes alight with warning.

Elara loved Baldrik.

Of that she was certain now.

The question was no longer whether she could win.

It was what she was willing to lose.

Lord Lanyard Darkoak's private apartment nestled atop a narrow, cobbled lane at Castellon's western edge. Shutters locked tight, a low fire murmured in defiance of the chill, its warmth barely a whisper against the cold stone walls. There were no guards, no servants—only stillness held tight within stone.

The chamber was a soldier's refuge, austere and disciplined. Rough stone walls carried faded banners of old wars.

An aging weapons rack leaned against the wall, its blades dulled but ready.

At the room's heart stood a massive oaken table, its weathered surface obscured by a map in oiled leather, tokens marking subtle alliances and veiled threats.

Lanyard paced, boots clicking in a measured rhythm. He paused at the table, studying the markers revealing the realm's fragile balance: Valen's black weasel pressed east next to Caerlyn's golden fox, Elara's silver snowflake near Castellon, Baldrik's stoic stag uncertain at the board's center.

The door eased open, quiet as a whispered prayer. Aulfis stepped through, cloak flecked with travel dust, eyes sharp yet tired. He locked the door behind him, the soft click a familiar ritual, then placed the key on its usual peg.

Lanyard's gaze remained on the map. "Hope you weren't expecting drills tonight."

Aulfis's lips curved faintly. "My sword's hung. I'm unarmed."

"You're never unarmed," Lanyard replied without turning. "Not with your training."

Aulfis's gaze flicked to Baldrik's marker. "Still watching him?"

"Someone must," Lanyard countered quietly, unyielding as steel.

Aulfis nodded, jaw tightening with grudging acceptance.

Lanyard gestured toward the hearth, where two cups and a bottle of dark ale waited. "Better than tavern swill. Hasn't poisoned me yet."

Aulfis poured smoothly, one eyebrow raised. "Thought tonight was supposed to be quiet."

"It is," Lanyard settled into his chair, fingers closing around the cup. "Quiet is when the most important things happen."

They drank in silence. Firelight shifted across the map. The third chair remained empty.

Two sharp taps cracked the quiet, precise as a blade striking stone.

Lanyard rose swiftly, opening the door without hesitation.

King Harald entered, and the room tightened around him. His cloak, damp at the hem, whispered softly against the stones.

His gaze took measure of the room, cold and deliberate.

His gaze settled on Aulfis. "You're here. Good."

"Always, sire," Aulfis replied evenly.

Harald didn't smile. He set aside a leather-bound bundle, the hilt of a sword just visible, and stepped to the table, brushing Baldrik's token aside with a dismissive flick. He unrolled a scroll bound with crimson twine.

"This," he said firmly, "is for neither the court nor the monks. Not yet. But it must exist."

Lanyard moved closer, and Aulfis leaned in, reading the writ inked in rich scarlet. The king's seal, the Thornsword Crest impressed in black wax, gleamed against the parchment.

Aulfis read the first line. Then again.

"Father."

"Yes."

"This names me heir."

Lanyard's eyes lifted slowly from the parchment to the king. He studied Aulfis a moment longer than courtesy required—measuring, weighing.

"The queen will not accept that," he said at last.

Harald did not hesitate. "She does not need to."

Aulfis's eyes flicked back to the parchment.

"It affirms what already is," Harald stated simply.

Aulfis straightened slowly, hand lingering on the scroll. "And Baldrik?"

Harald's voice was iron. "He walks with fire and monks. I'll not take that from him."

"But the realm—"

"Needs more than dreams," Harald said sharply. "It needs a sword in shadow, a ruler free of illusions."

Lanyard's gaze remained on Aulfis, still assessing.

Harald's voice lowered, intimate yet fierce. "You are no mere symbol."

Aulfis felt the words settle in his chest, heavy and unyielding, as if something vast had just been laid there and expected to remain.

"You are the crown," Harald continued. "Wear it proudly or cast it aside, but never leave it to gather dust."

Silence followed.

Then Lanyard spoke quietly.

"Do you understand what signing this does?"

Aulfis met his gaze. "It makes enemies."

Lanyard's voice hardened slightly. "It could make war."

Aulfis held his eyes a heartbeat longer. "I understand."

Lanyard stepped forward at last, producing an inkwell and a quill.

Harald signed first, each stroke like a sword laid to parchment.

Lanyard signed second, succinct and final. Then Aulfis. His hand shook briefly, steadied by sheer resolve. He wrote with quiet precision—no flourish, no hesitation.

Once sealed, Lanyard lifted the scroll and tucked it beneath a loose hearthstone into a narrow, iron-lined cavity.

Harald retrieved the leather-bound bundle and unwrapped it. A sword emerged, its blade clean and uncompromising, forged by Harald's own hand. The hilt bore a delicate script: *Maralei.*

He offered it solemnly. "Forged for a king who knows the price of a crown. Carry her name well."

Aulfis took it with awe, fingers tracing the engraved letters gently. "Mother," he breathed, raw.

Harald's gaze fell on the necklace at Aulfis's throat. He nodded. "Now she can still protect you, son."

Aulfis stood motionless, sword heavy in hand, heart heavier still. He sheathed it carefully, the scrape ringing like a vow.

The room held still, thick with the weight of decisions newly forged.

At last, Harald reached out and clasped Aulfis's shoulder—firm, paternal, final.

"You're a bastard no longer," he said gravely. "You're my legacy now."

Aulfis inclined his head slightly, resolve burning behind his eyes. "And your sword, if you'll have it."

Harald's lips twisted into a faint smirk, edged with dry humor. "Lanyard might dispute you for that title."

Lanyard merely raised an eyebrow, silently amused. He said nothing. Instead, he moved deliberately back to the table and lifted Baldrik's token from the table, setting it aside among the scattered pieces.

He opened a narrow drawer in the table and removed a carved piece: a rearing stag in black wood, its lines sharp and deliberate. He set it in place of Baldrik's token.

He looked to Harald and Aulfis. "Then let's begin preparing the realm you'll inherit."

His voice hardened. "And ensure the wrong crown stays off the wrong damn head."

The bells of Castellon rang out over marble terraces, their echoes tumbling down the terraced streets and climbing the city's fortified heights.

From the river markets to the hilltop battlements, the capital city stirred with anticipation. Banners snapped in the highland wind—black and silver for House Thornsword, emerald and reef-blue for the Vara Archipelago.

Balconies and parapets filled with onlookers. Petals tossed by eager hands scattered across the avenues, crushed beneath boots and hooves.

The main thoroughfare, normally cluttered with traders and townsfolk, had been swept clean and orderly, flanked at intervals by Eldaraine's ceremonial guard. Soldiers stood rigid, armor gleaming beneath the midday sun.

Black-dyed horsehair crests crowned their helms. Cloaks trimmed in silver thread fluttered as halberds lifted in synchronized salute.

Yet the Varanese delegation did not falter or break stride.

They advanced with unyielding poise. Unhurried. Purposeful. Unfazed by foreign grandeur.

At the forefront walked Queen Miroray Kaeleen. Her posture was impeccable, each step deliberate and assured. Tall guardsmen flanked her—silent warriors bearing ceremonial blades of sea-iron, their arms and faces inked intricately with dark, sinuous vines that spoke of deeds accomplished and oaths sworn.

Miroray's violet-blue eyes met each gaze, her expression composed and commanding. She wore flowing silks dyed in muted coral hues, accented with pearl-thread embroidery. Her wrists and throat bore subtle, carefully-chosen adornments of sea gems, coral fragments, and delicate silver chains, tokens of her authority and heritage.

Immediately behind her strode King Consort Tulavan Kaeleen. The serpent-carved sword slung across his back was no ornament—it was a promise. His ebony skin glistened beneath a crown of tightly-bound braids woven with brass cuffs and reef-cord. Tulavan's gaze was sharp and assessing, openly defiant beneath diplomatic decorum. He did not smile, nor did he need to; his presence was a statement that required no elaboration.

Behind them followed Fleet Captain Apeck and Varanese nobility—warriors in reef-hardened leather and ocean-forged steel, priests in coral-threaded robes murmuring blessings to gods unknown in Eldaraine. Whisperer Na'shivar drifted beside her, hooded and silent.

Queen Miroray wore no crown.

Her hair was braided in spirals of silver and sea-green. A necklace of mother-of-pearl lay elegantly upon her collarbone, each piece polished to a mirrored gleam.

Tulavan walked beside her, his posture slightly bent forward, lips moving beneath the rolling fanfare of horns. His voice was a rough murmur edged with skepticism.

Tulavan inhaled deeply, then exhaled through his nose. "All this wind," he muttered, "and not a lick of salt in it."

Miroray did not shift her gaze, nor did she grant him the acknowledgment he sought.

"Even their cheers sound rehearsed," he continued, glancing sideways at her, irritation flickering briefly in his sea-gray eyes. "Too polished. They're hiding something."

She still offered no reply, her expression unchanged—calm, distant, sovereign.

Tulavan scoffed lightly, shaking his head. "Damn continentals. Invite you all this way, and they don't even offer a drink before making you parade through their streets."

Miroray remained silent. Her focus was fixed, unwavering as the horizon, upon the marble steps looming before them, and the trio who stood atop them, waiting like stone sentinels.

King Harald dominated the scene, standing tall and imposing, his broad shoulders draped in a cloak of midnight velvet that snapped in the rising wind.

Upon the cloak rested the sigil of House Thornsword: a silver stag beneath a branching tree. His hand rested naturally on the pommel of his ceremonial blade, exuding quiet strength. His face was stern, unreadable, a mask of disciplined authority.

Prince Baldrik stood beside him, young in years but held rigid, his shoulders set too squarely for comfort, his jaw tight as if braced against a weight no one else could see. He wore a deep green doublet, buttoned high and belted tight at the waist, with a cream-colored cloak fastened at his shoulder. A sword hung at his side, understated but well-crafted. His eyes, sharp and watchful, tracked her approach without wavering. His expression was guarded, mouth drawn in a tight line, revealing nothing.

Yet Miroray's gaze lingered longest on the figure standing beside the king—Queen Avanna.

The queen stood motionless as carved marble, clad in a stately gown of white and sable silk, its high lace collar fanning behind her neck like the crest of a sea bird. A delicate circlet of silver rested upon her brow, gleaming faintly in the sunlight.

Her dark hair was carefully pinned high, woven through with thorn-like ornaments of polished black gold.

Her features were serene, painted with regal poise, yet beneath that carefully serene facade stirred a subtle dissonance—Avanna's stillness held a fraction too long, her breath measured with care rather than ease.

Miroray's brows furrowed minutely, but she masked her curiosity swiftly.

She lifted her chin slightly, settling her expression into one of serene neutrality. Whatever turmoil awaited her atop those stairs, she would meet it as she met the sea—unyielding, patient, and utterly prepared.

At last, King Harald stepped forward. The wind tugged at his cloak, snapping it sharply behind him as he descended the first few marble steps, his voice rang with practiced authority, clear and unwavering.

"Queen Miroray of the Vara Archipelago, High Voice of the Flamegrove, Sovereign of Vael'Shura and its sister isles—King Tulavan the Tidecaller, Co-Ruler of the Emerald Flame and Defender of the Southern Seas—you honor Eldaraine with your presence."

His words were formal, expertly measured, and perfectly neutral.

Queen Miroray inclined her head gracefully. "An honor returned, King Harald Thornsword. We arrive in peace, under full banners, and with no intentions beyond kinship." A brief hesitation—then softly, pointedly, she added, "And answers."

Those last two words lingered in the air, heavy as a brewing storm.

Then Queen Avanna descended two steps, her voice slicing across the silence with the precision of honed glass.

"Yes," she began, her tight smile devoid of warmth, "we are honored to receive you…"

A pause—sharp as a blade.

"…unannounced."

Another—sharper still.

"…unexpected."

Avanna's eyes flickered deliberately to the circlet of polished coral and volcanic glass woven through Miroray's braids, then slid pointedly to the man at her sister's side.

"…and married, I see. Congratulations are in order… *sister.*"

Miroray's jaw tightened subtly, the muscles clenching momentarily, though her expression remained otherwise unreadable.

Tulavan bristled, stepping forward. "The invitation to our wedding went unanswered—"

Before he could finish, Miroray's head turned slightly, her gaze piercing him like a blade of coral. The reprimand, swift and silent, forced Tulavan's words to die in his throat. He stepped back, swallowing visibly.

Those nearby noted his restraint with quiet intensity.

King Harald, unflinching and undisturbed, extended his hand—not to offer friendship, but simply to gesture.

"Welcome to Eldaraine," he said solemnly, "and welcome to our house."

He turned abruptly, cloak swirling dramatically behind him as he ascended the marble stairs without further remark.

Queen Avanna followed, her movements crisp and controlled, each step a precise statement of her displeasure.

Prince Baldrik trailed behind, silent and contemplative.

Miroray waited one deliberate heartbeat more, her face calm as moonlit waters—betraying nothing of the currents beneath.

Then, with Tulavan at her side, she ascended the stairs, her steps deliberate and regal. Behind them, the Varanese delegation followed, a tide poised at the brink, awaiting only the catalyst of the coming storm.

The long hall had cleared, save for flickering braziers and the rhythmic steps of distant sentries.

Queen Miroray walked beside her sister in silence, trailing half a step behind. Avanna's expression was unreadable, held taut with grace, but Miroray had seen masks like that before—on widows, dancers, and priestesses who'd lost their gods.

"Why didn't you write?" Miroray asked at last.

Avanna stopped mid-step.

"I did," she said, voice sharp enough to shear silk. "Dozens of letters. Not one returned."

"No messages from Castellon have reached us in over a season," Miroray said calmly. "And we sent our wedding invitation by royal vessel. Sealed and marked."

"Then it was intercepted," Avanna snapped.

Miroray raised an eyebrow. "And you thought silence was the better course?"

"No," Avanna said. "I thought it was your choice. The south has never cared much for its exiles."

The corridor seemed to narrow between them.

"You are not an exile," Miroray said firmly, her voice edged with earnest warmth. "You are always welcome home. Mother never exiled—"

"Mother gave me no choice, sister," Avanna interrupted sharply, eyes flashing with a sudden storm of resentment. "I had the right to be Queen of Vara. Mother chose to send me away."

Miroray stepped forward, her voice softer now. "Avanna… something's wrong. I can feel it."

"I'm tired," Avanna replied, her voice quieter now, brittle around the edges. Her gaze fixed stubbornly forward, avoiding her sister's penetrating eyes. "And the kingdom is cracking beneath our feet. But don't worry."

She touched Miroray's hand—gently at first, then with a little too much pressure.

"Baldrik will make it right," she whispered fervently. "He's strong. It won't be long now. And he won't be alone."

Miroray felt a knot tighten low in her chest, dread stirring there like something vast shifting beneath dark water.

"What do you mean?" she asked carefully, her voice steady despite the sudden, sharp unease.

Avanna's smile crept upward, unsettling not in its breadth but in its restraint, her eyes bright with a gleam that felt carefully held in check. "I mean… me. Baldrik and me. We'll steady the throne. When the time comes. It's not unheard of, sister."

Miroray's expression didn't change, but her heart stumbled in her chest. The breath she drew was shallow, held too long. "Avanna…" she said, the name an anchor and a plea. "You don't mean that."

Avanna looked at her, a restrained smile tugging at her lips, her certainty unyielding, as if the thought had been weighed and accepted long before this moment.

Miroray stepped closer, her voice low. "He's your son."

"I know," Avanna whispered. The word carried no shame—only conviction. The certainty of it made Miroray's skin crawl.

The air between them grew brittle, stretched thin by what neither would say.

Finally, Miroray placed a hand gently on her sister's shoulder, squeezing firmly—an anchor cast into stormy waters.

Avanna turned away, a low hum slipping from her as she walked.

The sound carried no true melody—fractured, uneven, like something under strain.

On the eastern terrace, King Harald and King Consort Tulavan stood side by side, overlooking Castellon's training yard below. The wind tugged at their cloaks, drawing chill air around their shoulders. Each man held a heavy goblet, the rich wine within warming more than just their throats.

Tulavan drained half his cup in a single swallow and scowled toward the distant city. "Back home, my voice only gets second say—if that."

Harald's eyes stayed fixed on the horizon, lips twitching into a faint smirk. "That so?"

Tulavan snorted softly. "Queen this, Queen that. Miroray gets the throne, and I get the chair beside it." He shrugged, humor darkening his tone. "At least here, the king wears the damned crown."

Harald chuckled, low and humorless. "Is that what you think?"

"Looks like it." Tulavan waved his goblet toward the disciplined rows of Castellon's guard, their armor gleaming sharply in the late afternoon sun. "Guards who never blink, banners that never sag, and a son who's got more jawline than judgment."

Harald raised an eyebrow, his tone dry, almost amused. "And what's your sage advice, oh seasoned husband of queens?"

Tulavan belched quietly, eyes twinkling with mirth. "Stag hunt. In five days. You, me, a few good spears, and woods free of politics."

"No Miroray?" Harald asked, his expression carefully blank.

"Gods, no." Tulavan grimaced exaggeratedly, his voice dropping conspiratorially. "That's exactly what I'm trying to avoid."

Harald studied him sidelong, eyes narrowed slightly. "Sounds suspiciously like a trap."

Tulavan met Harald's gaze, grin crooked and defiant. "Better than waiting around for one of yours."

They stood in companionable quiet, the wind filling the space where neither yet chose to speak.

Finally, Harald glanced sideways at the Varanese king.

"If the weather holds," he said slowly, deliberately, "and if you're still here."

Tulavan's grin widened, genuine amusement breaking through. "I like a place where the wine's warm and the women cold."

Harald clapped a firm hand on Tulavan's shoulder, a rare smile softening his usually stern features. "Then you'll love Castellon."

Tulavan gazed out over the land beneath the terrace, fields and distant forests stretching toward the horizon. "Your land's beautiful," he admitted grudgingly. "Nothing like the sharp reefs and angry tides I'm used to."

Harald nodded absently, sipping his wine. "The soil is fertile—grain, cattle, vineyards that stretch for leagues. Every generation builds something new, lays stones atop their fathers'."

Tulavan chuckled softly. "Sounds dreadfully boring. No hurricanes or sea monsters to keep life interesting?"

Harald's lips quirked, eyes glinting faintly with humor. "Only politicians and court intrigues. They're monsters enough."

Tulavan laughed outright, then fell quiet, sensing the shift in Harald's demeanor. Harald's expression sobered, his voice lowering, stripped of idle courtesy. "Why are you here, Tulavan? Unannounced, uninvited. I've heard you gave quite a scare to the watchmen at Eastmere. Twenty ships? Hardly a friendly visit."

Tulavan met Harald's direct gaze, humor evaporating swiftly. He shrugged, his tone blunt and unapologetic. "Sometimes friendship needs a strong first impression. Eastmere learned we're not just voices in the wind."

Harald raised an eyebrow, eyes narrowed, assessing. "Is that what Vara wants? To be heard? Or feared?"

Tulavan held the stare evenly, unblinking. "One tends to ensure the other."

Harald paused thoughtfully. "And yet, it's unusual. No warning, no letter. Not even from Miroray?"

Tulavan took another deep drink, gaze distant. "Not a word from Castellon in over a season. To me, silence is peace. But Miroray worried for her sister."

Harald frowned, a crease forming between his brows. "You mean no regular dispatches? Or merely letters between sisters?"

"Nothing," Tulavan said firmly, meeting Harald's eyes again. "Occasional scrolls from the Flamebound preaching why our gods are false, inventory demands from greedy merchants—but beyond that, absolute silence."

Harald considered this in silence, his eyes narrowing. "I'll have it looked into," he said at last. "In the meantime, you'll be accommodated in the finest quarters Castellon Shield can offer. Stay as long as suits you."

Tulavan raised his goblet slightly, eyes brightening again with cautious amusement. "And the stag hunt?"

Harald nodded, lips curving faintly in a rare, genuine smile. "Consider it done. You'll have a glorious set of antlers to adorn your hall entryway. And we use bow and arrow here, no spears I'm afraid."

They clasped hands firmly, the gesture brief but genuine.

They finished their wine in companionable quiet.

The private chamber smelled faintly of beeswax, cloves, and secrets, illuminated only by the flickering amber of a single lantern suspended from above. Thick velvet curtains muffled the sounds of the bustling palace beyond, cloaking the room in silence thick enough to swallow whispers.

Alerick lounged casually in the doorway, eyes half-lidded with practiced indifference. "You summoned," he drawled, voice smooth and deceptive. "I presume it isn't about tea."

Queen Avanna sat rigidly by the window, bathed in the shifting glow of lamplight. She held a crystal goblet loosely between slender fingers, its dark wine barely trembling despite the persistent twitch beneath her left eye.

"No," she said sharply, her voice fraying at the edges. "It's not about tea."

She gestured absently toward the table. "Wine?"

Alerick moved toward the offered goblet, then paused abruptly—a brief, vivid memory of what he'd done to the queen's own vintage. A courteous smile, betraying nothing, he withdrew his hand. "I prefer to keep a clear head when conducting business," he murmured.

He stepped fully into the chamber, the door sighing shut behind him. He sat across from her observing her with cool detachment, as one might watch a dangerous predator behind thin bars.

"There's a woman," Avanna began abruptly, gaze fixed somewhere distant. "She needs to disappear."

Alerick's lips curled faintly, amusement tempered by caution. "Disappear temporarily, or forever?"

"Forever," Avanna snapped harshly. "It must be clean. Final. I want grief, not closure."

Alerick raised an intrigued eyebrow. "Most prefer the opposite."

Her eyes narrowed. "I'm not most people."

"You've thought this through," he remarked quietly.

"I've given it some time."

"Who?"

Avanna's nails drummed lightly, briefly against polished oak, then stilled.

"Elara Icewind."

Alerick's careful mask slipped a fraction—just enough to lift one brow. He quickly composed himself, a quiet laugh escaping his lips. "If you wanted your son's hate, there are cheaper ways."

Avanna's jaw tightened visibly, wine trembling precariously in her grip. "Miroray arrives unannounced. Harald grows distant, silent—don't you see it? Mother sent me away once, easily enough. Perhaps Harald thinks he can set me aside—find something younger, more pleasing."

He regarded her neutrally, masking all internal reactions. A faint crease touched his brow, as if trying to follow her turn. "You think she's caught the king's eye?"

Avanna blinked, thrown off for a beat. The thought seemed to slip past her, ungrasped.

"No—no, that isn't it." Her focus snapped back, sharp and brittle. "I will not have a spectacle. No crowds. No whispers."

"You want subtly then."

"Yes," Avanna answered immediately, eyes distant. "No blades, no suspicious deaths in the dark. Make it tragic—an accident, a misstep, perhaps a robbery gone awry."

Alerick nodded slowly, contemplative. "A tragic romance gone wrong," he mused dryly. "Fitting."

He studied her carefully now. Her poise remained flawless, her voice steady, yet her eyes betrayed cracks like fragile glass. Her grip on the wineglass was strained, knuckles bleached white.

"You've changed," he remarked quietly.

"I've gained clarity."

He studied her a moment longer, saying nothing. The tremor in her hand was answer enough.

He set his hand on the chair's armrest, tapping it lightly. "These requests carry a cost, particularly involving those close to the crown. Potential queens are not eliminated cheaply."

"How much?"

He named his price deliberately high, expecting hesitation. "Two thousand now. Two more when it's done."

Avanna didn't even flinch. "Done."

Surprise flashed through him, swiftly hidden. He'd meant to dissuade her with the absurd sum, yet she met it with unsettling ease.

"Don't you wish to know the method?"

"No," she said simply. "I trust you."

Alerick smiled coldly, eyes glittering dangerously. "You're not afraid I might share our secret?"

"No," Avanna whispered, unwavering. "I understand exactly who you are."

He leaned forward slightly, voice velvet soft. "And who am I?"

"A man who values leverage as much as gold. Take both, and choose wisely whom you spend them upon."

For a moment, only the tap of his ring on the chair's edge lingered.

Alerick finally stood, offering a mocking bow, shallow and insolent. Before he reached the door, Avanna swiftly rose, moving to a heavy chest placed deliberately nearby. She withdrew two large sacks of coin, heavy with the unmistakable clink of royal gold, pressing them firmly into his hands.

"All king's gold," she affirmed softly.

The unexpected weight momentarily startled him. Yet outwardly, he maintained perfect composure, smoothly concealing the payment beneath his cloak.

As he stepped toward the door, Avanna's voice followed him, sharp yet distant.

"Make it look as though the Flames claimed her. I want Baldrik convinced."

Alerick glanced back once, his eyes cold, smile colder still.

"They always are," he murmured.

The door closed quietly.

Behind him, Avanna's wineglass slipped from trembling fingers, breaking against the floor.

She did not move, gazing downward, seeing only shards—beautiful and dangerous.

✶

The gardens beyond Castellon's southern gates lay basking beneath the golden wash of late afternoon, screened from the road by ancient stone walls thick with ivy. This was not the first time she had walked this path. Nor the second. Their meetings had become infrequent, carefully spaced, always harmless—wine, conversation, departure before dusk. Harmless, she had told herself.

Aulfis reclined comfortably on a finely woven blanket beside a low table generously laden with an array of pastries, honeyed fruits, delicate cheeses, and a crystal decanter of pale golden wine. His bearing was relaxed, an easy charm in his eyes as he watched Elara approach.

"My lady," he called warmly, rising fluidly to his feet, a practiced and inviting smile curving his lips. "I was beginning to fear you might reconsider."

Elara Icewind paused elegantly at the blanket's edge, her clear eyes studying him carefully, curiosity masked by practiced composure. "Reconsider what, precisely?" Her voice was smooth, subtly teasing yet guarded.

"Accepting an invitation from a presumptuous man," Aulfis answered lightly, his tone gently self-deprecating as he offered her his hand. "I could hardly fault you."

Elara's hesitation was slight, a fleeting heartbeat of uncertainty quickly masked as she allowed him to guide her gracefully onto the blanket. Her gown shimmered like molten silver, echoing her poised elegance in every subtle motion. She settled herself with the grace born of careful upbringing, though her gaze remained quietly vigilant, searching his features for hidden intentions.

"You are certainly confident," she remarked, her voice carrying an undertone of dry amusement, softening the guarded distance between them. "I have yet to determine if it's charming or merely pompous."

Aulfis chuckled richly, deftly pouring the wine into two ornate goblets, the sunlight catching in the liquid. "Could it not be both? Charm devoid of arrogance would make for terribly tedious company."

She accepted the goblet with a subtle incline of her head, eyes meeting his briefly over the rim, a flicker of amusement. "Then, I presume you are anything but tedious."

“I make a concerted effort to remain engaging,” he responded smoothly, reclining again with languid ease, his gaze holding hers with quiet intensity. “But enough of my humble virtues. Tell me, Lady Icewind—what truly intrigues you, beyond courtly strategy and impeccable decorum?”

She took a measured sip, allowing the thoughtful silence between them to expand comfortably. The sun warmed her skin, but her resolve held. “Is this your usual approach, then? Wine and flattery beneath flowering vines?”

Aulfis smiled indulgently, his eyes glinting with good-natured humor. “It seemed a fitting beginning. Does it offend?”

“Not offend,” Elara replied softly, her voice warming reluctantly, an admission of interest creeping into her tone. “Merely curious about where such beginnings might lead.”

“Curiosity,” he mused, leaning forward subtly as if sharing a cherished secret, his voice low and inviting. “A perilous trait in courtly life. Yet for you, I sense it serves as both armor and blade.”

She arched an elegant eyebrow, a faint smile escaping despite herself, the warmth of the day and the moment loosening her carefully woven defenses. “You presume much, Aulfis. Do you truly believe you have discerned so much from such brief acquaintance?”

“I don’t claim complete understanding,” he admitted openly, his voice earnest and quietly compelling. “But I find myself deeply intrigued. You cloak your truths behind layers of silk and practiced charm—much as I do myself. Yet, beneath those layers, something captivating reveals itself, if only for a moment.”

Elara's gaze softened slightly, surprise flickered—swiftly masked by guarded warmth. “Is this how you customarily court the ladies of the realm?”

He laughed softly, the sound rich and genuine. “Only those truly worthy. And even then, only rarely with such sincere honesty.”

She regarded him carefully, setting her goblet down with thoughtful deliberation. “Should I then feel honored, or wary?”

He leaned in slightly, eyes earnest yet invitingly gentle. “A touch of both might serve you best. But mostly honored—rarely do I share honesty so freely.”

“Then,” she murmured, her eyes steady, “it seems I am in esteemed company indeed.”

Aulfis hesitated just long enough for the quiet rustle of the garden's leaves to fill the silence, and then, moving with an unanticipated swiftness that startled her, he closed the distance between them. He leaned in and kissed her—light, deliberate, a question rather than a claim. Elara stiffened slightly in surprise, the initial shock giving way to a faint tremor of guilt. This was the line.

For the span of a heartbeat, she did not move. Baldrik's face flickered through her mind. The warmth of a morning ride. The weight of promises not yet broken.

She drew back first.

"Not that," she said softly. Not angry. Not breathless. Clear.

Aulfis did not chase the space she reclaimed. He nodded once. "Understood."

The moment cooled.

"Shall we walk back?" Aulfis asked softly, his voice rich and warm, holding no hint of regret as he rose fluidly, extending a hand toward her.

Elara accepted it, her touch more cautious than before, fingertips barely touching his, aware now of every subtle brush and sensation. Together, they began to retrace their steps, silence walking beside them but gradually becoming laden with words left unsaid, thoughts held captive by propriety and duty.

As they approached the imposing silhouette of the city walls, bathed now in the muted tones of dusk, Aulfis paused, turning towards her. His expression was open and inviting. "Would you consider joining me in my apartments? The evening still holds charm—perhaps another glass of wine, more of our conversation?"

Elara hesitated, her clear eyes meeting his steadily, the depths reflecting her inner turmoil. For a long moment, the world narrowed to just the two of them—the gentle cadence of their breathing, the careful expectation in his gaze. At last, she summoned a gracious smile. "Not tonight, Aulfis. Another time, perhaps." Her voice held warmth, cushioning the sting of refusal. "It truly has been a lovely evening."

Aulfis inclined his head graciously, an easy smile sliding into place, effectively concealing any trace of disappointment. "Another time, then," he echoed gently, the promise hanging pleasantly between them.

Their goodbyes were brief, she withdrew first. With a final shared glance filled with unspoken understanding. Elara turned to make her solitary journey back to Castellon Shield, her steps felt heavier than usual, each step heavier than the last.

She moved quietly through the darkening streets, her mind restless and tumultuous. She did not like that she had not moved away sooner. The memory of Aulfis's gentle kiss haunted her thoughts, a bittersweet temptation that she struggled to quiet.

Drawing a resolute breath, Elara steeled herself. As the gates of Castellon Shield loomed ahead, Elara understood the truth of it clearly: this evening had not been betrayal, but it had not been harmless either.

Aulfis remained where he stood long after she disappeared through the outer gate.

The last of the daylight thinned across the stone, washing the street in fading gold.

He did not move.

He only watched.

Bootsteps approached from behind.

Squire Torrin Lyonswark came to stand beside him, arms folding loosely across his chest. "Making any progress with the lady?"

Aulfis's gaze never left the gate. "Gradual."

Torrin gave a quiet grunt. "Gradual wins wars. But hearts?" He glanced sideways. "You mean to have it—or take it?"

Aulfis smiled faintly.

"I've already taken the throne from him," he said, voice calm as cooling stone. "I intend to take his love."

Torrin studied him for a long moment. "Careful. Hearts cut deeper than crowns."

"I know," Aulfis said. "But crowns don't keep your bed warm either."

They stood a moment longer beneath the dimming sky before turning back toward the city lights.

CHAPTER EIGHTEEN

Rain wept against the narrow panes of the servant's quarters, a gentle pattering that might have comforted some—but not tonight. Not in this room, where secrets clung to the air like smoke and guilt crept in through every crack. A single candle guttered on the sill, its flame casting long, nervous shadows across the worn floorboards and the pale, frightened face of the girl hunched there like a discarded doll, legs drawn up and shoulders shaking.

Lana clutched the small glass vial so tightly it threatened to crack in her palm. Her breath came shallow and uneven, each exhale trembling with fear that twisted like a living thing in her chest.

The Queen had screamed at the reflection in her mirror, called her own shadow a traitor, and accused a tapestry of whispering treason. And then, for the first time, she had called Lana by another name. Not as a slip, not in jest. Elara. The name had frozen Lana's blood, her stomach turning to water as panic clawed through her mind. Something inside her had folded, then dissolved, leaving only raw panic in its wake. She had stood there in stunned silence, watching the Queen tremble and snarl and clutch at her chest as though the very walls were closing in.

The door creaked behind her.

Serai entered quietly, her cloak dripping rainwater, her steps careful despite the years of discipline in them. Her face, schooled to calm, betrayed a tightness around the mouth—a sign Lana knew well. She paused a moment in the doorway, gaze settling on her daughter.

"Lana?" Serai said softly, voice low but firm. "What is it? What's happened?"

Lana didn't respond at first. She stared at her hands, at the thin glass vial clenched so hard it looked ready to splinter. Her lips parted, but no sound came. Her throat bobbed as she tried again.

Then the words tumbled out all at once, breathless and raw.

"It's gone," she blurted. "I gave it all. I... I thought it would help. I thought she'd get better, not worse. She kept screaming, and she threw a cup at the window, and she said the paintings were moving and called me... she called me Elara, Mother. She looked at me and I could see she didn't even know who I was."

Serai crossed the room in two quick steps, kneeling before her daughter, her heart tightening at the sight of Lana's distress. Her hands, warm but trembling slightly with suppressed worry, took Lana's fingers gently, trying to convey strength she wasn't sure she possessed. "How much? How many drops?"

Lana couldn't look her in the eyes. "All of it. She wouldn't calm down. I thought it wasn't strong enough."

The last of its contents had been emptied earlier that afternoon, when the Queen's moods had reached a fevered pitch of frenzied laughter and glass-shattering accusations. Lana had added a second drop, then a third, her fingers trembling the whole time. More than her mother had instructed. More than she understood.

"Lana..." Serai exhaled slowly, exasperation flickering beneath her worry.

She tamped it down, forcing her voice gentler as she tried to steady herself. "That wasn't for you to decide. You were never meant to handle such dangerous substances alone."

"But she was screaming, Mother," Lana said, her voice rising.

"She said the paintings were watching her. She called the fire 'a jealous serpent.' She threw a goblet and it shattered on the wall." Lana's voice cracked as she drew a shaky breath. "I thought another drop of the sedative couldn't hurt—maybe she'd finally rest. Maybe she wouldn't See me."

Serai's eyes narrowed slightly, her voice lowering cautiously.

"See you? What do you mean, 'see you'?"

Lana swallowed hard, then whispered, voice trembling, "She called me Elara. Looked right at me and said it, like she believed it. Said I was stealing her son. Dressing up in her skin."

Serai reached up and gently cupped Lana's cheek. "No one saw you administer it?"

"No," Lana whispered. "I was careful. I slipped it into her wine when no one was watching. She never noticed."

"Good," Serai said softly, though her voice carried little comfort. "Then we keep this close. No one must ever know what we've done."

Lana's lip trembled, her voice thickening with tears as she clutched tighter at her mother's hand. "But she's—she's slipping away, Mother. What if I've broken her beyond repair?"

Serai nodded, gravely, but a shadow passed through her eyes. "It was supposed to calm her," she murmured, voice low, uncertain. "A tincture to smooth her edges, to make her more manageable in court. Nothing dangerous. Nothing cruel."

She looked at Lana, then back toward the window, where rain blurred the outside world into a smear of grey and trembling light. "But this... what you've described?"

She hesitated. The candle flickered, and her reflection in the glass looked older than it had that morning. "I don't know what he gave us anymore. And that—not her words, not even her madness—that terrifies me most."

She drew in a slow breath. "It was supposed to be subtle. Safe. But maybe that was the lie—maybe the elixir was always meant to be loud, and we were the ones meant to sleep through it."

"But she's—" Lana's voice cracked. "She's not herself anymore. What if she never comes back? What if she forgets how to be... anyone?"

Serai looked away, her face unreadable. Then, very softly, she said, "Then she never comes back."

The words hung between them, bitter and impossible to take back.

Lana wiped at her nose with the back of her sleeve. "Is she going to die?"

"No," Serai said quickly, then hesitated. She knelt again beside her daughter, brushing a damp lock of hair from Lana's brow. "No, I don't think so." Her voice softened, trying to wrap reassurance around the uncertainty she felt. "She's strong, and her mind... it was already frayed. This won't kill her. But it may change her. I don't know for sure."

Lana looked away, the weight of those words sinking in. "It feels like I killed something," she whispered.

Serai rose slowly to her feet, smoothing rain from her sleeves. Her voice, when it came, was quieter than before, but steady. "You didn't kill anything, Lana. You tried to help. You trusted me. And if this was a mistake... it wasn't yours alone."

For the first time, her shoulders sagged slightly, her fingers curling loosely at her sides. Lana had never seen her mother look so tired.

She stared down at the empty vial. Her voice, barely audible, asked, "What do we do now, Mama?"

"We survive, and we don't say anything. Understand?"

Lana hesitated, her voice barely a whisper. "Even if it was poison? Even if we made her worse?"

Serai drew a breath, then exhaled slowly. "Even then. Because what matters now is what we do next. And what we do is endure. We stay silent. We protect each other."

Lana nodded slowly, biting her lip. "Okay. I won't say anything."

Serai turned to leave, but paused at the threshold. Rain still hissed against the stone beyond, and thunder rolled distantly like the mutterings of old gods.

"Come here," Serai said quietly.

Lana crossed the room into her mother's arms, burying her face into the familiar scent of herbs and candle wax. Serai held her close, strong and steady, but her eyes stared past the girl's shoulder, toward a future now soaked in uncertainty.

Her voice softened, meant only for the silence and the storm beyond. "You're still my daughter. No matter what we've done."

"I'm scared," Lana breathed.

"Good. That means you still know right from wrong. Just—learn when it's safer to pretend you don't."

In her heart, Serai did not pray.

She did not hope.

She clung only to the one thing that had ever guided her through locked corridors, whispered betrayals, and blood-washed stone:

Control.

But somewhere beneath that practiced stillness, something festered. A single thought, thorned and unrelenting, curled its roots into the quiet.

Faileas… what have you had us do?

Outside, thunder rolled again—closer now.

Rainwater tapped steadily through the worn stone arches of the lower breezeway beneath Castellon Shield. Shallow pools spread across the flagstones. Wind moved through the corridor in low, cold pulses.

Faileas leaned casually against one of the pillars, his arms crossed, a shadow where the torchlight didn't quite reach. The rain painted his cloak darker by the moment, but he showed no discomfort. His eyes tracked Serai's approach before her boots even struck the wet stone.

She moved like a storm—tight, fast, dangerous, barely contained.

"Lana gave her all of it," Serai said without preamble, her voice edged with frantic accusation, rain glinting sharply against her tense features. "All of it—and now the Queen is half-feral. She's raving, broken, beyond reason. That wasn't a sedative, Faileas—it was poison."

Faileas didn't blink, but something in his calm facade tightened, his eyes cooling in the flickering torchlight. He shrugged, slow and economical, a gesture that acknowledged her words without engaging them.

"You lied to me."

"I omitted what you didn't ask. Poison, sedative—words don't matter. Results do."

She took a step closer, fingers curled into fists at her sides. "You said it would calm her. That it would help her sleep."

"I said it would end the disruption," Faileas replied, his tone unchanging. "And it will."

Serai stared at him, searching for anything—remorse, doubt, humanity. But his face was a calm mask. A rippleless pond reflecting only what you bring to it.

"She's eleven. And you put murder in her hands."

"I gave you a choice," Faileas said smoothly, "and you made it. The Queen won't die, Serai. What's been done is done—and it can't be undone. But she'll live. If you're careful, so will the rest of you."

For a moment, Serai said nothing. Her breath trembled, then steadied. Her next words were quieter, colder. "If she talks—"

Faileas cut her off with a small lift of his hand. "If she talks," he said calmly, "the consequences won't be abstract. And you know this."

He stepped forward just enough to claim her space, lowering his voice until it carried weight rather than volume.

"I like you," he said. "Lana, too. But I don't like loose ends. Or sentiment."

Serai's jaw tightened.

"So be very sure," Faileas continued, "that what you whisper behind closed doors never finds the strength to walk."

Faileas paused at the edge of the breezeway, one hand lifting to adjust the hood that had slipped from his shoulder.

"One more thing," he said without turning. "If you speak of this—if Lana does—it ends badly. Be smart, Serai. Reins on both tongues. Yours and hers."

Then he stepped out into the rain beyond the arches, his footsteps swallowed by distance.

Serai remained, her hands slowly unclenching, the chill sinking deeper into her bones. The wind turned, catching the rain and flinging it sideways through the open colonnade, lashing her cheeks and soaking her collar.

She didn't move.

The stone beneath her feet no longer felt solid.

And for the first time in years, Serai wasn't sure if silence would be enough to protect them.

———— ✶ ————

The Great Hall of Castellon Shield's lower wing stirred with mid-morning intrigue. Sunlight filtered through stained glass, casting fractured color across polished marble as courtiers moved in deliberate clusters.

Lady Elara Icewind stood slightly apart, ocean-blue silk draped with deliberate restraint, her posture immaculate, her attention fixed not on the room but on a folded ledger held discreetly at her side.

"Careful," Lady Meyra Wynmere drawled beside her, plum-colored silk whispering as she leaned in. "You stare at numbers like that much longer and someone will assume you're plotting treason. Or marriage."

Elara did not look up. "If marriage balanced ledgers, I'd consider it."

Meyra smiled, sharp and knowing. "Ah. So it is numbers today. Not princes."

Elara exhaled softly. "Both, apparently. I was informed this morning my estates are being subjected to a final review—tenancies, tariffs, yields. Without notice. Without cause."

That earned Meyra's full attention. "Again?"

"A full accounting," Elara said quietly. "Surveyors sent to value the estate—lands, house, stables. Every acre priced."

Meyra clicked her tongue. "That's not accounting. That's pressure."

"Or impatience," Elara replied. "Someone wants certainty where there is none."

Meyra's gaze slid toward the upper galleries, thoughtful. "Funny how scrutiny always sharpens when a young prince starts looking fond of inconvenient women."

Elara finally looked at her, one brow arching. "Mind your tongue, Meyra."

Meyra only grinned. "Relax. If I meant Baldrik seriously, I'd have poured wine first. I'm merely observing. Courts do that."

Faileas stepped from the adjoining corridor at an unhurried pace, as though he had simply chosen this path by coincidence rather than design. His tunic was plain, his folio ordinary. Nothing about him invited alarm.

"Ladies," he said with a slight incline of his head. "A moment only, if you value survival over civility."

Elara turned first, recognition flickering and then smoothing into composure.

"Bold words, Faileas," she replied evenly. "This court holds grudges long and patience thin."

"Then I will be brief."

Meyra's smile sharpened. "You have our attention."

Faileas did not waste it. "The Queen has hired me to dispose of you, Lady Icewind."

Silence settled—tight, contained.

Elara's posture did not shift. "Yet you stand before me without a blade."

"I've been paid," he said. "Two thousand now. Two upon completion."

"What is this?" Elara asked coolly. "A crisis of conscience?"

"Not conscience. Calculation." His tone remained level. "A public death tied to the Queen's jealousy would fracture the court beyond repair. That serves no one."

Meyra stepped closer. "Gratitude won't protect her."

"Gratitude is irrelevant," Faileas replied. "Stability is not."

Elara studied him. "Are you advising me to flee?"

"No. I advise vigilance. The Queen has grown impatient. And unstable."

Meyra's voice lowered. "Then perhaps it is time the Queen found peace… one drop at a time."

Faileas' gaze shifted to her. "It has already been hastened. A child's fear accelerated the dosage days ago."

The words lingered.

Meyra frowned. "Then I will secure something stronger."

"It will not matter," Faileas said, certain. "The damage is done. Further doses will not deepen what is already broken. Nor will they kill her."

Elara's voice cooled further. "So you bring warning, but no remedy."

"I promised only to stall, not solve," he said. "Solutions require thought." A beat. "I will think."

He held her gaze briefly—not warmly, not softly, but with measured intent.

"In the meantime, Lady Icewind, avoid quiet corridors and unlit gardens. Impatience makes poor assassins."

Without ceremony, Faileas turned and blended back into the current of the hall.

———— ✶ ————

The trail beyond Glóshold sloped gently northward, threading through ancient pine and alder. Their budding branches whispered in the early light, the forest not yet fully awake. Rodrik left before dawn, accompanied by a guide sent from Glóshold—an older man named Thórleif, with a quiet manner and sure footing, charged with leading him to the summit of the Boulderfist trail and no further. Mist curled low over the trail, and the wind slept soundly in the trees—one last peace before the rise. The mead and supplies given to him by Vindrskar's people— topped off in Glóshold—weighed little compared to the promise he had offered—that should banners rise, the Wind-Sons would rise with him. That thought warmed him more than the morning fire had.

By midday, the land began to change. The dense woodland thinned, giving way to wide, rolling highland scattered with bramble and broken stone. Each step forward peeled back a layer of memory. He remembered other roads. Other boots beside his, long silent. Jarn and Velrik, who fell in the gorge outside Fennfield. Bryta—gods, Bryta—with her scarred knuckles and sharper wit. He missed her laugh the most. But it was Sigrún who lived deepest in him, lodged behind every breath.

She had been more than a wife—she had been his comrade in arms, his anchor, his equal. Fierce and unflinching, with eyes that held the clarity of winter skies and a voice that could rally warriors or quiet storms. They had fought together, bled together, built their quiet life between campaigns. She had known him in ways no one else ever would.

Her death had not been clean. Not honorable. Rodrik had seen the aftermath with his own eyes—Valen's doing, beyond all doubt. The how no longer mattered. Only the truth remained. They hadn't expected the wolf in her to die last.

He had built her pyre alone, stacking the wood with ritual care, placing her sword across her chest as the old songs taught. He said no words—none were needed. The flames took her. But the oath she left behind burns colder, deeper—in the marrow of his bones.

Gone in a heartbeat, taken by a man who thought his name meant he could never be touched.

Rodrik's jaw tightened. He had buried his grief with the ashes of his home, pressed the need for revenge beneath the weight of duty. But the name Valen still festered, a wound that had never closed.

When Rodrik read that name on the scroll, something aligned. The path north and the debt behind him were no longer separate roads.

Circus Valen.

Eirik had sent him south to see, to measure, and to return with truth—not to loose war on the strength of old blood and a single forged scrap.

Wise counsel. Careful counsel.

But the south was already rotting, and rot did not wait politely for better timing. If he turned back now with warning and nothing more, he would be handing stronger men to the slaughter unready.

He hadn't come north seeking vengeance. But neither would he pretend restraint still served the living. If the winds turned that way, he would not flinch.

A swollen stream cut across the trail, fed by melting snows in the high pass. The water surged dark and fast, white-lipped and wild. Rodrik stepped carefully across slick stones. The water clawed at his boots, ice snapping at each step as he balanced with the quiet precision of someone who had done this a hundred times.

Thórleif had already crossed ahead of him, waiting silently on the opposite bank with arms folded, as if unimpressed by the entire affair. On the far side, Rodrik looked back once—then pressed forward, falling in step with the older man.

In the waning light, he came upon the remnants of an old battlefield. Rusted iron jutted from the ground like the ribs of a buried beast. Bones bleached by time peeked through moss and loam. A weathered stone marked the dead—etched in the old runes, nearly swallowed by lichen. He crouched beside it, brushing the green aside—not to clean, but to say: I remember.

As twilight gathered like a breath held too long, the Boulderfists rose before him—shadowed, immense, ancient as the sky itself. Their snow-crowned peaks pierced the dusk like jagged spears. He found a lone tree clinging to a shelf of rock and set their small camp beneath its branches. Thórleif said little, as usual, unpacking his own bedroll with the mechanical ease of someone who had spent too many nights on cold stone.

Rodrik lit a small fire—just enough to heat water and steel. Above them, stars blinked into view, one by one, sharp as frost. To the north, green light shimmered across the sky in long, rippling veils—the aurora, the spirits of the dead, dancing in silence. He drew his axe, the blade catching the glow and starlight alike, and began to sharpen it with slow, methodical care. Thórleif gave a single approving grunt from across the fire, then muttered without looking away, "Spirits walk high tonight."

Rodrik said nothing. Some truths spoke better without answers.

After that, Thórleif fell silent again, eyes fixed skyward, as if listening to old voices only he could hear.

Rodrik paused his sharpening, eyes lifting to the slow dance of the aurora. For a long moment, he said nothing. Then, low and rough in his throat, he whispered a prayer to Sigrún—not for vengeance, not for forgiveness, but for strength.

"Hvar sem þú gengr nú, ást mín, ljósið leiði spor þín." – Wherever you walk now, my love, let the light guide your steps.

Tomorrow's climb would not be only stone and snow. Eirik had sent him south as a measured hand, to see clearly and return before pride or grief made fools of stronger men. By this time tomorrow, that road would be behind him.

Eirik had told him to see, to judge, and to return before grief made a fool of duty. Rodrik meant to cross anyway—and bear what followed.

The fire had burned low in the night, now little more than a ring of glowing embers. Morning light hadn't touched the eastern rim, and the cold crept through cloak and bone alike.

"Up," Thórleif said, nudging Rodrik's boot with the handle of a cooking ladle. "You'll want this in you. Warms the soul. It only gets colder and harder from here."

Rodrik sat up, rubbing a hand over his face as the wind tugged at the edge of his bedroll. He accepted the wooden bowl without a word, steam rising from the thick porridge inside. Oats, pine nuts, and a hint of salt pork—simple food, but it filled the gut.

Thórleif crouched beside the fire, gesturing northward toward the dim ridgeline just beginning to take shape against the pale sky. "Trail splits near the stone cairn. Stick to the left. The right's faster but turns slick once the sun breaks.

You'll hug a spine of rock for half a league—winds there whip like angry spirits, so mind your footing. After that, there's a shelf narrow as a butcher's smile, but steady if you don't rush it. We'll reach the final rise by dusk, if luck holds."

Rodrik ate as he listened, nodding occasionally. He had no illusions about the climb. These weren't hills. The Boulderfists had broken stronger men than he.

Thórleif stood and stretched, cracking joints like firewood. "I'll take you to the top, as promised. But beyond that—it's your feet and your gods."

Rodrik swallowed the last of the porridge, wiped the bowl clean with a scrap of bread, and stood.

"Fair enough," he said.

They broke camp in silence, the world above them turning from grey to gold.

The wind began before they reached the ridgeline.

It came low at first—a steady hiss threading through boulders and brush—then rose, gnawing at their cloaks and shouting down the quiet. Snow clung to the shadows, old and hard-crusted, while rock beneath their boots slicked with melt and treachery.

Thórleif moved with the grim certainty of a man who had walked these mountains too many times to trust them. Rodrik followed a step behind, his breaths sharp in his throat, boots striking stone in deliberate rhythm. The air thinned as they rose, cold as steel and dry as judgment, as if the mountain meant to strip flesh from bone without witness.

They crossed the spine Thórleif had warned of—a narrow fin of rock with nothing but sky on either side, the stone beneath their boots no wider than a blade's edge. Gusts howled across the exposed ridge, each one a sudden slap that stole breath and balance alike. Rodrik crouched instinctively, center of gravity low, fingers digging into frozen stone slick with melt. The wind tore at him, clawed into his cloak and tried to drag him into the open air, but he pushed forward like a fighter under a heavier blade. One misstep here would mean a fall long enough to name regrets—and scream them.

They paused beneath a leaning overhang to drink and catch their breath. Rodrik's fingers throbbed from stone-bite, his shoulders locked from hours of resisting gravity.

Thórleif passed him a strip of dried meat and muttered something about the old gods testing spine.

Late in the day, the wind grew frenzied, the path winding upward over jagged switchbacks cut into scree. Snow curled in ghostly eddies around their feet.

When they crested the final rise, twilight wrapped the peak in cold violet light. The world fell away on either side—to the south, the broken hills of Hravnskot; to the north, the vast, white sweep of Tuhkralin, rolling away into storm and silence.

Thórleif stopped there, stamping his feet against the cold to drive the numbness out. He gestured to a line of dark stones descending in a rough, deliberate path.

"From here, follow the guide stones. Easier going down. Harder to get lost if you don't rush it. Megi vindrinn finna bak þitt, ok steinarnir muna nafn þitt." - May the wind find your back, and the stones remember your name.

Rodrik appreciated the old tongue—and the weight of the words.

Rodrik gave a stiff nod, his face half-frozen beneath his hood.

They clasped forearms—short, hard—and held it a breath longer than necessary.

Thórleif turned back to the path they'd come from without ceremony. Rodrik watched him go until he became a shadow among stone.

Then he turned north and began his descent into Tuhkralin. He had not come this far to witness. Let Eirik judge him when it was done.

Mist veiled the Royal Stables as early sun painted the rafters. Soft morning mist curled gently around polished stone and weathered oak timbers, wrapping the stable-yard in a gauzy embrace. Servants moved purposefully, voices hushed but busy, quick steps scuffing softly on straw-covered cobblestones. Saddles of fine, polished leather were arrayed carefully along one wall, bridles hanging neatly beside them, each bearing insignia and embellishments declaring the status of their riders. The scent of oiled leather, warm hay, and sweat mingled with something colder—the taste before a storm.

King Harald stood poised near the last stall, sleeves rolled, one hand steady on the bridle of a massive elk-charger bred in the high fields of Timberwatch Hold. The beast snorted, stamping a heavy hoof, and Harald whispered low to calm it—words meant more for bonding than command. His dark riding cloak, trimmed in subtle silver thread, bore the royal crest discreetly embroidered upon his chest. He appeared at ease yet watchful, his eyes sharp and observant.

"You're lucky," said a voice beside him, dry with amusement. "Mine bit a groom this morning. Drew blood. I think she liked it."

King Consort Tulavan, dressed strikingly in his indigo and bone-white naval tunic with brass and coral decorations, leaned against the gatepost, nursing a clay mug of steaming spiceleaf tea. He looked oddly at home in riding leathers despite the jeweled cuffs still visible beneath his half-cloak.

Harald didn't smile, but his tone warmed. "Your grooms coddle them too much. Makes them soft and spiteful."

"Says the man who's hand-feeding his charger berries from the palace orchard."

"Bribes aren't softness. They're strategy."

"A king who bribes his own mount. Eldaraine must be thriving. All this peace—you'll have nothing left to conquer soon."

Before Harald could offer a reply, the stable doors groaned open. Lord Darkoak entered, cloak damp from the morning fog, expression bearing the weight of stone. Two palace riders followed a respectful pace behind, silent but purposeful.

Harald straightened. "You don't ride out to the stables for weather updates, Lord Commander."

Lanyard halted, gaze flicking briefly to Tulavan before settling firmly on the King. "Three reports in two days. All verified by separate agents. Villages along the Fernmarch, Wren's Edge, and Darnlow have suffered caravan attacks. Bread convoys. Timber haulers. Even a healer's wagon."

Harald's face did not change, but the stallion under his hand twitched restlessly.

Lanyard continued.

"Survivors describe the assailants as wearing royal uniforms. Crest and all."

Tulavan muttered, "Soldiers turned bandit?"

"No," Lanyard responded flatly. "They laughed while burning grain meant for Castellon. Stripped the wounded. One group left the king's seal carved into a tree. Crude, but intentional."

"False flags," Harald said, voice hardening. "Someone's sowing discord."

Lanyard nodded sharply. "I don't believe the men were ours. Neither do my captains. But someone wants the realm to believe otherwise."

Tulavan stepped closer. "You suspect Valen."

Lanyard's silence answered for him.

"Then I will," Harald turned, handing the reins silently to a groom. "He'd stage fires in his own fields if it meant owning the smoke."

"There's more," Lanyard handed Harald a scorched scrap of cloth bearing a partial crown crest. "Found nailed to a door in Wren's Edge. Message scrawled beneath: 'Your king burns your bread.'"

Harald's voice settled, firm and unyielding. "Double the northern patrols. Rotate southbound squads to the central range and post night watch at every waystone from Hillmere to the Fernmarch.

If any village sends smoke, I want a rider in my hall before the fire dies."

Harald stepped close until only inches separated them, his voice dropping, sharpened to a private edge.

"This part is not for council ears. You'll make yourself the point of contact—no intermediaries. Anyone with word of raiders, fires, or false banners reports directly to you. If they go around you, cut them out and seal the circle."

Lanyard inclined his head. "Understood, Majesty."

Tulavan whistled softly. "Someone's kicked the hornet's nest."

Harald's jaw flexed. "Let's make sure they regret reaching for the hive."

Harald turned back to his charger, voice firm. "Saddle the wind, Tulavan. The prey won't wait."

Captain Apeck broke the tension, amusement dancing in his eyes. "Horses, Tulavan? You sure you wouldn't prefer a boat? At least you'd know how to steer."

Tulavan smirked, playful irritation returning. "I've ridden before, Apeck. Unlike some, I don't need liquid courage to find my balance."

Harald chuckled softly, amusement returning to his eyes. "Darkoak, ensure the quivers are stocked properly with the stag arrows. I won't have the hunt ending before it starts because some idiot stableboy couldn't tell the difference."

"Already checked, Your Majesty," Lanyard replied smoothly, regaining his customary composure. "They are prepared."

Apeck shivered exaggeratedly, rubbing his hands together. "Tell me, is it always this cold in Eldaraine?"

Harald smiled slightly. "Brisk air clears the soul, Captain. Might even scour the salt from your lungs."

Tulavan chuckled, nudging Apeck. "It's not the salt that wounds him, Harald. It's the lack of Firewine at breakfast."

Laughter rippled gently among them, a momentary warmth against the morning chill.

All except Lanyard, who silently and methodically mounted his horse, ever vigilant.

Following suit, Harald, Tulavan, and Apeck swung smoothly onto their horses. Huntsmen, trackers, and guides formed ranks around them. The mounted group moved forward, riding out of the stables through Castellon's northern gate. Behind them, wagons rolled steadily, laden with camp gear and provisions, ready for the three-day pursuit.

As they turned north toward the dense hunting grounds, anticipation tightened, drawing them toward challenge, camaraderie—and the chase.

Night settled over the hunting camp, stars scattered across a field of black. Around a robust campfire, flames danced and crackled, throwing flickering shadows onto the circle of weary men gathered close for warmth and conversation.

King Harald leaned back, his cloak wrapped snugly against the night chill. His eyes reflected firelight, thoughtful and distant. Beside him, King Consort Tulavan stared into the flames, face aglow, lines of frustration etched into his otherwise stoic expression.

Captain Apeck prodded the fire with a long stick, sparks spiraling upward into the darkness. "Plenty of sign, but not a single elk to show for it. Are Eldaraine's beasts usually this shy, Harald?"

Harald's lips curled into a faint, knowing smile. "Elk in these woods aren't shy, Apeck—they're clever. Too clever by half."

Tulavan snorted softly, amusement breaking through his fatigue. "Maybe they're just wise enough to keep clear of a sailor on horseback."

Apeck chuckled ruefully, shaking his head. "And I thought I'd only have to worry about drowning at sea, not in embarrassment on land."

Lord Darkoak sat apart from the banter, quietly sharpening his hunting knife, the rhythmic rasp of metal on stone threading tension through the firelight. His eyes were intent on his task, features carved from stone, unreadable and aloof.

Harald stretched slightly, letting out a deep breath. "Tomorrow we'll push further into the northern woods. The trackers think we'll find the herd there. With luck, they won't evade us twice."

Tulavan nodded, his expression sharpening. "Luck, or perhaps more skill. We'll see if Eldaraine's elk can outrun Varanese arrows."

Apeck grinned broadly, nodding toward Harald. "If nothing else, the chase has cleared my lungs—even without Firewine."

Laughter eased the group, softening the edges of the day's disappointment. Even Lanyard's stern expression softened for a breath, a faint twitch at the corner of his mouth before he returned to his task.

Tulavan turned thoughtfully to Harald, the flickering firelight deepening shadows across his features. "How fares your kingdom, Harald? Your nobles behaving themselves, I hope?"

Harald gave a faint shrug, a shadow briefly crossing his eyes. "Eldaraine always grumbles, Tulavan. A kingdom without complaints would be suspicious indeed. Nothing but the usual grumbling from the royal houses. If they ever go quiet, I'll worry."

Apeck chuckled softly, leaning forward conspiratorially. "Grumbling nobles? Sounds like stormy seas to me. I've found such things rarely calm on their own."

Harald's smile was thin, though his eyes warmed slightly. "True enough, Captain, but storms pass eventually."

Lanyard cleared his throat pointedly, interrupting gently but firmly. "Gentlemen, we're hunting game—not gossip. Save the courtly games for stone walls."

The men exchanged amused glances, acknowledging the quiet rebuke. The night continued quietly, the fire crackling as conversation ebbed and returned. Beneath it all, anticipation held, waiting for morning.

The throne room was warm with light, high windows casting long bars of amber across the polished stone floor. The great chandelier of iron and glass hung steady above, its dozens of candle-flames flickering but unfazed—like courtiers trained not to flinch. A hush lingered in the gallery above, broken only by the turning of parchment or the shifting of velvet robes as nobles leaned to whisper.

The throne itself—a high-backed seat of carved blackthorn inlaid with gold—sat unshaken at the hall's apex. Upon it, Queen Avanna Thornsword sat poised, her bearing regal and calm. Gone was the disheveled specter of grief that had haunted the corridors since Miroray's arrival.

Today, she was lacquered perfection—gowned in sage green trimmed with ash-fox fur, her crown fixed and firm against a tight coil of braids. Her chin was high, her hands still.

To her right, seated in the Queen's Throne, sat her sister, Queen Miroray Kaeleen, draped in coral and silk. She sat with one ankle crossed over the other, expression unreadable but composed.

"Bring forth the next," Avanna said calmly, her voice carrying sovereign weight. Her tone carried no tremble, no twitch. If the court expected madness, they were sorely disappointed.

A steward stepped up, calling the name with a formal clarity: "Baron Bahlun of Westmere."

The man who approached was thickset and red-faced, bearing the stoop of one more used to shouting at grain counters than bowing to queens. His tunic bore the blue-and-copper sash of Westmere, though the fabric was worn at the edges. He knelt with effort, then rose stiffly, eyes darting to Avanna's face, then to Miroray's, then back again.

"Your Grace," Bahlun said, voice thick with restraint. "My apologies for the bluntness of my words, but the grain shipment—approved by the Crown for our western stores—has not arrived. The men sent to fetch it were turned back by the guards at Stonewatch. They were told no such quota had been approved."

Murmurs rippled across the chamber.

Avanna's expression did not flicker. "The quotas were confirmed by writ," she said coolly. "Signed and sealed. Have you brought documentation to challenge that?"

"I have," he said, motioning to his steward, who delivered a weather-stained scroll to the foot of the dais.

Avanna gave a glance to a page, who retrieved it and handed it to her clerk. The parchment was inspected in quiet, and a moment later the clerk stepped forward.

"This is not the crown's seal," the clerk said. "It bears the mark of House Valen."

Miroray's brows knit at that, and she glanced toward Avanna.

The Queen leaned back, one gloved finger tapping the arm of her chair. "Then your complaint is with Lord Valen, not the throne."

"Baron Bahlun. You have been lied to. I advise you not to place faith in false scribes. Return to Westmere. You'll have your grain. Twice what was promised. Directly from Lord Valens' stores in Fennmoor."

The Baron's eyes widened. "Twice, Your Grace?"

"Yes," Avanna said, her voice silk and steel. "And if Lord Valen would like to question that, he is welcome to do so. From the floor of this very hall."

The murmur sharpened—astonishment edged with the scent of retribution. Bahlun dropped to a low bow. "You are... most gracious, Majesty."

"Not gracious," Avanna said. "Correct."

As Bahlun withdrew, Miroray leaned slightly toward her sister, voice pitched just low enough for privacy. "That was generous."

Avanna's expression did not change. "It was precise. Generosity makes a spectacle of what is owed. This... was a correction."

A minor baron was called forward next—Lord Jarenth of House Merrowfield, a house so minor it was unclear why he'd been granted a voice. He bowed low, his embroidered cuffs frayed at the edge, his expression eager but uncertain.

"My Queen," Jarenth said, "there is troubling word from the southern trade route. Banditry has returned in force. Wagons burned near Rivermere. Herds scattered. The sheriff has asked for militia support—half a dozen knights, at most."

"Is this the same sheriff," Avanna asked dryly, "who last season blamed stolen calves on witches in the reeds?"

Snickers from the gallery above. Jarenth flushed.

"I… yes, Your Grace. But this time, there is smoke. And ash. And two dead drivers with arrows in their backs."

Avanna's eyes narrowed, just slightly. "Then let it be investigated properly. I will send Marshal Ryzen and a letter of inquiry. If more is required, I will see it done."

The baron bowed, grateful and dismissed.

There was a brief pause. Avanna turned her head slightly and offered her sister a smile. It was a real smile—or close enough to unsettle.

"When the matters of court are finished," she said, "I'd like you to join me in the solar. For tea. I believe it's been... too long since we've spoken properly. Sister to sister."

Miroray blinked, surprised. "Of course. I'd like that."

Avanna smiled. It was small, controlled, and for the first time in days, it reached her eyes. "Good. I miss the sound of your voice when it's not bound by politics."

Avanna looked back toward the court. "Let us proceed. I feel the day favors clarity."

The fire crackled, casting warm amber light across the polished wood and upholstered furnishings of Foxburrow's solar parlor. Sunlight filtered through narrow stained-glass windows, painting fractured gold and crimson across the floorboards. Shelves of old books and curios lent the space an air of quiet scholarship—removed from the rigid formality of throne rooms, yet capable of bearing dangerous truths.

Lord Quentyn Caerlyn stood framed by the mellow afternoon glow, his foxfur-lined robe catching the light. Above the mantle behind him hung the banner of House Caerlyn.

Outside, clouds gathered, dimming the sky to a muted gray.

A quiet knock sounded at the door, followed by the discreet entry of a steward. He bowed briefly before announcing, "Lord Branik Durnhart and Jorran Vey of House Durnhart have arrived, my lord."

Branik stepped into the room, iron-studded boots muffled on the thick rug. Lines of deep concern carved into his gruff features. Behind him, his advisor Jorran stood silent and alert, eyes wary, fingers twitching slightly as if prepared for unseen threats.

"What brings you to my home, Branik?" Quentyn finally asked, still gazing outward. "You don't like being far from the twins, which tells me either something has gone terribly wrong…or exactly according to plan."

Branik wasted little time, his voice low. "We have a serious problem—Lord Valen has moved beyond disruption. He's aiming at dominion."

Lady Caerlyn sat poised on a cushioned bench near the fire, a steaming cup cradled in her fingers.

Her brow knitted in thoughtful concentration, copper braids now muted by the subdued light.

Thistle Corven, the house spymaster, leaned unobtrusively against the wall, her presence felt more than seen.

"Speak plainly, Branik," Lady Caerlyn urged gently, eyes sharp despite her quiet voice. "You and Quentyn were both at the gathering when Circus proposed his plan. Quentyn briefed me afterward. He didn't mention any protest from you."

"I had no quarrel with disruption," Branik replied firmly, settling into an opposite chair with an air of unease. "But this—this isn't careful disorder. It's quiet conquest. Layered, calculated, and far-reaching. Valen is moving to claim everything."

Silence followed, broken only by the first patter of rain against the windowpanes.

Quentyn turned slowly from the window, brows raised. "Everything?"

Branik nodded grimly. "The grain market first, then trade. If Icewind buckles—and he circles her like a carrion crow—he gains leverage. Rumors speak of his hand behind Icewind's failed harvests—bad seed delivered knowingly to desperate stewards. Poachers thinning elk herds near Windmere, too convenient to be coincidence. He's not passively waiting for collapse. He's actively crafting it."

Quentyn snorted, eyes narrowing. "But Valen doesn't crave a crown. It's too cumbersome for him. He desires control, strings hidden in shadows, the crown upon a head he can command from afar."

Jorran spoke softly, arms folded in contemplation. "Starvation and silence are his weapons, not armies. He conquers with ledgers, not steel."

Thistle tilted her head slightly, her voice a dry whisper. "Charters drafted under his stewardship. Centralized grain control disguised as relief. At Goldacre, freshly cleared lands now host four silos and a barn large enough for livestock. Circus has never tolerated the scent of cattle shit. Which begs the question—what will he truly store there?"

Lady Caerlyn lowered her cup thoughtfully. "No one will oppose him openly. On parchment, his schemes read like mercy."

Branik's voice darkened further, a low growl threaded with alarm. "It's no mercy. It's a siege cloaked as stewardship.

"And whispers say he already has minor lords dancing to his tune—enough to tip the balance, crown or no."

Quentyn moved to a sideboard, uncorking a bottle of plum wine with practiced ease. "And here I thought treason would announce itself with war horns and banners." He poured carefully, his voice quiet but clear. "No, Valen won't wear the crown himself. He'll crown another quietly, gripping tight the leash."

Lady Caerlyn accepted her wine but did not drink. Her gaze remained steady. "We must choose. Watch quietly as the snake coils tighter, or begin sharpening our own fangs?"

Branik settled deeper into his chair, resolve replacing the worry etched across his features. "Then let this meeting be the first strike. Let Durnhart and Caerlyn share more than whispers—quiet readiness, watchful eyes, steel drawn in shadow."

Quentyn raised his cup, his smile faint and edged like a blade. "Foxes and wolves. The realm may soon regret teaching us to guard our tongues."

"Should we speak with Icewind?" Lady Caerlyn asked. "Or perhaps Wynmere?"

Jorran's eyes met Thistle's. A subtle nod passed between them. "One message for each. Carefully worded, without specifics. Enough to begin spinning a quiet web."

"I'll handle Wynmere," Thistle said. "They'll understand without needing it spelled out."

Jorran inclined his head slightly. "Icewind will require clearer words. I'll see to it personally."

Quentyn nodded slowly, eyes narrowed in consideration. "Elara has been staying frequently at the Shield of late. Best to reach her there."

Lady Caerlyn added, "And Alvis?"

Branik's expression darkened. "The King's brother is likely already fortifying Stormwatch. He's fiercely loyal to Harald and no friend to Valen."

Jorran added, "Dravik as well, it's unclear where his loyalty lies, however we should not discount him."

"Agreed. We should make clear to them we are not enemies. I'll dispatch riders north to Alvis and south to Dravik once we return to Highstone Manor."

Quentyn nodded. "It's vital Alvis and Dravik understand we're aligned in this."

They raised their cups together in quiet unity, the muted afternoon light catching in the plum wine, dark as velvet.

CHAPTER NINETEEN

Early evening sunlight streamed weakly through leaded glass panes into Avanna's solar, the faint golden glow already fading as clouds thickened beyond the balcony.

Queen Avanna sat at the ornate balcony table, her posture rigid, gaze fixed absently on the horizon, her usually immaculate braids slightly disheveled, pearls askew. The balcony railing sat deliberately low, designed not to block the view when one was seated. Her fingertips drummed restlessly against the marble surface, a subtle but telling sign of inner turmoil.

Opposite her, Queen Miroray reclined gracefully, her expression warm yet increasingly wary, violet-blue eyes fixed attentively upon her older sister's distant demeanor.

Nearby, Lana moved quietly, finishing the tea service with practiced grace. She poured carefully, the faint steam curling upward before setting the cup before Avanna. Then she stepped back at once, hands folded at her waist, eyes lowered, waiting to be called should the queens require anything further.

"You should see Kira, Avanna," Miroray coaxed gently, attempting to bridge the unsettling quiet. "She's sixteen now, grown tall and confident. Perhaps too clever—certainly enough to keep me on my toes. And Tika, that mischievous pet of hers, you wouldn't believe the trouble that creature causes. It nearly overturned the entire feast during the last celebration."

Avanna did not respond immediately, her gaze vacant, lips pressed tightly. Her fingertips paused their drumming as her expression became clouded with sudden confusion. She blinked slowly, looking around as if searching for something just beyond sight. "How is Mother? She hasn't written to me recently."

Miroray's brow furrowed deeply, her voice soft, cautious.

"Avanna... Mother has been gone a long time," Miroray said gently. "You know that. I think you're tired."

Avanna's gaze flickered with uncertainty, her eyes darting rapidly, chasing shadows of thought not fully formed. "She did. I saw the seal. The green wax. She always used green. Don't say she didn't. I remember."

Miroray reached across gently, her hand hovering near Avanna's, careful not to startle her sister. "Talk to me, Avanna. You've been slipping."

Avanna's confusion morphed abruptly into irritation, her eyes sharpening angrily as she withdrew her hand sharply.

"And what of Tulavan? Tell me of your new husband—our father's betrayer. How could you marry such a man, Miroray?"

Miroray's brows knitted tighter in confusion and mild distress, her response careful yet tinged with hurt.

"Avanna, what nonsense is this? Tulavan has done nothing but honor Vara, and our family. That's not just cruel, Avanna—it's false. You know it is."

Avanna seemed momentarily uncertain, her anger melting into bewilderment before abruptly shifting again. A jarring, sweet smile curled her lips. Her voice turned pleasant—deceptively so, as if nothing had occurred.

A faint shiver ran through her. She drew her arms closer, fingers brushing her sleeves as if surprised by the cold. "Be a dear," she said absently, eyes still unfocused, "and fetch my winter cloak from my rooms. The night air is rather cool."

"Yes, Your Majesty," Lana replied at once. She bobbed her head respectfully and hurried from the solar, the door closing softly behind her.

Avanna lifted her teacup, took a small sip, then set it down again. After a moment, she looked back to her sister and asked,

"And Kirahnae? How old is she now? She must be ten now?"

Unease deepened in Miroray's chest, her voice gentle but firm, eyes filled with cautious concern.

"Kira is sixteen," Miroray said softly. "She's nearly grown." Are you feeling unwell? You seem troubled."

Avanna's gaze grew distant again, her words quiet, wandering.

"I—I must have miscounted. Time seems different lately, doesn't it? Days slipping through fingers like grains of sand... Mother would say something about that, wouldn't she? Something wise and comforting…"

Miroray leaned forward, her voice full of gentle urgency. "Avanna, please listen to me. I'm deeply worried about you. Perhaps you should rest and—"

Avanna interrupted sharply, her voice abruptly suspicious.

"You wore that crown in your smile long before they gave you one, didn't you? Always Mother's favorite. You're here to take Harald from me, aren't you? To push me aside, just like her!"

Miroray rose slowly. Shock crossed her face—then eased, settling into gentle concern.

"Avanna, stop. Please—listen to yourself. Let me help you."

Avanna's voice trembled, eyes fixed with accusation.

"I know what you're doing," she said, low and tight. "I see it now. You want what's mine. You always have—Harald, Eldaraine… everything."

Miroray moved closer carefully, extending a calming hand. "Avanna, please—"

Avanna's breath caught.

Panic.

Threat.

She flinched as Miroray reached for her "Don't touch me!" Avanna shoved hard, a reflex born of fear. Miroray stumbled backward, eyes wide, arms flailing instinctively for balance. The low marble railing caught the back of her legs; she fell back, and for one devastating heartbeat their gazes locked, shock and betrayal etched starkly between them. Miroray's cry cut off as she went over the edge.

Avanna stepped forward and stared down, frozen, as if the world had stopped making sense.

Her chest heaved, breath rasping as if torn from her lungs. Her hands trembled uselessly, cold dread crawling over her skin as dark spots swam through her vision. Realization settled like ice in her veins.

Someone below screamed, as townsfolk started to gather.

Avanna did not move.

Then the moment lurched forward again. She stepped back from the balcony, turned toward the door, her voice pitching high.

"Guards! Guards! An assassin—someone has pushed Queen Miroray!"

The door burst open moments later, armed guards rushing into the solar, weapons drawn, eyes wide with alarm.

Avanna had collapsed into a chair, her body shaking uncontrollably, murmuring brokenly, "Assassin, assassin... my sister..."

Two of the guards moved swiftly to the balcony railing, peering down to see Miroray's body broken on the stone below, surrounded by startled onlookers as cries and murmurs rose and echoed back into the solar.

Air moved through the open balcony, cool against the sweat on her skin.

Lieutenant Leif, approached Avanna carefully, urgency straining his voice.

"Your Highness, what has happened?"

Avanna continued trembling, eyes glazed, whispering faintly. "Assassin... he took her... pushed her..."

Leif's voice tightened. He gripped her shoulders—firm, grounding. His eyes searched her face for a fraction too long before he spoke. "Avanna. Speak clearly. Who did this?"

The sharp urgency broke through Avanna's haze. Her eyes refocused slowly, locking onto Leif's face, her breathing slowing.

Her voice quivered, then found a narrow, brittle steadiness—words forming as if she were clinging to them for balance.

"I—I was too late. I came to meet Miroray—we were going to have tea, just… just be sisters again. Then—then there was a man. Big. Pale hair, braided like a northerner. He pushed her. She fought, gods, she fought—but he was too strong."

Leif's brow furrowed deeply. Something unreadable passed through his eyes—doubt, fear, love—gone almost as soon as it appeared. "Your Highness, why did he not attack you?"

Avanna hesitated, blinking as if waking. "He—he must not have seen me. When I shouted, he fled immediately."

Leif stepped back. He held her gaze a heartbeat longer than necessary, then nodded grimly, voice snapping into command. "Secure the castle! No one leaves until we find this assassin!"

Leif and another guard stayed protectively near Avanna, vigilant and tense, as the alarm spread rapidly throughout the castle. Marshal Ryzen entered swiftly, his presence commanding and authoritative.

Leif met Ryzen with a low, urgent voice. "Marshal," Leif pressed his hand to his chest with a sharp nod, "The Queen says she came upon a large man pushing Queen Miroray over the balcony. She claims he fled when she shouted for guards, possibly unaware of her presence. I've already ordered the castle secured—no one leaves until he's found."

Ryzen's expression darkened, eyes narrowing in immediate calculation. Turning quickly to another guard, he commanded firmly, "Send a rider to King Harald. He must return immediately."

"Yes, my lord, at once," he replied, turning sharply on his heel and departing swiftly from the room. As he did, the door opened and Lana stepped in holding the queen's cloak, nearly colliding with him as he brushed past without slowing.

Avanna straightened slowly, trembling hands gradually stilling. Her eyes cleared but remained oddly detached, calm settling over her features as she glanced around the solar, seemingly untroubled by the frantic activity.

"Miroray will handle Vara admirably until I visit again," she murmured serenely, her voice disturbingly tranquil. "She always manages perfectly."

Avanna's gaze shifted gently to Marshal Ryzen, a tranquil, unsettling smile forming on her lips. "Oh—Marshal Ryzen! I didn't hear you arrive. Would you like tea? Lana, pour some tea."

Her's eyes flicked to the cloak in the girl's arms. "Why do you have that?"

Lana stood just inside the solar. "Your Majesty," She said softly, confused. "You were chilled. You asked me to—"

"Of course," Avanna replied at once, the moment already slipping away. "Yes. Thank you." She sat gracefully smoothing her robes. "Pour some tea for me, would you?"

Marshal Ryzen's gaze settled briefly on young Lana, whose wide eyes flicked from the empty balcony to Avanna and back again. "See to the Queen," he instructed firmly. She dipped her head and moved inside the room.

Turning to Leif, he added quietly, "Remain here, Lieutenant. I'll post extra guards at her door."

Ryzen then gestured another guard forward, his voice low and authoritative.

"Have Queen Miroray's body collected respectfully and brought directly to the coroner's chambers. Summon cleaners to wash the stones below; they are to leave no trace behind."

The guard hurriedly bowed and departed swiftly from the room.

Ryzen lingered briefly, his troubled gaze resting on Avanna's eerily serene form. He exchanged a brief, meaningful glance with Leif before turning and striding out of the solar, his footsteps heavy with the weight of duty.

Outside, the storm broke. Rain lashing at the stone walls. A guard stepped over to the balcony and closed the doors, shutting the out the rain.

In her chair, Avanna sat sipping her tea undisturbed. Nearby, Lana stood ready to serve her queen, her eyes straying once—only once—toward the empty space where Queen Miroray had been.

West of Castellon, near the broken escarpments of Blackstone Ravine, the northern meadows stretched vast and vibrant—an emerald tapestry fringed by dense woodland, now transitioning gracefully from the soft embrace of late Bloomrise to the confident warmth of early Sunswell.

The air was rich with the scent of blooming wildflowers and fresh grass, tinged subtly by the earthy perfume of damp soil from recent rains. Gentle sunlight filtered through the canopy, illuminating patches of ground beneath towering oaks and slender aspens, casting dappled patterns of gold and green.

Amidst this idyllic landscape moved the royal hunting party, each clad in durable leathers and fine linens suited to the rigors of the hunt, quivers strapped firmly across their backs. King Harald's powerful bow, fashioned from seasoned yew and wrapped in supple leather, rested lightly in his grip.

Tulavan's bow was equally formidable, elegantly curved and lacquered, reflecting Varanese craftsmanship. Lord Lanyard Darkoak, observing closely, held a finely balanced hunting spear, its polished steel tip glinting softly in the filtered sunlight. Apeck choosing to observer rather than participate in the hunt, stood leaning against a thick alder, sipping on a wine skin he secreted away in his pack.

Each man moved with practiced familiarity: boots placed heel to toe to avoid snapping twigs, breaths slowed and timed between steps, eyes flicking briefly to one another for hand signals rather than words.

The tense silence broke briefly as Lanyard raised a swift hand, stilling the hunters instantly. He motioned carefully toward a dense thicket tangled with thorny bramble. Through the thorny screen stood a majestic bull elk, its great antlers sprawling upwards like the crown of a forest king.

The creature, regal and utterly oblivious, nibbled peacefully at tender new shoots of grass.

In perfect harmony, Harald and Tulavan drew their bows with practiced ease, smoothly notching arrows fletched with meticulously shaped feathers, their points honed razor-sharp for maximum precision. Their eyes locked on their shared quarry, their motions fluid yet subtly competitive—The elk offered more than meat—it offered proof. Of aim. Of dominance. Lanyard observed keenly, his mind drifting momentarily to his own first hunt with King Boris Thornsword, many years past. He had been younger then, a newly invited noble, unproven and eager.

Boris had stood much like Harald now—commanding yet measured, quietly confident, every action purposeful. Lanyard recalled clearly how the old king's presence alone had taught him the importance of quiet strength and silent judgment.

Watching Harald and Tulavan, Lanyard could not help but compare them to the formidable men he'd known, weighing their potential, measuring their worth. He recognized this hunt as more than mere sport; it was political theater, a delicate balance of power and pride, echoing lessons Boris himself had silently imparted that day long ago.

The moment stretched thin, tense, like the taut bowstrings held by both kings. Then, simultaneously, arrows flew with whispering precision.

They struck true with a solid, resonant thunk, the elk's body jolting sharply, muscles spasming before it collapsed, antlers sinking into soft earth.

Tulavan surged upright, his usually stoic face now alight with victorious exuberance, laughing heartily. Harald rose more slowly, a quieter but equally profound satisfaction marking his features.

Each man assumed himself the solitary victor, their mutual ignorance sparing them immediate disappointment.

Yet as they approached their fallen prey, their confident steps slowed, becoming hesitant, confidence bleeding into caution as the meadow held its breath, every small sound suddenly sharp against the open stillness.

Harald glanced briefly at Tulavan, their eyes meeting in cautious uncertainty, tension etched across their faces.

Tulavan's breath caught slightly, his earlier boasting shifting into wary hesitation as he exchanged a questioning look with Harald.

They moved closer, The space between anticipation and realization stretched tight—like the bowstrings they'd just loosed, until the truth of the kill became unmistakably clear, leaving them both momentarily speechless, suspended in stunned disbelief.

Two arrows stood embedded so closely together they seemed a single strike. Harald felt a brief pang of disappointment, quickly overshadowed by genuine admiration. A quiet chuckle rose in his chest, turning to full laughter as he met Tulavan's gaze, their brief rivalry dissolving into mutual respect.

"Dead center," Harald said with a grin, clapping Tulavan's arm. "Almost pity the beast. Almost."

Tulavan's smile returned, crooked and warm. "Yours flew sharp enough. Fate couldn't choose a favorite—so she split the prize."

Captain Apeck joined Lanyard, his grin wide and playful, though his eyes briefly flickered with unusual seriousness. "Two arrows, one kill. If that's not a sign, it's at least a promising partnership."

He paused slightly, his jest turning unexpectedly somber. "Gods help anyone who finds themselves facing you both." Apeck's smile lingered, but something in his expression hinted that he recognized the weight behind his own words.

Lanyard watched Harald and Tulavan carefully, noting thoughtful looks exchanged.

The huntsmen swiftly moved to prepare the elk for transport, while Harald and Tulavan shared a celebratory cup of wine. The camaraderie replaced competition, and for a brief moment, genuine laughter echoed pleasantly across the meadow.

Gradually, though, a subtle stillness crept through the trees; the rustling of leaves faded, the air holding tight as if anticipating what came next.

The serenity shattered violently.

A rider burst through the trees, his horse slick with sweat, flanks heaving, breath coming in desperate gasps.

The Castellon guard swung down too fast, nearly falling as he staggered forward, eyes wild.

"Your Highnesses!" he wheezed urgently. "The Queen—Queen Miroray... she's dead. Killed!"

Shock slammed through the group like a physical blow.

Tulavan froze mid-step, color draining from his face as his expression tightened into rigid stillness.

Harald felt a sickening twist in his gut, breath caught—like the world had locked around him. His jaw tightened sharply, eyes narrowing into steely resolve. His hand instinctively gripped the pommel of his sword.

He stepped forward, voice sharp. "Speak plainly! What happened?"

The guard sucked in a ragged breath. "An assassin, Your Majesty. Queen Miroray was thrown from the balcony. Queen Avanna witnessed it. A large man—gone before the guards arrived."

"Assassin?" Tulavan echoed, the word flat, edged with disbelief.

The guard nodded frantically. "The Shield is sealed. It is being searched every hall and chamber. Marshal Ryzen has ordered everything locked down until the man is found."

A heavy silence settled, stretching out painfully as the implications sunk deep into every man gathered, gripping them in tense uncertainty.

Lanyard's voice snapped sharply, cutting through their stunned paralysis. "Mount up. Now."

The quiet command broke their palsy like splintered glass, setting them into motion once more. Harald swung swiftly into his saddle, fingers tight on the reins as he fought to control the turmoil roiling inside him.

A dark suspicion clawed at the edge of his mind—could this be Valen's treachery, or something even darker stirring from Hravnskot?

Tulavan mounted in silence, each movement deliberate, jaw set as if motion itself were the only thing keeping him steady.

His thoughts turned immediately to consequence—plots deeper than a single death, fractures that could threaten the fragile peace between their kingdoms.

Around them, men scrambled urgently to their mounts, the sudden burst of activity cutting harshly through the lingering shock and disbelief.

Without another word, they turned swiftly and thundered back toward Castellon, urgency pounding beneath every hoofbeat, the meadow's peace swallowed in their wake.

The great gates of Castellon Shield yawned open like the jaws of a slumbering beast, torchlight flickering along its stone teeth. What should have been a triumphal return was instead shrouded in a grim pall. Guards stood like sentinels carved from stone, their faces masks of dread. Whispers darted through the gathered court, fluttering like uneasy birds before a storm.

King Harald strode forward first, mud-caked cloak trailing behind him, his eyes cold and grey. Beside him walked King Consort Tulavan, stiff-backed and silent, his dark eyes narrowed with suspicion, every muscle taut with barely contained tension.

Lord Lanyard Darkoak shadowed their steps, his gaunt face drawn tight, eyes flicking over every shadow, every face, calculating threats unseen. Captain Apeck followed, hand resting warily on his sword, geniality stripped away, replaced by grim determination.

The great hall stood heavy with silence, oppressive and suffocating. At the hall's far end, under a canopy of rich velvet and golden embroidery, Queen Miroray lay in solemn repose, her regal features serene in death. Candlelight danced across her peaceful countenance, illuminating the proud lines of her face and the opulent silk that enveloped her.

Queen Avanna stood by her sister's side, a specter in disarray. Her gown hung askew, hair unbound, eyes bright—yet vacant—as if watching something beyond the mortal realm. She whispered softly, as though speaking to someone just out of sight.

Guard Marshal Ryzen came forward, his posture disciplined yet visibly strained, tension etched sharply across his features.

He inclined his head respectfully. "Your Majesties," he began, voice tightly controlled yet edged with unease, "Queen Miroray fell from the solar balcony. Our investigation has uncovered nothing conclusive, but the circumstances are troubling and demand deeper scrutiny."

Tulavan turned toward Miroray's body, eyes scanning her still form, a hard, controlled intensity settling in his gaze. His voice was a blade, cold and sharp.

"What transpired, Marshal? Who was present when this happened?"

Ryzen hesitated, eyes shifting uneasily toward Avanna.

"Queen Avanna—Your Majesty—but she... insists Queen Miroray will provide answers herself upon her return."

Tulavan's head turned sharply, voice rising in barely restrained anger.

"Upon her return? Marshal, Queen Miroray lies dead before us. Speak plainly!"

Ryzen's jaw tightened, voice lowered further.

"Queen Avanna's mind seems… unsettled, she speaks as though Queen Miroray still draws breath and forbids any inquiries or further investigation."

King Harald moved carefully toward Avanna, each step deliberate, eyes searching her face for recognition or reason. Still speaking to Ryzen, "Marshal, have the grounds been secured?"

Ryzen nodded. "Yes, Your Grace. Castellon Shield is sealed. None enter or leave. Every room, every shadow is being scoured."

Captain Apeck spoke up. "Marshal Ryzen, my men stand ready. If you are in need."

Tulavan's voice broke through the heavy silence, sharp and commanding. "Captain Varyn. Marshal, take Captain Varyn of my personal guard. He knows my wife's habits and may notice something others might overlook."

Varyn stepped forward, bowing respectfully, his expression a mask of discipline beneath the clear pain in his eyes. "I am at your service, Marshal."

Ryzen inclined his head. "Your Majesty, that insight would be most valuable. Captain Varyn, your assistance is appreciated."

He bowed. "Your Majesty. King Tulavan." His gaze was steady. "Allow me to begin a thorough examination of the scene. I will pursue what answers may be found."

Harald stepped closer, voice lowered and firm. "Marshal, report your findings directly to Lord Darkoak. Answers must be found swiftly."

Ryzen nodded sharply. "Understood, Your Majesty."

Harald exchanged a dark, wary glance with Darkoak, whose face was a grim mask, neither men willing to voice what had begun to take shape.

Lanyard leaned close, voice a soft growl. "This goes beyond grief or madness. Something darker and deeper is stirring here. We must be cautious."

Harald nodded slowly, the weight of foreboding pressing heavily upon him. "Provide Marshal Ryzen any assistance he requires. We must find the truth of it."

"Yes, my king," Lanyard replied quietly, eyes narrowed in vigilance.

And as Tulavan stood rigid by Miroray's lifeless form, Avanna continued her quiet murmuring, her fractured smile fixed and distant, her gaze lost in shadows unseen by all others.

"Miroray will know," she whispered softly. "She will make everything clear."

The tavern was already loud with patrons, the air thick with malt, sweat, and the easy arrogance of men who believed the season itself favored them. Sunlight slanted through the open front shutters, catching dust motes and the pale edge of smoke curling up from the hearth.

Aulfis Brightoak leaned back on his bench, one boot hooked around the rung, a half-empty mug in his hand. Across from him sat Torrin Lyonswark—tall, all elbows and confidence, sandy hair pulled back from his face, a proper goatee framing a grin that promised trouble.

"You're telling me," Torrin said, incredulous, "that she rode, *then* doubled the price?"

Aulfis snorted. "She smiled sweetly. Like she was doing me a kindness."

Torrin laughed, sharp and unrepentant. "You should've walked. The smile's always the warning."

"This from a Lyonswark?" Aulfis arched a brow. "I thought you lot considered that a negotiation."

Torrin barked a laugh and knocked his mug against Aulfis's. "Sometimes the ride is worth more than the coin that bought it."

Around them, dice clattered, a lute struck up and failed, voices rose and fell. It was easy, familiar—two men killing time before duty decided to remember them.

Aulfis set down his emptied cup. "So, Kings Guard then?"

Torrin wiped his mouth with the back of his hand. "Ah, the trials went well," he said after a moment. "Or well enough. Still haven't heard a word from Darkoak, though."

Aulfis tilted his head. "If you've not been turned away yet, that's something. I could ask—quietly—if your name's still on the board."

Torrin studied him, then snorted. "Use that new title of yours to help a friend, eh?"

Aulfis was about to reply when his gaze slid, unbidden, toward the street beyond the open shutters.

A woman passed the window.

Silver-blue caught the light first. Then posture. Then the careful, practiced way she moved through the crowd as if every step had been weighed and found wanting.

Aulfis stilled.

Torrin followed his look, then smirked. "Don't tell me—"

"I'll be back," Aulfis said, already rising.

Torrin snorted. "No you wont."

Aulfis left his mug untouched and stepped out into the street.

"If she has a sister," Torrin called after him dryly, "I expect an introduction."

The market street bustled with sound and motion, merchants calling out over the steady churn of carts and feet. Merchants hawked their wares loudly, while children darted between carts and stalls, laughter ringing through the morning air. Yet Elara moved through the crowd at a measured pace, fingers tightening briefly in the folds of her skirt as she avoided meeting anyone's eye in her silver-blue gown like a ghost, her careful poise masking the storm of unease within.

A voice pierced through her tangled thoughts, familiar and smooth, a blend of charm and invitation. "Elara, what an unexpected pleasure."

Elara turned slowly, her heart giving an uneasy flutter at the sight of Aulfis near a fruit vendor's stall. His smile was effortless, confident—his blue eyes lingering on hers a fraction longer than courtesy required.

"Aulfis," she replied carefully, a courteous smile hiding the sudden knot of tension within her. "It seems Castellon grows smaller every day."

He approached with casual grace, his presence filling her space more comfortably than she would have liked.

"Small enough for fortune to favor me again. Perhaps you'll indulge me in a moment away from this noisy place. I know a quiet wine-house just off the market, quieter than this."

The thought of sitting, of quiet, tugged at her more than she liked to admit.

A flicker of caution whispered through Elara, yet it was quickly muffled by the inexplicable draw of his easy charm and the guilt-ridden curiosity she felt after their previous encounter.

"Perhaps just briefly," she conceded softly, her voice carefully controlled.

The wine-house lay tucked just beyond the market's edge, a narrow-fronted room with shuttered windows and a low murmur of conversation, scented with spiced wine and warm bread. They settled into an isolated alcove, Aulfis swiftly ordering a selection of rich wines and ales. He poured generously, pushing the goblet toward her, his eyes holding hers in a gaze that felt both comforting and dangerously persuasive.

Their conversation flowed easily, the wine warming her faster than she expected. It loosened the tight band around her ribs, softened the sharp edges of the day. She was not insensible—only tired, and grateful for the reprieve. A small, unwelcome doubt stirred.

She should have left sooner.

She did not move.

Stormvale Keep rose from the high ground like a watchful thing, its stone pale in the late Bloomrise sun, banners stirring lazily in the warming air. Below its walls, fields stretched green and orderly, the work of hands long accustomed to readiness rather than excess.

A rider arrived hard and fast, his horse lathered and shaking, iron-shod hooves striking sparks against the outer stones as he reined in. His cloak was torn by hard miles, his face drawn with the strain of a message that could not afford delay.

He was stopped at the gate by the head steward, Norwin Turik—a broad-shouldered man with iron-grey hair and the quiet bearing of one who had served House Thornsword for decades. Turik took in the rider's condition at a glance and did not waste breath on ceremony.

"I bear urgent word for Lord Thornsword," the rider said, breath still catching. "From Lord Durnhart. I beg audience."

The steward studied him a heartbeat longer, weighing urgency against risk, then nodded once. "You'll have it."

The rider was led through the inner ward and up into the keep, past stone warmed by sun and banners bearing the silver stag before the thorned tree, sigil of the House. Servants and guards alike made way without question.

Lord Alvis Thornsword awaited him in a solar overlooking the high fields, standing rather than seated, hands clasped behind his back as if he had already guessed the nature of what was coming.

The rider dropped to one knee.

"Speak," Alvis said.

The warning came plainly, without flourish. Valen's name. Quiet alliances. A design not to challenge the Crown directly, but to fracture it—turn Houses against one another, then claim their lands and holdings in the chaos that followed. Durnhart and Caerlyn had uncovered enough to know they were not partners, only pieces set upon a board that had never been theirs.

Alvis listened without interruption. His expression did not change as Valen's treachery was laid bare; only his eyes hardened, as if an old suspicion had finally been given shape.

"I am not surprised," he said when the rider finished. "Valen has always mistaken patience for loyalty."

He turned then, pacing once across the chamber before stopping at the window. "Tell Lord Durnhart this: House Thornsword does not bend to Valen's designs. Nor will it stand idle if the Crown is threatened."

The rider inclined his head. "He asks only that you wait—for now. And be ready."

Alvis considered that, then with a look of determination said, "That much, I can promise."

Emberfist was carved into the cliff like a wound that never healed. Black stone rose sheer from the Narconian Edge, its battlements stacked vertically, banners bearing the black hawk snapping in the hot wind that rolled up from the Scorchlands below. Nothing approached the fortress unseen.

The rider was admitted without delay.

He was brought into a narrow receiving chamber cut directly from the rock, cool despite the heat outside. Lord Dravik Narcona waited within, hands clasped behind his back, posture rigid, his expression unreadable beneath the heavy brow that had made lesser men falter in war councils.

The rider knelt and delivered his warning.

Valen's name. Quiet alliances. A plan to fracture the realm and claim what remained once blood and confusion had done their work. Durnhart and Caerlyn had sent him, believing Narcona might yet choose the Crown over the game being played around it.

Dravik listened in silence. When the rider finished, he inclined his head slightly.

"I understand," Dravik said. "You have carried your message well."

Relief touched the rider's face.

Dravik's mouth tightened almost imperceptibly. "I regret the hardship of your journey. It was… unnecessary."

A guard stepped forward.

The blade came across the rider's throat in a single practiced motion.

The rider gasped, hands flying to his neck as blood spilled between his fingers, dark and sudden. He staggered, dropped to his knees, eyes wide with disbelief as he looked up at Dravik.

Dravik met his gaze without flinching.

The light faded from the rider's eyes. He pitched forward, striking the stone floor with a dull, final sound.

"Have someone clean this up," Dravik said as he turned and left the chamber.

Jorran reached Castellon Shield at dusk, the outer towers already casting long shadows across the lower courts. He gave his name and business at the gate and was passed inward with the brisk efficiency reserved for messages that carried seals rather than gossip.

Icewind's apartments lay quiet.

A chambermiad met him in the antechamber, expression apologetic before a word was spoken. "Lady Icewind has not been in residence since midmorning," she said. "She departed without escort."

Jorran frowned. "Without word?"

"Without destination," she corrected. "She travels often between holdings."

Elara's chambers themselves bore no sign of haste—no overturned chair, no discarded cloak. The windows stood open to the evening air, curtains stirring faintly. Everything was as it should have been.

Which troubled Jorran more than disorder would have.

He lingered only a moment longer, weighing delay against distance. Then Jorran turned sharply on his heel. Leaving the chambermaid behind him.

By the time the gates of Castellon Shield closed behind Jorran, the light was fading from the sky.

He rode west, hoping—without reason—that he would reach Lady Elara in time.

✶

"You must try this one," Aulfis insisted, refilling her goblet once more. Elara hesitated this time before accepting it. Her laughter came easier than it should have. Her judgment felt warmer, looser, less disciplined than she preferred.

Eventually, Elara placed a hand on the table, steadying herself as the realization crept through her muddled thoughts. "I should return," she murmured, her voice soft and uncertain.

Aulfis rose smoothly, offering his arm. "Of course. Allow me to guide you back."

She hesitated, then took his arm, leaning against his strength as they left the tavern.

Outside, the city had softened into twilight, streets bathed in shadows, the air cool against her flushed cheeks. But the streets felt unfamiliar, winding differently than she expected.

"This isn't—" she began uncertainly, confusion breaking through her haze. "This is not the way to Castellon Shield."

"It's close," he replied evenly. "Rest a moment at my apartments, and we'll continue."

A pulse of alarm moved through her—clear, sharp, undeniable. She could have pulled her arm free.

She did not.

Instead, she let him guide her onward.

Inside his private chambers, the click of the door shutting behind them echoed through her clouded mind. She turned, suddenly aware of the quiet intimacy of the room. "Aulfis, perhaps—"

His hand brushed her cheek, and this time she did not step back. "Just a moment, Elara. There's no harm in resting briefly."

She knew what the room meant. She knew what stepping further would cost. His touch did not drag her; it waited. The choice hovered between them.

"This is wrong," she said, more clearly than she intended.

He held her gaze. "Then say no."

Silence stretched.

She should have stepped away.

She should have left.

She did not.

He didn't pull—he waited.

She met his eyes and felt the last barrier tremble. This was the edge. This was the cost.

"If I stay," she said quietly, the words steady despite the heat in her veins, "this changes everything."

"It already has," he answered.

Another heartbeat passed.

She kissed him first.

It was not desperate. It was deliberate.

When he drew her down with him, it was because she had closed the distance. It was easier, in that moment, not to argue with herself.

She chose it—for one reckless, exhausted moment, she decided not to walk away.

Morning arrived without mercy. Sunlight cut through the curtains, stark and unforgiving. Elara woke with the weight of another body beside her and knew—before memory fully assembled—exactly what she had done.

She slipped from the bed, gathering her clothing with hands that did not feel entirely her own. She did not look at him. She did not want to see his face attached to what she had chosen.

In the mirror, her reflection stared back—pale, eyes sharp with accusation. No one had forced her. No one had tricked her. She had crossed the line herself.

"What have you done?" she whispered—not to the room, but to the woman in the glass.

She dressed quickly, movements precise despite the tremor beneath them. Panic pressed at her ribs—not fear of him, but fear of consequence. Baldrik's face rose unbidden in her mind. The look in his eyes when he had said he loved her.

She swallowed hard.

She fled his room, pulling the door closed with aching care. Each click of the latch sounded like a verdict.

Inside, Aulfis did not sleep.

He lay on his back, staring at the ceiling, listening to the retreat of her steps. A slow breath left him—not laughter, not tenderness, but satisfaction settling into place. The board had shifted. Exactly as he intended.

As she left the apartments, she never saw the figure standing quietly in the shadows. Lord Darkoak watched her depart, his features set in grim, unreadable intensity. His eyes shifted toward Aulfis's chamber, calculating the implications with cold, methodical precision.

In silence, Lanyard stepped back into the shadows, eyes narrowed, already measuring the damage done.

⁂

The corridors of Castellon Shield lay silent, shadows clinging to the stone walls. Lord Lanyard Darkoak moved swiftly, the whisper of his boots absorbed by plush carpets. He paused before King Harald's study, the oak door standing closed and unyielding. With a determined breath, he knocked firmly.

"Enter," Harald's voice came, gruff and weighted with exhaustion.

Lanyard stepped within, the door clicking shut behind him, sealing them in privacy. Firelight cast shifting light across maps, parchments, and worn spines. Harald stood near the hearth, silhouetted against the flames, his broad shoulders set beneath the strain of recent days, a goblet held loosely in his grasp.

"My King," Lanyard began softly, his voice measured and precise.

Harald turned, eyes narrowing beneath furrowed brows, firelight catching the lines of worry and fatigue. "Report, Lanyard. How fares the investigation? And the mood of the realm?"

Lanyard moved forward, hands clasped respectfully. "The investigation remains inconclusive, though suspicions continue to mount. Unrest stirs among the people, tension held barely in check. Miroray's death—"

"I know," Harald interrupted sharply, fatigue heavy in his voice. "And Tulavan? His anger remains unchecked?"

"Indeed," Lanyard replied gravely. "He has insisted upon remaining in Castellon, determined to see justice done. Word has already been dispatched to Vara; Princess Kirahnae will oversee the islands in Tulavan's absence. Effectively, she rules as queen now."

Harald sighed deeply, shaking his head slightly, the weight of recent events pressing upon him.

He allowed a brief silence to settle, absorbing the strain of the kingdom's turmoil before shifting to more immediate concerns. "Kirahnae's ascension will not please Tulavan. His pride and anger will only deepen. More complications we scarcely need."

Lanyard nodded solemnly. "A delicate matter indeed. Tulavan's rage will not easily abate, especially with his authority challenged."

After a moment's silence, Harald straightened, shifting to another pressing concern. "Enough courtesy tonight, Lanyard. Between treachery and Avanna's unraveling mind, patience has worn thin. Is there more?"

Lanyard hesitated only a heartbeat, choosing his words carefully before speaking plainly. "Aulfis has lain with Lady Elara Icewind."

The king fell silent, the air tightening between them. Harald's knuckles whitened around the goblet as his jaw tightened in restrained fury. "You are certain?" he finally asked, voice dangerously quiet.

"I witnessed her departing his bedchamber," Lanyard confirmed, his tone calm but unyielding. "Disheveled, visibly unsettled—clearly compromised."

Harald's breath hissed sharply, frustration simmering beneath his control. He turned abruptly, gripping the edge of the hearth, knuckles white with tension. "Damn him," he growled, his voice low and lethal. "Now—of all times—when every corner of this castle hides a blade."

Lanyard stepped forward, straightening his shoulders, jaw tightening as urgency sharpened his voice. "Aulfis's pride swells unchecked, Harald. The prospect of the throne has emboldened him. Icewind complicates matters further. Her influence is volatile and unpredictable; she risks igniting wider harm."

Harald took a slow, measured breath, the cumulative crises weighing heavily, deepening the weariness on his face as he considered Lanyard's words. "Lady Icewind complicates matters considerably," he said carefully. "Your recommendations?"

"Act swiftly and decisively," Lanyard advised firmly. "Separate Aulfis from Elara. Reinforce the consequences of his reckless decisions. Monitor Lady Icewind closely—if necessary, remove her from the influence she holds over our future."

Harald's eyes narrowed thoughtfully. "Have the auditors concluded their review of her accounts yet?"

Lanyard shook his head slightly. "I expect their report within the next few days, Your Grace."

"Good," Harald murmured darkly, a hint of grim satisfaction creeping into his voice. "If the situation is as dire as we suspect, this may provide the means to lessen her influence, if it must come to that."

Unseen in the shadows beyond the doorway, Queen Avanna pressed her hand tightly against her lips to stifle the gasp that threatened to betray her presence. Her pulse surged with the panic of unraveling control. Baldrik—her son, her future, slipping further from her control. "It must be me," she breathed in a voice edged with quiet resolve, a promise as cold as ice. Silently, she retreated deeper into the darkness.

Inside the study, Harald lifted his gaze, meeting Lanyard's steady eyes. "Very well," he conceded grimly. "I leave this matter in your hands. Watch them both closely, and ensure that this indiscretion does not deepen our wounds."

Lanyard inclined his head sharply, eyes hard with resolve, "As always, Your Grace. I will see it done."

Lady Meyra Wynmere's chambers were softly lit by late afternoon sunlight slipping through silk curtains. A faint trace of lavender lingered, soothing yet at odds with the tension Elara carried as she stepped inside.

Meyra glanced up from her writing desk, the quill halting mid-stroke as her keen gaze took in Elara's guarded distress. Setting the quill aside with practiced calm, Meyra rose gracefully, an inviting smile curving her lips. "Lady Icewind," she said warmly, her voice touched with a gentle humor, "this is a pleasant surprise, though your face suggests otherwise. What's happened?"

Elara hesitated, the rigidity of her posture betraying the emotional battle she fought internally. "Forgive me, Meyra. I find myself needing counsel from someone I trust."

"Then you've chosen wisely," Meyra replied smoothly, moving swiftly to guide her friend toward a plush, cushioned chair near the hearth. "Sit. Whatever weighs on your heart, speak plainly; you have my confidence and my ear."

Elara sank slowly into the offered chair, her hands nervously smoothing the folds of her gown. Her eyes searched the woven rug beneath her feet, as if its tangled threads might untangle her own. She drew a careful breath, lifting her gaze hesitantly to Meyra's expectant expression. "I've made a mistake," she confessed softly, her voice edged with raw honesty. "One that cannot be undone."

A flicker of curiosity crossed Meyra's features. "A mistake? You, Elara? That is unexpected."

A flush of embarrassment tinged Elara's pale skin, highlighting the internal struggle before she finally spoke, her voice barely more than a whisper. "I spent a night with someone… someone who complicates matters far beyond mere gossip. Someone who was not Baldrik." She swallowed. "I knew what I was doing, Meyra. I knew it would change everything. I simply… was not thinking past the moment."

Meyra's brows lifted in surprise.

"I see," she said carefully.

Meyra paused, seeing genuine turmoil on her friend's face. "Elara, you're truly troubled. What is it?"

"It's Baldrik," Elara admitted, eyes darkening with vulnerability. "I fear what this might do to him—to us. He's already standing at the edge, ready to disappear into the Flamebound Order. If he learns of this betrayal, it may confirm every doubt he has about his place here. I can't bear the thought of losing him—not like this."

Meyra leaned forward, her demeanor turning serious, eyes sharpened with calculation and empathy. "Elara, secrets have a cruel way of growing claws. Keeping this hidden could poison the very thing you wish to protect. But you must also consider the court, the kingdom. The ripple effect of your confession will not stop at Baldrik." She paused, her expression turning more serious. "And if he chooses the Order anyway? What then, Elara? Monks cannot have relationships—not in any intimate sense."

Elara looked away, her gaze distant. Memories of Baldrik's quiet words, his gentle touch—the way his sincerity made her feel seen—flooded her mind. The thought had crossed her mind before, yet hearing it voiced aloud pierced deeper than she anticipated.

Elara's expression twisted with frustration and despair. "I know that all too well. But this guilt… Meyra, it's suffocating. No one forced me. No one tricked me. I stepped over the line myself. How can I build a future with Baldrik if it's founded on deception?"

Meyra studied her friend carefully, weighing loyalties and courtly repercussions. "Elara, consider carefully. Your standing at court is already precarious, and this revelation could further destabilize your position. Yet, Baldrik is wise and compassionate. Honesty, difficult as it may be, can become a powerful tool. But you must tell him soon, before he finds out from another source. If Baldrik learns of this second-hand, it could end disastrously. Better that he hears it from you, in your words, and sees the sincerity in your eyes, rather than feeling ambushed by whispered scandal. If your aim is truly to hold onto him—to maintain his trust and the kingdom's favor—truth might indeed be your strongest tether."

Meyra smiled, admiration still there—but it did not reach her eyes. "You are stronger than you know, Elara. But before you go, there is something else you must hear. It is not why you came—and I wish it were not mine to tell."

She moved to the window, drawing the curtain aside just enough to glance outward, as if choosing her next words with care. "A rider came to me last night," she said. "A woman—Thistle. House Caerlyn's spymaster. She brought disturbing news. Valen is working quietly," Meyra said. "He invited the great houses to that gathering under the guise of shared grievance—encouraged them to undermine the crown just enough to stain their own hands. But it was never partnership. It was bait."

She turned back, eyes sharp. "While our attention was fixed upward, he moved beneath us—through the minor houses. Pressing debts. Manipulating charters. Eroding borders piece by piece. When the crown moves against those who answered his call, Valen intends to step in as savior and claimant alike, taking what remains."

Meyra turned back to her, expression hard now. "There are whispers he has had a hand in the failed crops. In the sudden rise of poaching. In disruptions meant to look like misfortune—designed to weaken estates already marked."

Her gaze sharpened. "Including Icewind."

Elara let out a breath that was half a laugh, half a curse. "Flames take him," she said quietly. "All of it—the lies, the rot, the quiet knives."

Meyra's eyes met Elara's, steady and unflinching. "Lords Durnhart and Caerlyn have seen through Valen's game. They are with us. For now, we do nothing. We wait."

Elara's breath caught. The relief she had begun to feel shattered, replaced by something hotter—anger, sharp and sudden. "So while I wrestle with guilt," Elara said, voice tight, "the ground beneath my feet is being cut away." Her hands curled in her lap. "Harald is already moving to seize my lands. And now I learn Valen has been bleeding my estate for years."

Elara surged to her feet, anger breaking free at last. "We wait?" she snapped. "Meyra—my family's estate is already lost. The crown means to seize it soon. I've lost Baldrik. My home. My land." Her voice cracked, fury bleeding into despair. "My title. That disgusting parasite has ruined me. What more do I have to lose?"

Meyra crossed the space between them and caught Elara's hands, gripping them firmly. "Your soul. Your strength," she said quietly. "We wait because the time is not yet right. And because if Valen learns we see him clearly, he will destroy what little remains. We cannot move against him yet."

Elara's breath came fast, then slowed as she stared into the hearth fire, its flames snapping and shifting before her eyes. When she finally spoke, her voice was low. "What do I have left, Meyra?"

Meyra did not hesitate. "You have me."

Elara drew in a long, steadying breath.

Then another.

She straightened, something new settling behind her eyes as she turned back from the fire. "I'm not finished yet," she said.

Meyra's voice was steady. "No, you are not. We are not."

✶

CHAPTER TWENTY

Rain muttered against the tall windows of the Queen's solar. Candlelight gilded the marble floor in trembling pools, and the scent of lavender oil and wine clung faintly to the warm air.

Baldrik stepped across the threshold with the uncertain composure of a man summoned to a battlefield with perfume on his collar. The chamber was quiet, save for the patter of rain and the low crack of a nearby hearth.

He remembered when this room was filled with warmth—when his mother would sit in quiet authority, her presence steady and assured, when her eyes carried clarity instead of obsession.

The change had been sudden. Jarring. As if a door inside her had slammed shut overnight. She had withdrawn almost at once. The air had become thick with incense and restless thought. What had once been a place of retreat had become something else entirely—watchful, inward, wrong.

Not age. Not time. Something sharper had taken hold.

He had tried to dismiss the signs—the abrupt mood swings, the pacing, the fixation on Elara and the Flamebound. He marked it as the strain of court, the mounting pressure on the kingdom in recent weeks. Exhaustion. Grief sharpened by pressure.

But the look the chambermaid had given him tonight, careful not to meet his eyes, stripped that comfort away. Whatever had taken hold of Avanna was not slow. It was not fading.

It was accelerating.

His mother sat before a massive mirror carved from silver pine, its edges traced with stormglass and soft gold. She did not turn to greet him. She sat draped in an unlaced pale silk nightgown and an unfastened dressing robe. Her reflection revealed shadows beneath her eyes, fine lines of strain cut deep, and trembling hands that betrayed a quiet desperation. Her hair, usually coiled with precision, hung loose over one shoulder in rippling obsidian waves. She did not meet his eyes—only her own in the glass.

"You came."

Baldrik hesitated before answering. "You summoned me."

"I thought you might ignore it. After all, you've been ignoring everything else lately."

Her voice was smooth, layered in weariness and wine. A goblet sat on the low table nearby, its lip stained dark as old blood. Beside it, a bottle of Firewine—drained. The lingering scent of it stirred something sour in his gut.

He stayed by the door. "Your chambermaid said you weren't well."

"Does this look like illness to you?" she asked, rising slowly. Her robe slipped, silk whispering against her skin like smoke with nowhere to rise.

Baldrik looked aside instinctively. "Mother… perhaps this isn't the time."

Avanna turned from the mirror, facing him now. Her bare feet whispered over the stone as she walked closer. "No, it never is. Not when the crown is in question. Not when your loyalties lie tangled in monk robes and courtesan lace."

He stiffened. "You asked to speak with me. Not accuse me."

She stopped a few feet away. Close enough for the fire to catch in the sheen of her gown, the thin silk clinging to her frame in a careless exposure that stripped the moment of dignity. She unsettled him, a strange mix of grace and unraveling. Something too wrong to ignore.

"Do you remember what you said to me the day they made you swear the Oath of Lineage? You were twelve. They draped you in your father's old cloak, and you shook beneath it like a bird too small for the sky. You said, 'I don't want to be king, Mama. I just want you to be proud of me.'"

Baldrik swallowed hard. "That was a long time ago."

She stepped closer. "Not long enough. Not to me."

Baldrik kept his voice calm. "You should rest."

"Don't patronize me." Her voice cracked slightly, then steadied like a blade re-honed. "I was a queen when they still called you 'boy.' When your father was still weeping over his forge like a drunk poet. I built this court while men fumbled for power. And now, I watch my son run from it like it burns him."

Her fingers brushed the air between them, not quite touching. Her breath reeked of wine.

He remembered when those hands had wiped blood from his scraped knees. Now they hovered like blades waiting to be drawn. His throat tightened.

She smiled without love or kindness. It was the smile of a woman who had bled for her crown and would bleed again. A queen who had given everything except surrender.

He took a careful step back. "You're drunk. And grieving. This isn't you."

"It *is* me," she said. "Clearer than I've ever been. Do you think I don't see what you're doing? The Flamebound? That little Icewind leech clinging to your arm? You think she loves you for your heart? No, my sweet boy. She saw the crown you cast aside and reached for it like any good survivor."

Baldrik's expression hardened. "You don't know her."

Her mouth curled, bitter and precise, like a cut drawn with ink. "Oh, but I do. Darkoak saw her creeping from your brother's chambers, skulking like a thief in borrowed silk. And Darkoak doesn't guess. He names what most men pretend not to see."

Baldrik's brow knotted sharply, confusion edging his voice. "You of all people, Mother, should know I have no brother."

Avanna snapped forward, eyes ablaze. "You do, Baldrik—Aulfis."

"Aulfis?" Baldrik echoed, genuine disbelief clouding his face. "My cousin, you mean?"

"No," she hissed, voice low and biting. "Your brother. Your father's bastard. And your little distraction has been warming his bed for who knows how long. A neat little hedge against a failing future."

Baldrik flinched visibly, fists tightening until his knuckles paled. "Lies," he rasped softly.

"Truth," Avanna pressed, stepping closer with venomous certainty. "You imagined you were her only flame. You believed she would choose you, despite everything. But she didn't, Baldrik. She chose herself. She always will."

His breath came sharp, strained by denial. "Even if you believe that—she would never—no, you're wrong. She's not like that. You must have misunderstood. Or someone lied to you."

She erased the space between them, her robe brushing his tunic, the heat of her body catching through the silk, her face tilted upward inches from his. "You remind me so much of your father," she murmured, one hand sliding onto his chest. Her eyes searched his with something that wanted to look like affection and failed.

"She moved on, Baldrik. To new blood. She saw your doubt and chose certainty. The throne will not wait for boys to find themselves."

Her other hand rose, fingertips brushing his cheek.

Baldrik's heart thrashed against his ribs, disgust crashing hard against disbelief. Every nerve screamed to pull away, but shock pinned him where he stood.

"Still mine," she whispered. "Still perfect. We could rule together, you know. This kingdom, this legacy. You need only claim it—and let me crown you with my own gentle hands."

With a sudden, reckless tug, she loosened the robe and let the silk pool soundlessly at her feet. The gesture was raw, misjudged, and unbearable.

He saw only how far she had fallen.

He recoiled sharply. "What are you saying?"

"That no one understands you as I do. Not Elara. Not the monks. Not even your father. You are mine, Baldrik. You were made from my blood, my pain. And I will not let them take you."

He stepped back, voice rising. "Stop. Mother please. This is madness."

Her eyes burned fiercely. "I *gave* you everything! And you would throw it away for some cloistered flame and a broken girl warming your father's bastard's bed?"

"Enough!" he roared, voice cracking through the room like thunder.

She froze, stricken.

"I trusted you," he said, voice unsteady. "I looked to you. But this—this is something else."

Baldrik turned, heart pounding, breath ragged. For one terrifying moment, he felt like a child again—twelve years old, sitting at her feet while she whispered stories of kings and legacies. But this was not that woman. This was something broken wearing her voice.

"Do not summon me again. Not like this."

Baldrik moved toward the door.

Her voice lashed after him, sharp and ragged. "They'll burn you! Your precious monks—and the kingdom will burn with you, Baldrik!"

He glanced back, disgust and sorrow etched into his expression.

"Baldrik," she pleaded, the sharp edge in her voice collapsing into something thin and aching.

"Please… We could rule together."

He hesitated only a heartbeat, then turned away, closing the door firmly behind him.

Avanna stared into the emptiness, shoulders twitching under an invisible weight. Then it struck her—cold, clean, unbearable. Even this had failed. She had played her last card, and still he had gone.

"You were mine," she whispered, her voice thin, nearly lost beneath the storm outside.

In the corridor beyond, Baldrik sagged against the cold stone wall, heart hammering painfully in his chest. He pressed a palm to his forehead, breath hitching. Something inside him cracked—not loudly, not violently, but forever.

Trust and belief collapsed all at once, confirming every doubt he had tried to bury. He needed air. Distance. And more than either, he needed the truth from Elara's own lips.

The rain fell harder, its rhythm steady and relentless, washing away nothing.

Baldrik moved through darkened corridors, each step deliberate, his heart fractured and unsteady. His mother's words echoed in his mind, sharp and poisonous, carrying with them the unbearable possibility that the woman he loved had betrayed him.

His breath was shallow, his pulse a war drum pounding in his ears as he finally stood before the ornate doors of Elara's royal apartments. They were engraved with intricate silver vines, delicate yet unyielding—much like the woman beyond them. For a moment, his knuckles hovered, shaking visibly in the pale lantern light. Then, with quiet resolve, he knocked, each strike softer than the last, echoing gently through the stillness.

The door opened slowly. Elara stood in the frame, caught off guard. Her eyes were wide and uncertain, her usually poised face was stark with anxiety. Her dark hair fell loose around a face pale with worry and exhaustion.

"Baldrik?" she whispered, her voice small and careful. Her eyes searched his, desperate for answers. "What's wrong?"

"We need to speak," he said quietly.

Elara stepped aside, opening the door wider. Candlelight filled the room. As she closed the door gently behind him, she studied his face with growing alarm.

"What's happened?"

He took a long, slow breath, gathering what remained of his courage. "My mother told me something."

"Your mother—" she began, then faltered, her gaze darting away nervously before returning to his. "Baldrik, she isn't well. She—"

"She told me you've been with another man." His voice cracked slightly, carrying all the pain of betrayal. His eyes held hers with one last wounded plea. "Tell me it isn't true."

The world seemed to freeze. Color drained from Elara's face. Her lips parted, trembling, but no denial came. Her silence stretched between them, heavy with a truth neither dared speak.

At last she spoke, her voice fragile, almost broken. "Baldrik… I—"

"Please. No lies, no denials. I deserve the truth from you. Just this one thing."

She looked away, eyes brimming with tears, hands twisted **tight** together. Her breathing was uneven, panic in every trembling inhale. When she spoke again, it was barely audible, a confession torn from her with palpable agony.

"Yes," she said. "I wanted to tell you myself. I wasn't ready. I never meant to hurt you."

"But you did."

Tears spilled down Elara's face. Her body shook as she reached instinctively for him, then hesitated, pulling her hand back sharply, as though she feared contaminating him further.

"I know," she whispered raggedly. "I know, and if I could undo it—"

"You can't." His voice was barely above a whisper now, soft but absolute. "We can't."

He did not move toward her.

"I loved you," he said, and the words sounded torn out of him. His chest tightened hard enough to hurt. "I cannot build my life on this. Not on doubt. Not after this."

Her knees gave beneath her. She caught the edge of a chair, fingers slipping against polished wood, but the strength went out of her all the same. She struck the stone hard, silk doing nothing to soften it. The shock ran up through bone and spine, but she barely felt it. The breath left her in a broken sound she could not swallow back.

He turned away.

"Baldrik!" Her desperate call pierced the quiet just as his hand found the latch.

He paused.

For one suspended moment, he saw it as he had wanted it: her beside him, not here in this room but somewhere beyond the reach of court and crown, somewhere honest, where love might have been enough. He felt the shape of that life collapse inside him, not all at once, but deeply enough that nothing in him could pretend it still stood.

His mother's madness. The crown he had never wanted. And now this.

Whatever still reached for warmth inside him drew back all at once. Not dead. Not gone. Just shut behind something hard and cold.

He did not turn around.

"Goodbye, Elara."

The door closed behind him.

Elara sank deeper onto the cold, unforgiving stone, her body shuddering with grief she could no longer control. Her fingers grasped blindly at emptiness, as though she could still catch hold of what had already slipped irretrievably away.

Not only him. Not only the man she loved.

The future she had wrapped around him went with him too—whatever fragile shape of safety, love, and belonging she had let herself believe might still be hers.

Her dark hair spilled around her, tangled and wild like shadows cast from lost dreams, a shroud to hide her from the cruel truth.

The candles burned low. Her sobs filled the room.

Marshal Ryzen stepped onto the solar balcony, the wind tugging at his cloak. Lieutenant Cecilia followed close behind, amber eyes narrowed as she scanned the marble flooring. Squire Tollin moved silently, absorbing each detail, while Captain Varyn stood near the balcony's edge, his posture rigid and professional.

Ryzen knelt, gloved fingers resting briefly on the railing. His brow furrowed slightly. "The railing is untouched," he noted quietly. "No scratches, no scuff marks—no evidence of a prolonged struggle here."

Lieutenant Cecilia crouched low, studying slipperl prints pressed faintly into the dust on the marble tiles. "Two sets of prints. One steadier. The other breaks near the edge."

Tollin crossed to a small tea table. He lifted a delicate porcelain cup, glancing at the dried film within. He gave it a cautious sniff, then a brief touch to the tongue before spitting. He wiped his mouth with the back of his hand and gave a small shake of his head.

"Two cups poured," he said. "One untouched, tea gone cold. The other partially consumed. Nothing bitter or foul."

He turned to Captain Varyn. "Captain, was tea something Queen Miroray often shared with Queen Avanna?"

"Rarely," Varyn said. "Queen Miroray typically valued solitude during such moments. However, she would not refuse an invitation from her sister." "Queen Miroray typically valued solitude during such moments. However, she would not refuse an invitation from her sister."

Ryzen looked over the balcony's edge, measuring the drop. "The fall was straight downward, close to the balcony's edge. The body fell near the wall. Not the drop I'd expect from a running leap."

Lieutenant Cecilia stepped beside him and followed his gaze. "She didn't slip naturally. No scuffs or desperate marks suggesting accidental loss of footing."

Cecilia's eyes flicked to the railing. "Height's wrong," she murmured.

Ryzen's mouth twitched, just barely. "Royal privilege. Safety should not obstruct the view." He glanced at her. "Explain."

She rested a hand lightly against the stone. "This comes low." She looked to Varyn. "The Queen's height?"

Captain Varyn answered after a beat. "Of the Kaeleen daughters."

Cecilia didn't look at him. "Not helpful."

A faint exhale from Varyn. "Near a head taller than you, Lieutenant."

Cecilia nodded once, already measuring. "Then this would have caught her mid-thigh." Her gaze returned to the drop below. "If she went off balance here… she'd have nothing to brace against. No chance to recover."

Ryzen studied the railing a moment longer. "Caught off-guard. There may have been a brief struggle."

Tollin shook his head slightly. "There's no sign of that, sir. Table and chairs are undisturbed. Not even the tea's been spilled." He glanced once more over the setting. "Doesn't feel like a struggle fits this."

Varyn spoke then, careful with the question. "Queen Avanna mentioned an assassin. Could someone have entered unnoticed?"

Ryzen shook his head slightly, "Guards were stationed at the door. No intruder was seen or heard. Climbing would require equipment, there would be marks—something obvious."

Cecilia's voice was firm. "No rope marks. No disturbance along the stone. Climbing this in daylight without notice would be unlikely."

Tollin slowly shook his head as he completed his examination, silently confirming Cecilia's findings.

Ryzen let a breath pass before he spoke. "We have no sign of an intruder, yet Queen Avanna insists otherwise. We assume nothing yet."

Tollin silently gestured toward a slipper partially hidden beneath a curtain near the balcony's edge. Ryzen moved closer, carefully examining the slipper's curious placement. "The slipper sits wrong. Not where I'd expect it if she went over by choice."

Cecilia glanced at Ryzen. "An impulsive act?"

"Possibly," Ryzen said. "But speculation alone is worthless. We need clear, tangible proof."

Captain Varyn spoke. "Marshal, will you uncover the truth?"

Ryzen met Varyn's gaze and nodded once. "We will, Captain."

He straightened, already turning back to the chamber door.

He paused a step later. "And the handmaiden?" Ryzen asked without looking back. "The one assigned to the Queen's chambers. Lana."

Cecilia answered at once. "We spoke with her. She was sent from the room shortly before the incident—asked to retrieve Queen Avanna's winter cloak from her private chambers."

"She heard nothing?" Ryzen asked.

"Nothing," Cecilia confirmed. "She returned moments after the guards were called. Claims she saw no one enter or leave in her absence. No raised voices. No disturbance."

Ryzen nodded once, filing it away. "Then her absence matters."

"Lieutenant Leif should be our next priority," he added quietly.

He turned back to the balcony rail, eyes tracing the empty air beyond it.

Night draped the abandoned theater in thick velvet shadows, broken only by the pale flicker of distant lanterns casting weak light upon the worn wooden stage. Dust motes floated gently in the air, caught in the spectral glow, swirling lazily like ghosts too weary to fully manifest. Rows of empty seats sat silent witnesses, draped in darkness, their velvet worn and threadbare, whispering of faded grandeur.

On stage, Prince Aulfis Thornsword paced impatiently, his breath misting lightly in the chill. The training sword in his grasp was worn smooth from countless hours of drills, though in his hands tonight, it felt clumsy, inadequate. He thought bitterly of his recent elevation to next in line to the throne; authority was finally his by right, yet here he was, still being schooled like a common squire.

Across from him, Master Daelchi Junfolda stood calmly, bare-handed, eyes sharp and alert, posture spare and efficient, as if excess motion offended him.

"Again," Junfolda instructed, his voice steady and flat, stripped of patience or indulgence. He shifted effortlessly into a defensive stance, balanced perfectly on the balls of his feet, every muscle subtly tensed beneath the folds of his robes.

With a snarl of impatience, Aulfis lunged forward, training blade sweeping horizontally with a wild arc aimed at Junfolda's midsection. A crisp whoosh cut through the air, followed by the sharp clap of Junfolda's open palm meeting polished wood.

He pivoted efficiently, redirecting the blade downward with a subtle twist of his wrist and a sidestep that placed him safely to the side. The sword struck with a jarring crack, its shock racing up Aulfis's fingers and wrist. The prince stumbled forward, balance compromised, seething with embarrassment.

"Again," he said. "You are late to every movement. Control precedes strength."

Aulfis spat a curse, cheeks flushing crimson beneath his dark gaze. "Your philosophy bores me, old man. Strength is forged in steel, not poetry."

The training master tilted his head a fraction, expression unchanged. "Steel answers the hand that wields it," he said. "Your hand is unsteady."

Rage flared. Aulfis launched a flurry of strikes, each slicing the air with desperate precision. His master's feet moved with disciplined economy, stepping fluidly around each thrust and slash, palms connecting firmly with the wooden sword, each deflection deliberate and decisive. The stage echoed with rhythmic slaps and thuds, creating a haunting percussion of combat.

"You're slow, Aulfis," he said, stepping aside with minimal movement, placing himself just beyond the prince's reach. "You are letting anger decide your timing, that is weakness."

Roaring in frustration, Aulfis surged forward, his movements devolving into frenzied hacking. He flowed around him with practiced economy, never still, never cornered. Every parry was exact, every dodge a quiet lesson—each miss another crack in Aulfis' pride.

"Enough," Junfolda finally snapped, voice sharp and immediate. "Stop. You are done."

Aulfis screamed in rage, discarding the blunt training weapon with a clattering echo that reverberated through the empty theater.

Storming toward his belongings at the edge of the stage, he gripped the hilt of Maralei, the blade his father had forged for him. Its weight settled into his hand cold and familiar, carrying all the pride and expectation bound up in it.

His hand hesitated, trembling slightly as a flicker of doubt surfaced through his anger. For a heartbeat, the weight of it struck him—the line he was about to cross. But pride roared louder than conscience, and the whisper of doubt was drowned in heat and inheritance.

He drew Maralei sharply from its sheath with a hard ring that cut through the silence.

His master stiffened slightly, eyes narrowing at the sight of real steel. "Put it away," he said. "You are not prepared for that blade."

"Maybe it's your judgment that's dulled, old man," Aulfis said, lifting the blade between them. His voice rang with borrowed steel, though his pulse thudded with doubt. "Defend yourself." Aulfis sneered coldly, newfound authority bolstering his voice, though his heart pounded with sudden uncertainty.

Without further hesitation, Aulfis sprang forward. Maralei cut through the air in fast, vicious strokes, his reach and anger driving every one of them. His master's feet shifted rapidly, his body angling away from each strike with deft precision.

Palms open, he pushed the steel aside, deflecting each blow inches from his body. Each contact rang sharp, edge scraping skin and hardened callus.

"Enough," he warned again, breath heavier now, sweat glistening at his temples. "You are reaching beyond your discipline."

Blinded by fury and pride, Aulfis pressed harder, drowning what little doubt remained beneath a fresh surge of rage.

In a desperate gambit, he feinted left, then spun on his heel and brought Maralei up in a diagonal cut toward the man's midsection.

His master, precise footwork momentarily disrupted by the sudden feint, reacted an instant too late.

The blade pierced flesh with a muted, sickening squelch, sliding deep into Junfolda's abdomen. Time seemed to slow as warm blood flowed over Aulfis' fingers, the shock of violence momentarily overwhelming him.

Junfolda's eyes widened in shock, breath catching sharply in his throat, a strangled gasp escaping—an unguarded sound that seared itself into Aulfis' memory.

For a breathless instant, Aulfis froze. Shock washed through him—hot, disorienting—as he realized what he had done. His grip did not loosen, not at once, as if his body had failed to receive the same command as his mind.

"You should have moved," Aulfis said, the words brittle and rushed, as if spoken to fill the silence rather than wound. His hand jerked back then, too late to undo anything.

His master staggered back, slipping from Maralei's unforgiving edge, collapsing onto the wooden stage with a dull thud. Blood spread across the stageboards beneath him, darkening the wood, seeping slowly between the worn planks as if the theater itself were swallowing the moment.

Aulfis stood rigid, breath uneven. Something twisted in his chest—shock, disbelief, a flicker of something he refused to name. He forced it down, straightening, schooling his expression into stillness.

He stepped back, staring for a heartbeat longer than necessary. Then he wiped the blade mechanically and sheathed it, the motion stiff and precise.

His footsteps echoed hollowly as he strode from the theater, leaving the lifeless body sprawled on the stage behind him.

Lanyard's private apartments were bathed in the dim glow of evening, the room heavy with shadow. Dark oak furniture stood heavy and unyielding, their silhouettes casting long lines across the flickering firelight. The fire crackled low in the hearth, giving more glow than heat.

The door swung open abruptly, and Aulfis entered with an air of smug self-assurance. Fresh bruises marked his knuckles, yet he moved with casual arrogance, appearing unbothered by the marks of his recent training.

Lanyard turned slowly from the hearth, eyes narrowing slightly. "Your session ran late."

Aulfis shrugged without concern, dropping onto a sturdy oak chair near the fire, legs stretched out, owning the space. "Junfolda insisted on extra drills. I obliged him."

"Generous," Lanyard said dryly, eyes tracing the fresh bruises. "Did he impart anything useful?"

Aulfis laughed lightly—a cold, hollow sound. A flicker of discomfort briefly disturbed his composed facade. "He tried. Always pressing discipline. Control." He paused, eyes glittering in the firelight. "It failed him tonight."

Lanyard stilled, sensing the shift beneath the prince's tone. "Explain."

Aulfis waved a hand, careless, fingers trembling before stilling. "I killed him," he said, inspecting his nails with forced indifference. "He was slow. Call it an accident, if that helps."

The room fell silent. Lanyard's expression hardened, irritation cutting through the shock. His mind moved quickly—not to grief, but to consequence. An Aynaraq Tidewarden master dead on Eldaraine soil was not a private matter. His gaze fixed on Aulfis, already measuring the cost.

"You're certain?" Lanyard's voice was low and tight.

Aulfis's smile was slow. "Training accidents happen, don't they? He won't be correcting anyone else."

Lanyard's jaw tightened. "Junfolda was skilled." A beat. "Such accidents are rare."

Aulfis shrugged. "Skill isn't always enough. He preached strength and clarity, but he was fooled by a simple feint. He fell. Weakness shows."

"You concealed it?"

Aulfis shook his head. "No one saw. You taught me the value of discretion."

Lanyard stepped forward. "And yet—you feel nothing?"

Aulfis stood abruptly, shadows shifting behind him. "Feel?" His voice sharpened, then wavered for a breath. "He was a master who failed. If he had been stronger, he would still be alive."

Lanyard studied him, irritation and unease tightening together. He had shaped this boy—tempered him, sharpened him—but not this. Not the ease of it.

"Junfolda was a good man," Lanyard said. "And he answered to Aynaraq. That alone makes this a problem."

Aulfis spun, eyes hard, fists clenched. "He was not strong enough. Weakness does not serve our house. You taught me that."

Cold realization settled in Lanyard's chest. The line he had drawn had been crossed—cleanly, without hesitation.

"Strength without control is a disaster," Lanyard said. "Be careful, Aulfis."

Lanyard's hand curled into a fist. He had sharpened the blade. And now it cut.

Aulfis's lips curled faintly. "Compassion gets in the way. I won't repeat his mistake."

He paused, gaze sharpening. Something new settled behind his eyes—cold, steady, and not yet named.

"And where is the body now?" Lanyard asked.

Aulfis glanced back over his shoulder. "Where I left it. You should attend to it. I'm going out."

Lanyard exhaled slowly. Another quiet cleanup. Another line crossed. "Very well."

He did not move. He watched the prince go, each footfall echoing sharper than the last. Silence pooled around him, cold and heavy.

The crown had not yet touched Aulfis's brow, yet already Lanyard saw the outline of a problem that would require constant restraint, careful guidance—and, if needed, force.

✶

Late afternoon sunlight washed Lord Valen's estate in deceptive gold. From his veranda, he surveyed the domain briefly—statues, clipped hedges, and stone arranged to impress.

He observed the king's soldiers at his gates, their polished armor shining—polished, official, infuriating. Their presence grated, a silent challenge to his authority. Valen's fingers tightened around his crystal wineglass, then deliberately relaxed. He took a slow sip.

"My Lord," came a voice smooth and precise. Rennic stepped onto the veranda, impeccable as ever.

Valen turned, the unease already buried. "Smudge."

Rennic inclined his head respectfully. "The militia are in position, my lord. Taverns, market stalls, the west grove. They're playing their roles: overeager, bumbling, harmless. Some have begun mingling with the king's soldiers at your gates. The soldiers appear convinced."

Valen nodded, though a sliver of doubt slipped through. Had every militia man been thoroughly vetted? One misstep could unravel everything. His expression did not change.

His gaze flicked briefly toward Rennic. "Has that militia man—Braddock, the one with the loose tongue—been dealt with?"

Rennic's eyes narrowed slightly as he recalled. "Yes, my lord. He proved… less than durable."

Valen gave a slight nod. "Good." He paused.

"Ensure they blend seamlessly," Valen said. "Let them ask naive questions, tell foolish jokes—keep them believable."

He led the way into his inner chamber. A room designed to overwhelm and distract, heavy with wealth and control.

Crossing to a carved sideboard, he opened a small lacquered box and revealed a row of glass vials nestled in dark velvet. He took one between two fingers, then held the box slightly toward Rennic.

"Mix this with my private wine reserve—half a bottle per cask. Have the militia deliver them as goodwill gestures."

Rennic's eyes sharpened slightly. "And the bodies, my lord?"

Valen's lips curled, not in warmth but with the faint satisfaction of a man already counting the dead. "Bury them discreetly in the dry grove. Keep their uniforms—folded neatly. And return them here."

Rennic nodded. "Of course, my lord."

As he turned, Valen's voice followed, quietly commanding. "Let them savor their downfall."

Rennic paused briefly, then departed quietly.

Valen returned to the veranda. He watched the soldiers again, noting the small gestures that irritated him. He took another measured sip of wine as dusk crept across the estate.

"Loyal dogs," Valen whispered calmly, malice subtly coloring his tone. "Easy to tame. Easier still to put down."

Evening shadows stretched across the grand banquet hall, cloaking the quiet preparations for Queen Miroray's wake. Candlelight flickered as servants arranged floral wreaths, positioned ceremonial objects, and set tables with solemn care. Grief mingled with political obligation, creating a palpable tension.

King Harald stood overseeing the meticulous preparations, his face steady yet etched with weariness. His bearing conveyed the heavy burden of political sorrow rather than personal mourning, as though the loss represented a duty fulfilled rather than a heartache borne.

King Consort Tulavan stood a short distance away, rigid as a drawn blade, his attention fixed on the center of the hall where the wake would soon be held. His jaw was set, his expression tight with restrained fury rather than grief.

"How long," Tulavan said at last, his voice clipped and cold, "does your investigation intend to linger, Harald?"

Harald turned to face him, choosing his words with care. "As long as it must," he replied evenly. "Queen Miroray deserves truth, not haste."

Tulavan's gaze sharpened. "She was my queen," he said. "And every hour without answers invites rumor."

"I will not trade certainty for speed," Harald answered, his tone firm but controlled.

Tulavan held his stare a moment longer, then looked away toward the bier, his anger unresolved but contained.

Lord Lanyard approached with measured tread. "Your Majesty, might I have a moment?"

Harald nodded wearily, stepping aside slightly for privacy.

"Speak."

Lanyard hesitated briefly, then spoke low and discreet. "Prince Aulfis has killed Master Junfolda, his instructor."

Harald's eyes narrowed sharply, his voice strained but steady. "How?"

Lanyard exhaled slowly. "He claims it was an accident during training, but his demeanor troubles me deeply. There's a darkness growing in him."

Harald's brow furrowed, his voice low with concern. "This darkness—explain further, Lanyard. Speak plainly."

"He has grown increasingly reckless, Your Majesty," Lanyard said. "He ignores my warnings. He's become arrogant, dismissive. Whatever restraint once guided him is slipping—and that concerns me."

Harald gazed toward the candlelit hall. "This is troubling. He is our heir—our future. If this recklessness continues, it threatens the realm itself."

"Yes, Your Majesty," Lanyard affirmed solemnly, his voice heavy with the weight of the task before him.

A servant interrupted discreetly, whispering into Harald's ear.

"Your Majesty, Faileas requests an audience."

With a quiet breath, Harald nodded.

"Send him to me." He gestured for Lanyard to remain close, and the two men stepped discreetly into an alcove partially hidden behind columns and drapery.

Faileas approached quietly, dressed to blend with the crowd. No title. No livery. Just a shadow come to speak truth. He bowed slightly—enough to acknowledge royalty.

"Quickly Faileas, I am rather busy," Harald commanded curtly, his voice tinged with the impatience of a man burdened by too many secrets and decisions.

Faileas's gaze remained steady, his eyes tight with things unsaid. His voice was flat.

"The Queen hired me to kill Lady Icewind."

Lanyard's mouth twitched. "So," he said, voice dry, "someone finally chose not to look away."

Harald's features hardened into quiet fury. "The Queen of Eldaraine should not be hiring assassins."

The words landed hard—proof the rot had reached the throne.

Lanyard narrowed his eyes skeptically, suspicion clear in his voice.

"And you're telling us this? Isn't silence the sacred creed of your kind?"

Faileas paused, his control slipping for a brief moment.

"It is. We never speak." He hesitated, letting the weight of his next words fill the silence.

"Then why break it?" Harald demanded sharply, suspicion mingling with curiosity.

"She's like a sister to me," he confessed quietly. "The day her family perished in flames, I pulled her out. I raised her quietly, hidden in shadows. If I allowed this, I may as well have left her in the smoke."

Silence held. Lanyard finally broke it, his tone dry. "Even blades can hesitate. Flame help us all."

Harald studied Faileas with calculating intensity. "You've bought her one chance—no more. I won't risk civil war for sentiment."

Faileas inclined his head respectfully, the weight of his decision clear in his quiet determination. "I ask for no mercy, only to prevent a grave mistake. You'll find a bag of two-thousand gold pieces in your map room. I've returned the Queen's payment."

His words were steady but heavy, an unspoken vow lingering beneath.

Without another word, Faileas bowed briefly, turning swiftly to vanish into the hall's dim embrace.

Harald stood a moment, the anger settling into something colder.

"Avanna is to be watched," he said quietly. "Not openly. No whispers. No panic. But she does not move without us knowing."

Lanyard inclined his head. "It will be done."

"And Junfolda?" Harald asked.

"Handled," Lanyard replied. "We will honor him. Aynaraq will hear what we decide they hear."

Harald's jaw tightened once, then eased. "See that they hear it late."

From the hall, Tulavan's voice cut through the murmurs again—sharp, impatient.

Harald exhaled, burying the rest. "We end this quickly. Give him his rites, then send him home."

Lanyard's expression did not change. "As you command."

The King straightened and stepped back into the light. Servants moved around the bier, candles flaring to life one by one. Tulavan stood waiting.

There would be time for reckoning later. For now, there was only the wake—and a realm that could not afford to fracture in full view.

CHAPTER TWENTY-ONE

Baldrik stood within the Grand Citadel's sacred gardens as late light filtered through the lattice of ancient trees. Leaves shifted in a steady hush. Distant bells marked the hour. Beyond the outer walls, storm clouds gathered, low and heavy, their thunder restrained but near.

Footsteps approached—measured, familiar.

"I have made my choice," Baldrik said at last, facing Kælric's searching gaze.

Kælric studied him, unreadable. "The Flamebound path is not lightly chosen. Why now?"

Baldrik's hands tightened briefly at his sides. "Because I kept telling myself there was more time. That I would know when it was right." A beat. "There is no right. There is only what I keep walking past every morning pretending it isn't there."

"And you believe the Order alters that?"

"I believe it gives me something I chose." Baldrik said it plainly, like a man who had turned the thought over a hundred times and worn it down to its simplest form. "Everything else was decided before I had a say in any of it. I want one thing that isn't."

Silence held between them.

"Is it selfish," Baldrik asked, "to step away from what the realm expects?"

Kælric's answer came without softness. "Selfishness is taking without regard for cost. You are not taking. You are relinquishing."

He did not look away. He watched for hesitation—for the smallest fracture in the prince's resolve. He found none.

"And Elara?"

Something moved across Baldrik's face—brief, unguarded, the ghost of a deflection that never quite formed. Then it was gone. His jaw set. "Elara walks her own road. Mine no longer runs beside it."

Kælric watched him carefully. "She mattered."

"She does. She did," Baldrik said evenly. "Which is why distance was necessary."

Kælric gave a single nod. No comfort offered.

Baldrik drew a slow breath. "I have weighed it. The cost. The loss. I do not mistake the price."

"Good," Kælric said. "Mistaken sacrifice breeds resentment."

Baldrik lifted his chin. "Then let it be sacrifice, not escape."

A pause.

"What if I am wrong?" Baldrik asked quietly. "What if resolve fails me?"

Kælric's gaze did not waver. "Resolve fails when it waits for certainty. The Flamebound walk because they commit. Not because they are assured of victory."

The answer did not ease him. It was not meant to.

"And if this choice leaves only regret?"

"Then you will carry it," Kælric said. "Regret is a weight like any other. It does not excuse you from the road."

Thunder rolled faintly beyond the walls.

"And the Queen?" Kælric asked.

Baldrik's fingers curled once, then stilled. "My mother is unwell. I cannot mend what I did not break."

Kælric inclined his head, accepting the boundary.

"I have chosen," Baldrik said.

Kælric stepped aside. "Then return in five days. Prepare yourself. Speak what must be spoken. When you cross this threshold again, there is no retreat."

Baldrik met his eyes. "I understand."

He turned and left the garden without hesitation, his steps even.

Kælric remained where he was, watching the path empty. The air held the weight of coming rain.

Meyra hesitated at the threshold of Elara's door. The house, once warm with quiet elegance, felt altered—quieter, thinner. She stepped inside, her gaze moving over carefully arranged furniture and precisely drawn drapes. At a glance, nothing was amiss. Yet too many doors stood closed—doors she remembered always open—and the silence between the walls carried more weight than it should.

She found Elara sitting by the hearth in the parlor, staring into the dying embers of a sparse fire. Her usually composed form seemed diminished, shoulders slumped beneath the weight of an invisible burden. The delicate fabrics of her gown, though impeccable as always, now seemed to hang loosely upon her frame.

"Elara?" Meyra spoke softly, her voice gentle, careful not to startle.

Elara slowly lifted her eyes, their cool gray depths shadowed by a pain that went deeper than mere weariness. Her voice emerged hollow, a whisper frayed by despair. "Meyra. It's over."

Meyra moved closer, kneeling beside Elara's chair and placing a comforting hand gently on her friend's knee. "What's happened?"

Elara's gaze drifted briefly around the parlor, lingering on the doors purposefully shut to conceal the barrenness beyond. "My title, my estate—everything is slipping away. The Queen's scrutiny of my ledgers has tightened like a noose. I've been forced to sell heirlooms just to remain afloat."

She hesitated, her elegant hands trembling as she wrung them together nervously. "And now… Baldrik." Her voice broke slightly, barely audible. "He has left me."

Meyra's heart twisted with sympathy, and she tightened her grip reassuringly. "Elara…"

Elara's calm mask finally cracked fully, and she allowed a shuddering breath to escape, shoulders shaking with suppressed emotion. "I had thought him a means to restore my house, a way forward. But he became… more. So much more. I never meant—" she paused, drawing in a sharp breath as though speaking aloud made it unbearably real, "I never meant to fall in love."

Meyra gently squeezed her hand. "No one ever does."

"I controlled everything else," Elara whispered bitterly, a note of self-reproach coloring her words. "Every move calculated, every alliance carefully weighed. Yet, the one thing I could not foresee—my own heart—has undone everything."

"Not everything," Meyra said. "You still have your mind. That hasn't been taken. You've faced worse boards than this."

Elara met Meyra's gaze, her cool grey eyes reflecting the embers' faint glow. "Perhaps," she murmured softly. "Yet, the emptiness around me echoes louder each day. Every sold heirloom, every closed door, every silence amplifies my loss." Elara's voice faltered, just slightly. She looked away, toward the hearth. "And Baldrik is gone. He will choose the Flamebound, I am certain. He was so cold Meyra." For a breath, her composure slipped—eyes bright, lashes wet. Then she swallowed, straightened, and the moment sealed itself away as if it had never surfaced. "I misjudged the board."

Meyra reached out, gently brushing a lock of hair from Elara's brow, speaking with calm determination. "You're not alone. I'm here. We'll find a way."

Elara managed a faint, sad smile, the ghost of her familiar charm briefly surfacing. "Good," she said quietly.

The two women sat quietly as the fire dwindled lower. The silence did not lift the weight in the room, but it made space for it—broad enough to breathe, narrow enough to endure.

Elara wiped the tears from her cheeks, not decisively but with something closer to habit. For a long moment she did not rise. When she finally stood, it was slower than usual, as though testing whether her legs would obey. She smoothed her dress out of reflex rather than pride, fingers lingering briefly in her hair before falling still. The control did not return all at once—it settled in layers.

"You're right," Elara said, more evenly now. "I still have my mind. That's something anyway."

Meyra watched her friend with cautious optimism, curiosity mixing with admiration. "What's your next move, Elara?"

Elara's gaze swept over the empty room, a sharp appraisal in her cool eyes. "Baldrik is gone. Most of my possessions are sold. The stables are empty. The fields neglected." She drew a breath. "Facts."

Meyra stepped closer, her voice gentle yet filled with readiness. "Then what can I do to help?"

Elara turned, not sharply but with a steadier focus than before. "We think," she said. "We plan. Quietly. From where we still have reach." The words felt less like a rally and more like a necessity. She drew a slow breath. "Wine would help. Join me."

Meyra returned the smile, raising her brow slightly. "To whatever's left."

The two women moved purposefully to the veranda, glasses in hand, overlooking the quiet, moonlit grounds. The soft night air carried the distant fragrance of jasmine, mingling peacefully with the charged anticipation of their plotting.

The quiet was soon disturbed by footsteps on stone—measured, unhurried, and entirely expected. Alerick stepped onto the veranda without pretense, his presence announced by neither stealth nor ceremony.

"Alerick," Elara greeted evenly, eyes sharpening with recognition. "You bring news, I trust?"

Alerick inclined his head, expression neutral, professional. "Good news, my lady. The King has been informed of the Queen's contract on your life. You are safe. For now."

Elara stared at him, the news taking a moment to settle. Relief did not bloom—only a slight easing at the edges. A breath left her, almost a laugh but not quite. Meyra lifted her glass. "One less problem ."

Elara met Meyra's gaze, steadier now. "For the moment."

They tapped their glasses lightly, the sound small against the night air, and drank.

The problems were not gone. The losses were not mended. Nothing had been restored.

But the board still existed.

Elara set her glass down first.

"Valen thinks I'm finished," she said quietly. "The Queen thinks I'm contained. Let them think it."

Her gaze drifted over the darkened grounds—not softer, not broken.

"We don't recover," Elara continued. Her voice had not risen. If anything it had dropped — leveled out into something that had shed the last of the evening's grief like a cloak left on the floor. "We reposition."

The moonlight lay across the grounds below, indifferent and clear.

Meyra set her glass down beside Elara's. "Then tell me where we start."

Their voices lowered. Not with hope—with intent. The problems were not gone. The losses were not mended. Nothing had been restored.

But the board still existed.

The map room lay quiet in the late hour, the walls close and the shadows deep. Maps lay dormant across the long table, their markers immobile, silently recounting earlier heated discussions. A soft crackle from the hearth lent warmth to the silence, casting flickering amber reflections upon aged vellum and polished iron.

Lord Darkoak entered without ceremony, carrying the quiet weight of unpleasant duty. Under his arm rested several worn ledgers stamped with the sigil of House Icewind. His expression was grim, the firelight carving deeper lines into his seasoned face.

Harald did not raise his head at Lanyard's approach. He stood leaning over a far table, silvered beard catching fragments of firelight, tracing troop paths with a gloved finger, his eyes intent and unmoving.

Lanyard cleared his throat gently, yet purposefully.

Without looking up, Harald spoke, voice low and weary. "She's ruined, isn't she."

"Beyond creative accounting," Lanyard replied, dry as winter steel. "Three years of falsified harvest yields. Foal projections inflated beyond reason. And the lesser houses' ledgers cooked so badly I can practically smell the char."

Harald sighed deeply, his shoulders tightening with reluctant resignation. "And the verdict?"

"Utterly bankrupt," Lanyard said. "Far beyond land-poor. Crown taxes unpaid. Estate maintenance in arrears. And a sizable loan to Lord Valen who would happily strip Icewind bare."

Harald's jaw tensed visibly as he absorbed the grim reality. "And the estate?"

"Legally yours to claim," Lanyard said, voice even, void of sentimentality. "The law is quite clear."

The king exhaled slowly, deliberately, as if releasing a private weight. "And Elara herself?"

"Still occupying royal apartments," Lanyard said, disapproval carefully contained. "She wears dignity like armor while the estate collapses beneath her."

Harald raised his head finally, a silence hanging heavily between them, unbroken save for the quiet, steady crackling of the hearth.

Lanyard reached into his coat, carefully setting the detailed audit scroll upon the table. His gaze was firm, unwavering as it met the king's. "Shall I arrest her, Your Majesty? Bring her before the court and make the lesson plain?"

Harald's voice, when it came, was resolute yet tempered with something unspoken. "No."

Lanyard's jaw tightened, frustration simmering beneath his disciplined exterior. "She lied to the crown—and still sleeps on royal sheets."

"She's hardly the first," Harald said quietly.

"She lied directly to the Queen," Lanyard pressed.

Harald's eyes lifted to Lanyard's, deep and clear as ice, reflecting both strength and the quiet turmoil beneath.

For a brief moment Lanyard said nothing.

Harald had seen the way the prince watched her across crowded halls, the way Baldrik's attention bent toward her like a compass finding north. Love made men reckless. Kings least of all could afford it. "And my son loves her."

He turned away, striding slowly toward the grand window, arms folded tightly across his chest as he stared into the darkness outside.

"Seize the estate quietly. No fanfare," Harald said. "Move her possessions to the royal apartments. Make certain the vultures understand the carcass has already been claimed."

Lanyard's surprise was evident, though he masked it swiftly beneath disciplined neutrality. "You're letting her keep the royal rooms?"

"I'm keeping her close," Harald said quietly. "Within the Shield. Where I can see her."

Lanyard considered the answer, eyes narrowing slightly as the implications settled. Then he nodded in agreement. "A satisfactory arrangement."

King Harald turned back to face his most trusted advisor, his gaze steeled with unwavering resolve, aqua-blue eyes unyielding in the soft firelight. "Good."

Marshal Ryzen entered Queen Avanna's chambers with measured steps. The candles were lit too brightly for the hour, their reflections multiplying Avanna endlessly across mirror and gilt until it was difficult to tell which image was the queen and which were only echoes.

She sat at her vanity, spine straight, hands folded around a silver comb. Her eyes were fixed on her reflection, unblinking, as though she feared what might move if she looked away.

"Your Majesty," Ryzen said, stopping well short of her reach. "You said there was someone else in the room," he said mildly. "Before the fall."

Avanna turned slowly, as if the motion required rehearsal. Recognition came in pieces. "Marshal," she said. "Have they found him?"

Ryzen inclined his head slightly. "Where did he stand?"

Her fingers slid along the comb's teeth. "He was there," she said. "I felt him. Big. Heavy. Like a door closing."

Ryzen repeated his question, "Where exactly?"

"Behind her," Avanna answered at once—then hesitated. "No. In front of me. Or—" She stopped, breath shallow.

Ryzen waited. He did not fill the space.

Avanna's gaze drifted back to the mirror. Her mouth twisted, the reflection answering her a half-beat too late.

"She was smiling," Avanna said. "Because she thought she'd won. Because she thought she could take it."

Ryzen kept his voice neutral. "Take what, Your Majesty?"

"The throne," Avanna said at once. "Harald. Everything." Her fingers clenched around the comb. "She always wanted what was mine. Always."

Her breath caught. "I wouldn't—she couldn't have it. He is mine."

Ryzen took a step closer—not toward her, but toward the mirror.

"And you?" he asked quietly. "Did that upset you?"

Her grip tightened. The comb bit into her palm. "I told her to stop."

"And did she?"

"Did she what?"

"Stop."

Avanna grimaced, "Of course she didn't. Miroray always had to have her way."

"What did you do when she didn't?"

Avanna's mouth opened. "I—" Closed. Truth struggling with confusion.

Outside the chamber, questions were being asked again and again—of guards, of servants, of the girl Lana. The answers shifted, blurred, bent. No hand reached from shadow. No footstep crossed the threshold. Every path folded back on itself.

Avanna swallowed. Her reflection seemed suddenly too aligned, too singular. The room was quiet for a long time.

"There was no one else," she said slowly, as if testing the words for weight.

Ryzen felt the air tighten.

"No assassin," she continued. "No man in the dark." Her voice thinned. "Just… us."

The realization did not strike like lightning. It seeped.

Her eyes sharpened—not in madness, but in unbearable clarity. "I touched her," Avanna whispered. "I remember her sleeve. I remember the sound."

For a breath, she held together.

Then the knowledge finished its work.

Her shoulders folded inward as though struck from within. "Flames," she breathed. "Miroray. I didn't— I didn't—"

Ryzen stepped forward only long enough to take the comb from her hands and close it away. "That's enough," he said quietly.

Her grief twisted, words dissolving into sound, apologies breaking apart before they could form meaning.

"Stay close," Ryzen told Lt. Leif, voice low. "Her Majesty does not leave these chambers. Not alone. Not for any reason. Keep the balcony barred."

Leif acknowledged silently, stepping gently yet firmly closer as Avanna dissolved into quiet, wrenching sobs, her murmured apologies spilling helplessly into the shadows.

Ryzen stepped into the corridor, releasing a weary breath into the echoing silence.

The weight of the tragedy pressed upon him, no lighter for being named. There had been no assassin. No hidden hand. Only a queen, a dead sister, and a truth too terrible to survive intact.

Avanna had not been struck down by the truth.

She had touched it—and shattered beneath the weight of it.

The conspirators gathered in a shadowed alcove within the throne room wing, discreetly apart from the milling courtiers and solemn-faced attendants. Marble columns pressed in close, their polished surfaces catching torchlight that flickered and broke across faces held too near one another. The ceiling above was lost to shadow, felt rather than seen.

Lord Circus Valen stood by one of the polished columns, fingertips idly tracing the cool marble, his gaze sharp and predatory. Nearby, lesser conspirators shifted uneasily, careful not to draw attention. Rennic approached silently, stepping from the deeper gloom beyond the corridor, eyes glittering with fresh intelligence.

"About time," Valen remarked, voice deceptively calm, though a subtle tension rippled beneath it. "I loathe these little excursions. Too close to the crown. Too far from my walls."

Rennic's lips curled faintly, a razor's edge of a smile. "I come bearing truths, my lord, and they seldom travel swiftly."

"Then speak your truths," Valen drawled, composing himself, eyes narrowing with calculated interest. "What fresh news stirs our noble king?"

Rennic drew closer, his movements deliberate and smooth, voice barely above a murmur yet weighted heavily with significance. "Harald's grip tightens—not only does he patrol the northern routes more fervently, but he's personally scouring the accounts of minor houses. Most notably, Lady Elara has drawn his suspicion. And she has been kept company by the King's bastard."

Valen's eyes flashed sharply, the corner of his mouth twitching with amusement. "Elara and Aulfis? So, she's bedded both brothers, knowingly or otherwise. Tell me, does she have any notion about Aulfis' true heritage?"

Rennic shook his head slightly, his tone edged with cold certainty. "It appears not, my lord. Her actions suggest ignorance rather than cunning. It would seem she was seen to be heavy with drink."

Valen chuckled softly, eyes alight with genuine entertainment. "Clever, even when she isn't trying. She becomes more desirable by the day. How certain are you?"

Rennic inclined his head slightly, voice quiet and assured. "Certain enough to stake our plans upon it. And there's more—Aulfis grows dangerously unpredictable. His training master has gone missing; whispers speak of the boy's temper, quick and fierce as wildfire."

Valen straightened slightly, anticipation flickering in his gaze. "Unpredictability can be an asset."

Rennic paused, a calculated moment to let his words resonate. "The master's disappearance remains contained—for now. Only a few know, and fewer still understand what it means. That ignorance is our advantage. When the truth surfaces, it will not arrive as fact, but as rumor. Fear will follow suspicion, and suspicion will find its mark. Harald's authority hangs by a thinning thread. One pressure point, pressed with care—and the crown crumbles. Worse still, it may not remain an internal matter. When Anyaraq learns of it, they will demand answers. Or restitution if it turns grim. Either will serve us."

Valen leaned in subtly, the predator within him fully engaged. "And how precisely will you push?"

Rennic turned slightly, disdain briefly flashing in his eyes. "Nothing spoken, nothing planted. For now, we hold the silence. Let the court remain ignorant while the ground is prepared."

Valen's smile thinned, interested rather than displeased. "You would wait."

"I would shape the moment," Rennic replied. "If he is dead, and the news is allowed to surface, it must do so sideways—half-heard, poorly sourced, impossible to pin. Rumor, not revelation. Suspicion will do more damage than truth ever could."

Valen nodded. "And Aulfis?"

Rennic's mouth curved faintly. "He will be the story they want to believe. Unchecked temper. Violence poorly restrained. Enough shadow to make every glance feel dangerous."

Valen allowed himself a small, predatory smile. "Elegant. But caution must be our watchword. Timing, Smudge, is everything."

"Precisely," Rennic said. "The wake will soften them. Grief dulls scrutiny. By the time the whispers begin, the court will already be leaning toward them."

Valen straightened his cloak deliberately, eyes gleaming with ruthless determination. "Then we prepare. Position your agents, but keep them quiet. Let silence do its work first."

Rennic bowed slightly, his voice a silk-wrapped blade. "Consider it done, my lord. Harald may soon discover that the heir he cherishes is the very flame that will burn him."

As the conspirators dispersed into the shadows, Valen noted the subtle shift in the throne room's mood. Nobles gathered, their voices kept deliberately low as they drifted toward the warmly lit main hall, where Queen Miroray's wake was to begin. With a final, meaningful glance exchanged with Rennic, Valen smoothly joined the throng, ready to weave his presence into the fabric of intrigue. The realm balanced on a knife's edge, and Valen intended to be present when it tipped.

The grand hall of Castellon Shield was cloaked in solemn dignity, softened by the golden glow of countless candles shimmering within polished silver sconces and ornate candelabras. Heavy banners of Eldaraine's green and black woven alongside Vara's emerald and reef-blue draped from towering ceilings, whispering a silent elegy of unity and mourning. The mingled fragrance of polished oak, melting wax, lilies, and sea orchids permeated the air, invoking memories of the queen now lost.

Guests gathered quietly, their voices hushed in reverence, clustering along extensive tables that stretched the length of the grand chamber. Nobility wore expressions of tempered sorrow, their garments rich yet muted—deep velvets, somber silks, and dark satins chosen to honor the gravity of the moment rather than personal vanity. Occasionally, soft laughter or whispered remembrances gently broke the stillness, poignant glimpses into personal grief amidst collective mourning.

At the elevated head table, King Harald sat with commanding stillness at the center, his solemn presence grounding the hall.

To his immediate right, Queen Avanna sat rigidly poised, her striking beauty rendered cold, her eyes distant and enigmatic. Beside her, Prince Baldrik maintained an impassive visage, though his thoughtful gaze betrayed subtle unease.

Lord Lanyard Darkoak sat vigilant and unmoving beside Baldrik, his sharp eyes carefully monitoring the hall and rarely straying from Harald's side.

Seated to Harald's left, visiting royalty occupied places of honor with poised decorum. King Consort Tulavan wore his irritation with quiet dignity, his ebony-toned features feigning profound sadness.

The banquet began earnestly, a low, steady murmur of restrained conversation filling the hall. Respectful tranquility reasserted itself, though beneath it unspoken tensions lay coiled and waiting.

Elara's gaze drifted, more than once, toward Baldrik. Her expression remained composed, but her gaze lingered a fraction too long before she forced it elsewhere. Baldrik, keenly aware of her attention, maintained a determined distance, focusing instead on his whispered discussion with Lanyard. He did not look at her.

Seated beside Elara, Meyra observed the exchange and, after a moment, intervened. With practiced grace, she placed a hand on Elara's wrist and shifted the conversation to safer ground, drawing Elara's attention away from Baldrik's pointed absence.

At another table, Lord Valen sat at ease, his stillness deliberate rather than relaxed. He did not fidget or look about; his impatience showed only in the slow, deliberate tap of one finger against the polished tabletop, a rhythm of contempt rather than nerves. Beside him, Rennic sat silently, an unremarkable presence among the house Lords and Ladies who spoke in cautious tones.

Elsewhere in the hall, Lord Quentyn Caerlyn and Lady Olivia sat deep in earnest conversation with Lord Alvis and Lady Sarah Thornsword, their voices discreet yet charged with urgency.

"I have complete faith in Harald," Alvis asserted firmly, his eyes unwavering. "He has always foreseen threats and reacted decisively. Our king will manage whatever arises."

"Certainly," Quentyn responded respectfully, his voice hushed yet deliberate, "but I must admit a recent discussion with Lord Durnhart troubles me deeply. He spoke at length of Valen's quiet efforts to undermine several lesser houses—pressuring them toward dependence on the crown, then positioning himself to absorb what remains."

Lord Alvis stroked his chin thoughtfully, the weight of the moment settling on his features. "Branik's message reached Stonewatch days ago. There has been movement in the north," he said quietly. "My riders along the passes report increased Hravanskot presence—organized, watchful. I have kept the roads secured, but the pattern is not reassuring."

Lady Caerlyn spoke with genuine concern. "Indeed. Our merchants report that all trade with Hravanskot ceased abruptly and without explanation. Whatever is happening there is deliberate, not accidental."

Quentyn leaned forward, his brow furrowed as the threads began to tangle in his mind.

"If Valen is already undermining the lesser houses," he said quietly, "it is not unthinkable that he would look beyond our borders as well. The Hravnskot movements—trade cut, forces gathering—could be another of his ploys."

Olivia turned to him at once, her expression calm, almost indulgent.

"Husband," she said gently, "you give Circus too much credit."

Alvis inclined his head in agreement.

"She is right," he said. "Lord Valen is crafty, yes—but even the Hravnskot would not have dealings with him. Whatever stirs in the north is its own matter."

Their conversation lingered, casting a deeper shadow of unease over the banquet hall, subtly intensifying the tension that threaded quietly yet unmistakably through the room.

The banquet passed with quiet dignity, the hall settling into an understated rhythm of muted conversations and the gentle, rhythmic clink of silver against porcelain. A temporary calm lay over the gathering, masking deeper tensions beneath carefully maintained decorum, the shared grief of Miroray's loss uniting even the most disparate factions.

At the high table, King Harald observed the hall thoughtfully, his expression a studied mask of quiet authority. Lord Darkoak had quietly risen and now stood vigilantly behind Queen Avanna, his silent, protective presence casting a reassuring shadow over the royal couple.

Harald leaned subtly toward Avanna, voice low with reflective intimacy. "Remarkable to see Lord Valen tonight. I don't believe he's ventured from his fortress in nearly two years."

Avanna inclined her head gently, eyes distant yet warm. "Indeed. It is good to see your brother Alvis here as well. Familiar faces bring comfort." Her voice lowered, tinged with quiet confusion. "And Miroray... It will be wonderful to see her again. She must be delayed—perhaps by a storm over Vara?"

Harald froze. Just for a breath. Then nodded slowly, his jaw tightening around silence he dared not break.

He gently covered her hand with his own, his voice softly reassuring. "She'll arrive soon, Avanna. Patience, my love."

Avanna relaxed marginally at Harald's calming reassurance, though a flicker of uncertainty lingered in her eyes.

Harald straightened with deliberate grace, sharing a subtle, questioning glance with Lanyard. "Everything ready?"

Lanyard nodded imperceptibly, his confirmation firm and silent.

King Harald stood, raised his goblet and tapped it lightly with his ring. The sound, clear and resonant, spread through the hall, immediately quieting all conversations and turning every eye toward him with expectancy.

At her table, Elara held herself very still, composure practiced and deliberate. Her gaze flicked once toward Baldrik, noting the careful control in his expression before she looked away again. She kept her hands folded in her lap to stop them from moving.

Lord Valen, seated with deliberate stillness, let his eyes narrow thoughtfully. He leaned subtly toward Rennic, his voice sharp with guarded curiosity. "Now, what do you suppose is about to unfold?"

Rennic's reply was measured, a faint, enigmatic smile on his lips. "Perhaps something seismic enough to drag even you into the daylight, my lord. Change rarely asks permission."

Valen grunted quietly, one finger tapping the table with unhurried contempt, his gaze fixed on Harald. "Indeed."

At another table, Quentyn exchanged a wary glance with his wife before turning discreetly to Alvis, his voice cautious yet charged with subtle urgency. "Harald seems particularly resolute this evening. Do you think this concerns the northern troubles?"

Alvis shook his head slightly, his confidence unshaken, voice steady with conviction. "My brother never acts without careful reason. Whatever he reveals tonight will be significant, beyond mere formality."

Olivia's expression clouded with unease, her attention returning to the high table.

"Whatever he intends, I pray it brings stability rather than further uncertainty."

Their conversation quieted, each noble's attention drawn irrevocably to Harald, the entire hall poised in silent anticipation, awaiting the king's words with bated breath.

Marshal Ryzen entered quietly at the rear of the grand hall, his presence instantly drawing Lord Lanyard's sharp, vigilant gaze. Their eyes locked briefly, exchanging a swift, practiced communication. Ryzen's expression was somber, the gravity in his eyes enough to confirm that contingency plans were no longer hypothetical. Lanyard maintained his stoic demeanor, giving a brief, solemn nod that carried heavy finality.

Without a spoken word, Ryzen made a subtle signal to his guards. They moved efficiently, positioning themselves subtly yet deliberately around the king's table, their readiness apparent only to those paying close attention.

King Harald shifted, posture straightening further, his presence radiating quiet authority. He addressed his guests with practiced composure, his voice steady and resonant.

"Once again, I thank you all deeply for gathering here tonight, during this solemn hour. For some, this marks your first visit to Castellon Shield. Welcome. For others," Harald's penetrating gaze settled upon Lord Valen, "it has been far too long."

Valen inclined his head slightly, eyes narrowing with cautious interest, curiosity simmering just beneath his polished exterior.

Harald continued, his voice steady but carrying a measured weight. "We gather under shadow. Queen Miroray Kaeleen of Vara was a sovereign of rare discipline and strength. Her loss is not Vara's alone, but felt across these halls as well."

He turned slightly, acknowledging the Varanese delegation. "To King Consort Tulavan Kaeleen—you have my court's respect and my condolences. To my queen, Avanna—your sister is honored here, and her name will not fade in silence."

A brief pause, then, formal and deliberate: "Long live Queen Kirahnae Kaeleen."

Cups were raised across the hall, the toast moving like a quiet tide. Tulavan lifted his cup a fraction slower than the rest, jaw set, the motion deliberate rather than willing—but he drank all the same.

Harald took a measured drink and let the moment settle before pressing on, his tone sharpening just a fraction beneath the courtesy. "As you are all assembled, it seems appropriate to make an announcement of considerable significance."

Lord Darkoak stepped forward, presenting Harald with a meticulously prepared scroll, its official seal gleaming faintly in the candlelight. Harald accepted it solemnly. As he unrolled the scroll, he slowly lifted his gaze—tension tightening the hall like a drawn bowstring.

"A new royal succession has been decreed," Harald's voice echoed clearly through the vast chamber, each word landing heavily upon the attentive ears. "Henceforth, the line of succession shall stand thus: First Heir—Aulfis Thornsword."

Aulfis emerged confidently from behind the king, his expression carefully poised between humble acceptance and thinly veiled triumph. His gaze swept calmly over the stunned nobles, taking in their surprise without reaction. His eyes found Elara's stunned look. A faint smile touched his lips—brief, proprietary, and gone.

A sharp, collective gasp rippled across the hall, then broke into urgent whispers. Faces turned, eyes wide, disbelief passing in quick, frightened exchanges.

Elara's stomach twisted—not in fear, but recognition.

"No!" Queen Avanna's voice pierced the silence, raw and trembling, a jagged blade of grief and fury. She sprang to her feet, her chair scraping sharply across the polished marble floor, eyes blazing with defiance and despair. "This cannot stand! I refuse to accept this outrage! Aulfis is no son of mine, no rightful heir. You cast aside your own son for a bastard, Harald!"

The hall erupted—gasps swelling into shocked murmurs and anxious whispers. Nobles exchanged panicked glances, unease and disbelief clouding their refined features. Guards tensed instinctively, their hands subtly shifting toward weapons as an unseen storm gathered strength.

Lanyard stepped urgently forward, his voice firm yet tempered by practiced diplomacy. "Your Majesty, please, this is neither the time nor place—"

"Be silent, Lanyard!" Avanna's command sliced sharply through his plea, eyes wild and unbridled. "I will not be hushed! I will not stand idle while you toss my son aside for a common-born bastard. This is madness!"

King Harald's face grew cold, eyes hardening to steel. His voice, clear and cutting, carried the unbending authority of a ruler forced to decisive action. "Enough, Avanna. Your outburst shames the memory of your sister and disrespects this gathering." He inclined his head sharply toward Marshal Ryzen, whose guards had already moved into position with practiced efficiency. "Escort the queen to her chambers at once."

Avanna's eyes widened in shock and betrayal as she was restrained. Her resistance was futile; her furious protests filled the air, then faded into anguished silence as she was led away. Her voice echoed painfully, leaving a chill that settled over the grand chamber.

The room went utterly still. No lord or lady moved; breath caught, eyes fixed, as though the hall waited.

Elara sat frozen, her features drained of color as the weight of it settled. She stood abruptly, her chair striking the floor behind her, and left the hall without apology.

Meyra half-rose from her seat, her voice gentle yet insistent, calling after her, "Elara, wait!" But her plea was swiftly swallowed by the escalating turmoil filling the hall.

Baldrik watched her go and for the first time, did not look away.

Rennic's gaze followed Elara's fleeing form. Without uttering a word, he rose fluidly, moving with quiet purpose through the chaos, a shadow slipping after hers.

The chamber fractured—voices rising, shock spilling into open confusion. Lords leaned toward one another, whispers sharpening into something louder, less controlled.

Harald did not speak.

He stood, unwavering. Steady.

The sound ebbed, uneven at first, then faltering as attention drew back toward the royal table. One by one, voices died beneath the weight of his stillness.

When he spoke, it was quiet—and carried.

"Attend."

The single word settled over the hall, firm as iron.

Only when silence returned did he continue.

"Second Heir—any future children of Aulfis. Third Heir—my steadfast brother, Prince Alvis Thornsword."

Harald paused, letting the implications settle.

A stunned silence descended, the shock of Harald's words gripping the hall.

"The line stands as declared," Harald said, voice firm and unyielding. "Beyond this, succession shall follow the laws of Eldaraine, as it always has."

Aulfis stood tall and collected, observing the turmoil he had indirectly incited with serene indifference. A faint smile flickered across his lips, barely perceptible yet deeply provocative.

"Did you have any knowledge of this?" Quentyn's voice was taut with incredulity, his gaze sharply questioning Alvis.

Alvis shook his head slowly, astonishment etched deeply upon his usually calm features. "I swear, Quentyn, Harald kept his plans hidden even from me. This revelation strikes me just as sharply as it does you."

Lord Valen leaned forward intently, his eyes glinting with keen, dark amusement. He murmured quietly to Rennic, voice rich with intrigue, "Harald has truly outdone himself tonight. What fascinating turmoil he's unleashed."

CHAPTER TWENTY-TWO

Elara Icewind stood in the shadowed hall adjoining the grand banquet chamber, the echoes of chaos still ringing sharply in her ears. Torchlight danced restlessly along the stone walls, casting erratic shadows. Each breath dragged slow and heavy, tasting faintly of smoke.

Her fingers clutched the heavy velvet curtain that separated the hall from the banquet room, knuckles pale and trembling. Through a narrow gap, she glimpsed fragments of the lingering turmoil: King Harald's stern commands, Avanna's shrill, defiant curses, and Prince Baldrik—quiet, resolute, unreachable.

Baldrik had chosen the Flamebound Order, relinquishing crown and comfort alike. The revelation of Aulfis' royal blood—his smug satisfaction, his calculating eyes—had been a dagger aimed precisely at her chest. The world she'd meticulously crafted crumbled swiftly beneath her feet, leaving her balanced over something vast and cold.

"My Lady," a voice murmured smoothly behind her, sharp as steel.

She spun, heart jolting sharply against her ribs, finding Rennic Stride leaning casually against the far wall, half-hidden in shadow. His expression was unreadable; his eyes were alert, assessing rather than amused.

"Not now, Rennic," Elara managed, her voice brittle, more plea than command.

"But Lady Icewind," he said softly, stepping forward into the flickering torchlight, his posture impeccably poised. His fingers brushed lightly at the dust on his sleeve as if this moment were merely a trifling inconvenience. "Now is precisely the time."

Elara straightened her shoulders, summoning what remained of her dignity. "I have no desire for your games tonight."

"Games?" Rennic's brow arched elegantly, his mouth settling into a faint, controlled line. "No, no games tonight, Lady Icewind. Merely advice from a concerned friend." His words slid like silk over a blade.

"Friend?" Elara's laugh was bitter, harsh. "If your friendship were a wine, it'd reek of spoiled poultry and bile."

Rennic's expression never faltered. If anything, his expression remained steady, unoffended. "Call it what you will, Elara, but surely you realize the ground beneath you is shifting. Hesitation won't hold the floor tonight."

She looked away sharply, the image of Baldrik's solemn resignation burned vividly into her mind. "Action? The only action left is to survive."

Rennic tilted his head slightly, watching her with focused attention. "Precisely. And survival demands aligning yourself swiftly with power. Real power. Aulfis now holds the royal favor."

Her stomach lurched, sharp and violent. For a heartbeat she could only stare at him, revulsion flaring hot and immediate. "Aulfis?" she hissed. "Are you mad?" Her voice shook, fury cutting through the fog of shock. "After what happened—you would have me stand beside him?"

"Arrogance and cruelty," Rennic said evenly, "have always found their way into crowns."

Elara's breath came fast, unsteady. Anger warred with something colder as she met his gaze, fury slowly giving way to calculation. "You expect me to bind my fate to such a man?"

"I expect you to see clearly, Lady Icewind. You've always understood necessity. Consider this merely another necessary maneuver." Rennic stepped closer, voice dropping lower, dangerously intimate. "You know what chaos unchecked can do. Aulfis requires guidance, subtle yet firm, and you possess the rare talent of steering even the most stubborn hearts."

She drew a shuddering breath, heart aching at the raw pragmatism he laid before her. "Baldrik—" Her voice faltered. Her eyes burned, vision blurring as his quiet resolve rose unbidden in her mind.

"Chose the Flamebound. He chose exile from worldly power." Rennic did not lean closer. His voice lowered all the same. "You need not follow him. Love fades. Power lasts."

Elara turned away, pressing her palm briefly to the stone wall as if grounding herself. Tears welled despite her, hot and traitorous. Her pulse thundered, disgust still sharp—but beneath it, unwelcome thoughts began to surface. Images flickered through her thoughts—her estate crumbling, her name sullied, Baldrik's quiet resolve, and Aulfis' cold, triumphant smile. Survival, Rennic had named it correctly. The word echoed, ugly and persistent. Survival was an ugly game, yet one she had always played exceptionally well.

Slowly, Elara lifted her chin and scrubbed the tears from her cheeks with the heel of her hand, stubborn and unapologetic. The revulsion had not vanished. She simply locked it away with the other things she could no longer afford to feel. "And your advice, Rennic? Your true aim?"

His expression shifted—subtle, almost imperceptible. Relief first. Then calculation settled quietly behind his eyes. "Our interests align," Rennic said simply. "I would see you remain standing when others fall. Aulfis will need restraint—direction. You are uniquely suited to provide it."

"And when it all turns to ash?" she asked softly, eyes searching his for honesty she knew she wouldn't find.

"Then you endure," Rennic replied. "Intact. Relevant. Safe. Power is never gentle, but it can be shaped."

A brief pause, then, almost offhand: "Bailen—Flame keep him—was always deft with ash." His gaze held hers a moment. "I see that much of your father in you."

Elara stood silent a moment longer, the sound of distant commotion fading into something sharper—quieter, more dangerous. Her heart still ached, but she felt it now for what it was: a liability. A mistake she had allowed herself to indulge.

Baldrik's name lingered at the edge of her thoughts. She did not reach for it.

She let it fall.

What remained was clearer. Colder.

She met Rennic's gaze squarely, something within her settling back into place—the part of her that survived, that endured, that calculated when others faltered.

"Very well," she said firmly, her voice steady, stripped of what had wavered before. "I won't be erased, Master Stride."

Rennic inclined his head once, precisely. "I was hoping you wouldn't, Lady Icewind."

She turned and looked back into the throne room, watching the nobles gather themselves and depart, the aftermath settling like dust after a storm. Baldrik had vanished from his seat, King Harald was deep in discussion with Lord Lanyard and Marshal Ryzen, while King Tulavan stood nearby, his face contorted with unmistakable anger. And Aulfis—Prince Aulfis, she supposed bitterly—sat smugly, leisurely finishing the remains of a meal abandoned in the chaos, as though the bedlam around him were of no consequence.

Elara straightened her spine, her jaw tightening once. The last of the softness left her expression.

"So be it," she said, not as surrender—but as decision.

With measured steps, head high and expression set, she re-entered the hall—not as she had been, but as she needed to be—and walked toward the royal table.

⁂

The air inside Queen Avanna's private chambers was oppressive, thick with incense and unspoken grief. Shadows draped the stone walls like mourning veils, broken by restless candlelight. Rain battered the windowpanes—relentless, accusing, cold.

Queen Avanna paced feverishly, her movements sharp and erratic. Her eyes glittered, fists clenched tight enough to tremble. She whipped around at the sound of the chamber doors creaking open, lips curled back in disdain.

King Harald entered first, weary yet resolute. Behind him, Lord Darkoak stood watchful. Last came King Consort Tulavan, shoulders tense beneath his cloak, anger evident but held in check by respect for Harald's dominion.

"Have you come to apologize for this insult?" Avanna's voice sliced through the heavy silence like a blade. She laughed sharply, pacing a tight circle. "Confined like a common traitor in my own chambers?"

Harald stepped forward, his voice low and firm, grief pressing at its edges. "Avanna, we must speak of Miroray."

"There's nothing to discuss!" Avanna snapped, venom dripping from each word. "Miroray is alive, resting in her chambers. Your suspicions are treachery, Harald—nothing less."

Harald exhaled slowly, eyes darkening as patience thinned. "Avanna, Miroray is dead. You must face this truth."

"She is not dead!" Avanna's voice erupted, echoing fiercely against the stone walls. "I spoke to her mere moments ago. Do you dare call me mad, Harald?"

Tulavan took two steps closer, his restraint cracking. "Queen Avanna, this farce dishonors Miroray's memory. She deserves justice—not this poison of lies and cowardice."

Avanna whirled toward Tulavan, her gaze fiery with contempt. "Justice? You dare speak of justice, Tulavan, standing among traitors? Miroray breathes still—perhaps you should reconsider your allies."

Tulavan's jaw tightened sharply, anger finally breaking free. "Harald, this is what your silence has wrought. If you will not command your queen, then your grip on this kingdom is already slipping."

Harald raised a hand sharply, silencing the rising voices. Fatigue weighed on him, but his words rang with quiet authority. "Enough.

Avanna, for your own safety and the safety of Eldaraine, you will remain confined until clarity returns."

"You would imprison me?" Avanna's voice trembled with betrayal, fury crackling around her. "Your queen—your wife?"

"For your protection," Harald repeated, his tone heavy with sorrowful resolve. "And that of the realm."

Tulavan finally broke, his voice thunderous with grief and rage. "This is cowardice, Harald! Miroray deserves truth, not your empty words and meaningless gestures."

Lanyard moved swiftly, placing himself firmly between Tulavan and Harald, his voice quiet yet sharp as steel. "Mind your place, Tulavan. Remember whose court you stand in."

Tulavan bristled but stepped back, visibly struggling to rein in his fury.

Harald met Avanna's gaze one last time, regret etching deep lines into his features. "Until you can see clearly, Avanna, I must confine you."

Avanna stood frozen, disbelief and defiance battling fiercely within her. "You will regret this betrayal, Harald—I swear it."

Harald turned toward the door, his shoulders bowed beneath an invisible weight, his voice a quiet, bitter acknowledgment. "Perhaps I already do."

As Harald exited, Lanyard and Tulavan followed closely behind. Harald paused briefly at the threshold, his voice low but unwavering as he addressed the guards outside. His gaze settled on the man at their head.

"Lieutenant Leif," he said. "You will command the watch here."

Lieutenant Leif straightened at once. "Yes, Your Majesty."

"Do not leave her unattended. Keep two guards inside at all times. I do not care if she is bathing or entertaining a steward—do not let her out of your sight. Do you understand?"

"Yes, Your Majesty," the guards responded, their voices firm and unwavering.

Inside, Avanna unleashed her fury. With a cry of rage, she seized a crystal goblet and hurled it against the wall. Glass exploded—the final fracture of her mind, beautiful in its violence, sharp in its sorrow, utterly and irreversibly broken. Her chest rose and fell in ragged breaths, eyes blazing with bitter, unyielding defiance.

"Traitors!" she screamed, her voice echoing hollowly in the empty chamber, amplifying her isolation and despair. "All of you—traitors to the true crown!"

⸻ ✶ ⸻

Tulavan strode through Castellon's shadowed corridors, each step echoing sharply, grief and anger held in a vise. Beside him walked Captain Apeck, his face drawn, the lines around his eyes deeper than usual. Their silence was heavy, charged with emotions neither man wished to give voice to.

They arrived at the chamber holding Queen Miroray's body. Sea Serpent Fleet guards stood sentinel, their shoulders rigid, eyes downcast and filled with sorrow.

"Bring her," Tulavan commanded, his voice low and fierce. "We leave this place."

With profound reverence, the guards carefully lifted Miroray's lifeless body. Their movements were tender, burdened by sorrow and respect, as though she were fragile porcelain rather than fallen royalty. Tulavan watched in silence, jaw set hard. When he spoke, his voice was stone. "Castellon has betrayed us, Eldaraine has taken our queen. They have sealed their fate."

The procession moved silently, a funeral march echoing through the halls, grief and wrath hanging thickly in the air. Apeck kept pace, unease tightening his features. Though sorrowful, his heart recoiled at the grim certainty he saw in Tulavan's eyes.

Outside, beneath storm-heavy clouds, carriages and horses borrowed from Eastmere awaited, drivers and attendants rigid with tension, sensing the volatile undercurrents in the air. Miroray's body was placed into a waiting carriage with utmost care, covered reverently in a cloth bearing Vara's emblem, a stark symbol of their tragic loss.

As they mounted their horses, Apeck finally broke the oppressive silence. "Tulavan," Apeck said quietly, "we return home. But must this mean war? Think of Vara's children. Our islands."

Tulavan halted, bitterness tightening his voice. "Miroray deserves justice," Tulavan said. "Eldaraine has shown their true face. We must prepare."

"Yet," Apeck interjected carefully, voice quiet but firm, "Kirahnae is queen now. She may see things differently. She may seek peace."

Tulavan's gaze hardened, his words quiet and edged. "Then that, too, will be corrected," Tulavan said. "By storm or steel. I will see Vara ruled by one who remembers what was taken. Kirahnae is young, untested. She cannot see clearly. I will not allow hesitation or childish sentiment to weaken Vara. Eldaraine will pay in blood for Miroray."

Apeck paused, loyalty warring with dread. "War is a dangerous path, Tulavan. Justice, yes—but at what cost?"

Tulavan's voice sharpened, anger flaring as Apeck questioned him. "The cost has already been paid, Apeck. Miroray's life was taken unjustly, without cause or honor. Do you expect me to return home and forgive?"

Apeck stared back, recognizing the depth of his friend's grief, finally nodding with somber acceptance. "As you command."

The carriages lurched forward, wheels creaking, hooves striking stone. Tulavan's gaze remained fixed ahead, unblinking, his mind already charting the tides of retribution, each wave a promise of reckoning. They would reach Eastmere in three days, and from there, Vara would return home beneath banners of mourning and vengeance. First on Tulavan's list was Kirahnae. The throne of Vara would not be allowed to hesitate.

Queen Avanna's chambers were cloaked in a brooding silence, shadows flickering with the candle flames. Avanna sat rigid and regal, brittle as ice, her gaze fixed on Lieutenant Leif.

Leif stood at perfect attention by the heavy wooden door, every muscle in his frame rigid, his expression a mask of disciplined calm. He met Avanna's penetrating stare without hesitation, understanding the subtle gesture of her slender fingers curling inward—an unspoken command he'd long been trained to recognize.

With practiced authority, Leif turned to the other guard on watch. "Give us a moment, Stellan" he said.

Stellan hesitated, "The king's orders—two at all times."

Leif stepped closer, voice low and final. "I assume the responsibility. Outside."

Stellan bowed sharply and withdrew, the door closing with a heavy, measured sound.

Avanna rose, the whisper of silk barely audible. Fury sharpened into calculation. "Leif," she breathed, her tone a dangerous blend of command and seduction, "we must speak openly now."

Leif inclined his head respectfully. "As you wish, my Queen."

"Harald has betrayed me," she said. "He confines me, shames the crown, and mistakes restraint for weakness. Eldaraine will pay for it."

Leif's jaw tightened, something deeper than loyalty flickering behind his discipline before he forced it back into place. "My allegiance has always been yours, Your Majesty," he said, and the words carried more than oath before he mastered himself. "Only yours."

"Then you understand what follows." She did not raise her voice. "Harald must be removed. I ask whether I can trust you."

Leif's eyes never wavered, his voice firm, steeped in resolve despite the weight of the command. "Your will is my duty. Say the word, and I will make this night his last."

She rested her hand briefly on his armored shoulder—command, not caress, though she felt the tension it sparked and did not withdraw. "Eldaraine needs resolve," she said. "Stand with me."

Leif swallowed once. "If you command it, I will see it done."

Avanna inclined her head, satisfied. "Then wait. Choose the moment."

Leif bowed and returned to his post, duty settling like a weight across his shoulders.

Beneath Castellon Shield, buried deep where the stone swallowed sound and breath alike, lay a torchlit chamber carved more for penance than confinement. Damp streaked the mortar like veins, fed by centuries of rain tapping a rust-wreathed grate far above. Torchlight didn't banish the dark so much as make it ripple.

Marshal Ryzen stood just outside the bars, arms folded across his chest, posture rigid with unspoken frustration. A single torch guttered on the wall, casting the boy's face in slow, flickering shadow.

The boy sat slouched on a narrow bench of stone, no older than sixteen. Straw clung to his hair and sleeves. His eyes were rimmed red, but he didn't cry. Not anymore.

Boots echoed down the hall—not rushed, not hesitant—just the sound of inevitability approaching.

The guards at the archway snapped to attention.

King Harald stepped into the cell block like a verdict wearing a royal cloak—calm, final, unquestionable.

His cloak drank the damp from the air as he passed, rain steaming faintly from the fur lining. He stopped in front of the cell, said nothing at first—just studied the boy. The silence didn't intimidate. It evaluated.

Ryzen let it linger before speaking. "Your Majesty," he said, quiet and even. "This is the one. Page of the Shield. Name's Truin. Caught red-handed, behind a bakery Your Majesty. Fire still warm when we pulled him away from the smoke."

The King turned slightly. "What bakery?"

"Thamer's Hearth. The one with the green-tiled chimney."

"And the letters?"

"Royal. Seals broken, wax melted into the stones. Most already turned to ash."

Harald faced the boy.

His voice was measured, neither cruel nor kind—just clean as drawn steel. "Do you know what you burned, boy?"

The page nodded, slowly. "Not what they said, Your Highness. But… I knew where they were from."

"Then why take them?"

The boy's fingers twisted in his lap. Shame clung to him like soot. "I… I was told to."

"By whom?"

Ryzen's voice was low, almost too quiet. "He's not the spark. Just the ash trail."

"I don't know. Just a voice. A shadow in the alley behind the Blackmill stables. Never saw his face. Just said if I pulled letters marked 'Vara' or anything with a wine crest and put them in an empty barrel behind the Iron Cup, I'd get a silver for every day I did it."

He looked up then—eyes wide, frightened. "But… I can't read, Your Highness. So, I just took them all."

The King didn't blink. Didn't scowl. Just asked, simply: "And this shadow gave no name?"

"No, Your Highness. Just the coin."

A long pause. Harald's gaze shifted to Ryzen.

"You suspect Alerick?"

"I do. But I've no proof, Sire."

"Of course not." Harald's mouth tightened. "Proof is never his style."

The King turned slightly. "The barrel?"

"We checked," Ryzen said. "Owner of the Iron Cup says all barrels are handled inside the pub now. Delivery, collection, even empties. Said a few weeks back someone made off with a full one, so he stopped leaving them in the alley."

"So no barrel."

"No, Your Highness."

"Who supplies Iron Cup with their wine?"

"Wynmere mostly. Durnhart and Lesserin through Foxburrow to a lesser extent." Ryzen reported. "I could have my captains question lady Wynmere in the morning."

"No," Harald said. "No. that wont be necessary. We have cut the chain."

Harald let the silence stretch again. It wasn't meant to frighten. It was a net—wide and silent—to see what twitched. The page didn't dare speak.

Finally, the King nodded once. "Thank you, Marshal."

He turned, cloak trailing softly across damp stone.

As he reached the archway, Ryzen spoke behind him. "And the boy, Sire?"

Harald stopped. Didn't turn back.

"Hold him. Feed him. Come Bloomrise, let him go."

Ryzen's brow furrowed. "Just like that?"

The King's voice didn't soften. Didn't harden either. "He's a boy who followed coin, not treason. Let him live with the ash on his hands. It will cling longer than any chain."

Then he left, judgment trailing behind him like a second cloak.

The torch behind him hissed, as if it agreed.

And in the quiet that followed, the boy wept—not loud, not broken. Just quietly enough that no one offered comfort.

Only Ryzen remained, watching with a soldier's stillness.

He did not speak.

Only listened as the last embers crumbled softly beneath the boy's boots.

Nightfall settled over the Citadel, torchlight marking a winding descent toward the inner sanctuary below. Baldrik stood at the mouth of a chamber carved deep beneath the Flamebound Citadel, stone walls slick with condensation, the air cool and mineral-thick beneath the incense.

Moisture gathered in the mortar lines and clung to the ceiling in dark beads, catching the light in dull glimmers. The space felt older than the halls above it, older than the citadel itself. Not grand, but enduring. Sound seemed to sink into the stone rather than echo.

Kaelric placed a hand on Baldrik's shoulder. "Fear is natural. Do not let it command you. Tonight is not spectacle. It is relinquishment."

Baldrik nodded, drawing a deep, steadying breath. "I understand."

They moved forward into the chamber. In its center lay a circular basin, filled with fine white sand, surrounded by carefully arranged stones etched with ancient runes. At the chamber's edges stood the Flamebound monks, silent and watchful, each holding a torch blazing brightly, flames dancing in reflection against the chamber walls.

An elder monk stepped forward, his voice resonant, echoing off the stone. "Baldrik, son of Thornsword, you stand at a crossroads. To join the Flamebound is to step into fire and relinquish what binds you. Step into the circle. Enter without retreat."

Baldrik stepped hesitantly into the sand-filled circle, its grains cool beneath his bare feet. The monks moved ahead simultaneously, each torch igniting a line of oil hidden beneath the sand, setting the edges of the circle ablaze. Flames rose quickly, forming a ring around him, sealing him within a circle of fire.

Baldrik's heart raced, but he steadied himself, focusing on Kaelric's calm, unwavering gaze.

Kaelric spoke firmly but gently from beyond the flames, his voice clear over the crackling fire. "Speak what binds you, Baldrik. Name it."

Baldrik closed his eyes, the heat intensifying around him, flames leaping higher with each breath he took. He raised his voice, hesitant at first, the heat wavering around him. "I fear my inadequacies." The heat surged upward, crackling fiercely.

He spoke louder, with growing strength, his voice rising over the flames' powerful climb. "I fear failing my father's expectations." Another surge of fire encircled him, heat swirling yet not scorching. His voice swelled, resonating clearly, infused with raw honesty. "I fear betraying my own heart." The flames roared higher, blazing intensely around him. "I regret the moments I let others hold the quill of my story." Each confession rose into the roar of the fire.

As he spoke, the flames rose higher, heat enveloping him but not burning. Smoke thickened and drifted low across the sand.

Kaelric's voice rose again, guiding him deeper into introspection. "Now, Baldrik, state your truths. Who are you beyond titles, beyond lineage?"

"I am Baldrik," he declared, his voice raw yet resolute, his skin prickling as if brushed by heat too close for comfort Each breath scorched his throat, the air heavy and punishing as he drew in strength to continue. "Not merely a prince, not merely the blood of my father. I choose my own path—a path guided by truth, tempered by discipline, and forged by fire."

For a moment Baldrik feared the flames would incinerate him entirely; his skin felt as if it were blistering, the scorching air clawing painfully at his throat as he fought for breath. Panic pressed in hard, a raw instinct to flee screaming through his limbs.

He remembered the words spoken to him seasons before.

"When the fire finds you, do not run from the pain. Follow the smoke."

Baldrik forced his eyes open. Through the wavering heat he saw it then: smoke curling low along the stone floor, slipping between the tongues of flame in a thin, deliberate line along the stone floor.

He stepped toward it.

The pain sharpened as he moved, heat biting deep, but he did not turn away. He followed the smoke, one measured step at a time, letting it guide him through the narrowing ring of fire. The blaze thinned along the line of smoke, leaving a narrow seam through which he moved.

Behind him, the fire surged upward—then settled back into the ring, and guttered out, leaving Baldrik beyond the circle, shaking, breath ragged.

The monks stepped back, bowing in solemn acknowledgment. Kaelric approached, his expression composed, though something measured flickered behind his gaze. "Welcome to the Flamebound, Baldrik. Your trial by fire is complete."

The chamber stilled. When Baldrik drew a steady breath again, he stood in shadow and stone. The heat had passed, though its memory lingered in his bones.

Baldrik knelt solemnly in the quiet chamber, the atmosphere heavy with reverence and ritual silence. Kaelric stood behind him, a ceremonial blade glinting in the soft torchlight. Baldrik closed his eyes, feeling the gentle but firm grasp of Kaelric's hand on his shoulder, grounding him.

With solemn precision, Kaelric raised the ceremonial blade and drew it through Baldrik's hair, severing each lock cleanly at the nape. The strands fell softly around him, a quiet rain of relinquished identity. In silence, Kaelric gathered the sheared hair and placed it into a glowing brazier.

Flames caught instantly, rising in a controlled bloom that cast flickering light on Baldrik's face. He watched without flinching as his past curled and blackened in the fire, the scent of smoke mingling with the incense-laden air. Nothing remained but ash.

Kaelric approached once more, carrying the Flamebound robes with respectful reverence. Baldrik rose slowly, the cool stone beneath his feet contrasting sharply with the remembered heat. With deliberate care, Kaelric draped Baldrik in the simple robes, their weight settling across his shoulders.

"With these robes," Kaelric said, "you leave behind what you have relinquished. There is no retreat."

Baldrik adjusted the robes carefully. He met Kaelric's gaze, steady and resolved.

"Your trial by fire is complete." Kaelric affirmed quietly. "Your true journey begins now."

Baldrik stepped into the courtyard, the night air a tranquil balm after the searing heat. The monks greeted him warmly, their gentle smiles offering reassurance and respect, their murmurs of welcome filling him with a quiet peace.

Elara stood alone in the echoing silence of her home, now emptied of everything that had once filled it. Each room whispered with memories, carrying the faint echoes of her brothers' laughter, their mischievous feet pattering through corridors as their mother's voice playfully scolded them from afar.

The faint scent of bread and lavender still lingered in the air., pulling her back to mornings filled with warmth and light.

She could still hear the resonant timbre of her father's voice drifting from the study, grumbling quietly over dwindling horse feed and worrying about another harsh winter. The comforting rustle of his papers and the familiar scrape of his pen offered an ephemeral moment of comfort, fleeting yet achingly clear.

Her eyes wandered over bare walls, once adorned with vivid tapestries and proud banners, now stark and accusingly empty. Her gaze settled upon the single portrait defiantly remaining—a family captured forever in happier times. Approaching carefully, her heartbeat quickened, throat tightening as she reached out. She lifted the portrait from its hook, fingertips brushing each painted face. The joyful sparkle in Deklan's eyes, Odin's perpetual curiosity, her father's quiet strength, and her mother's radiant warmth—all were frozen in an idyllic moment, untouched by the harshness that had since fallen upon them.

"I'm so sorry," she whispered, tears blurring her vision. "I kept my promise as long as I could." She drew a breath. "I will find another way."

A sudden wave of nausea swept through her, a sharp reminder of the weeks gone silent. Her hand instinctively pressed gently against her abdomen, her heart pounding with a blend of fear and cautious wonder. She had told no one, guarding this fragile secret closely, unsure yet profoundly certain that her life had irrevocably changed.

Outside, the muted rumble of wagon wheels and hushed murmurs from the waiting servants signaled the inevitable end. The empty rooms seemed to echo louder now. The silence pressed in around her, heavy with memory. Summoning her resolve, Elara took one last, lingering look, committing every detail to memory.

With the portrait wrapped carefully beneath her cloak, she stepped into the crisp air. Aulfis stood waiting, a solitary figure among the servants and wagons. His posture was confident, his expression unreadable. He extended his hand, an offer she understood.

She hesitated for only a heartbeat, meeting his gaze with quiet defiance, understanding the choice she had made. Resolutely, she placed her hand into his. His grip closed—firm, claiming.

Behind them, a member of the King's Guard hammered a placard onto the heavy oak door, each strike resounding like a judgment echoing deeply within her. The stark proclamation read, bold and unapologetic: "Lawful seizure by King Harald Thornsword, King of Eldaraine."

Elara refused to look back, her chin held high as she stepped away from the hollow remnants of her past. Her heart was heavy yet resolute, burdened by loss but also ignited by fierce determination. She would forge a new path, not merely surviving, but thriving.

Aulfis guided her to the waiting wagon with quiet authority, helping her into it before mounting his horse with practiced ease. The wagon rolled forward, wheels groaning softly against the packed dirt road, a solemn procession beneath a sky heavy with uncertain promises. Aulfis rode ahead, posture rigid, setting the pace for Castellon. Elara watched the road unwind, her thoughts no longer reaching for what she had lost.

Baldrik's name surfaced once—unbidden, unwanted.

She did not follow it.

She let it pass like smoke on the wind.

What remained was clearer. Colder. Certain.

This was not surrender.

It was correction.

She had followed her heart once.

She would not do so again.

The game had not ended.

It had only changed.

And this time, she would play it as she was meant to.

She did not look back.

He descended alone.

The path winding from the Boulderfists was barely more than suggestion—an ephemeral trail of crumbled shale, slick ice, and half-swallowed cairns lost beneath the timeless embrace of snow.

Every step demanded vigilance. But Rodrik did not fear falling; he feared wasting time, squandering the precious minutes that stood between him and answers hidden by the cold.

Below stretched the Tukrahlin Tundra, an endless expanse of stark whiteness and oppressive silence. It was a place that sunlight abandoned, leaving behind only shades of ash and bone. Even the sky seemed weary, drained of color and life, whispering an exhausted sigh across the horizon.

Snow hung motionless in the air, suspended as though held by the land itself. The cold had long since shed its cruelty, becoming something ritual and omnipresent. It was a presence Rodrik could feel—ancient, enduring, and watchful.

He passed a weathered stone marker, buried up to its neck in frost. Faded runes were etched into its face, half-erased by centuries of relentless wind. A spiral claw symbol, worn yet resilient, still lingered defiantly. Rodrik did not touch it, nor did he speak. He had always respected things that outlived men.

By midday, the wind shifted. Less biting now, more curious, sharper. He paused atop a ridge where the snow had drifted waist-deep, compacted to the hardness of granite. From this vantage, he could see distant ice fields glinting to the northeast, broken by obsidian-black rock and ominous bone totems—driftwood structures lashed together with sinew, antlers carved and hung like silent warnings.

No footprints disturbed the pristine landscape—not of beast nor man. Kneeling beside a narrow, shallow furrow in the snow, Rodrik pressed two fingers into the crust. Soft, wind-blown, fresh. Yet no marks indicated passage. Whatever moved through here left no trace—or hid it deliberately.

Rodrik rose again, the frost-heavy cloak clinging to him. His gaze swept the desolate horizon, eyes narrowed with cautious contemplation.

Far beyond the pale curtain of drifting snow lay the fabled capital, Qilauriq—the Place of the Northern Breath. Here, in this place of utter stillness, it seemed as distant as a forgotten dream.

A sudden gust yanked his hood back, whispering past his ear—not a natural wind, but something speaking in a tongue older than man. He stood unmoved, voice barely more than a murmur above the ice crackling in his beard.

"Tell your stories, then."

For a time, he walked in silence, the wind filling the space where thought once lived.

Eirik's voice lingered there—steady, measured, warning.

Do not be the axe.

Rodrik's jaw tightened.

He had tried that path. Tried distance. Tried solitude. Tried to let the world rot beyond his reach.

It had found him anyway.

Valen had seen to that.

The memory came unbidden—firelight, blood, the stillness where his wife should have been. Not grief. Not anymore.

Something colder.

Something patient.

Eldaraine was rotting from within, and men like Valen fed on it. Left alone, they would choke the realm and call it order.

Eirik would read banners.

Rodrik would raise them.

The North would not stay silent forever.

His course turned, subtle but certain—not toward retreat, nor report, but toward something older. Toward allies who did not bow to southern crowns.

Toward war.

If Valen stood in its path…

Rodrik's expression did not change.

All the better.

And he walked on.

www.ingramcontent.com/pod-product-compliance
Lightning Source LLC
LaVergne TN
LVHW041249110826
845146LV00005BA/1282

* 9 7 9 8 9 9 5 5 0 9 1 0 3 *